The Fake Out

BOSTON REVS THREE OUTS BOOK 2

Jenni Bara

The Fake Out

Boston Revs Three Outs Book 2

Copyright @ 2024 Jenni Bara

Line Copy and Proof Editing by VB Edits

Final Proofreading by Jeffrey Hodge

Interior formatting Saras_pa_services_and_designs

Cover by Chelsea Kemp

E-book and Hardcover by Saras_pa_services_and_designs

ISBN: 978-1-959389-15-6 (ebook)

ISBN: 978-1-959389-23-1 (paperback)

ISBN: 978-1-959389-22-4 (hardback)

Jennibara.com

DEDICATION

*To everyone afraid to make
their dreams happen....dare
to leap because even if it's
scary it can be the best
thing that ever happens.*

Playlist

Flowers - Miley Cyrus

Shake It Off - Taylor Swift

Does to Me (feat. Eric Church) - Luke Combs

Start of Something Good - Daughtry

You're On Your Own, Kid - Taylor Swift

Pieces of Me - Ashlee Simpson

i like the way you kiss me - Artemas

Enchanted (Taylor's Version) - Taylor Swift

Centerfield - John Fogerty

Sand In My Boots - Morgan Wallen

Gotta Be Somebody - Nickelback

Rumor - Lee Brice

Chasing Cars - Snow Patrol

They Don't Know About Us - One Direction

Crazy for This Girl - Evan & Jaron

Shut Up and Dance - WALK THE MOON

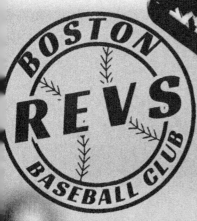

BOSTON REVS BASEBALL CLUB

REVS | BANDITS
JULY 1ST | 6 PM

LINEUP

COACH: TOM WILSON #49

1	KYLE BOSCO #29	RF
2	JASPER QUINN #16	1B
3	EMERSON KNIGHT #21	3B
4	ASHER PRICE #5	C
5	HENRY WINTERS #44	2B
6	EDDIE MARTINEZ #30	SS
7	COLTON STEWART #23	DH
8	TRISTIAN JENNER #27	LF
9	MASON DUMPTY #22	CF
P	CHRISTIAN DAMIANO #35	P

CONTENTS

Gianna

1

"Seven months," I whispered. Swallowing hard, I choked back the wave of nausea that rushed through me as I processed his words. How was it possible that I'd been totally in the dark for so long?

With a loud sigh, he sat back and crossed his arms over his broad chest, making his polo shirt pull tight along his shoulders. Jake was the type of guy who got away with things because he was pretty. Not rugged, not sexy, not suave, but pretty. And it worked for him. Blond hair with just enough wave to make it look like he'd spent time crafting the perfect style. High cheekbones, straight nose, white teeth. But even pretty couldn't fix *this*.

"Tell me you're joking," I finally snapped, causing a few heads around us to turn our way.

Jake shifted in his seat and angled toward me. "Here we go with the bitch face," he huffed under his breath.

I heard it a lot. Resting bitch face. As if I had no control over it, when the truth was that the expression was purposeful. Sad was pathetic. Angry was powerful. Plus, if anyone deserved to be bitched out, it was Jake Caderson.

With long, thin fingers, he tapped the white tablecloth so hard that the ice in his water glass rattled. "Don't make this a bigger deal than it has to be."

1

A scoff escaped me at those words. He had to be joking. He acted as if I were overreacting. As if we hadn't been planning to move in together this weekend.

My gritted out "Are you fucking kidding me?" didn't *feel* like an overreaction.

I opened my mouth, ready to lay into him, but my soon-to-be ex-boyfriend held up a hand, cutting me off.

"I brought you here to tell you about Libby in hopes that you'd be reasonable about it. The last thing I want is for you to embarrass us both." He lifted his chin, gesturing around my favorite restaurant.

I'd been coming here for birthdays and celebratory dinners most of my life. The little family-owned Italian restaurant with the best manicotti in all of New York. The same manicotti that was trying to work its way back up my throat.

I pushed my plate toward the center of the table, hoping that would end my desire to throw up. But it did no good. The marinara wasn't causing the nausea. It was the realization that Jake had spent last night in my bed, knowing what he was planning to do.

What an asshole.

And who in their right mind chose a person's favorite place to do something like this?

Saturday and Sunday, as in three days from now, we had plans to move into our new apartment. Since my dad was selling his house and Jake's lease was up, we had spent weeks this spring looking for a new place. A little over a month ago, I'd found the perfect spot.

I swallowed the lump in my throat and breathed past the hurt clinging to the mad growing inside me. My hands shook, so I fisted them in my lap. There was not a world where I would look anything but pissed off.

"I have no intention of embarrassing myself." Teeth gritted, I looked across the restaurant, unable to even stand the sight of him. A huge part of me wanted to toss my cosmo in his face and storm out. But more words had to be said. One sentence could end an eighteen-month relationship, but it didn't untangle it.

"Glad we agree." He nodded. "I didn't plan to get Libby pregnant —it was supposed to be a quick fling you never found out about."

My hands twitched toward my drink again, because *what the fuck?*

"But now that she's hit the third trimester, she's making more demands. I'm sure you can be sympathetic to that."

Sympathetic? To whom exactly? Jake? My attention was drawn to the knife on the table. *What was the minimum sentence for assault in New York?* Maybe a jury would be sympathetic *to me* for castrating him.

"The last few months have been rough for her."

Oh, he meant sympathetic to *Libby*. Not happening. Though the bulk of my anger was directed toward him, the woman he was cheating on me with knew we were together. So I had zero sympathy for either of them. Jake and I worked for Doucette Designs in New York City. He was a vice president of design, while I was an artist on staff. Libby worked in legal in the corporate office in Pittsburg. She came out to New York fairly often for new client contracts, although I hadn't seen her in a couple months. Probably because she was showing and knew she'd better steer clear of me.

"So," Jake hedged with a long breath out, "for obvious reasons, I had Stan take your name off the lease."

My attention snapped to his face as my stomach sank. He was rigid in his seat, his muddy brown eyes darting around like he was planning a quick escape. My heart pounded like an angry bass drum, the deafening sound starting in my chest and moving to my ears.

He did not just say he stole *my* apartment. Right?

"Stan did what?" Stan was the realtor that Jake insisted we use when I found the perfect place. The top two floors of a brownstone that had been converted into an apartment with two bedrooms and an open kitchen and living area with an actual working fireplace. It was over the budget we'd set, but I'd had money saved and used it to pay first and last month's rent and the realtor fees. From there, we could split the rent and make it work. I had been nervous about it, but Jake had talked me into trusting our relationship, trusting in the two of us enough to make the two-year lease commitment. With my money…

My stomach roiled, and the manicotti threatened once again to make an appearance.

What was I thinking?

He finally looked at me, his jaw locked tight. "I'm the reason we passed the credit check. I'm the tenant they wanted. And since Libby is transferring to the New York office—you know, because of the baby— she's moving in with me." His eyes narrowed. "And you can't afford the rent on the place on your own."

It galled me that he was right. Without shutting off my cell phone and Netflix and selling my car—and eating nothing but ramen for the next two years—I couldn't afford it. I'd used the eleven thousand dollars I'd saved while living at home with Pop for the last few years to get us locked into the lease. Because I'd *loved* the place.

And I couldn't stop myself any longer. I pushed to my feet, grabbed the almost full martini glass, and threw my drink straight into his face.

"What the *hell*," he sputtered, swiping at his eyes as the pinkish liquid ran down his pale cheeks.

"I better get my deposit back. And the realtor fees I paid." I swiped my purse from the table and stomped out, head held high, as the people at the surrounding tables gawked. Oddly enough, I wasn't at all embarrassed.

I drove home, fueled by a mix of the adrenaline and the desperate need for comfort.

In the driveway, I scanned the under-contract sign in the yard. Although the idea of moving had been scary, my brother and I had pushed for Pop to sell this place.

He'd had a heart attack at the end of February, and since the best cardio rehab in the country was in Boston, my brother, Chris, convinced Pop to make the move. He hadn't even been in the rehab facility a whole ten weeks before he found a new home. Between all the Boston Revs baseball games he could attend and the time he spent with Chris, his sunshiny girlfriend, and their pet puffin, Pop was as happy as I'd seen him in years.

He deserved retirement and all the happiness that came with it. As a teacher and coach, as well as a single parent for the past twenty-two years, he'd done more than his fair share of struggling through life.

The only issue was that he was closing on the house in a week. On June first, the house I grew up in would have new owners, and I'd be homeless.

I shuffled inside and closed the door behind me. Other than my bedroom and the sofa Pop didn't want, the house was mostly cleared out. We'd been planning to use Jake's furniture in the new place.

I took a deep breath and swallowed back the pain ricocheting through me. I should call Mila; she'd eat ice cream with me and tell me I was too good for the jerk. But her gentle sweetness would probably make me cry, and I wanted to be pissed, not sad. Linc would have no problem heading out to a bar to get drunk. But I couldn't make either call. The *I told you Jake was an ass* conversation he'd insist on wasn't one I could stomach right now.

Deep down, I had known it for a while. But I was almost thirty, and at this point, good enough seemed like all I was capable of having. That thought had another shot of anguish ripping through me. *No one should settle.* My family and friends had been telling me that for years. But so many people, including me, would kill for a man who was fairly good-looking, somewhat successful, and half-decent in bed.

I scanned the shell of a room. Six days to find an affordable apartment in New York. Like that wasn't an impossible task. I swallowed and closed my eyes. Staying with Linc wasn't an option. He and his boyfriend were in an adorable studio in Brooklyn with no space for guests. Mila might let me crash for a day or two, but she had two roommates, so that wasn't a long-term fix.

But fuck my life. There was no way I could find a solution today.

What I could use was a hug. But in this house, even when I wasn't alone, hugs were few and far between. I couldn't ask for a better family, but neither Pop nor Chris was the touchy feely type, and like so many times since my mom died, I craved a hug. Not that I'd whine about it.

Nor would I harp on any of this. I was pissed and embarrassed, but what I didn't feel was the soul-crushing sadness that should come with losing the man that I was supposed to love. That probably said more than I was ready to admit about my relationship with Jake. But it didn't change the fact that tomorrow morning, I had to go into work and face him—along with the rest of the office—and somehow come to terms with the fact that the very pregnant woman my ex had cheated on me with would now be working in my office daily. After I dealt with all that, I had to find an apartment. Hopefully one without a security deposit, since I couldn't imagine Jake rushing to give my money back. I had a work bonus coming, but not until I finished my current project a month from now.

But whatever. I wasn't going to let an asshole ruin my life.

"I've got this." I squared my shoulders and put on my tough-girl mask as I whispered to the empty room.

Emerson
2

AT THE SOUND OF KEYS JINGLING IN THE LOCK, I SET THE WOODEN SPOON on the counter and jogged for the door, bumping my shoulder on the archway when I slipped past. As I swung it open, Gianna's big brown eyes widened and her keys landed with a clink on the gray carpet of the building's hallway. She blinked twice before her expression morphed into a scowl.

"What are you doing here?" she demanded, like I was the one out of place when in fact she was the one that just left New York to move up to Boston.

Chuckling, I crouched and picked up the keys by the silver baseball bat key ring. "I know." I tossed them at my roommate's sister, and after a quick bobble, they were firmly in her palm. "I wonder how I get to live here too."

Stepping back, I waved her inside.

I shouldn't play into the nothing in my brain assumption, but correcting people was pointless. Plus, it was true. I had been playing pro baseball for just over a year and I still hadn't gotten used to my new status. It was wild to me that I lived in a two-thousand-square-foot apartment with a stellar view of Boston Harbor, a doorman, and

7

people who carted our shit around. It seemed more like a fleeting dream than my reality, and I wasn't sure that would ever change.

"I thought you'd be out with the team, bar hopping or whatever." Again, her snippy tone seemed to imply that I wasn't allowed in my own apartment.

"Nah. Come in." I nodded at the guy in the maroon coat standing behind her in the hall. "If you leave it all here," I said to him, tipping my chin at the three bags, two enormous suitcases, one box, and the weird narrow, flat bag, "I'll get it."

"I can do it." Gianna crossed her arms under her ample tits, the move pushing them up into the scoop of the purple sweater.

I forced my eyes up to her face, which was set in a glare, her attention firmly fixed on me.

For the life of me, I had no idea why I loved that glare so much. Clearly, I was a glutton for punishment. From the moment I met the woman, the daggers she shot my way had settled firmly in my stomach, making my body come alive. But I'd worked hard to ignore the sensation, even though I wasn't normally a man who overlooked the possibility of pleasure. What I was, though, was loyal, and she was my best friend's sister *and* she was spoken for. Even if Chris and their pop kept calling the guy she was with a shitty human being, it was her choice, not theirs. I'd never met the dude, so I had no room to judge, and I couldn't imagine she didn't care about him, because a woman as strong-willed, talented, and sexy as Gianna could have her pick of guys.

"I'm sure you can carry all your bags alone"—I smiled again when she looked like she might snarl at me—"but I hate being a dick. And if I left you to lug around all your shit into the apartment alone, that's exactly what I would be." I shrugged. "I know it's selfish and assholey of me, but you'll just have to take one for the team and let me be a gentleman."

She blinked those big brown eyes flocked by the longest lashes I'd ever seen twice. "Uh…"

I loved confusing her almost as much as I loved her glare. Yeah, there was definitely something wrong with me.

"Excuse me." The man behind her gently prompted Gianna to move into the apartment so he could unload the bags.

"Thanks, man." I slipped my hand into my back pocket to pull out my wallet, but before I could pull a few bills out, she handed him a small wad of cash. Chris, my roommate, had told me to take care of it. But I had no interest in fighting about stupid shit like her brother would. If she wanted to tip the guy, then more power to her.

The door closed, and the rush of air sent her floral scent my way. It took more strength than I'd like to admit to fight the responding shiver that wanted to rush through me. Orange blossoms. The woman always smelled like citrus blooms. And damn if my dick didn't notice.

Nope. *Ignore that shit, Emerson.* After yesterday's game, Chris had told me that his sister needed a place to crash for a few weeks. And since my best friend spent 90 percent of his time at his girlfriend's apartment, he was more than happy to let Gianna stay in his empty room. As much of an ass as the guy pretended to be, he had a heart of gold, especially when it came to the people he cared about. And his sister fell into the top three of that list. Although he thought I'd be annoyed, I was thrilled about my new living arrangements. Not that I'd admit it to him.

"I'm so excited you're here. Bring it in." I opened my arms.

I was a hugger, and I was an asshole using this moment as an excuse to touch the woman whose curves had haunted my thoughts for months.

With a step back, she glared at me. "What?"

I waggled my brows. "Let's hug it out." Moving toward her, I doubled down.

She crossed her arms and shook her head. "No."

I'd known this woman for years, but even now, I wasn't sure if she was like Chris and didn't like to be touched, or if she just didn't like the idea of touching me. Either possibility sucked.

"Your loss. I'm an A-plus hugger." I dropped my arms to my sides and went for her bags, watching my steps and moving carefully. The last thing I wanted was to make an ass of myself in front of the goddess in my foyer.

I made the first trip to her room without incident, but by trip number three, my mind was wandering to thoughts of dinner, my family and the call I'd promise to make, the next episode of the show I'd started last night, my contract issues, my roommate, and tomorrow's game.

As all those thoughts swirled in my mind, the bag I was carrying knocked into the doorframe, sending me bumping back against the door, which caused it to go flying against the stopper stuck to the wall behind it. As a loud thunk echoed, I held back a grimace.

Instead, I smiled wide. "Let's get the base pumping." This was my go-to reaction, joking and making the best of my inability to pay attention to whatever the fuck I was doing.

Gianna didn't even crack a smile as she stepped through the doorway. Instead, she scanned her temporary room with narrowed eyes and a tight jaw.

As she assessed the space, I took her in. She always looked so damn good.

I snorted quietly at the lackluster word. Sinful. That was better. She was all smooth skin and fuck-me curves. The fitted purple sweater hugged her full tits in a way that had the buttons down the front looking like they could pop with just a flick of my finger. The fabric ended at her stomach, playing a wonderfully awful game of peek-a-boo with her belly button. Her wide hips and that fucking ass encased in tight black leggings tempted me to do terrible things. I bit back a groan. I had no right to fantasize about her ass the way I did.

Taken.

I silently chastised myself, like I did every time I was near her. The woman had a boyfriend, and I respected that. The boyfriend was a safe buffer. No matter how hot Gianna was, no matter how badly my body begged to be near hers, I wouldn't cross that line. Which was good, because Christian would rearrange my pretty face if he had even an inkling that I had jacked off to thoughts of his sister. I got it. I wouldn't want a guy like me screwing around with one of my sisters either.

"Emerson?" My name on her lips almost sounded like a snarl, yet tingles shot through my extremities. Damn, why did everything about this chick need to be such a fucking temptation?

"Mariposa?" I cocked a brow, not bothering to fight a smile as she glared at the nickname I was fairly certain she didn't understand.

"Is my brother using my bedding?"

Oh. That was the reason for the frown.

"No." I shook my head. "I changed the sheets and stuff earlier. I wasn't sure what time you'd get in, and if it was late, I didn't want you to have to deal with doing it."

A small crease appeared between her brows as she looked from the bed to me. The movement caused her silky brown hair to float around her tits and sent another blast of orange blossom wafting my way.

"You…" The word died on her tongue, and she frowned again.

From the moment I met her, every kind gesture I'd directed toward her was met with some form of cactus-like prickles.

"Anyway, sorry if I didn't get it right." I rubbed at the back of my neck. "You probably would have done it better. I've never quite understood what hospital corners meant. I always just do the quick tuck and go. Just like a girdle."

Like a girdle? What the fuck was I saying? Gianna's presence always left me off-kilter. I had to get out of the room before she could get worked up and pull out all that sass. If I didn't, I'd do something stupid like tell her she was so pretty it made my chest hurt.

Without my permission, my eyes zeroed in on her round ass, and instantly, my dick got heavy in my jeans. Shaking the image from my head, I turned to the door.

It was going to be a long fucking month, and yet I couldn't stop myself from smiling about it.

Gianna

3

HE'D MADE MY BED? I DIDN'T KNOW WHAT TO DO WITH THAT. NO ONE had ever done that stuff for me. Not since my mom had died. Maybe Pop did at first, but I couldn't say I remembered that time well. Tension knotted my shoulders as I twirled a single curl around my finger and surveyed the pink flowers on the bedding. Each time I visited my brother, I used my own sheets and quilt. I'd brought an extra set from home the first time I visited and had left them here so I didn't have to bring them back and forth. He always let me have the bed, and I couldn't stomach thoughts of what might have happened on the sheets, even if he'd washed them. Chris was the bigger germophobe of the family, but I hadn't escaped the neurosis completely.

I had my own things, and bedding was one of them. Rationally, I understood that the staph infection my mom caught after coming back from a tropical vacation with Pop wasn't likely from the sheets and towels at their hotel, but ten-year-old me was convinced the infection that caused her to become septic came from sleeping in strangers' germs. And I still struggled with the idea of germy sheets.

Jake had always mocked me for packing my own sheets and towels when I traveled. Clearly he, along with most people, didn't understand

13

the sheer amount of rank strangers' excretions that were forever on hotel room sheets.

I fought a shudder at the thought.

"Let me know if you need anything."

I spun in time to see Emerson clip his shoulder on the doorframe as he hurried out of the room. The guy chuckled at the clumsy move but didn't slow or turn back.

My brother's best friend was...different. When I met him a few years ago, I was confused. The man had the uncontainable energy of *Winnie the Pooh*'s Tigger and the dopey happiness of my least favorite *Friends* character. He was so freaking irritating, with his constant chatter and exuberance for life. To this day, I couldn't wrap my head around how my grump of a brother had bonded with Mr. Happy Pants.

Whatever. This was temporary. Before long, I'd move on to my new place.

Chris had told me to adjust his stuff any way I wanted, so I headed for the dresser, skipping the top drawer, because that was typically the drawer people kept personal shit in. I had zero interest in discovering items that would make me want to burn my eyes out.

Drawers three and four seemed safest.

I yanked the third one open, finding two pairs of sweats. The drawer below it was half filled with athletic shorts. Quickly, I made a stack and shelved them in his almost-empty closet.

Clearly my brother didn't spend much time here anymore. Not that I was surprised. It had been obvious to all of us long before Chris copped to it that Avery was destined to be his better half. Now that they were done hiding behind this best friend bullshit and he was with her, it didn't shock me that he was all-in. Chris was a forever-type person. It was only a matter of time before he popped the question.

My brother was picky about who he let into his circle, but once he welcomed a person, that was it.

And besides Avery, Emerson Knight was also solidly in Chris's circle of forever, even if I didn't understand why. Though I guessed I didn't need to understand. If my brother trusted him, that meant Emerson was good people.

I peered over my shoulder toward the center of the room.

And he'd made my bed…

Not to mention he hadn't made a single snide comment about my quirk.

Shaking my head, I turned back to the task at hand, ignoring the weird flutter in my chest at the thought. As I organized, Avery texted that she and Chris were bringing Pop by for dinner. I hadn't seen him in a few weeks, but according to Chris, he was getting stronger every day.

I finished unpacking before I pulled out my phone to check in with my friends. Once my family descended, I'd be too busy trying to figure out dinner. Knowing Chris, he'd show up and expect food to magically appear.

Me: Made it - all settled.

My phone instantly buzzed with a FaceTime request.

Struggling to decide whether I wanted to roll my eyes or sigh, I clicked Accept and was greeted by spikes of platinum hair and a pair of bright blue eyes.

"Where is he? And is he shirtless?" Linc craned his neck like he was trying to look around me. "I've heard his thing is, like, nakedness." His brows were in his hairline as he blinked at me in anticipation. "Don't be stingy with the views, Gi."

"How many times have I been here before? You know I've never seen him without clothes, so don't believe everything you read." I huffed.

According to Linc, gossip on all the socials was that Emerson liked hanging out in his birthday suit while he was at home. But I couldn't imagine my brother would put up with that shit. Sounded to me like the wishful thinking of millions of people. And I guess, in a way, I could understand it. Not that I felt the same way. But his goofiness aside, it was impossible not to notice that the man was sexy as sin. Even I'd had trouble looking away from the corded forearm muscles as he moved my bags.

The image on the screen went blurry, and then Mila appeared on the video chat.

"Bored of Boston?" Her tone was hopeful, like she'd be thrilled if I said I was ready to move back to New York already. It must be nice to live in that kind of fairy tale land.

"Linc is just hoping for man chest," I explained.

"Trying to make Eli jealous?" She cocked her head, half of it disappearing from the screen, and worried her bottom lip. Probably concerned he'd hurt his boyfriend's feelings.

We were an odd group, the three of us. I'd met Linc at cosmology school over ten years ago. These days, he was a highly sought–after stylist at the biggest Moxie Salon in New York, and I'd never be able to repay him for the wonders he worked on my hair.

Though he'd clearly flourished in his career, it turned out that I hated peopling too much to stay in the business of cutting hair. So, six years ago, I'd gone back and taken art and design classes. That was when I met Mila. Soft-spoken and careful with her words, with her French braid, baggy clothes, and dreams of being an elementary school art teacher, she was the antithesis of me. Linc met Mila, cut her long, drab hair into a cute little bob, and dragged her out into the world of the New York bar scene. And since then, we'd been together.

"Oh, Eli is fine with me being a creepy stalker." He rolled his blue eyes. "Babe!" he yelled. "Care if I check out some professional baseball guy's chest without his knowledge or permission?"

In the background, Eli responded, but his words were impossible to make out.

Linc turned back to us, his eyes twinkling below the silver loop through one brow. "He said *whatever*."

"Be nice to him." Mila shook her head. "I miss you already, Gi. You should come back."

I'd stayed with Mila for a few days after my father's house sold, but then I'd finally bitten the bullet and called my brother. I wasn't thrilled to have to mooch off Chris, but an apartment in the city was impossible to find on such short notice. I had some work to do for the Boston Zoo anyway, so the temporary move four hours north wasn't really a big deal.

"I'm hoping to find a place near you before July." But August was more likely. Jake still hadn't reimbursed me, though he swore he'd have it soon. With him, that meant it could be tomorrow or next month. "Plus, I'm glad to be away from Jake for a while."

"What did the tool bag do now?" Linc smirked. "His standing hair appointment is next week. Wouldn't it be funny if I had an off day?"

My stomach sank. "Don't get yourself in trouble. He's not worth it."

"Debatable." Linc tossed his head back and let out the most terrifyingly evil laugh. The *I intend to mess with you so good* meaning behind it sent shivers down my spine.

"Seriously, what did he do?" Mila asked this time.

I lowered my focus, unable to look at them, and shook my head. Libby flaunting her engagement ring, then her friend's comment about my size. I tipped my chin up, determined to cling to the anger coursing through me and not let anything else in. "Nothing out of the norm. He sent me to get the group's coffee order, and while I was gone, he handed out housewarming invites." I sighed, still beyond annoyed that he was living in the apartment I'd found and paid for. "Plus, he took me off the denim company project. That one I was really excited about. Apparently *they* don't like my vision."

Linc snorted. "Definitely gonna be half-blind next Wednesday."

I didn't want to chuckle, but it was hard not to. Messing with Mr. Perfect's hair would be funny. Even so, Jake would be livid, and then he'd try to get Linc fired.

"No need. I'm busy working on the zoo project for the next couple of weeks, so I'm free of his harassment. And I'm sending my résumé to every graphic design firm in New York. A new job is at the top of the list, right after new apartment," I muttered. New job, new place to live, new relationship status, all at the same time. Ironic for a woman who didn't like change.

"If my lease was up anytime soon, I'd move in with you," Mila assured me. It wasn't the first time she'd said it, but her lease wasn't up for renewal until October, and there was no way I'd live in my brother's apartment for that long.

"I know." I gave her a smile. "But I'm going to be thirty in a few weeks. It's time I adult and get my own place." And I'd been looking forward to having a place to make my own.

After realizing I didn't want to cut hair, I'd moved back in with Pop so I could work part time while getting my degree. It had made sense. Then, when I was hired at Doucette Designs after graduation, I stayed so I could double down on my efforts to pay off my college loans. And in the end, it was the best decision. Because now I was debt free.

The house I'd grown up in, that my mother, with her artistic hand, had decorated, was always more of a way to remember her, to be surrounded by her. It was why it took Pop and me so long to let it go. But now that he'd sold it, I could live in a place that felt like *me*. Jake the jerk wasn't part of the plan anymore, but that didn't mean I couldn't create a home for myself.

"So." Linc waggled his brows. "Can we get a tour of the temporary place?"

"No."

"Come on," he moaned, tipping his face up to the ceiling. "I want an up-close and personal view of the hottie you get to call a roommate."

I was not harassing the guy. It was bad enough I was encroaching on his space. I refused to be an annoying fan girl like that. Chris hadn't paused to ask Emerson if it was okay before he agreed to let me stay me. And when I mentioned that his roommate might not love it, Chris assured me that Emerson was pretty much never home, so it wouldn't be a thing.

"We are not harassing anyone today."

Linc cupped a hand around his mouth. "*booo*," he chanted.

I rolled my eyes. "Goodbye." With that, I ended the call and headed out of Chris's bedroom to figure out dinner.

As I stepped out into the hall, Emerson's voice flooded my ears. If I didn't know he was such a goofball, I might find the deep, rumbling tone attractive. Halfway down the hall, the smell hit my nose, making my mouth water. Garlic and cream.

I peeked into the kitchen, finding Emerson standing at the counter. He was tall and broad and far too happy-looking. The spoon in his hand was so at odds with the bat or mitt I was used to seeing him

18

with. Even so, he looked just as comfortable in the kitchen as he did standing by third base.

As I stood at the door, his mouth moved, words that I couldn't catch passing quickly through his lips.

It wouldn't shock me if he was talking to himself. It seemed on par.

That thought left me as I got another whiff of the delicious aroma wafting around me. The smell screamed alfredo, which was one of my faves.

When I came back to my senses, he was still talking. That's when it hit me. I wasn't catching the words because he was speaking in Spanish. He'd grown up in Puerto Rico, so it made sense. Quietly, so as not to interrupt him, I slipped over to the fridge to grab a water.

"Come say hi," Emerson said in English, his green eyes focused on me. "Otherwise they'll accuse me of sneaking a girl around my apartment, and my mother will give me a lecture about not stealing free eggs." With that, he shifted his attention back to the counter and his phone, that I now realized was balanced against a bottle of olive oil. "This is Chris's sister, Gianna."

With one long arm, he pulled me close. His fingers skimmed the strip of bare skin between my sweater and leggings before he grasped my hip, holding me in place. The warmth of his palm heated my skin, even through my thin black pants.

I tensed at first, unused to physical contact. But I forced myself to relax as he pulled me closer so that I appeared on-screen beside him. A different spice hit my nose as his solid body pressed lightly against my own, causing my stomach to flip.

I swallowed hard and willed my body to remain relaxed. I'd never been this close to him. And I wasn't sure I liked it. My last two boyfriends hadn't been super touchy outside of sex, and after so long, apparently, my body didn't know how to react to a normal touch.

"Hi!" came a chorus of female voices. And I was met with smiling faces and bright, happy eyes that matched Emerson's. A mix of browns and greens.

"These are my sisters, Isabella, and Yevette, and my mom." As he introduced them, he tilted his head just enough that his breath skated along my cheek.

I cleared my throat and tried not to inhale his intoxicating scent. "Uh. Hi?"

"Wow, I totally didn't expect you," one of his sisters said. She looked younger than the other. Maybe seventeen.

"How do you make your hair do that?" This from the other sister, who couldn't have been much more than eighteen herself.

"You have really long lashes," the first said.

My stomach knotted a little tighter with each comment. I wasn't sure whether they were dishing out compliments or criticisms. Teenagers were hard to read. Before I could decipher their intentions, a male appeared, hovering behind the three women, standing a head taller than them. He narrowed his eyes, then he snickered and said something I didn't understand.

Emerson's mom whacked the guy in the chest, and in response, he barked out a laugh and shook his head.

"Enough." Emerson chuckled easily. "Chris and Avery are going to be here soon, so I'm hanging up. Love you all."

As the crowd on the other side of the screen shouted Spanish phrases, he ended the call, and the room went quiet.

"My brother Andre was the guy who showed up at the end. I love them all, literally couldn't pick a favorite, but they are a lot." With a shrug, he dropped his arm from my waist.

At the loss of his touch, my skin cooled, and a shiver coursed through me. It was almost like I missed it.

Get a grip Gianna. People were always weird around my brother now that he played professional baseball. There was no way I'd act like that with Emerson.

With a shake of my head, I wandered over to the stove and peeked into the saucepan. "Are you making dinner?"

Nerves skittered through me. What was I supposed to do if I didn't have to make dinner?

He chuckled again. "Somebody should, and we can be sure your brother won't."

Of course Chris wouldn't cook. The man couldn't even scramble eggs.

I snorted, and a wisp of my asymmetrical bangs floated into my eyes. Without a pause, Emerson brushed them back, his fingertips gently skimming along my temple.

Our eyes met and locked, and a strange warmth spread through me. From this close, I could make out a small fleck in his right iris. He froze in place, his teeth pressing into his lower lip as his hand hovered just above my shoulder.

The air in the kitchen electrified, and his lips parted like he might say something, but before he could, the door opened, and we jumped apart.

"Bambi?" my brother called, stepping into the room.

Emerson spun toward the stovetop, blinking and swallowing audibly. Completely ignoring Chris, he cracked the knuckles on one hand, then the other. Odd. He almost seemed nervous. Or was he uncomfortable?

Chris gave me a chin tilt, which was the warmest kind of welcome anyone but his girlfriend could expect. "Oh, hey, Gi. Didn't realize you were here already."

"I told you she texted when she got here," Avery called from the entryway, where she was holding the door as Pop came in.

Chris met my eye, silently telling me not to offer my help. My father was stubborn, and any help we offered would be met with a brush-off. Avery was one of the few he let do anything for him.

I tried not to frown at the slowness of my father's movements. He was without his walker, which showed that he was getting stronger, but it hurt to see him this way. He'd lost so much weight in the last few months. All his life, he'd been solid, but now his polo hung loosely off his frame. And he'd aged. Like instead of the *damn, he can't be sixty*, it was more like *damn, he's sixty*.

I took a deep breath and moved hesitantly toward him. "Pop."

"I will not break in half, girlie." Even though the tone had a bit of reproach to it, my dad smiled at me. It was virtually impossible to knock the positivity out of him.

I leaned in, attempting to give him a hug, but all I got in return was a shoulder squeeze. Sadness wormed its way into my brain, despite my best efforts. He smelled like home and the comforting scent of Old Spice. Missing was the hint of cigarettes that used to float around him, but that was a positive. I needed Pop around for a while more. I didn't feel like I was ready to be without his support, so I was thankful he'd quit that shit and was taking care of himself.

"Smells amazing, as always, Em," Avery said from behind us. "How can I help?"

Emerson angled close and brushed his lips over her cheek in greeting. Shockingly, my overprotective brother didn't even react. Chris just grabbed a beer out of the fridge as Emerson gave instructions and Avery moved to drain the pasta.

A flash of jealousy hit me. But I wasn't sure whether it was because Avery and Emerson fit in the dynamic of my family in this setting better than I did or because of how close the two of them were. Maybe it had more to do with the happiness that floated around the room so thickly it was suffocating.

"I thought we'd gotten past your dislike of Avery," my father mumbled beside me.

Heart lurching, I spun to him and opened my mouth, but I quickly shut it again. I'd never *disliked* her. She was just tiny and perky and full of sunshine. And as someone who was none of those things, my insecurities ran rampant around her. Pissed was easier than vulnerable, so that had always been my default setting. But I had tried to swallow that back.

"Avery's great," I said. She clearly loved my brother and was there for him no matter what. That was all I could hope for him. She didn't give a shit that he was a famous baseball player or how much money he made. She just adored Chris for who he was. That honest devotion was hard to find.

"Then don't scowl at my girl, Gi." Chris smirked. Which was weird. I wasn't used to my brother being happy. Frowning, glaring— that was his norm. But the smile he shot me as he opened his beer was out of place. So was the way he took a sip and then passed the bottle over to Avery like he hadn't spent decades being adamant about not sharing food and drinks. "You don't need to spread cranky all over just because you broke up with Jake."

I glared. I wasn't cranky about Jake.

"Chris," my father chastised.

At the same time, Emerson dropped the knife he was using to dice the chicken, sending it clattering to the floor.

"Shit," he muttered, crouching and swiping it off the tile.

"You okay?" Avery asked.

"You know me." He chuckled, the sound forced rather than easygoing like it usually was. When he moved to the sink, his green eyes met mine with an intensity I'd never seen from him before.

"I saw some of the partial designs for the new exhibits," Avery chirped, breaking the weirdness that had settled over the room. "They're perfection. The way you tied in the animals and the sponsors is incredible. Even unfinished, I'm blown over," she gushed as she plated the pasta.

"See?" My brother frowned at me as he grabbed two plates and moved to the table. "I keep telling you that you're good at that. I know shit, and I'm not biased."

With a nod of agreement, Avery picked up the beer and another plate and followed him.

Since Mom died, Chris and Pop seemed to double their effort to be supportive of my creative side. She and I had shared the passion. My brother and my father were the sports guys. Art was our thing. It wasn't so much unbiased support. It was more that after she died, they always tried to fill the void she left behind.

"I can't wait to see them," my father added, slowly shuffling over to the table with a bottle of water.

"Same." Emerson's deep voice rumbled through my body as he followed me into the dining room.

Before I could answer, Chris said, "Oh, Bambi, I Venmoed the grocery money for the week."

With a look at Emerson, who stood in the doorway carrying two plates, I frowned and turned to my brother. "Why?"

"What do you mean *why*?" His dark brows pulled together. "That's how we do food."

"But you don't live here…"

He scoffed. "I'll be around, and plus, I'm covering yours."

Irritation made my blood heat. That's exactly what I thought. "No." I hated his steamrolling.

"You moved here to save money, so I got the food. Don't be annoying." Chris snapped the napkin onto his lap and turned his attention back to Avery, who was settling next to him.

Emerson cleared his throat.

I whirled on him, fisting my hands on my hips. "I'm not letting him pay for everything."

His eyes softened, the green turning a mossy hue, and he nodded. "I get it. Chris steps in and takes care of people without thinking about how it might make them feel."

That was exactly it. But I didn't want to burden my brother when he was already letting me stay here.

Emerson dropped his voice lower. "But he *doesn't* live here, so you and I will work it out. Venmo goes both ways." With a smile, he passed me one of the plates he was holding. "Now enjoy dinner, because I'm almost as good a cook as I am good-looking."

I scoffed, fighting back the smile wanting to work its way across my lips.

Angling in, he gave me a once-over. "The grin is cute, but I prefer the full smile. That, Mariposa, is showstopping." With a smirk, he left me standing there in shock.

Did my brother's best friend just flirt with me?

Emerson
4

"BOSCO, DAMIANO," COACH WILSON BARKED.

Curious, I surveyed him from across the locker room. Usually, I did my best not to insert myself into issues that didn't involve me, but pregame was boring as shit. Sitting around made me crazy. I didn't want to plan for the game. I just wanted to play it.

"Hannah needs you two for a social media promo."

"No fucking way." Chris's head snapped up from his phone, where he was probably texting with Avery.

Tom Wilson, who happened to be Avery's dad, glowered at his pitcher. But he didn't take one step across the royal blue carpet. He simply crossed his arms and tipped his chin up. Like a warning from the general—no words needed.

Chris swallowed audibly and slumped into the white folding chair set up in front of his locker. "No disrespect, but Coach, Hannah and I have a deal. I don't stir up shit, and she doesn't make me perform like a trained monkey."

As much as I loved the guy, he was a dick.

"I'll be the monkey." I hopped up from my own chair and gave Coach a smile. Hannah's media stuff was usually fun, and I had no interest in sitting around for the next six hours, waiting for the game to start. Last week I'd volunteered to sit in the dunk tank. I had a blast while hundreds of fans under twelve tried their hand at hitting the bull's-eye. Might have been my favorite pregame activity so far. Though right up there with it was making balloon animals for the opening of the puffin exhibit at the Boston Zoo. And the event where we ran bases was amazing. Honestly, now that I was thinking about it, there was no way I could choose a favorite.

Coach gave me a clipped nod.

"So it's the A-team, then?" Kyle Bosco, who normally enjoyed the chaos of Hannah's ideas as much as I did, came up beside me and held out his fist, looking to bump knuckles.

Instead, I wrapped an arm around the right fielder in a half hug, half hair rub. "You know it."

He pushed me away and turned back to his locker to fix his hair. "Fucker."

"Don't worry, dumbass, he didn't mess up your perfect highlights," Mason Dumpty, our center fielder, mocked from the couch he'd settled into a few minutes before. He'd spent the last thirty minutes stomping around looking for his folding chair. I was pretty sure only Bosco thought the hide-the-chair game was fun.

Bosco glared. "I do not get my hair highlighted, but I don't wanna look like shit on Insta or YouTube."

I snickered and ducked so the towel he pitched at me hit our new first baseman, Jasper Quinn, instead. The kid had just graduated from college and had only been with the team for a few weeks. My hope was that trading Deckato, the seasoned veteran, for the young kid was a way to free up some money to extend my contract, but thus far, my agent had heard nothing.

"Stop dicking around and get going." Coach Wilson pointed out the door.

Cringing at the reprimand, I headed out to find Hannah in the tunnels, with Bosco hot on my heels.

"Traded spots again?" Hannah arched a thin brow at me. It had become a regular thing, me covering for my best friend with her.

"You prefer me anyway." I smirked.

"Fans like Dragon." Hannah shrugged, brushing her dark hair over one shoulder.

Despite my best efforts, a lump lodged in my throat in response to that simple comment. I wasn't the fan favorite. Even at the start of my second season with the team, I was still the new kid. It shouldn't have bothered me. I'd sported the title from the time I was drafted out of high school. Until now, I hadn't thought twice about it. But the idea that the Revs didn't think I was worth a contract renewal hurt. After this season, I was up for my first extension since I'd moved from triple-A to the majors. The thought that they wouldn't bring me back was like lead in my stomach.

"Fans love me," Bosco scoffed.

"The ball bunnies love you," she corrected. "As long as it's not Tristian, I have no preference."

Our head of PR and the left fielder had some sort of history. And it wasn't good, from what I could tell. But it made sense. Tristian was a tool.

Without another word, Hannah spun on her heel and took off.

"So, how's living with Gianna?" Kyle waggled his brows at me as we followed after Hannah.

I shot him the side-eye. Loaded question. Like I would tell Mr. Gossipy anything about how I felt about my new arrangement. Plus what could I say, mostly I was tongued idiot around her. I wasn't sure I could be anymore awkward if I tried.

"Chris said she ditched her boyfriend, so living with that goddess sounds like a good time."

"She makes our apartment smell like oranges," I said vaguely. Figuring he wouldn't know what to do with that.

"Huh. Citrus fruit." He nodded. "I can see it."

"Let's go Tweedledee and Tweedledah." Hannah pushed open the door to the team room and held it for us. "Let's try to get through this without it being a thing."

The normal three-person media crew was standing in front of a rectangular table set up in front of a banner with a Revs logo behind it.

Kyle stepped up to the table and eyed the two Revs scarves draped over it. "What are these?"

"They're blindfolds," Hannah said.

"Kinky." Turning on his heel, Kyle smirked at her.

"No." Hannah huffed a breath through her nose, her jaw locked. "Not kinky. Fan friendly." She held up a hand. "All-age fan friendly."

Before Kyle could piss her off, I grabbed both scarves and turned to him. "Let's do tradesees." With a step closer, I held one scarf out and reached for him.

"The fuck?" He reared back, bringing his hands to his head to protect his hair.

"You do me, I do you. I'll be careful of the hair," I promised, knowing it was his thing.

Kyle yanked the scarf I was holding out from my hand. "Do me first. I'm not letting you blind touch my hair."

Hannah huffed a breath. "Neither of you are *doing* each other."

Snickers echoed around us as one of the women from the crew came over and took them out of our hands. She waved us behind the table and showed us the marks on the floor where she wanted us to stand.

"This is going to be a blindfolded taste test. I'll feed one of you, then you have to explain to the other what it is. That person then has to guess the food."

"Easy." Bosco nodded. "We're on the same wavelength. We back each other up, so we've got the silent communication down."

"Hell yeah," I said, pounding his fist. It was true. With me on third base and him in the outfield behind me, we relied on each other pretty heavily and had worked well together since I was brought up to the Revs.

Quickly, the crew blindfolded us both. I guess it made sense. This way, neither of us had to blindfold the other without being able to see. Even if it would have been more fun our way.

Hannah did a countdown and then gave a welcome spiel before she dove into the game. "Okay, Emerson," she said, using her media voice, "here is the first plate."

"Plate?"

What was she talking about? Was it a baseball reference?

While I was expecting a forkful of food to be placed in my mouth, what I got instead was a push to the back of my head. Caught off guard, I didn't have time to fight it before my face was smashed into a puddle of goo on the table in front of me.

"Hannah." I jerked back and gasped through the cold, slimy film covering my nose and mouth.

A deep laugh erupted, sending a hint of irritation through me, but that fizzled quickly. I couldn't say I was shocked that Mason Dumpty had shown up to watch whatever this was. Like I said, Hannah's shit was always entertaining. She was good at her job. And fans loved all the activities she roped us into. I should have anticipated something ridiculous. She was great at making them laugh.

"This is why I say no to this shit," my grumpy roommate said. Clearly, Mason hadn't come alone. Chris almost sounded amused.

Smiling, I licked at the gooey substance still coating my face. "Not everyone can be as fun as me. And I've got a long tongue, so I'm best suited for this one anyway." To emphasize my point, I stuck my tongue out as far as it would go and swiped at the food again.

"Remember, Emerson," Hannah said, chuckling, "you have to describe it to Kyle."

Describe it. The flavor hadn't registered, so I licked my face again.

"Cold mush," I guessed.

"What?" Bosco asked.

Hannah hummed. "Try again. Be more descriptive."

This time, I was more prepared. Carefully, I lowered my face and sniffed without making a bigger mess. Strawberries, maybe. Tentatively, I lowered my face and stuck out my tongue.

The goo was cold. Creamy. Kinda sweet. But sorta tart. I licked again. Oh, wait. "I know—it's yogurt." Yes. Nailed it. Definitely yogurt. I sat up straight and grinned. "Strawberry Greek yogurt."

"Jesus," Chris muttered. "You're supposed to describe it and have him guess."

"Oh, oops." I chuckled. I'd forgotten that part.

Hannah sighed. "Okay, let's try again."

Beside me, Bosco's chair scraped along the floor like he was scooting closer to the table. "Don't worry, babe, I got this."

"Okay," she said. "Right here."

For a moment, the room was quiet. Without my sense of sight, my hearing improved. I could hear breathing and the soft shuffle of footsteps.

The peace was broken when Bosco crowed. "Oh! It's what you eat with beans."

Lips pressed together, still tasting the strawberry yogurt, I racked my brain for a food similar to the yogurt's texture that would go well with beans. "Crème."

"What is that?" Bosco asked with a laugh.

"It's like a mix of sour cream and cheese."

"No. Not that. You eat this with beans."

"Crème," I said again. Because that's what went with beans. Everyone knew that.

"No, this is crunchy."

Crunchy? What the hell kind of crunchy food went with beans? Uh. I'd already messed this up once. I wasn't doing it again. "Chips?" I guessed, but wouldn't I have heard him chomping if he was over there eating chips?

"No."

Frowning, I turned his way, even though I couldn't see him. "Tortillas?"

"No. Like *this* and beans."

I clapped my hands, shooting up straight. *Yes.* I had it. "Pork."

"No! It's white, and you eat it with beans, and it's crunchy, not creamy."

"Uh, it's only crunchy if it's made wrong," Mason mumbled from the other side of the room.

What was it? "Uh…" I scratched at my head, at a loss.

"Rice," Bosco said, his tone laced with annoyance.

Hannah groaned.

"Rice?" I said, wishing I could yank this blindfold off. Mason was right. Rice shouldn't be crunchy. I'd never had crunchy rice. If Bosco hadn't thrown that out there, I would have gotten it.

"I want a do-over," Bosco demanded. "He should have gotten that."

"No, it's Emerson's turn," Hannah said.

"He should have gotten that. I want a do-over."

"Okay," I agreed with an easy shrug. I could go without having my face shoved into another plate of food, and Bosco clearly needed the win.

"Fine," Hannah said.

I waited and listened, this time to the sound of him chewing.

"They're salty. And small. And a snack."

"Fritos."

"No."

"Sunflower seeds."

"No. They're shaped like…" Bosco hummed, then chuckled. "Like a dick."

"Banana?" I guessed.

"No. Smaller. Like a dick on a… mouse."

Hannah coughed, and the room broke out in laughter.

"Mouse dicks?" I asked, confusion and amusement teaming up and making me laugh.

"Kinda. I don't know. Just think dick on a mouse. But salty and crunchy."

Elbows on the table in front of me, I racked my brain for foods that were dick shaped. "Oh," I said, clapping. "Cashew!"

"Yes! That's what I'm talking about." Kyle drummed both hands on the tabletop, making the whole thing vibrate.

"We can't use that." Hannah scoffed over the noise.

Kyle's drumming came to an instant halt, and the room went quiet again. "Why?"

"We can't go on social media talking about rodent penises. I specifically said this activity was approved for all ages."

Bringing my fist to my mouth, I swallowed back a laugh at the reproach in her voice.

"Fine. Give me another. I'll keep it totally G-rated," he demanded. The dude was probably the most competitive member of the Revs.

Hannah sighed, but a moment later, there was a shuffling of feet. Then she murmured words I couldn't make out.

I laced my fingers behind my head and waited while he shuffled around beside me.

With a snap of his finger, Kyle said, "It's what Gianna smells like."

"Oranges." The word left my mouth instantaneously.

"Jesus," Chris muttered. "Neither of you should know what my sister smells like."

I winced. Shit. I probably answered that a bit too fast. But I'd spent the three days since she'd moved in immersed in that scent. Every detail of it was lodged in my brain. "I live with her, man." With a yank, I pulled my blindfold off and searched the room for him. "Even though I'm not eating the flowers, I can't help but smell the bouquet."

He blinked, and his entire body went rigid, but after a couple of heartbeats, he relaxed and shook his head. "Whatever the hell that means. But yeah, okay." Then he turned his death glare on Bosco. "Stay away from my sister."

Shit. Gi would hate that. Chris liked to issue demands, and already, it was obvious to me that Gianna wasn't big on being told what to do.

"She can take care of herself, man," I said. "And you know she'd cut out your tongue for trying to be her boss."

Chris scowled, but then he shrugged. "Probably."

"Well," Hannah muttered, "this was a disaster. Let's just hope we can edit it into something somewhat usable."

With a wave to the crew, she started cleaning up, and they followed her lead.

Chris shuffled closer. "Sorry, man. I'm not trying to give you shit," he said, shocking the shit out of me. With one hand in a pocket, he scratched at the back of his head. "You're doing me a solid by letting her live with you. I know she's a pain in the ass."

She really wasn't. I'd hardly seen her in the three days she'd been there. I wasn't home much, and when I was, she was usually camped out in her room.

"It's not a big deal." I shrugged. "If the place didn't smell like orange blossoms all the damn time, I wouldn't even know she's around."

Which was good. Because now that I knew her boyfriend was out of the picture…nope. I wasn't even thinking about it. She was a sexy, talented woman who'd no doubt easily find another guy to worship her. And for so many reasons, that guy couldn't be me.

Gianna

5

I stood at the massive wall of windows, studying the Boston skyline. The zoo sign needed finishing touches, but the skyline had been screaming at me for hours.

It could be a challenge to channel creativity into what I was forced to do when deadlines and client demands became the priority. And I'd learned not to ignore inspiration for too long, or I'd get all gummed up. Then nothing I painted or drew would be anything but trash, whether for myself or for the job.

The zoo signs were going well. I'd have no trouble finishing the detailing before opening night under the stars next week. Even if I gave myself the night off.

My mother always said that food feeds the body, but creativity feeds the soul. And my soul felt bruised.

I was hopeful that being in Boston would give me a break from dealing with Jake on the regular, but even while I worked remotely, he emailed and called me multiple times a day. Almost like he was checking in on me. Like he was concerned that I wasn't doing my job with the zoo. I'd never given anything but a million percent to any of my designs, so the distrust was unnecessary and frustrating.

33

Between dealing with my asshole ex—who, although didn't leave me heartbroken, definitely left me feeling dumb and unwanted, not to mention embarrassed—and not having a place or space that was my own, failure hovered strong. I needed some soul food. And in this moment, between the view and some angry music, I found some peace.

I lifted my brush again and turned off all thought. The yellows blended into the grays and blacks, giving light to the buildings. My lips moved along with the words to the Miley Cyrus song, as if they had a mind of their own, while I worked. I had just finished lighting the buildings when a noise in the kitchen startled me.

I turned and jumped when I caught a glimpse of a figure standing at the counter. My heart pounded, even as he came into focus and I realized it was Emerson.

Pausing the music, I shot him a glare. "How long have you been standing there?"

He shrugged. "I'm not good at time."

Lips parted, I sucked in a breath, ready to lay into him. But I had no idea how to respond to that. He couldn't mean he didn't know how to read a clock. That would be ridiculous.

"Sorry." The corner of his mouth lifted slightly. "Didn't mean to interrupt."

"You didn't. It's just weird that you're standing there." I pressed my lips together, squirming as he watched me with a look of concentration on his face.

What was he hoping to see? I was a mess. I could guarantee I had paint on my face. It tended to happen when I got into a design. Hackles raised, I braced myself for him to comment on it, to mock me. He wouldn't be the first.

But rather than criticize me, he took a swig of his water and shrugged. "Standing is not weird. Juggling would be. Especially since I'm not good at it."

The air whooshed out of my lungs, and I dropped my shoulders, confused. "What?"

His face lit up in a full smile. "Crazy, right? I should be excellent at it. I catch balls for a living. But it's the damnedest thing." He chuckled deeply, and although I wasn't following him, the sound rumbled through my stomach. The man was oddly sexy. "Every time I try, I toss those balls up and they just rain on my head like bird shit."

I scoffed. What did he expect me to say to that? *It's cool that you're a bad juggler*? Or *Yeah, I hate being dusted by bird droppings*?

"Well, I'm just gonna zoom over to the shower."

I set my paintbrush down and turned. "Didn't you just shower?"

According to Chris, the guys always hit the showers after a game. It was why they took so long to get to the team room.

"Nah, locker room showers are typically just a quick rinse-and-go so I don't stink." He waved his hand in front of his nose. "Between the dirt and sweat"—lips quirked on one side, he made a clicking sound—"it's no bueno."

I huffed a laugh. "I grew up with Chris. I get it."

His eyes twinkled as he full-on laughed. "Yeah, I knew for sure Avery loved him when she ended up in the closet with him after the game but pre-shower."

A shudder ran through me. Those were details about my brother I had no interest in.

"Anyway, this is my wind-down shower. So..." He held his arms out on either side of him and took off, making a motor noise.

For several seconds, I stared at the empty space he'd left behind. Was he pretending to be a plane? Whatever he was doing, he'd left me all kinds of off-kilter.

Finally, I flicked the music back on and focused on my painting again. I'd only just gotten back into the zone when a loud pounding interrupted me.

I growled and tossed my brush down. I swore if a neighbor was here to complain about my music, I might chew them out. It had been a long day already, and I didn't have time for idiocy.

I yanked the door open to a guy in a gray polo, a pair of shorts, and the brightest blue Revs socks I'd ever seen.

"Where is Mr. Damiano?" he asked.

Great, a fan. I'd dealt with enough of them in my life, so I'd gotten pretty good at scaring them off quickly.

"Not here." I crossed my arms and arched a brow, making sure to don that mask Jake had mistaken for resting bitch face.

"Someone must be," he said, craning his neck and peering into the apartment, "because, clearly, you haven't showered."

My shoulders tightened in irritation. "Excuse me?" This guy was something. Yeah, I may be dotted in paint, and I was sporting leggings and T-shirt, but I wasn't disgusting.

He pushed past me and moved down the hall.

"Listen, asshole," I said, but my words were drowned out as he beat on Emerson's bathroom door.

"Shut the water off now," the guy barked, not looking back at me.

An instant later, the water stopped, but that didn't stop the fucker from pounding on the door. He only dropped his hand when it swung open and Emerson appeared.

My mouth went dry at the sight of him. My roommate had a white towel wrapped around his waist, and there were streams of water running down his broad shoulders, silver chain around his neck, over his tan chest, and settling into the divots of his abs. Without my permission, my eyes followed the drops as they continued their journey.

My perusal came to an abrupt halt, though, when he cleared his throat. Sucking in a breath, I forced my eyes to his face, finding him smiling sweetly at me. I ground my teeth. Dammit. He'd caught me ogling him. He flicked his hair back, flinging water on the dude who was hovering too close to the doorjamb.

"You're causing a flood downstairs," the dick growled.

Emerson blinked in confusion, and his smile fell. He opened his mouth, but before he could get a word out, the fuckface continued his tirade.

"It doesn't take a genius to know to shut off the water when there is a leak."

In the next heartbeat, the light left Emerson's eyes. Fuck, the look was all wrong on him. Sad Emerson shouldn't exist.

The defeat in his posture sent my blood boiling. I'd had enough. Yanking on the guy's arm, I spun him toward me. He stumbled, but caught himself quickly and pulled his thin arm out of my grasp. The glare he hit me with was surely meant to intimidate me, but clearly, he didn't know who he was dealing with.

"Listen, dickwad," I gritted out, pulling my shoulders back and tipping my chin to towel-clad Emerson, who was still dripping water all over the floor beneath him. "This poor guy just finished winning a game for a team you like, if your socks are any indication." I pointed down to the high socks and shorts look this tool bag was failing to pull off. "All he wanted was to unwind. The only way he could have known a pipe was leaking was if he could see the fucking future. And as quirky as he is, I don't get the genie lamp or a wizard vibe. Do you?" I lifted my brows.

The man's only response was sputtered nonsense.

"That's what I thought." I took a step closer. "So maybe calm the fuck down and think twice about yelling at the person paying rent for an apartment you apparently don't take care of very well."

At this point, my finger was slammed into the man chest, but I wasn't done. I'd show this douche—

My tirade was cut off by a chuckle in my ear and a strong, damp arm wrapped around my waist. Normally, I'd flinch away from a germy shower towel because they were almost as bad as sheets, but the warmth of his body above the white fabric froze me in place.

"Thanks, Mariposa," Emerson said, pulling me away from the assholey little man.

His breath ghosted across my ear, and I fought the shiver that tried to race down my spine at the sensation. Leave it to my body to betray me when this overzealous puppy stuck in a gorgeous man's body touched me.

Rather than release me, he kept his arm wrapped around my midsection, and though I could have been hallucinating, I swore he brought his nose to my hair and inhaled.

Holy. Shit. Did he sniff me? Did I smell? Oh shit. The comment he'd made about the shower flashed through my mind. I had showered early in the day. But maybe I'd worked up a sweat—

"If you've got your woman under control—"

My body clenched for a totally different reason, and I pushed at his arm, ready to toss my gloves and show this man just how out of control I could be.

But Emerson stepped around me and stood between us, protecting the idiot who clearly had a death wish. I stepped to one side, but Emerson reached one large hand back and set it on my hip, his fingers biting into my skin, stopping me.

The contact sent my heart tripping over itself, distracting me from the moment.

"I'm sorry, sir," Emerson said, keeping his tone polite, as always. "But regardless of the state of my relationship with Gianna or any woman, I'd never attempt to control them. I find most of the female population way more capable than us idiots."

His disarming smile had the guy snorting. But my stomach flipped at Emerson's statement and the respect in his tone.

He released me, and with both hands up in front of him, he stepped back toward his room.

"Why don't you relax in the living room, sir? Give me a second to get dressed, and then we can talk. I'll do whatever I can to help." He smiled like a big, dumb dope at the man who had been nothing but awful since he stepped into the apartment.

"Well." The man shifted on his feet and pursed his lips. "The people who live below you are Revs fans. I'm sure an autograph from your roommate would go a long way in smoothing things over."

The light in Emerson's eyes dulled, but he nodded and pasted a phony smile to his face. "Done. Dragon always has a few signed photos around."

Five minutes later, the asshole left happily, with Emerson's promise to not use the bathroom and a handful of signed pictures of my brother.

"There's no way I would have given him my brother's autograph," I said as soon as the door was closed. "I was seriously considering castration."

Emerson chuckled. "Really? I totally didn't get that vibe."

I rolled my eyes. "I didn't like how he was talking to you."

The corner of Emerson's mouth lifted just a bit, drawing my attention to his strong jawline and the fine layer of scruff there. Normally, facial hair looked messy, but the dark shadow on Emerson's otherwise innocent face worked.

"The way you stuck up for me definitely roller-coastered my stomach. I'm not sure anyone has ever fought like that for me."

My shoulders tightened at his words. Seriously? I narrowed my eyes at him. This guy was sweet enough to cause a toothache. How was it possible that he didn't have an army at his back?

He shrugged. "I stay out of the way and do my best to keep people smiling."

I assessed the happy man in front of me, taking him in from head to toe. I would never have guessed by his constant positivity that he'd had a hard life, but suddenly, I was questioning a lot of things.

Jaw locked, I asked, "What does that mean?"

Emerson shifted on his bare feet and pressed his hands together in front of him. The pop of his knuckles as they cracked filled the silence around us.

"Emerson?"

Finally glancing my way, he sighed. "I'm the oldest of four. My mom's time was stretched thin, and I didn't need her to protect me. She had other people to worry about."

His focus drifted over my shoulder, like he couldn't look at me and say the next words.

"I was seventeen when I moved to triple-A. They treated me like a goofball kid, teased me endlessly. So I leaned into it. Made a point to make them laugh so that they didn't hate me."

My heart ached at the words and the hint of sadness in his usually jovial tone. "What?"

"Gianna." He finally met my gaze, his normally bright green eyes tinged with brown looking almost muddied and hollow. "I was a kid, on a team full of men. I had no friends and barely any life skills. But I made sure they'd never have to go out of their way to do shit for me. The last thing I wanted was for them to resent me, so I stayed out of the way."

Emerson

6

Dammit. It killed me to see that pitying look in her eyes. Like she thought I was pathetic.

Shifting on my feet, I dropped my focus to the floor between us and cracked my knuckles again.

The truth was that, until I was twenty and Chris joined the team, I didn't have a single friend. I was just the stupid kid who was fast as hell. I played shortstop at that point, and nothing got past me. I led triple-A in steals for three seasons. Even then, I ran a faster forty than most of the guys in the majors. None of that made me friends. At seventeen, I didn't know shit about anything. I played with twenty-five years old who were jealous of my speed and spent their free time in bars I couldn't get into. Who had girlfriends and one-night stands and affairs.

At that point, I'd only ever kissed two girls. I was immature and naïve and not suited for life with the big boys. I made bad jokes and tripped over my own feet when I wasn't on the field.

Though being so out of my element at seventeen had made me who I was now at twenty-six. I'd never fit in, and now, I didn't try to. But I clung to the solid friendships I'd made during my time with the Revs.

41

The guys I played with, especially Chris, were more like family than teammates.

So regardless of how adorable Gi looked with paint on her fingers and shirt and the yellow streak on her cheek, I'd stay away. Even though my heart had skipped when she jumped to my defense, the last thing I wanted to do was piss her brother off. Even if parts of me, especially the parts below the waistband of my gym shorts, wanted to.

But with one last long look at the woman whose brown eyes were narrowed in confusion, I shrugged, playing off the depth of this conversation. "Anyway, I find you catch more flies with honey."

"Bees," she corrected.

"What?"

"It's bees. You catch more bees with honey than you do with vinegar. My father's been telling me that my entire life."

I chuckled. My mom was the queen of getting the expression wrong. And I'd admit I did sometimes too, but this time, I was pretty sure it was Gi who was wrong. But the woman was known to be stubborn, and I didn't want a fight. "Well, seeing as I'm allergic to the bees, I'll leave those for you and Pop," I joked. "I'm starving. Feeling a grilled cheese?"

She blinked at me in response.

When she didn't answer the question, I cleared my throat and headed for the kitchen. "How about this? I'll make a few, and if you feel up to one, you can have it." Bending at the waist, I pulled out the flat pan. "And since I totally messed up your night, I'll be quiet and let you get back to your masterpiece."

She shot me a withering look, her lips pursed and her dark eyes hard. "No need for sarcasm."

"Trust me, that wasn't sarcasm. Your work is damn good, Gi," I assured her, rummaging in the fridge for cheese. I dug out the cheddar, gouda, and pepper jack. The combination was perfect and gave the sandwich just a bit of a kick.

When I glanced back up, she was still standing in the center of the room, glaring at me.

Head tilted, I assessed her. "What?"

"I can't tell if you're being serious." She crossed her arms, and even in the damn oversized T-shirt, I could clearly see the outlines of her full breasts.

For a heartbeat, my eyes lingered on the lace I could just make out through the white fabric. But with a mental kick in the pants, I spun away and ran a hand down my face.

"I'm dead serious." Instead of heating the pan, I went back to the fridge for a beer. Damn, did I need a drink. I pulled out two and held them both up. "Preference?"

She frowned at the Bud Light, then the Sam Adams lager. She grabbed the lager and went for the drawer where we kept the bottle opener. I couldn't blame her for her choice. Bud Light kinda sucked. But it fit into my meal plans during the season a little more easily, so it worked out in the end. I cracked mine and took a pull.

"Are you the one who frames them?" she asked.

Though the question could have been viewed as cryptic, I didn't have to ask her to elaborate. We had three of her oil paintings hanging around the apartment.

"Does it kill the image of your brother to know he doesn't do it?" I chuckled.

Christian could give two shits about decorating this place. If it was up to him, we'd have the ping-pong table and a couch and a TV.

Maybe it was because I'd been on my own so long, or maybe it was just the need to spend time in a place that felt like home since I was so far away from my family. Either way, I couldn't live in a sterile, empty box.

Quietly, she scanned the open living area and sipped her beer. "You have good taste."

I smirked. "And you have a lot of talent."

The way her cheeks turned pink was as attractive as it was surprising. With a finger twirling a single curl, she looked away. Gianna always seemed sure of herself, so the uncertainty in her expression and posture were shocking.

Her brother and her dad sang her praises, so one would think she'd be used to the compliments. Unless, maybe, they were the only ones?

Christian had always bitched about her ex-boyfriend being shitty and unsupportive.

"Did your guy not tell you that all the damn time?"

She looked up at me and opened her mouth quickly, but instead of replying, she sighed. Her brown eyes swirled with so many emotions, but I didn't know what any of them were. They were all new to me, because normally, all I got from her was pissed off.

I set my beer on the quartz countertop and waited, watching her. She dropped her attention from my face again, tracking the lines of the hardwood floor below her feet. Finally, she glanced at her drink and slowly lifted it.

"My friends told me he was jealous." She took a sip of her beer, and a small crease appeared between her eyes, but she still wasn't looking at me. "I made a lot of excuses for why he didn't like to give compliments." She paused again and took another sip of the beer. "But I realize now that he's just an ass."

I chuckled. Sounded like everything I'd heard about the guy. I moved to the bread drawer, deciding that since she was opening up some, I'd push my luck. "What made you decide that?"

"A few weeks ago, he took me to my favorite restaurant, and in the middle of dinner, he told me he got someone else pregnant and was moving in with her." Her tone was matter-of-fact, but the words were like nails ripping through my ears.

I was halfway back to the counter when the bread slipped from my hand. Letting it fall to the floor, I spun back to her. My heart hammered oddly as an irrational anger gripped me deep in my chest. "The fuck did you just say?"

"I know." She slammed her beer onto the counter and then bent to retrieve the bread. "Total ass, right?" She shook her head and passed it back to me.

"Uh…" That was the understatement of the century. But also, Christian was the most overprotective person I'd ever met, so… "How is it your brother didn't eviscerate him?"

Her eyes widened for a second in surprise, but she quickly schooled her expression and hit me with the glare I was so familiar with. "I'm not telling him." With her arms crossed over her body again, she jutted one hip in a way that screamed *fuck off*.

I swallowed, digesting her confession and wondering what the hell to do with it.

"Look," she said, interrupting my thoughts, "it's embarrassing, and I don't want—"

"Gianna," I said, keeping my tone soft.

She didn't glance up.

"Gianna," I said more forcefully.

This time, her brown eyes lifted, tracking over my bare chest before finally meeting mine.

"His shittiness isn't a reflection of you," I said, fisting a hand on the countertop. "It's on him." With my other hand, I gently snagged hers and gave it a squeeze. "You are a talented, fierce, gorgeous woman, and you deserve a hell of a lot more than that."

Her lips parted on a quick intake of breath. Besides our hands, no parts of us were touching. Even so, my entire body heated. The air around us buzzed. Her pupils dilated, making it obvious that she could feel the electricity coursing between us too. All I had to do was tug on her hand and let her fall into me. Then I'd claim her mouth. She'd welcome it. I'd welcome it.

But I wasn't going there.

I released her hand and quickly stepped back.

She blinked several times, like she was returning to reality, then her mouth fell into a tight line. "Right." She nodded. "Still, none of it is Chris's business."

Nodding, I turned to the stove.

"I'm gonna…" Without finishing her sentence, she padded away, the sound of her feet on the floor almost imperceptible.

I wanted to kick myself, but what the hell should I have done? Kiss her? If she were any other woman, that's exactly what I would have done, because I wanted to so badly. But Christian was my best friend, the guy who'd been there for me when I literally had no one. And I wouldn't fuck that up by casually hooking up with his sister.

Regardless of how impressive and fucking gorgeous Gianna was, I didn't have more than causal in me. My contract with the Revs was up in four months, and if that didn't get extended, I had no idea what I'd do or how I'd support myself, let alone have the bandwidth to care for another person while I was going through that crisis. Gianna wasn't the type to need to be taken care of, but she deserved a partner who had a purpose. One who brought value to the relationship. Not an unemployable slouch who'd mooch off her. If baseball didn't work out, I didn't even have a degree to fall back on. Unlike most players, I'd skipped college to play in the minors. If baseball was no longer a possibility, then who was I?

With each day my agent heard nothing, I felt less confident that I'd be a Rev next year. There weren't other teams lining up either. My only option would be to go back to the minors. Spend ten months in some small town far away.

I glanced over my shoulder at Gianna, who was at her easel across the room again. Her back was to me as she stared at the painting in front of her. The skyline on her canvas was more interesting than the one out the windows. Her ability to pull things in and make them more was awe-inspiring. All her work was filled with this emotional vulnerability that she rarely expressed anywhere else. A softness that I could only guess lurked under the surface. And shit, if it didn't fascinate me.

As much as I couldn't cross lines with her, I couldn't leave this awfulness hanging between us either.

"Want to learn to flip grilled cheese?" I asked.

Her head snapped my way. "What?"

I pulled the pan off the stovetop. The buttered bread had heated enough that all three layers of cheese were starting to melt. I held it out above the counter so she could see, and with a flick of the wrist, I tossed the bread into the air and caught it again, uncooked side down.

Almost unwillingly, her mouth pulled up at one corner. "Tricky."

I nodded. "Want to learn to be tricky too?"

Finally, I got an almost full grin.

"What makes you think I need to learn?" With one brow lifted, she pushed off her small stool and strode toward me with a look of determination in her eye.

I set the sauté pan down so she could grip the handle. In one smooth motion, she picked it up and flipped the grilled cheese again.

46

Eyes rolling, she scoffed. "You're not the only one who can do tricks."

"Damn, girl. Nice." I laughed, elated not only because she could do it, but because she'd so willingly come over to play with me. "Can you do two flips?"

She sighed like I exhausted her, but instead of turning on her heel and walking away like I expected, she took the pan back. Turned out she could flip twice, so I did a triple flip and handed the pan back. But she didn't have my skills. She gave it a good old-fashioned try, then tried again as we finished up the sandwiches, but she couldn't beat me.

Once we had our sandwiches on plates, I wandered to the living room. "Want to watch a movie?"

Rather than giving me a firm answer one way or the other, she shrugged and eyed the television.

Taking that as a yes, I pulled up my watch list.

The second the list appeared, she let out a harsh scoff. "I'm not watching Avery's movies."

With my lips pressed together, I scanned the screen. It was loaded full of several of the best rom-coms out there. "I love these. I couldn't pick a favorite. You've heard me talk about the chills I get from a good happily ever after." A sigh escaped me, unbidden, and I couldn't help but smile. I loved seeing people end up happy. It was a drug I couldn't get enough of.

"They depress me."

"Depress you?" I shifted on the couch and frowned at her. Of all the snarky responses I could have predicted she'd come up with, that wasn't one of them.

She picked up the sandwich, keeping her focus trained on it, clearly trying to ignore my question, and took a bite. "Wow, Em, these are really good."

I'd humor her for a minute. "It's the pepper jack. Perfect little kick to the gooey goodness."

After her second bite, she hummed. "I think it's the play between the Gouda and the jack. You get that savory strong flavor, but with the bite of the spice in the jack."

"Exactly." I took a swig of my beer, preparing to return to my question. I wasn't sure why I was harping on it, other than I wanted to understand Gianna.

This same need to know more about her had hit me the first time I saw her artwork. The depth of the dark water, almost lonely in front of the city of Boston, with its bright shiny lights, had entranced me. Like it was speaking to me because, so often, I felt like the water. Alone in a crowd. When Chris had told me that his sister painted it, my heart lurched oddly in my chest. I'd always thought Gi was beautiful, but since that moment, I hadn't been able to curb my curiosity about her.

"So," I hedged, "why are rom-coms depressing?"

She huffed and glared at me for a full minute, slowly chewing. Finally, she set her sandwich down, wiped her hands, and sat back against the sofa cushion. "When you never get the happily ever after, it's annoying as fuck to have to keep watching it happen for everyone else."

Her tone might have been biting, but the vulnerability in that statement stole the smile off my face.

"I never get that." She picked up her grilled cheese and pointed it at the woman who was practically glowing with happiness on the screen.

It was like a knife to the chest, knowing that the men in her past hadn't made her smile. I was nowhere near stable enough to be a forever guy, but I made sure I always left any woman, whether I hooked up with her or not, with a smile on her face. Bringing joy to the people around me was a privilege. And it sucked that no one had gone out of their way to do that for Gianna.

"You'll find it someday." Even with her rough edges, she more than deserved to be loved fiercely. She stood up for people, and she worked hard. I surveyed her, taking in her dark hair, her dark eyes, the serious expression. She had that spark—not happiness; more like heat. Everything with her was hot, and I loved basking in that glow. The prospect of getting burned gave me that same rush that I experienced every time I kicked off the bag to steal the base.

She snorted. "Whatever you say."

Maybe that was what I could do for her in the next few weeks. Show her she deserved more joy.

Gianna

7

"That man is like lightning." The voice had me glancing up from my phone. Avery's friend Wren was staring down at the field from our box. "I bet he steals second before the first pitch."

"No," Avery shook her head. "Em always waits at least one pitch. He loves the fake out too much to go too soon."

Wren chuckled and cocked a knowing brow. "That's true. He's mastered the art of the fake out."

Avery giggled in response, clearly understanding the joke there that made no sense to me.

I bit back a huff. I didn't want to be annoyed with them, but I felt out of the Emerson loop, and that was…oddly frustrating.

He was oddly frustrating. I couldn't get a read on the guy. After last night, maybe I really did understand what they meant by him being good at the fake out. Twice between the building's super storming in and the end of the night, I thought he was about to kiss me. Both times, he pulled away and went back to his friendly, goofy self. It left me feeling dumb for reading into something that clearly wasn't there.

I had planned to just avoid him today. The team was leaving on a five-day road stretch, and my hope was that when he got back, we'd

49

both have forgotten. But I'd already promised Avery that I'd come to the game with her and Wren and Wren's parents. She was convinced Wren and I would get along.

She promised that we had similar interests in art and fashion, and I wouldn't say that she was wrong. Wren worked at the Boston Auction House, facilitating the sale of artwork. And even while attending a baseball game, she had a classy air around her. The high-waisted pants and a silk tank top she'd chosen, along with a pair of wedges, made her look more ready for lunch at the country club than a sporting event.

I had considered not wearing this sundress to the game, knowing Avery always opted for jean shorts and my brother's jersey, but as adorable as she looked in a jersey, those things made me look like I was wearing an oversized box. Now that we were here, with Wren and her parents dressed to impress, I was glad I'd stuck to my favorite blue sundress.

"Look, he's already playing with him." Wren tipped her chin to first base.

Down on the diamond, Emerson crept away from first, leaving just the tip of his cleat on the bag. He was smiling and joking with the first baseman while he waited for Mason Dumpty to get up to bat.

"Walking Em seems dumb." Avery shrugged. "Chris stresses when there's a threat of a steal on first base. It's odd to do that on purpose."

I didn't follow baseball enough to add to that comment. I probably should know more. My dad had coached high school ball until his heart attack, and obviously, Chris had played his whole life, but sports just weren't my thing. Even if I had knowledge of it, at the moment, I was too preoccupied with watching Emerson in his pinstripes as he shifted two lengths from the base with a smirk on his face.

I could tell he was messing with the first baseman just by that expression. He moved a bit farther from the bag, taunting the pitcher. All over the stadium, fans were pointing at him. Like they were just waiting to see him make his move. Or maybe they just liked the view.

Couldn't blame them for that.

His long, lean body looked good in the white stripes, but his uniform hid the tight muscles I knew were beneath. Swallowing, I tried to push away the memory of how he looked sprawled out on the couch shirtless as he ate his grilled cheese last night. How the light caught the silver chain on his neck. How every chuckle tightened the muscle and deepened each cut of abs that lined his torso. How his corded forearms lifted the bread to his full lips.

How much my body heated in his proximity. At some point during the night, a switch flipped in my mind. Since I'd met him, I'd known that my brother's best friend was a gorgeous guy that women every-where wanted, but last night, I found myself falling into that category. Suddenly, I craved him too, and I didn't know what to do about it.

My plan for the evening had been to finish my painting, but instead, I found myself one cushion away, trying not to laugh along with him and enjoying myself while watching reruns of a show I'd seen multiple times.

And now I found I couldn't look away from the third baseman.

He shuffled two steps farther, and the pitcher turned, but by the time the ball left his hand, Emerson was already back on base. With a grin, he waved his hands, and the fans cheered. The Bandits' first baseman tossed the ball back to the pitcher and glared at Emerson. That look, though, didn't stop him from immediately doing it again. He continued his taunting until the pitch count was at two balls and two strikes.

Then as the pitcher started his wind-up, Emerson's lunge got just a hair deeper, and the muscles of his ass tightened for a split second. Then he was moving.

In a blink, he was racing for second. Before the ball even got to the catcher's glove, he was dropping to the dirt, and in the most graceful motion I'd ever seen from Emerson—hell, from any man—he slid toward the bag and popped up to stand back on both feet just as he reached it. The drop-and-lift was pure art in motion. Fluid like the swell of an ocean wave.

The stadium broke out in cheers for yet another stolen base. But Emerson just wiped at the brown dirt on his chest and smirked at the second baseman.

"See?" Wren hollered as she clapped loudly. "Told ya. He's got to be close to leading the league. That man has moves."

"Ones you've seen?" Avery teased.

Of their own accord, my shoulders went rigid. I had no claim on Emerson, but as I studied the tall, thin brunette, my hackles rose. Her straight, bluntly cut black hair just brushed her shoulders. Her almost jet-black eyes popped because of her very naturally applied makeup. High cheekbones, small nose, and deep red lips. She was willowy in a way I'd never have any hope of attaining, even if I lost fifty pounds. If she was Emerson's type, then I definitely wasn't.

And I wanted to smash something.

She whacked a hand lightly against Avery's arm. "I do not sleep with Daddy Wilson's boys. Unlike you, I follow his rule."

My shoulders dropped slightly at the relief I didn't want to feel in that statement.

Avery groaned. "Stop calling my father Daddy Wilson."

Wren's red lips pulled up in a smirk, and she tapped one long red nail against them. "But I do love to watch his boys play."

Tom Wilson had his own box at the stadium. From the looks of it, it was for Avery, who attended just about every home game. Since Pop had moved to Boston, she'd made sure to include him too.

He was currently sitting outside the box in the open-air seats with Wren's parents. From the way he chatted with them, it was clear the three of them did this a lot. Pop was as laid-back and casual as a guy could get, while Wren's parents looked like they were headed to an upscale restaurant after the game.

At the crack of a bat, I zeroed in on the field again. The ball soared high into the sky, straight over the wall at left field, and into the water beyond.

The crowd erupted, the whole stadium alive and roaring.

"Mason's bat is on fire," Wren cheered as Avery screamed.

I tracked Emerson as he rounded third and headed for home. After crossing the plate, he turned back, and when Mason's foot touched the white pentagon, both guys jumped into the air, crashing chests and laughing. Music pounded through the stadium so loudly the seats vibrated. The guys knocked cleats again and broke into an obviously planned dance. They shuffled to one side, their arms moving and their shoulders bouncing in sync, all the way to the dugout as "Shut up and Dance" blared around them.

The crowd was on their feet, bopping right along with them as they hammed it up.

"They're cute, aren't they?" Wren asked, zeroing in on me in my periphery.

Brows pulled together, I turned, eyeing her first, then Avery. "Uh, yeah, I guess."

"I love when they do 'Moves Like Jagger,' although this is a close second." Avery giggled.

"They have perfected it this season," Wren added.

With a nod, Avery shook her empty beer bottle. "Anyone want another?"

We both declined, and as she wandered off, I couldn't help but turn back to the field.

I'd watched this game my entire life, but suddenly, it all felt different. And I had no idea why.

A handful of Revs players poured out of the dugout and attacked both men with back slaps and giant hugs. The crowd cheered, but for one second, Emerson turned and looked up at us. Almost as if he could see me from way down there. What a silly impossibility. I'd mentioned I was coming today, but I hadn't told him where I was sitting. Still, it felt like he was looking at me, so I lifted a hand and gave him a tiny wave.

He lifted his chin in response and flashed a smile.

My stomach flipped. Holy shit. He *was* looking at me.

"Emerson has never bothered to look this way before, but I swear that's the fifth time he's done it today." Wren's dark eyes ran over me —from the hair I spent forty minutes curling down to the strappy wedges on my feet—before she focused on my face. I braced for a snide comment about why Emerson would be looking at me. "He told me about your paintings."

My spine went straight. That was the last thing I expected her to say. "What?"

Nodding, she tucked a strand of hair behind her ear. "We were at a bar a few weeks ago. I asked him about the image on his phone's lock screen. It's an oil painting of the stadium from the water?"

My heart clenched. I'd painted it for Chris last year, and I'd been shocked to find it framed on the wall of his apartment. The bigger shock, though, came yesterday, when I discovered that Emerson was the one who framed it.

"He has a photo of my painting on his phone?" Quickly, I scanned the field, but he was gone.

"He said something about how the water spoke to him."

I swallowed back the emotion welling up inside me at that thoughtful statement. I remembered feeling that way when I saw one of my mother's paintings. Wildflowers. Nothing crazy. Still, something in the way they blew so freely in the breeze called to me. The canvas was still with my dad, hanging above his bed. But the feeling of being captivated by the emotion of the painting was something that had stayed with me.

My mother had always said the mark of a true artist was creating strong feelings in the people viewing the work. Good or bad, it didn't matter. It was the ability to evoke the emotion that was so special. I had come home from second grade crying that someone had called my painting from art gross and told me they never hated something more. But my mother insisted we have a celebration for me that night because my work had spoken so deeply to someone.

"Avery told us you were a graphic designer. I didn't realize you painted too."

I was jarred back to the moment by the question. "It's just a hobby." Shrugging, I nervously twirled my hair. Wren worked with well-known art and artists. The Boston Auction House sold paintings worth thousands, even millions. I painted for the enjoyment, not to make money.

With a slow nod, she snagged her purse from beneath her seat. Then she pulled out a white card and held it out to me.

I cocked my head, confused, but took it from her anyway. Her name was embossed in gold in the center of the thick cardstock. Beneath it, her title, assistant acquisitions manager, was printed. I looked back up and scrutinized her, unsure of what to make of it.

"I help a lot of people sell their hobbies. If you ever find yourself interested in the idea, call me."

A tiny part of my heart soared. How cool would it be to say I'd sold a painting? Especially through the Boston Auction House.

When I quit styling and went back to school, my dream had been to work in graphic design so I could pay the bills and still have time to work with oils and canvas. Maybe start selling them at fairs or to small shops. One professor had encouraged me to do something with my art. But at the time, my boyfriend, Ron, had sneered and scoffed at the idea that I'd ever expect to make money off my silly paintings. I'd given Jake a painting of the New York skyline for Christmas, and he'd kept it in the back of the closet. And then, somewhere along the way, I'd decided that my hobby wasn't something more than a method I used to relax myself. The thought of trying to sell my work and discover no one was interested? Or having Chris and Pop be the only ones to bid on it? It terrified me. Any time I thought about it, I was filled with an intense feeling of dread.

I cleared my throat, slowly shaking my head. "I don't think so."

With a hand on my forearm, she gave me a warm smile. "Keep the card. You might change your mind."

I slipped it into my pocket, but I very much doubted I would.

Emerson
8

AFTER MASON'S HOME RUN DURING THE FOURTH INNING PUT US IN THE lead, we stayed that way. And although it was a win, we lost Mason in the middle of the game, which put a damper on all our moods. He made an amazing flying catch that saved the lead, but he fell on the way down and knocked himself out. So after the game, we all headed down the tunnel, trying not to stress about our teammate who was at the hospital being checked out.

That was what I should have been focused on. Mason and his injury. Instead, all I could think about was long hair, brown eyes, and gorgeous curves. Because all game long, I was looking up to the box where I knew Gi would be.

Pop and Avery had come to most home games this year. I knew where they sat, and there was no doubt in my mind that Gi would be with them. I hadn't meant to focus on her, but time after time, my attention shifted up to the box.

As if controlled by an invisible force, I couldn't stop myself. She felt it too. I wasn't dumb. At this point in my life, I knew when a woman was attracted to me. I heard the quick intakes of breath, saw the way her focus dropped to my mouth before she caught herself. I'd even seen her pulse pound against the smooth skin of her neck.

Restraining myself around her was torture. One I had little experience with. Being young and single, I rarely had to avoid attraction. If it was there, then I acted on it. This situation was causing my hyperfocus, which normally only existed on the field, to kick in. I wanted to think about anything—anyone—else. But my thoughts constantly drifted to the swell of her hips. The fullness of her thighs. The soft mounds of her breasts. Her plush pink lips. Even the way the skin pulled across her cheekbones.

God, I was becoming obsessed.

But a fling with Gianna would muck everything up. From the dawn of baseball, drama fucked with a team dynamic more than any other issue. I'd seen it over the years, teammates fighting over a chick. Guys vying for a position. Or the same salary. I'd gone out of my way to avoid falling into those kinds of traps and instead focused on being grateful just to be on the team and be part of the group.

But as I stood in front of my locker, cracking my knuckles, I was thinking about the best ways to make my best friend's sister smile. About the way her teeth would press lightly into her bottom lip as she shifted closer to me.

Shit. I dropped my head back. I needed to stop.

A hand landed on my shoulder, startling me.

Twisting, I huffed a breath.

"Looks like you might get lucky and get a room to yourself for the entire five-day trip," Bosco joked.

Mason and I were typically roommates on the road, but Bosco was probably the guy's best friend. And in his normal way of deflecting his concern, Bosco joked around.

"Don't be a dick, Streaks." Eddie Martinez, our shortstop, shook his head. "A reporter might hear you and print God knows what about you being an insensitive prick."

"He's just making margaritas out of the lemons that life is tossing our way," I said, smiling at the guys.

"Lemonade," Bosco corrected, dropping his head and giving it a shake.

I shrugged. "I didn't think you drank that shit, but sure, if that's what you want."

"You're such a dumbass." Bosco whacked me on the side of the head.

In a flash, I turned and jumped on his back to bear hug him.

He grunted and whipped to one side, but I held tight, rubbing against him. "Get your half-naked ass off me, fucker."

"But I'm such a good hugger," I laughed as I finally let him squirm away.

"Better you than me," Chris muttered from his own locker.

A loud clap had us all looking over to Coach Wilson, who was standing in the doorway. "We've got the room cleared to give you all an update on Dumpty."

The silence was instant.

Wilson cleared his throat. "Officially, he's day to day while he's being monitored for a mild concussion. Unofficially, he's not traveling with us, and he'll be out for at least five days. He's definitely got a concussion. A shoulder tear is possible. They're waiting on the MRI results." Wilson crossed his arms and rocked back on his feet.

Dread washed over me as I rubbed at the back of my neck. A tear would be season ending. Losing Mason, one of the team's best batters, would make it impossible to make a playoff run this season.

"We're hoping for the best," Wilson said, his hands on his hips.

"Does he have someone to stay with?" I asked. Like me, his family was far away and unlikely to make it to him tonight.

"Miller and Langfield are with the training staff at the hospital," he said, referring to Cortney Miller, our GM, and Beckett Langfield, the team's owner. "I think the plan is to take him back to Miller's place."

Bosco snorted. "Oh, he's gonna get to go to the momcom."

"Wouldn't let Cortney or Beckett hear you mock any of them," Asher Price, the team's catcher, warned.

Cortney and Beckett had ended up falling for women who were best friends, and the families lived in side-by-side brownstones. There were rumors that the houses were connected, but I'd only been to Miller's place once and hadn't seen it.

Their girls made up half of what Bosco referred to as the momcom.

There were two other women in that group, and when both Beckett and Cortney had started dating Liv and Dylan, the four women were living and raising their seven kids together in a single brownstone. Although most of my teammates scoffed at the idea, I thought it sounded like fun.

"Streaks is just sore he didn't get to join the mommune when the lovely Delia picked Enzo DiLuca," Martinez joked, leaning back in his white folding chair now that he was dressed after his postgame shower.

"Please," Bosco scoffed. "Can you honestly see me seriously dating anyone, let alone a single mother?" He shuddered at the idea.

I *couldn't* see it. The man was allergic to not only commitment but any sort of responsibility that wasn't baseball related.

"But like I said"—Bosco pointed at me—"you're going to have your own room this trip. You better go out and find someone to enjoy the luxury with."

I smirked. Because, sure, there had been a time when that would have been my thing. But I was weirdly unexcited about the idea now.

Emerson
9

Me: Everything going okay with the bathroom?

Gi: Besides opening up the wall and fixing the pipe, they haven't done anything, so it looks like you're going to be stuck using my bathroom when you get back.

Me: I'll use the kitchen sink to brush my teeth, and I can shower in the locker room at the field. I won't bother you.

Gi: I'm not that bad to share a bathroom with...

Me: But you don't know that I'm not.

Gi: GIF of eye roll

STREAKS ADDED DRAGON TO THE CHAT.

Streaks: Where we all heading?

Dragon: Why did you put me in this chat again? I'm not chasing ball bunnies with you

Angel Boy: They added me and Martinez, and we're married with kids.

Streaks: We're on the road

Streaks: Guys your better halves are at home

Streaks: There is no reason you can't hang with me

Streaks: Bambi and I will handle all the women don't worry

Martinez: I'm about ten years too old to keep up with you, Streaks.

Streaks: I'm older than you

Angel Boy: Pretty sure you still think you're 22.

Streaks: Look who's got the dad jokes

Angel Boy: Emoji of a middle finger

Streaks: Seriously no one will go out with me?

Dragon: Nope

DRAGON LEFT THE CHAT.

Streaks: Bambi?

Streaks: Man????

Streaks: Where you at?????

Martinez: When I saw him earlier, he said he was ordering room service and going to bed.

STREAKS ADDED DRAGON INTO THE CHAT.

Streaks: Do you see that, Dragon?

Streaks: Your boy is staying in…

Streaks: He might be dead

Streaks: We must check on him!!!

Dragon: For the love of God, he's a grown-ass man. He doesn't need checking on. Gi and Pop just left Avery's, and I'm FaceTiming her, so leave me alone

DRAGON LEFT THE CHAT.

Streaks: Sucks to be you Angel Boy

Angel boy: Why? I'm not in the room with him. I'm at the bar with Martinez and the new guy having a burger and a beer.

Streaks: Seriously?????

Angel Boy: Selfie of Asher Price, Jasper Quinn, and Eddie Martinez at a high-top

Streaks: Fuck you very much

Angel Boy: GIF of a guy falling over laughing

Martinez: We're at Taps on 8th. We were about to tell you.

Streaks: Be there in five

Streaks: Assholes

Gi: Good game. Congrats on your 15th stolen base.

Me: Wow you watched it?

Gi: Avery had Pop and me over for dinner.

Me: Ah, so not by choice.

Gi: GIF of an eye roll

Gi: They still haven't been back to work on the bathroom.

Me: I'll check in with them when I get home.

Gi: Sorry - you're probably out having fun - I'll let you be.

Me: Picture of himself sitting shirtless on his hotel bed.

Gi: I swear Chris talks about how you're always out at a club or a bar...

Me: Not feeling it lately.

Gi: How come?

Gianna
10

THE BUZZING OF MY PHONE IN MY HAND STARTLED ME SO BADLY I JUMPED.

Why was he calling me? Emerson had texted randomly while he'd been gone for the last four days, but he hadn't called. I glanced down at my tank top and shorts with a wince. My hair was a mess, and I was covered in paint. Even my chest had green streaks on it.

Frowning at the phone, I slid the button to answer the FaceTime request. "What's wrong?"

For a beat, he blinked at me, silent, then he cleared his throat. "Nothing. I just thought that if we were chatting, this would be easier."

"We're chatting?"

He leaned back against his headboard and crossed his arms over his bare chest. He was on the slim side, but that didn't mean he wasn't cut. I tried not to focus on the swells of muscles that rippled across his arms as he got settled. Instead, I focused on his green eyes, bright and sparkling as always. Did he wear contacts or use special drops to make them do that? Because mine had never twinkled like that.

He chuckled. "What do you call it when two people are asking and answering questions back and forth?"

I rose a brow at the mocking tone, but he just smiled in return.

"What are you painting?"

"I didn't say I was."

"Oh, I didn't know you were into war paint. Looks cute on you." He leaned closer to the screen like he was trying to get a better look.

"Did you call just to mock me?" I crossed my free arm over my chest and huffed.

His attention drifted low, and he sucked in his bottom lip, but quickly looked away from the screen. "I can't remember why I called." He shrugged, glancing back at the phone. "Are you finishing up the zoo signs?"

"No," I breathed, officially giving up trying to understand why he'd called. "They're already done." I turned back to the painting I was working on for Pop for Father's Day. He'd always loved the house in the spring, when the weeping cherries and daffodils bloomed. So this last year, I took a picture, and I'd been working on recreating it on canvas for him. "The Zoo is supposed to be hanging them for Friday night."

"I can't wait to see them. I'll have to swing by one of these days."

Brows pulled together, I set the paintbrush back down. "The Revs have a table. Are you not coming?"

He had his own life, and my event probably meant nothing to him. But an annoying little part of my brain was whispering its disappointment as I realized he wouldn't be there. I ground my teeth. No, I wouldn't let him have this effect on me. The last thing I needed was to develop a crush on my brother's best friend. The sexy professional baseball player that half the city probably lusted over.

"Nah, they invite the big names to those things." He shook his head, and I heard the popping of his knuckles, although I couldn't see his hands on the screen.

"What?" Emerson Knight was a big name. No one got fans as excited when they walked into Lang Field as he did. He was great at getting the crowd on their feet and dancing, and when he was on base, the whole stadium held its breath, waiting for him to steal. Not to mention the man's stupidly beautiful face peppered the Revs' socials.

Yes, annoyingly, I was checking them for glimpses of him now. Another thing I needed to stop, since there was no good reason his dopey smile and silly antics should interest me so much.

"You know." A single-shoulder shrug. "Price, Damiano, Martinez,

Bosco, and Dumpty. The fan favorites." He said it without a trace of emotion, but his matter-of-fact attitude was belied by the way he ran a hand down his face.

As I watched the way he shrugged off the topic, anger on his behalf coursed through me. Had no one ever told him he was in the same league as those guys?

"Anyway." He moved on before I could say anything. "Maybe one day when I'm home, you can take me and show me the signs. I really do want to see them." A soft smile graced his lips, but the light in his eyes had dulled. "But I'll let you get back to your work. I didn't mean to interrupt. I guess I just missed seeing the daggers you love to shoot my way."

Shit. I schooled my expression. Yes, I'd been glaring, but it wasn't directed *at* him.

"Have a good night, Mariposa." That smile went even softer, and then he ended the call.

It sucked that he wasn't going out. Not because I had these weird feelings about him, but because it seemed like he wanted to go.

My focus shifted to the black frame on the side table next to the sofa. Inside it was my painting of Puff, mid-jump off a rock. Emerson was as weirdly excited about that bird as my father was. And almost as much as Avery and Chris. What if I asked for a plus-one to the zoo event? I shook my head. I didn't even know if Emerson would want to go. I glanced down at my phone and pulled up my friends' group text.

> Me: Would it be weird to ask to bring someone to the thing on Friday?

> Linc: Ummmm 'scuse me? A DATE???

I blew out a breath, considering the best way to word it. But before I could respond, my phone was buzzing again. I sighed but accepted the FaceTime request and propped my phone up beside me.

"You are at your most adorable when you're covered in paint." The dreamlike sigh floated from Linc's lips. "It's so obvious that you were born to be an amazing artist." He clapped his hands. "But more importantly, tell me the date is with the naked roommate."

"He's fully clothed all the time." I growled the lie. Because, though I'd never seen him naked, he did wander around shirtless a lot. Enough that I was beginning to think the rumors about him not being big on wearing clothes might be true.

"It's too bad. I've seen pictures, and that man is really good-looking." Mila, who'd joined the call too, waggled her brows.

My hackles rose, though I wasn't sure whose statement caused the response. Either way, I snapped. "He's also really good at baseball and just a nice guy."

"No longer claiming he's weird?" Linc's left brow rose almost in time with the corner of his mouth.

"Shut up." I sighed. "He's..." What was the best way to describe him?

Mila smiled, and Linc almost squealed.

"I love this so much," he gushed. "It's going to be the best roommates-to-lovers story ever. I totally prefer MM to MF, but if it means you getting a happily ever after, I'd be game for MF."

I tossed my hands in the air. He would never let it go. "No. My comment about him being a good guy is just that. Don't make this a thing."

"You asked about a date," Mila reminded me gently.

"No, I asked about bringing a..." I had no clue how to describe Emerson at the moment. "Friend?"

Linc scoffed.

Mila gave me a placating smile. "Linc," she soothed, "give it some time and don't push. Remember, she did just get out of a terrible relationship."

"Thanks," I muttered. Although that wasn't the issue either. It had been almost a month since everything with Jake had gone from present to past.

"Best way to get over someone is to get under someone else." He paused. "Or over them. Or beside them. Or inside them." His eyes lit up and his mouth popped open. "Or—"

"There is no way there is another *or* in that," I huffed. "Just forget I asked."

"You realize that's unlikely to happen, right? Linc gets excited about this stuff." Mila's blond bob bounced as she shook her head. "Remember the gym sub?"

"Ohmygosh." He rushed the words together without a breath. "You two would have made such pretty babies."

I rolled my eyes. "Mila went on one date with the guy, and there was no spark."

"Yeah, it was pretty dull." Mila shrugged.

"Not in my mind."

"See what I mean?" Mila asked, moving in closer to her phone's screen.

"I'll make it easy. Let it go, or you're uninvited to the get-ready party." I turned back to my painting and studied the details, considering what it was missing.

"But you need your glam squad," he whined.

"I don't *need* my glam squad, but I'd like them, so they need to act like adults." I dipped a clean brush into the pink paint on my pallet and added a hint of it to the flowering tree, smudging in the brighter color with an almost white pink.

My phone buzzed again, rattling on the table beside me. The notification that appeared at the top of the screen made my stomach sink. "What the hell now?" I muttered. It was past ten o'clock. "I gotta go, guys. It's the asshole."

"Jake?" Mila asked.

I nodded, setting my brush down. "He better be giving me an update about my deposit."

I hung up and flipped over to Jake, tapping the speaker button.

"Hello?"

"Hey, Gigi."

It was nice to be able to admit that I hated that nickname. Through our relationship, I'd tried to make myself not want to frown every time he used it, but now I could just scowl, and it didn't matter.

"Got my money for me?" I asked.

"Next week," he promised.

I glanced at the date on my phone, mentally noting the date seven days from now. I was going to lose my shit if I didn't get it back by then.

Brush in hand again, I turned back to the pink tree, blending the colors until it was a deep rose, giving it depth.

For a long moment, I worked in silence.

"Are you there?" Jake finally asked, his voice tiny.

"Yes." I wasn't the one who'd made the call. I didn't know what he wanted me to say. And it wasn't going to be *hey, buddy, how have you been?*

"Well, uh. Okay." He stumbled over the words.

I waited again.

He sighed. "Listen, about Friday…"

Ah. I understood what this was now. "It won't be weird," I assured him. "Don't worry."

"Of course not." He cleared his throat. "But the thing is, Libby and I decided we should be attending events together."

I gritted my teeth. Great, I'd get to spend the night with the happy couple. At least the assigned tables were ten tops. I'd have other people to be buffers. The idea of bringing a date flashed through my mind again. I eyed the counter where I'd laid my red dress…

An image of Emerson in a dark suit floated through my head. The way he'd smile down at me as he stood next to me. My heart skipped at the idea of his hand resting on the small of my back. I swallowed.

"Gigi?"

Jake's voice startled me back to the conversation.

"Okay, go with Libby. Not an issue." Maybe even call her Lili or Bibi. I didn't give a shit.

He let out a long breath. "Thank you for understanding. I thought you were going to fly off the handle at the idea that she'd take your seat."

I blinked, and my heart lurched. "Wait…what?" I cocked my head to one side so quickly my messy bun bounced.

"Since the zoo account is getting so much publicity, the firm is sending all the big guns. It was just supposed to be you and me, but now the higher-ups are attending."

He couldn't be saying…

"So thank you for letting Libby have your ticket."

He was saying it. My hand tightened around the narrow brush as fire ran through my veins. "Jake, this is my account. *I* brought it in. *I* did all the work."

After doing the sign for Chris and Avery's puffin exhibit, the zoo asked me to update the signs throughout the whole park. Like a loyal dumbass, I'd brought the account to the firm. Without me, it wouldn't have even been a thing.

"Right, right." He brushed that off like it didn't matter. "We aren't taking credit. Everyone will know it's your thing. And we can send you pictures of the event."

The wooden handle of the paintbrush between my fingers cracked from the pressure I was putting on it. "Jake," I gritted out, setting down the broken brush.

His tone hardened. "You're going to be difficult, aren't you? You have to learn to let me go, Gigi. No one likes the pathetic girl who can't move on when it's over."

The effect his words had on me was so visceral I reared back as if he's physically reached through the phone and hit me. I didn't care about seeing Jake. In fact, I'd rather he not come to the event. But he was overseeing the project, so I'd come to terms with his presence. Regardless, his position with the company didn't take away my right to go.

If I threw a fit, I'd get a seat at the table. Because, after all, I'd single-handedly landed this account. But if I did that, Jake would twist my reaction and make it look as though I was a jealous ex who wasn't over him.

Apart from his calls and emails, I hadn't thought about Jake in the last few days. I didn't miss him, and I definitely didn't miss the way he treated me. If I'd learned anything over the last few weeks, it was that I should have ended things a long time ago. I wasn't heartbroken; I was embarrassed and pissed. It had taken far too long to figure it out, but the truth was that I hadn't loved him, no matter how much I tried to make myself.

But did I want to deal with rumors of being the jilted ex? No.

"Trust me, I'm long over you," I muttered.

He chuckled. "Sure."

Was it actually so hard to believe? My temper flared, the fire inside me raging, and the words slipped out before I could stop myself.

"I've actually been seeing someone. It's fine if I don't go to the zoo thing. It'll be the perfect opportunity for the two of us to do something else."

He snorted again. "I'll believe it when I see it. But whatever you say. As long as we're on the same page with Libby taking your seat and you not throwing a fit, you can live in your fantasy world."

"Right." I bit the word out. Every part of me wanted to tell him to go fuck himself, but I needed this job. I hadn't had one hit on my résumé on Indeed or any updates from the recruiter I'd spoken with. Apparently, the industry was oversaturated. And the idea of quitting my job without another lined up was scary as hell. I couldn't not have an income.

"Don't let this mini meltdown of yours affect your work. I need those images for the Java project by Monday."

"Right." I kept the single word short, but I tempered my tone into something mostly professional.

The way Jake made every project funnel through him was frustrating. I provided him with a design, and he went to the customer with it. Then he'd come back to his team with changes and tweaks. Technically, overseeing the designs and communication was part of his job, but for the artists, having no contact with the customer made the work harder and extended timelines. One of the reasons the zoo project had been done so quickly and efficiently was because I'd gotten to speak directly to the zoo's team. Since I was the one who'd brought them in, they'd specifically requested that I be their point of contact. If only that could happen more often.

Abruptly, Jake cleared his throat and said, "Night."

When the room fell silent, my eyes moved to the clear bag holding the red dress I'd picked up from the tailor today. I had splurged on it, especially since I'd paid extra to have it taken in so that it fit better. It was the kind of dress that would make an ex-boyfriend suffer. Originally, that was my thought. But every time I envisioned a set of eyes roaming over me, they were green, not brown. And the truth was that I didn't care much about what Jake thought. Though that didn't mean I wouldn't mind seeing a day when karma would bite him in the ass.

Emerson
11

"Hey, Bambi." Chris stepped into the apartment and closed the door behind him with a gentle kick. "Where is Gi?"

I shrugged. I hadn't seen her. If I had to guess, she was avoiding me. My decision to FaceTime her two nights ago was a spur-of-the-moment thing. We were chatting, and I just wanted to hear her voice. So I'd called. It took less than a minute to gather that she didn't view it as a welcome interruption. That hurt, but I'd done my best to push the pain away. I had never wanted to just talk to a woman before, so I'd never done anything like that. And immediately, I regretted it. Her discomfort was palpable, and the conversation was stilted.

Plus, I'd hardly been able to focus because her tits were trying to burst out of that tiny shirt she was wearing. It was all I could do to not stare at them. As soon as I'd hung up, I'd gotten into the shower to jack off, pretending it was her huge tits and not my hand rubbing my dick.

I was at a loss for how to handle my thoughts and reactions to her. All kinds of emotions rushed through me every time I even thought about the woman.

We'd gotten in late last night from the road stretch, and when I got home, her door had been closed. Since my bathroom was still out of commission, I'd skipped the shower I usually took to unwind and had just gone to bed. The last thing I wanted to do was bug her again. So

75

far today, I'd been home from the day game for thirty minutes, and the whole time, her door had been shut tight. Again. So the chances were good that she was avoiding me. But most days, she did spend a lot of time in her room, so maybe I was overthinking it.

I scratched my head.

"Is she not home?" he asked again, yanking his phone out of his pocket.

He was tapping at the screen when a door opened down the hall. "*I'm here*. You don't need to be an asshole." Gianna stomped barefoot into the room. She was dressed in black leggings and a matching crop top, and her nails were painted a bright red.

Without my permission, my imagination ran wild, picturing her scratching those nails down my chest, then gently wrapping one soft hand around my dick.

I glanced away before I swallowed my tongue or my eyes bugged out of my head. Every article of clothing the woman owned was created to be a torture device especially for me. So why the fuck did I spend any time she wasn't around desperate to see her? I'd be walking around sniffing oranges if I wasn't careful.

Teeth gritted, I kept my attention fixed on the table in front of me and cracked my knuckles.

"I thought you said she wasn't home." Chris scowled at me.

"Clearly I am," she snapped.

I'd yet to get a single word in, but with the two of them, that wasn't unusual.

"You really need to find someone besides me to cut your damn hair."

"You know I don't like people to touch me. I don't give you shit about constantly getting new sheets everywhere you go. Don't give me shit either," Chris muttered, his mouth falling into a tight line.

This was normal for them. The bickering. So it made no sense that I had to fight to stay in my seat and appear unconcerned rather than tell Chris to fuck off. What made my reaction even more strange was that I never argued with him. Hell, I owed him so much.

I rubbed a hand down my face and pulled out my phone to distract myself. Once I'd unlocked the screen, I read through my sister's text messages. Isabella was graduating from high school soon and wanted to make sure I'd be there. Like I'd miss it.

"You've been doing it for ten years. I don't see why it's an issue now."

"Chris." Her voice got louder, grabbing my attention.

Quietly, I watched the interaction. If he overstepped, then, brother or not, he'd have to leave. I didn't even care that this was his apartment. I would toss him out.

But they both just stood, arms crossed, glaring at each other. Like a contest. Finally, Chris broke.

"You can't mean that I should find someone new today," Chris scoffed. "We have your thing tomorrow, and I need it cut."

Gi huffed, and her shoulders dropped. "I don't get why everyone loves you. You are the worst. But fine. I'll cut your hair." She spun on her heel and stomped out of the room. "But I will *not* be the one sweeping it all up," she shouted as she stomped down the hall.

"I don't get why she's so mad." Chris pulled the stool Gi used for painting off the tarp and brought it to the center of the room.

"When did you ask her about the haircut?" I knew from experience with my own sisters that sometimes it was just timing.

He shrugged. "I told her I was coming like a half hour ago."

"Oh." I tried not to, but I couldn't help but laugh. He was such an idiot. "That's probably why she's pissed."

"What?" He lifted a hand and cocked his head.

"Typically, when you want a favor from someone, you *ask* them." I shook my head but still chuckled. "You can't just *tell* them. Don't be a dick."

Eyes narrowed, he scanned the room. "Huh." With that, he pulled out his phone and busied himself with it.

With a shrug at his profile, I turned back to mine, but a second later, my scrolling was interrupted by loud, thumping steps.

"Why are you such an asshole?" Gi barked as she appeared again. "You seriously sent me a text *now*, asking whether this was okay?"

I was entranced by her, as usual, as she juggled the brush, her phone, a small black case, a bag, and some black piece of fabric that was slipping from her arm.

Shaking myself from my stupor, I hopped up and darted toward her, tripping on the leg of the coffee table and stumbling before I righted myself and closed the distance.

Her brows pulled together as I got closer. "What?" she snapped.

I held out my hand, and though she glowered at me, she didn't put up a fight as I grabbed the black fabric before it could fall to the floor.

"Let me help, Gi," I said quietly.

Almost imperceptivity, she nodded, pressing her lips together and ducking her head.

As I took the case from her, my fingers brushed against the back of hers. Instantly, goose bumps burst across her soft skin. With my heart in my throat, I took in the pebbled skin of her arm, slowly working my way up to her shoulder, then zeroing in on her breasts. Through her bra, I couldn't tell, but I was dying to know if her nipples had hardened. And I was dying to wrap my lips around one and suck. Desperate to make her moan my name.

Like she could read my mind, her breath hitched. The sound forced me to lift my gaze up to the hollow of her throat where her pulse pounded. I took in her plump lips and her pink cheeks, then my gaze skated higher. Until finally, our eyes met. Her pupils were blown wide, eclipsing her dark irises. Her lids were heavy, her long lashes fluttering. I wanted to lean close. Press my lips to hers. Feel every soft curve of her body.

I brushed my thumb over the back of her hand again, and she shifted closer.

"What are you doing?" The sound clawed at my ears, and on instinct, I jerked back, heart pounding and stomach sinking.

Chris was in the damn room.

My head snapped around to her brother. His narrowed eyes flicked between me and his sister. Fuck. Could he tell what I had just been thinking? I swallowed. No way. Not if I acted normal.

"Nothing." I shrugged. "I was being a gentleman. Helping her so she didn't drop shit."

The crease between her brows was back. "I wasn't going to drop anything," she said, tearing the case from my hand and stomping toward her brother.

I fought the smile forming on my lips as she set down the case and the bag, then discreetly checked the floor around her, clearly realizing she was missing something.

"You're right. You definitely weren't going to drop it," I assured her as I balled up the black piece of fabric and tossed it to Chris.

"You could just accept help," he muttered to his sister.

"Did you actually want me to cut your hair?" Gi crossed her arms and lifted her chin.

Chris held his free hand up. "Truce?"

"Just sit down and stop being annoying." She pointed at the stool, and he complied, passing the black wrap to her as he did.

While she swung the fabric around and hooked it around his neck, I moved back to the sofa and pulled up Instagram to kill time.

Hannah had uploaded a reel featuring the mascots, along with Quinn, Price, and me.

The Revs mascots were a trio of revolutionary soldiers dressed in regimental uniforms under baseball jerseys.

Quinn and Price and I were each teamed up with one mascot to run a relay race. I'd joined the drumming soldier with the throwback jersey, and he and I had crushed it.

Quinn was young, and Price might be the big bat of the team, but I had the speed. And although my fun-loving drummer dropped his sticks early on and had to stop to pick them up, putting us in last, I'd made up the time, and we'd pulled off a win. The drama the mascots launched into had me chuckling. The one on the horse stomped around in circles, and the third flailed on the ground, throwing a tantrum.

"You excited about Friday?" Chris asked over the snipping of the scissors.

Gianna was silent, and although I was trying not to intrude on their conversation, my ears perked up at her lack of response, because she had sounded excited a few days ago.

"Why are you pouting?"

"I'm not."

I didn't look her way, but I didn't need to in order to gauge her mood. I could hear the frustration in her tone. Once again, I wanted to tell Chris to back off. But he wouldn't. He was the type that dug in full force. The dude had waited a year for his girl. Trust me, he didn't let anything go.

"What's the deal?" he demanded.

She sighed, and in a quiet voice I'd never heard from her, she said, "Jake uninvited me."

I whipped around so hard I nearly fell off the sofa. At the same time, Chris pushed to his feet, glaring at her. "The douches did what?"

"It's Doucette. Not douche," she growled.

I wasn't sure why she always pronounced the word that way. But every time Chris called the company a bunch of douches, she always corrected him.

"I'm fine not going," she said, though she kept her focus on the scissors in her hand and shifted on her feet, looking anything but fine.

"What do you mean?" Chris crossed his arms under the black cape, puffing up in his typical overprotective way. "This event is to show off the new signs—that *you* made—and you're telling me you're not going?"

She swallowed, and for a second, I thought she might cry. The thought of it was like a knife to the chest. That wasn't Gianna. She used anger to hide her emotions and always kept her head held high. But I knew how it felt to work as hard as everyone else yet not get the same credit. It was a punch to the stomach, and although I was used to it for me, I wanted better for her.

But like a switch flipped, she pulled her shoulders back, and that chin, which loved to lift in indignation, rose a fraction. Her eyes hardened, and any hint of vulnerability was gone before most people would have even noticed. "It's to raise money for the zoo. This has nothing to do with me. The event was planned long before I agreed to paint a few signs."

"No." Chris shook his head. "You didn't just paint a few signs. You practically rebranded the place. This is bullshit. Bambi," he called over to me. "You're taking Dumpty's spot at the gala Friday, right?"

I nodded.

"Got a date?"

Gianna zeroed in on me. No, I didn't have a date. I'd thought about asking her dad if he wanted to go. He was the type of parent who would like to see his daughter's hard work celebrated. But I hadn't gotten a chance yet. Hannah had only sprung the invitation on me yesterday at the relay race with the mascots. I was rarely invited to the big things, but since Mason was still recovering from his concussion, they needed another body.

"Dude, the question isn't a hard one." Chris shook his head.

"No, Dragon." I cleared my throat to answer him, but I kept my eyes on his sister. "No date."

Gianna's shoulders relaxed just a bit, and though she was still scowling, the look softened a fraction.

"Great." He lifted a hand from under his black cape and waved it between the two of us. "You two can go together."

"No." Gianna spit out the word fast.

My stomach sank. She was attracted to me. I had no doubt. But apparently I wasn't the type of guy she'd want on her arm at such an important event.

"Why the fuck not?" Chris glared at her.

I lowered my head and rocked back on my heels. I didn't need an explanation. I understood, and I couldn't be upset with her for not wanting to bring the class clown to the formal event.

"It's your thing," Chris argued. "You *will* be there."

"Well," Gianna said, worrying her lip, "it's dumb. But my temper got the better of me…"

What did her temper have to do with anything? She was cute when she was fired up. All glary and ragey vibes.

Though in this moment she was the opposite of fired up. My heart hurt as I watched her twirl a long strand of hair around her finger nervously.

"Just spit it out." Chris frowned.

Her eyes flicked to me for one second before she looked down at her feet. "Jake was being an ass, so I might have told him I was dating someone."

My heart clenched. She was dating someone. Already? When the hell had that happened? Fuck. My stomach sank, and a wave of anguish ran through me. I couldn't have her. I knew that. But it hurt anyway.

"So?" If they didn't share several features already, the way he sneered the word just like she would have would be enough to make it obvious they were siblings.

A kernel of irritation hit my stomach at the idea that Chris didn't care that she was dating again. Since the second she'd arrived, he'd been all about the team staying away, yet it was okay for some stranger to take her out?

She flung her arms out. "So? I can't show up alone." Her arms dropped, along with her chin. "Jake already thought I was lying."

"You *were* lying," he said with all the confidence of a guy who was aware of the facts.

She was lying. I shouldn't smile, but I couldn't help it. She wasn't dating someone. Thank fuck. And also, I was an idiot. Just because she wasn't dating someone didn't mean I could have her.

Arms locked across her chest again, she popped one hip. "I don't want *him* to know that. So if I go, it'll have to be with my 'boyfriend.'" She used air quotes around that last word.

"I can do it." I couldn't have stopped the words if I tried.

Gianna and Chris turned to me in unison, wearing matching masks of confusion.

"I'll pretend to be the guy you're dating." Because that meant that, for one night, I could touch her. I could rest my hand on the swell of her hip. I could hold her hand. Whisper in her ear. Smell her perfume. Wrap her in my arms while we danced.

For one night, I could pretend I could have her.

Gianna blinked.

"I can fake it," I assured my best friend.

"Perfect." Chris lifted his fist up to me. "I owe you, bro."

I shook my head, even as I tapped knuckles with him. He didn't owe me shit. In fact, this was the opposite of that. I owed him for suggesting Gianna go with me. I'd do just about anything to be close to her, even if it was all pretense. And instead of being an obstacle in my path, he'd just given the opportunity to do it.

Fuck. I was a shitty friend.

"Are you sure?" Gianna whispered.

Chris shook his head and blew out an exasperated breath. "Don't look a gift horse in the mouth."

She whacked him on the head. "Shut up." When she looked my way again, still waiting for my response, her deep brown eyes were filled with so much uncertainly. It was an emotion she worked so hard to hide. And yet, in small moments like this one, it shone so brightly.

"Gianna, I'd be honored to pretend to be the lucky guy who gets to date you."

The worry faded from her expression, and the corner of her mouth almost lifted in a smile.

My stomach flipped at the sight. Because it almost seemed like she wanted to go with me.

"Great." Chris clapped his hands and plopped back onto the stool. "You can do his hair too."

"What?" Gianna's gaze shot to me.

"He needs a trim before tomorrow," Chris said. "And he won't have time to get in anywhere else. So you might as well." He waved a hand at the floor. "I'll even sweep that hair too."

She turned hesitantly to look at me, her pleading gaze silently begging for me to give her an out. But if I agreed with Chris, then I'd get her hands on me.

"Do you mind?" I asked.

Slowly, she sucked her bottom lip into her mouth and shook her head. "Let me finish him."

"Thanks." I smiled, hoping she could see the earnest appreciation I felt.

With a brief nod, she turned back to her brother.

It took her another few minutes to finish up his cut, and then he and I traded places. I hadn't put on a shirt after my shower, and a thrill shot down my spine when she fastened the cape around my neck and her fingertips brushed against the skin there. Her hands froze for one breath before her thumb rubbed just below my hairline. My heart pounded.

"Just clean it up?" she whispered the question.

Swallowing thickly, I nodded.

As she ran her fingers through my hair, I had to fight a shiver. It was far too easy to imagine another moment, where her hands were in my hair. Where it wasn't clinical judgment but a meaningful moment, where she'd pull my mouth to hers. I glanced up and locked in on the way her teeth pressed lightly against her full lips, imagining that lip between my own. Where instead of fighting this need, I simply gave in and let myself ride the high of it. My skin tingled.

I heard the snipping, but I was in a world where nothing existed but her touch. The drag of her nails against my scalp, the brush of her fingers along my skin. When she stepped in front of me, I got an eyeful of her tight cropped shirt. My hands itched to touch her. To feel more of the soft skin peeking out between her black shirt and leggings. My mouth was almost lined up with the pale flesh. The urge to press my lips against it was almost impossible to resist.

Slowly, I lifted my hand from under the cape. My fingers barely brushed the smooth skin. The harsh suck of her breath echoed through me. Goose bumps broke out on that inch of skin, leaving me desperate to touch her again.

"Anyone want a drink?" Chris yelled from the kitchen, jarring me back to the moment. To the reason I wasn't touching her.

An electric energy pulsed through the space. My hand still hovered in the air between us. My heart hammered in my ears. Her eyes met mine, and she swallowed.

"Anyone?" he called when we didn't answer, like he was oblivious to the tension in the air. Could he be? Because to me, it felt like thick smoke hovering over all of us. I dropped my hand, and Gi glanced away.

"No thanks," I croaked, then cleared my throat.

"I'm fine." Gi's attention refocused on my hair. Shoulders back, she lifted her arms. Her hand brushed my ear, sending a shiver down my spine and launching my heart into overdrive. She froze in front of me, her breath catching once more.

Haircuts were supposed to be a mundane chore. This felt anything but. Instead, the interaction was charged, and a blazing fire burned inside me.

When her finger brushed the back of my neck, my cock pulsed. I shifted on the stool, thanking God I was covered by the damn cape, because my dick was tenting my shorts. I couldn't stop the images of her hands running down my body from playing in my mind. Visions of her looking up at me as she dropped to her knees between my thighs. The way her tongue would run slowly along her lips before she leaned forward and took me into her mouth.

I fisted my hands in my lap. I couldn't meet her eyes. If I did, I knew what she'd see. I was half-terrified and half-thrilled by the idea that my desire would be reflected in her gaze.

She ran her hand along my jaw to my chin and lifted, turning my head one way, then the other, her fingertips soft like silk against my rough skin. Tilting at the waist, she lowered herself and studied my hair, looking from one side of my face to the other like she was checking the evenness of the cut. Fuck. The scoop of neckline hung loosely, giving me a fantastic view of cleavage. My mouth went dry. I longed to run my tongue across the perfect swells. To feel the weight of her tits in my palms. To tease her nipples with my tongue until she writhed against me.

Blinking myself out of the fantasy, I forced my eyes up, only to find her watching me with a heated intensity that seared straight into me.

"Do we really not have any Easy Out?" Chris called.

With a quiet gasp, Gianna jumped back.

Her brother stomped around the island back to us.

I cleared my throat, silently telling my dick to shut it down. "I'll put it on the grocery list."

"Great." Chris dropped onto the couch and reached for the remote. "Avery's out with the girls tonight, so how about a movie night?"

Normally, I'd be all-in, but tonight, I didn't want to hang out with my best friend. At the moment, all I wanted to do was pull his sister onto my lap, strip her down, and let her ride my dick until we both came.

I was such a shitty friend.

That should be my new mantra. I should tattoo it on my eyeballs so that every time I looked at her, I'd be reminded to stop. But as I studied her—the concentrated expression as she focused on my hair—as I was hit with yet another whiff of her orange blossom scent, all I cared about was seeing her smile.

"How about we watch that one about the next civil war?" I suggested.

She smirked, and I felt like I'd gotten a win.

"Or the new thriller that Netflix just released." Gianna turned away to pull out the clippers.

"Sure." Chris flicked through the list of movies until he found the one she wanted.

The scrape of the clippers sent another wave of shivers through me, but it was nothing compared to the pressure pounding in my dick. I needed to cool off.

When the buzzing finally stopped, I breathed a sigh of relief.

"You're done. Might want to hop in the shower to rinse off the stray hairs."

Yeah, shower. Cold shower. And then movie night with Damiano siblings.

Gianna
12

Me: I'm going to the thing on Friday after all.

Linc: !!!!

Linc: Why aren't you answering?

Me: We're watching a movie.

Mila: You and Emerson?

Me: And Chris

Linc: Damn I want to be in the middle of those two. Lucky Bitch.

Mila: Chris is her brother...

Me: Exactly <barf emoji>

Linc: You say potato, and I say penis.

Mila: I can picture Gianna's face right now.

Linc: The eye roll, right?

Me: Sigh – ANYWAY I know we said we'd do a dinner and hotel night...

Mila: You should be at your event.

Linc: Back to the glam squad! I will make you so hot Jake's head explodes.

Mila: I thought we didn't care what Jake thinks.

Me: We don't.

Linc: Oh wait till you see the hair cut I gave him yesterday.

Linc: GIF of Disney villain laughing

Mila: You're lucky you didn't get fired.

Me: Chris is giving me the evil eye because my phone keeps going off - so are we good for tomorrow? I'll come by the hotel with my stuff to get ready if that's cool

Linc: Oh no way. We are coming to you. We want to see the naked roommate.

Mila: Wait did we figure out who the date is?

Linc: It's hot roommate.

Mila: Is it? I thought he wasn't going.

Me: I will come to you – seriously - see you tomorrow.

GIANNA LEFT THE CHAT

Emerson
13

At the sound of the knock, I moved to the door. Thank fuck. This had to be the contractors finally here to fix the bathroom. There'd been a hole in the wall for more than a week now, which meant I'd been using Gianna's shower since I returned from our road stretch. Tonight, at least, she was headed out to get her hair done, so I wouldn't be annoying when I used her bathroom.

She was in the shower now. I'd given up actively trying not to picture her with her head tipped back and water trailing down her body. Over the swell of her breasts…

Fuck. The floor came up really fast as I crashed down. I glanced around. I wasn't sure if my toe had caught the carpet or if I'd hit the coffee table. Either way, I needed to stop thinking about Gi when I walked around, or I might break a bone.

Another knock cracked through the air, louder this time, and I jumped up and rushed that way.

When I pulled the door open, I pressed my lips together, confused.

A man with a platinum-blond mohawk spiked a good four inches off his head stood before me in a pair of ripped skinny jeans and black combat boots. His black lips lifted into a huge smile as one pierced brow arched on his forehead.

"Emerson Knight. I knew you didn't wear clothes." He clapped, the sound echoing down the hallway and the movement drawing my attention to his black cropped shirt. With a grin, he turned to the small woman next to him. "The sneaky bitch has been holding out on us."

"Yeah." The woman, who looked like a blond Snow White with very porcelain skin and a cute button nose, sighed dreamily, her doe eyes drinking me in.

There were lots of internet rumors about me and walking around the house naked. Probably because I spent much of my time in the locker room in boxer briefs. But I had no interest in addressing the topic with these strangers. Plus, I wasn't currently naked.

"I always wished I could pull off the skinny jeans," I said, eyeing his white pants. There. Topic changed.

The man sank his teeth into his bottom lip. "Ooh, baby, with those thighs." He kissed his fingers, then held his hand up and made a flicking motion.

"Exactly why they never fit." I waved them inside.

"Do you always let random people into your house?" Mila asked.

I chuckled, closing the door behind them. "Does Gi normally take pictures with random people and use them as the background photo on her phone?"

Linc smirked at me. "She talks about us."

Not a lot, in all honesty. She didn't say much about anything, but she'd mentioned her friends coming up from New York. "I thought I was picking her up at your hotel in a few hours, so I didn't expect you. But the more the merrier." I tilted my head toward the kitchen. "I made food for Gi and me, but there's enough to share. Hungry?"

I wasn't sure how they would feel about arroz con gandules, but I never minded feeding people.

"Oh, I love food. Especially food I don't have to cook. Eli is great in bed but a total mess in the kitchen." He moved past me. "We'll make Gi a plate, and she can eat while I style."

I followed him into the kitchen and pulled out a few bowls.

"Is it fried rice?" Mila asked, peeking into the pan. "It smells amazing."

"No, it's better," Linc assured her as I passed him a bowl. "It's peas and pork. The second you take a bite, you'll feel like your mouth died and went to heaven."

"Like your tongue is dancing to a good salsa."

"Yes." Linc lifted his fist, and I pounded it. Once he'd spooned the rice dish into a bowl for him and another for Mila, he strode out of the kitchen. "Grab a few water bottles, Mila. Emerson, you get yours and Gi's, and we'll get this show going." He lifted both bowls without looking back and moved toward the bedrooms. "Which one is hers?" He lifted his nose into the air and sniffed. "Never mind. I can follow the body wash. It's so damn strong."

Two bowls in my own hands, I followed.

He turned into Gianna's room. "Hey, babe."

"Linc?" Gianna cracked the door to her bathroom open, and steam billowed around her. "Wasn't I meeting you at the hotel?"

My breath caught, and my feet stuttered to a stop, causing Mila to crash into the back of me.

Wet skin. Small white towel strappy wrap thing hugging her body. Lots of wet skin. And orange blossoms.

My brain should have worked better than that. Typically, it could form complete thoughts, but in this moment, all I could process was the way the white terrycloth hooked over her shoulders and Velcroed precariously between her big breasts. It was like the smallest towel dress ever created.

"Uh." Gianna shifted on her feet, and I drank her in, practically drooling over the swell of her hips and the bare skin of her soft thighs.

I fought the groan trying to work its way out my throat. "Sorry," I choked out, glancing at the bowls in my hands. "We were bringing food. Probably should have knocked."

Stuttering, I stepped back, but as I did, I tripped over the short woman behind me. With a stammering apology, I sidestepped and walked into the bed.

Shit. I halted all movement and shut my eyes, breathing in a long breath to calm myself down.

A warm palm pressed into my arm, garnering my attention. When I opened my eyes, the first thing I saw was a set of bright red nails against my bare skin.

She reached out and took the bowl from me. "Thank you," she said quietly.

Her damp hair hung around her shoulders, and her face was shower fresh. Water still clung to her eyelashes. Nothing like the perfect hair and makeup she normally sported, but she was just as beautiful. And standing this close to her made my heart race.

"I'm gonna throw clothes on." She set her bowl on the dresser, then shuffled into the closet and shut the door. I wanted to follow her. See the white towel fall to the floor. Touch the skin she kept hidden beneath it. I wanted to bury my head between her thighs while I devoured her pussy. Relish the taste of her as she came all over my face, screaming my name.

"Want to hang with us while we get her ready?" Linc's voice startled me back to the moment.

I cleared my throat as I blinked at the closet door. "Sure." Then, with a long breath out, I dropped to the bed. Apparently, I was a complete glutton for punishment.

Gianna
14

"DUDE, YOU SHOULD TOTALLY COME," LINC SAID OVER HIS SHOULDER AS he wrapped the wand around a strand of my hair. "It's November, so the season will be over. It's going to be sick. Everyone needs to do Jazz Madrid."

"Spain's on my list."

My stomach had done nothing but somersaults since I'd stepped out of the closet. When I was fully dressed and ready to face my friends, I found Emerson perched on the bed, chatting with Linc about his trip to Spain this fall. Their conversation only paused while Linc dried my hair. During that time, Mila and Em dove into a conversation, though I couldn't hear what they were saying over the noise of the hair dryer. From my vantage point, all I could tell was that they were both chuckling. Not that I was surprised. Positivity oozed from both of them. As soon as he shut the dryer off, Linc was back on Em about Spain.

I hadn't realized Emerson wanted to travel. I hadn't had the time or money to travel much yet, but I had a list too. I wanted to paint the northern lights. See the sun set over the pyramids. Watch the rain run off a heliconia flower.

"And stick men, man," Linc said. "They are a must for a jazz lover."

Emerson's deep chuckle warmed my belly.

"You can't peer pressure him into tagging along with you," Mila warned.

"Oh, I totally can." Linc waved her off.

"Okay. Rephrase." She held up a hand, palm out. "You shouldn't."

"Nah." Emerson waved her off. "I wouldn't be opposed, exactly. I just have to figure some stuff out before I lock much in."

The thread of uncertainty in his voice made my stomach clench. What did that mean?

I turned to ask, but Linc yanked my head back. "Do not move. But let's explain that, Knight, because our girl is curious."

"I am not," I snapped.

Linc cocked a brow, silently calling me a liar. Okay. Fine. Maybe I was.

"It's not a big thing." Emerson shrugged a shoulder, going for nonchalant. "My contract is up at the end of the year. And it's starting to look like Boston isn't going to renew it. So I'll have shit to figure out."

This time when my head whipped toward Emerson, Linc didn't stop me.

"What?" I demanded.

He lifted that shoulder again and set his bowl on the nightstand. Then he stood and cracked his knuckles, avoiding eye contact. "It's okay. I'm not the playmaker or the big bat. The payroll is high, and if they have to cut me to make it work, I get it."

"Idiots." I glared. He wasn't the big bat or the playmaker, but he was fast. And on top of that, he led morale for the team, and the fans loved him. Those things were worth hanging on to.

Two lines formed between his brows, and his throat worked as he swallowed. "They actually aren't, Gi. Miller and Langfield are smart. Honestly, there isn't a better front office in the league. They will do the right thing for the team. I respect that. It just might mean that I'll be moving in November, not going to Spain." He shrugged again. "It comes with the job."

He said it like it didn't matter. But his green eyes were dull, and the smile he shot my way was forced.

"I can't believe they would let you go. Ever," I said, working hard to keep the anger out of my voice.

Emerson's response was another small smile.

Since I'd moved in, he'd done nothing but build me up. Chris had always said his best friend was the biggest supporter to the people around him. The first to congratulate one of the guys on a great play or over personal achievements. He was the guy who'd start a flash dance in the stands to celebrate a teammate's home run. If only he recognized his own self-worth as easily as he did others'. It was a habit I was trying to create, but it was a challenge, and I hated that he had to fight the struggle too.

"Well, this got heavy," Linc announced after a long moment where Emerson and I just stared at each other. "Let's lighten things back up. Two truths and a lie!"

Mila groaned. But he went on before anyone spoke.

"I'm a bottle blond." He released another curl from the wand. "I got Eli's name tattooed on my dick before he even agreed to date me. And—"

Mila choked on her water, sputtering and coughing as it dripped down her chin.

Yeah, that was a truth. I knew it, and so did she. The shocked response probably had to do with him so easily admitting that insanity to a virtual stranger.

"Three." Linc went on as he spun my hair around the wand. "I've googled you, looking for naked pictures."

Emerson snorted, shaking his head. "Hope you didn't waste too much time on that."

Linc pouted, his lower lip sticking out as he peered over his shoulder. "Oh, I wasted way too much time. Sadly, I didn't find a single one."

"Nah, man." Emerson took a drink of his own water and screwed the cap back on. "I have a younger brother and sisters who look to me for direction. Not to mention all the kids who look up to professional athletes. The last thing I want is to be a shitty example."

From the moment I met him, I'd seen him as a lighthearted goofball, but the more time I spent with him, the more I realized it was a façade. He was so much more. Responsible, thoughtful, compassionate, all while maintaining the ability to make people laugh and feel good about themselves.

Linc patted my shoulder and then fanned himself. "That's like hot dad vibe. Who knew being responsible made my dick wanna cha-cha?"

"Linc," Mila chastised. "Not everyone gets your sense of humor. And the game's over. You're gonna make Emerson uncomfortable."

"Not at all uncomfortable, bebé," Emerson assured her.

Instantly, a pit formed in my stomach. Baby, or at least that's what it sounded like, rolled off his tongue easily and often. He used it on women all the time. Always with the flash of a flirty smile. For years, I never even noticed that he did it. But now, as much as I tried to fight the feeling, it bothered me. I wanted to be on the receiving end of that smile and flirting. Yet he'd never used the term for me.

It wasn't until Linc pulled on my curl and I found his eyes in the mirror that I realized I was pouting over it.

"Nah, I'm still in the relaxed phase of my social life." Emerson chuckled.

I strained to hear every word of the quiet conversation from across the room.

"Makes sense," Mila said. "You have enough pressure with baseball."

"Give me ten years. I'm sure I'll be singing a different tune. Right now, I don't have the bandwidth for something serious."

Linc leaned forward and brought his mouth close to my ear. "Do you hear that, Gi?"

"What?" I whispered, making eye contact in the mirror again.

"That man is primed and ready to be the rebound fling you need to put Jake so far in the review mirror it will be like he never existed." He waggled his brows and shook my shoulder in emphasis.

I scoffed, elbowing him. "Just because he doesn't want a relationship right now doesn't mean he wants a fling with me."

Linc's deep chuckle was evil, and his eyes flashed with mischief. "Biatch, that man almost passed the fuck out when he saw you in your towel robe. Trust me. He wants to experience all the parts of you."

"No he doesn't. Stop it." I locked my jaw, set on shutting him up, but I couldn't stop my eyes from wandering to where Emerson sat on the bed, chatting easily with one of my best friends. As their conversation continued, he glanced my way and smiled, and a minute later, he excused himself to grab his clothes so he could shower.

As soon as the water was flowing in the bathroom, my friends lost their minds.

"Gi," Mila stage whispered, eyes glued to the door like she was afraid he was going to come out. "You totally need to hook up with that guy!"

"I told you," Linc sang, waving the hair wand in front of him.

I sighed, even as a lump lodged itself in my throat. "Stop it."

Ignoring my directive, they kept up with the chatter until the water shut off. Finally, probably worried Emerson would overhear, they shut their traps. But when he opened the door, I couldn't look away. He was dressed in a pair of gym shorts, just like he'd been before, but all his tanned skin glistened, still damp from the shower. His shoulders, tight chest, and six-pack abs were all on display.

For a heartbeat, he stood in the doorway, eyes locked on me. I couldn't drag my attention away as one corner of his mouth kicked up in a smile and he ran a hand over his well-defined chest.

"I'm gonna get dressed." With that, he ambled across the room, and as he passed me, he settled his hot palm over the small strap of my tank top. When he dug his fingers into my skin and squeezed gently, my heart skipped. My breath caught and froze as I stared into his eyes in the mirror. "Looking good, Mariposa."

His deep voice echoed through me, but before I could even react, the warmth of his hand left my skin, and he walked away.

The second the door shut behind him. Linc fanned himself. "I'm telling you—you need to jump that man."

I glared, choking down the desire that single touch had ignited in me. Turning back to the mirror, I forced myself to refocus and let Linc finish before I put on my dress.

When I stepped out of the bathroom in the red satin, both Linc's and Mila's eyes snapped wide.

"Too much?" I skated my hands down the fabric over my hips. The dress was fitted through the hips before the slit up the thigh let the satin flare out to the floor. The dip of the neckline wouldn't be too much on most, but being an F cup since I was thirteen meant that sometimes I had to be careful about the line between hot and too much.

"No, but damn, Emerson might die." Linc laughed.

"Did you do the bend and shake?" Mila gently asked, confirming that I wouldn't fall out of my top.

I nodded. Spanx with supportive cups were my friend.

"Now go out there and convince that man he needs his hands all over your curves." Linc waggled his brows.

I rolled my eyes, but when I walked out of my room into the open living area and found him dressed in his black-on-black suit, it was hard not to want to agree with my friend.

There was fire in Emerson's eyes as they hovered over me. The way they paused at the neckline of my dress, then slowly scanned down to my hips and back up, had my body heating.

He cleared his throat. "You. Are. Gorgeous."

Stomach flipping, I stepped closer. In that moment, it felt as if he wanted me. But in the next second, he spoke, and the words were like a bucket of ice water poured over my head. "The idiot ex is going to hate himself, and I'll play my part to make him jealous."

A lump formed in my throat. Was that all it was to him? Oh course. That was what he'd agreed to do. So I pulled my shoulders back, harnessing my *don't fuck with me* vibe and shielding myself against the emotions threatening to ravage me.

"Ready?" I asked.

He watched me carefully for a minute, his expression thoughtful, before he nodded and turned to my friends. "It was nice meeting you both. If you want to hang here, feel free."

"We're headed back to the hotel to change, then going bar hopping." Linc rubbed his hand together. "Need to find my girl a hookup."

"It's funny how we have such different plans for the same night." Mila's eyes were bright as she turned to us. "Have fun."

"I left my keys if you need them," I said with a quick hug to Linc.

After I wrapped Mila in a hug too, Emerson opened the door and ushered me into the hall.

He was quiet on the elevator, cracking his knuckles and keeping his focus fixed on the number panel in front of him. I'd never seen him this nervous.

Once we settled back into the black Mercedes, I broke the silence. "You okay?"

He nodded and cleared his throat. "I've just never done a formal event like this before."

I frowned. Never? Chris did them all the time. "How is that possible?"

He rubbed his hands on his pants and then looked at me out of the corner of his eye. "The team usually calls on me for the funny stuff, like a pie in the face. I'm not the guy who goes to the big-ticket fundraisers. And you—" He took me in, his gaze searing me as he looked his fill. He forced a swallow and met my eyes. "You are so beautiful it makes my chest hurt."

My heart squeezed in response to the quiet comment. Beautiful wasn't a word I heard a lot. Pretty or curvy, maybe. But no one called me beautiful. Cheeks heating with a combination of embarrassment and pleasure, I reached up to touch my hair before I remembered that Linc had done it. The last thing I wanted was to mess it up.

"Sorry," Emerson said, his face set in an earnest frown. "I just want to be a good date, not the dumbass who crashes into a table or tells a stupid joke. I just want you to be proud that I'm the guy on your arm."

That caused a totally different kind of pang in my chest. Every line on his face was etched with worry. It was a look I'd never seen on the always smiling man. "Emerson," I whispered, grasping his hand. His fingers were long and firm as they wrapped around mine. "Just be you, and we'll have a good time." When the worry in his expression didn't ease, I added, "I don't think you're a dumbass at all—I just really like hanging out with you."

That's all it took for the crease between his brows to disappear and his shoulders to lower. In the space of a breath, his eyes were back to shining with the sparkle that was so intrinsically Emerson.

"I like you too, Gianna," he said softly, squeezing my hand.

Those words, coming from the guy who was just my fake date for the night, settled way too deep in my chest.

Gianna

15

"It's so cool, the way they take the little balloons and make them look like sparkles and stars." He'd relaxed by the time we pulled up in front of the zoo, as if he'd simply taken me at my word. It was the honest truth. I was happy to just be with him.

I ran my hands over the tight red material of my dress, willing myself to settle. The huge sign above us that read *Boston Zoo* was probably the biggest piece I'd ever completed. The way the animals peeked out from behind the letters made me just as happy today as it did the day I'd finished the design. But obviously, I was riding a high caused completely by the fact that my work was on display in downtown Boston.

"You did good, Mariposa." With a smile, Emerson squeezed my hand. "Really damn good. Be proud of yourself."

We stopped there for a moment to take pictures for his mom and sister, and once he was satisfied with the number he'd taken, we wandered under the silver, gold, and black balloon arches and into the event.

"What's your favorite animal?" he asked as he surveyed the table cards and picked up two with puffins on them.

There was no question that the theme for the players' table would be that bird. I swore every one of the guys was obsessed with Puff. The bird had become an honorary member of the team after my brother had accidentally hit him with a pitch last year. It was hard not to love the Atlantic puffin. Even I had to admit the little guy was adorable. And currently, everyone was on puffin baby watch, because any day now, Puff was going to become a daddy.

"Wait…" Emerson grabbed a card with a python off the table. When I'd called Jake a month ago, asking about what animal the firm would want, he'd insisted on the snake. His favorite. How fitting that an image of the slithering, shudder-inducing creature was printed beside his name. Although the comparison might not be fair to snakes. They'd never done anything to warrant being associated with him.

"Are you telling me the name of this place is actually douches?" His eyes were wide. "I thought Chris was just messing with you all this time."

"It's Doucette," I corrected.

He blinked and then started to chuckle. "Douches."

"It's Da-shh-eee-ttt." I rolled my eyes.

With a yank, I took Jake's card out of his hand and put it back on the table. Of course Jake wouldn't be here yet. The man loved to be fashionably late. He thought it made him important to have people wait on him. My brother's head had almost exploded last Thanksgiving because Jake had been an hour late and hadn't even bothered to apologize when we had to hold dinner.

Continuing my perusal, I scanned the rest of the cards, quietly admiring my own artwork.

"Why did management choose a duck for their table?" I asked when I noticed the mallard printed on each place card.

"Beckett loves them." Emerson tucked the two cards into his inside jacket pocket. "Rumor has it he slept with a stuffed duck until he got married."

Squinting, I waited for the grin or a laugh. But his expression remained neutral. Seriously? The broody billionaire had slept with a stuffed animal for forty years? "Are you messing with me?"

Emerson's only response was a smile.

"No way." I shook my head.

He shrugged. "Just what I heard. You still haven't told me—what's your favorite animal?"

"I'm not sure I've ever really thought about it." I perused the area, stopping on the sign I'd created for big cat alley. "Maybe a leopard."

Slipping his hands into his pockets, he rocked back on his heels and nodded. "Capable. Independent. Fierce. Just like you."

"I don't know about that." I chuckled, pushing away the slight discomfort that ran through me in response to his compliment. "They're graceful in their movements, though. I like watching them. How about you?"

"I can't pick one." He lifted his chin, zeroing in on my brother, who was standing across the room with a black bird on his shoulder. "Puff's one of my favorites, of course," he said confidently. "But I love bears. They're so much fun to watch. And monkeys." His eyes widened. "How could anyone forget the monkeys? They're crazy. And giraffes. Ever fed a giraffe?"

I shook my head but chuckled at his excitement. Of course he couldn't pick one. To Emerson, just about everything he encountered earned his awe. That outlook on life was so foreign to me, but it was hard not to admire him for it.

As we walked farther into the zoo, the area opened up into a beautiful, wide wooded space. Fake trees, flowering bushes, and rocks served as decorations and created an atmosphere reminiscent of an enchanted forest.

"Wow, it doesn't even look like the zoo anymore," Emerson said.

About fifty tables were decorated in black and gold and silver, just like the balloon arch, and beyond them was a dance floor and a stage. On one side, several tables were loaded with cellophane-covered baskets. And in each of the four corners was a bar. The scene was gorgeous, and since it was a clear night, the stars, although few and far between because of the city lights, shone above us.

Emerson's hand found the small of my back as he guided me toward his teammates. We'd barely said hi before Hannah Erickson, ever on the job, asked Emerson to help her with content for the Revs' social media.

Without hesitation, he jumped in, and the next thing I knew, he and

Puff were doing a choreographed dance. Two head nods, a shake back and forth, and three spins.

A laugh bubbled out of me as I watched. It may have been the cutest moment I'd ever witnessed.

"Wait, the beginning glitched. Can you do it again?" Hannah asked, her blue eyes focused on the screen of her phone as she tapped one black stiletto on the bricks below her feet.

"Anything you need, bebé," Emerson assured.

That one word had my spine snapping straight. How was it that two tiny syllables could cause so much annoyance?

The team's head of PR was beautiful. There was no denying that. Tight black dress that ended just above the knee. Brown hair in a high ponytail. She looked buttoned-up and professional, yet also elegant. I hated that I felt jealous. And I couldn't help but be reminded of another buttoned-up professional who was always dressed in black. It was dumb. I wasn't dating Emerson, and he wasn't Jake. Not to mention, Hannah seemed nice. Nothing like Libby. I shook it off and scanned the tables again, eager to take my mind off the situation.

"Em, I'm going to look at the baskets." I nodded toward the far side of the room and stepped that way.

"I'll just be a sec," he assured me before turning back to once again dance with the bird.

It blew me away that he hadn't originally been invited to this event. If he weren't here, who would have danced with Puff for the Revs social media? Chris sure as shit wouldn't have done it. And although Kyle Bosco was known for his antics, he looked pretty content where he was cozied up to the gorgeous blond I was pretty sure was a model I'd seen on a magazine cover or two. From what I knew of the guy, I couldn't see him leaving his date for a bird.

I glanced back at Hannah again, who was barking out orders. Did she have the first clue just how incredible Emerson was? I hoped so.

Giving him his space to be the Boston Rev goofball everyone knew and loved, I scanned the baskets and tickets for a variety of sporting events and shows. But nothing really caught my eye.

A few members of the zoo's board mingled nearby, as well as a few people from the zoo's marketing team I'd worked with. Before long,

Emerson appeared at my side, and instantly, he was chatting up anyone who came our way. We wandered from one table to the next, bidding on a couple of items that jumped out at him, before he ushered me over to our assigned table. After dinner, the president of the zoo stood up to give a quick call for donations. He even thanked the firm for the amazing job on the rebranding.

"He should have fucking thanked you by name," Chris muttered from my left side.

"They said they wouldn't name people for fear of missing someone." That's just how things were done at these events. And plenty of people had come over to thank me and praise my work already.

"That's bullshit." Chris shook his head and glared at the zoo president, who was still yammering on.

"Agreed," Emerson whispered.

"We should say something." With a grunt, Chris pushed his chair back.

My heart skipped. I absolutely didn't want them to make a scene.

"Didn't Walter come talk to you?" Avery asked, peeking around my brother.

"He did," I assured her, grasping Chris's arm to keep him from standing.

She whacked his other arm. "It's the way her company does this stuff. Don't be difficult."

Scooting his chair in again, he slumped. He meant well, and I appreciated the support. As annoying as Chris was, he was also my biggest champion.

And having an ally in Avery was a relief. If she didn't approve of my brother stepping out of line, then he wouldn't say a word. Avery was the only person in the world who could truly control him.

"You going to dance with me?" Emerson gently bumped me with his shoulder.

"Not likely," I joked. "But I'll grab refills for both of us."

"Want me to get it?" he offered, brows lifted high.

I shook him off with a smile. He'd gotten the last one, but he'd had to go back again after he dropped my drink halfway back when someone pushed their chair out quickly and Emerson bumped into it.

It was easier if I did it myself. So, with a small, reassuring squeeze to his arm, I stood and headed to the bar. As I stepped up, I recognized Jake's boss waiting for the bartender.

"Hello, Mr. Whittemore," I said, stepping up to the bar next to the president of Doucette Designs.

He turned away from the liquor, scanning my face with a polite, impersonal smile, clearly not recognizing me.

"Gianna Damiano?" I prompted.

His face remained blank.

As disappointment swirled inside me, I forced myself to keep my tone friendly. "I worked on this project."

"Oh, yes." He smiled. "That's right. You assisted Jake with the signs. I didn't realize any of his artists would be here."

My smile slipped as my heart splatted on the floor beneath me. So Jake hadn't given credit to me on the project like he promised he would.

"Well." He picked up two wineglasses off the bar and lifted them. "Have a good night, miss."

I forced a smile, but suddenly, a drink didn't sound so appealing. Turning away from the bar, I scanned the event space again, stopping on the table with the snake design rising up from the large floral arrangement in the middle. A few people milled around the ten chairs. Did any of them know that I'd created every design for the new signs on my own, or did they all assume it was Jake?

"Gianna?" a singsong voice called behind me.

Although I didn't recognize the voice, I turned at the sound of my name. A woman with wild red curls and a bright smile approached. Her hunter-green dress ended mid-calf, the color complementing her pale skin perfectly. She was pretty in the wild child way, but I didn't have the first clue who she was or how she knew my name.

"Yes?" I asked, fighting the urge to cross my arms to brace myself for the impending uncomfortable conversation with a stranger.

She held a hand out to me. "I'm Dylan." Her voice was friendly, and from the positive vibes radiating off her, she was clearly comfortable, as if she knew me and we were going to dive into a conversation we'd had a dozen times.

Even after studying her and shaking her hand, I was still at a loss for who she was.

"The confusion is vibrating off you like a bass drum beat." She smiled. "Although you don't know me, I think you probably know my fiancé, Cortney. He played with your brother before he moved into management."

"Oh." This was Cortney Miller's soon-to-be wife. I hadn't met her, but I'd heard a lot about both her and her daughter. "My brother says Willow is the sweetest baby ever."

She chuckled. "I think her daddy would pounce on anyone who claimed anything different. Even if he's a baby hog and tries to keep everyone at arm's length."

"Well, new baby, germs. I get it." Although kids weren't in my immediate future, I could imagine myself worrying about the same kinds of things someday. If I ever had the opportunity to have a family. My lack of urgency about kids had been an issue with Jake. He was a few years older than me and thought kids were more of a now thing, while I thought they were more of a later thing.

"I absolutely adore the signs. It's like the universe brought us together for this new fun project I have." She beamed at me.

I blinked. Project?

"Oh, I should probably explain it." She laughed. "I'm opening a daycare facility at Lang field."

I fought the frown at the stadium name. Seriously, the Langfields had named their ballpark *Lang Field*.

"I own a company called Little Fingers," Dylan said, launching into a detailed story about how she and her friend had started a preschool that, over the years, had grown into six, with another in the works. And how the universe had provided exactly what they needed each step of the way. "So now it's provided you."

I blinked again. I didn't want to be rude, because maybe she'd found me on LinkedIn or Indeed, since I was job hunting, but working in a preschool setting was the last thing I was interested in doing. And to be honest, I'd probably be terrible at it.

"I see where you're going with this, and what I should have said was that I'm looking for someone to design a logo for our Lang Corp location."

"Oh." I nodded, flooded with a sense of relief. "Okay, well, if you reach out—" I snapped my mouth shut. Because when the zoo had contacted me, I'd encouraged them to reach out to the firm to make plans. But why? There was no clause in my contract that said I couldn't work on side projects, and what loyalty did I have for a company that had literally uninvited me from the event held by a huge client that I had personally brought to them and worked with every step of the way? Not only that, but Jake had taken me off the two big accounts that I had pitched last month. So why would I actively work to bring them business? The president didn't even know who I was.

I glanced around the room, stopping at the table decorated with snakes.

"That whole area is a murky cloud of grays and blacks." Dylan waved her hand. "I don't jibe with auras like that." She winced. "It really crushes all my pretty teal. But your orange is like a beacon. Passion with just a pinch of red. You remind me of my friend Delia."

I had no idea what she was talking about. My dress was definitely red, even in the low lighting, not orange. Then again, hers wasn't teal; it was more of dark green. But she was right. That table was full of dark suits and black dresses.

"I get that tonight is a big night for you, so I don't need an answer now." She passed me a white card. "But I hoped you'd wanna come by one day. I wrote my address on the back of Cortney's card. Just slip it right in." She pointed at my chest. "You'll remember it later when that dress comes off, and it falls to the floor. The universe will put me back in the center of your mind."

She pointed again to my chest, one brow arched, so I obeyed, slipping the card into my bra.

"Great." She clapped. "My phone number is on there too. Just swing by anytime. I'm sure the universe will make sure I'm home."

"It will *what*?"

Her pretty gold eyes, full of more knowledge than I ever hoped to possess, sparkled. "Don't worry," she assured me with a pat on my arm.

"Firefly." Cortney appeared beside Dylan then, towering over both of us, tall and impressive in his navy suit. I'd mostly seen him with his typical man bun, but tonight, his golden hair hung down past his shoulders. "What did she say?"

"Oh, nothing yet. But she's gonna come over soon."

The confidence in Dylan's voice shocked me. I'd hardly said anything, so how did she know I'd show up?

"She needs some time. Not everyone can feel the way auras mesh so clearly. It took you a while too. But she'll get there. Don't worry." She lifted on the toes of her flip-flops—the last thing I'd expect her to wear with such a formal dress—and gave him a quick kiss on the neck. Then, grasping his hand, she turned back to me. "We'll see you later."

As they wandered away, his large hand settled on the small of her back and he leaned down, bringing his mouth to her ear. The way she beamed up in response showcased just how much love coursed between the two of them. It almost seemed like a blanket wrapping them tight and keeping out anything else.

"What are *you* doing here?" The high-pitched female voice was like an ice pick to the temple. The sound had my hackles raising and instantly sent me back in time to a moment in New York weeks ago.

"What are you doing here?" The voice curled my toes.

"I work here, Libby." I didn't turn away from the coffee machine as I filled my cup. All week, I'd been waiting for this moment. The day after Jake had broken the news over dinner, he'd announced to the staff that Libby was moving to the New York office. He'd also switched out all the photos in his office for ones of the two of them. Like he could rewrite history and convince the world that the two of them had been legitimately dating rather than cheating.

"I thought you were in Boston so that we didn't need to deal with this weirdness," she huffed.

With a deep breath in, I turned and took in her small frame. She'd always been petite, and in one of those awesome fuck-yous from the universe, she was a tiny, cute pregnant person too. Her belly rounded like a little basketball so that from the back, she probably didn't even look pregnant. I hated her even more for that. Even at seven months pregnant, her belly was smaller than mine.

"I'll be working on the zoo stuff after today." If only I could have made it that one last day without seeing her.

"Libby!" another voice called and Nina popped her head into the break-room. "I heard congratulation are in order. Let me see the ring."

Ring? My stomach dropped to the floor. No way. Jake had always claimed he wouldn't rush into marriage. He wanted to live together for at least a year before taking the leap. "Testing compatibility," he'd always said.

Libby lifted her hand and set it on her little bump, smirking at me. The large diamond sat on a gold band. "He asked last night when we officially moved in together. You should see our new place. It's perfect."

My eyes stung, but I refused to do anything but lift my chin and lock my jaw. I pictured a tree falling on the house. Crushing the adorable brownstone I'd found. That was all it took to lift my mood and stop the tears from forming.

"Oh, Gianna. I didn't see you there." Nina's eyes widened, and she stepped back.

"How is it possible you missed her? She's the size of two normal people." Libby scoffed.

I pulled my shoulders back and kept my head high. I hadn't been insecure about my weight since high school, and I wasn't going to let bitchy women change that.

"I'm headed out." Of the breakroom, the office, New York. I wanted out of all of it.

Nina couldn't meet my eyes as she stepped out of the doorway so I could pass.

"God," Libby groaned in a stage whisper. "I don't get why Jake was ever with her."

"At least you'll always know he traded up."

Their laughter echoed down the hall.

"Gigi," Jake snapped from his office. "Can you please do a coffee run—"

"GIGI?" JAKE'S VOICE BROUGHT ME BACK TO THE MOMENT.

I blinked, bringing the couple in front of me into focus. I almost didn't recognize Jake. Instead of the perfectly quaffed style he'd worn since before I met him, he had a buzz cut.

With a harsh breath in, I gaped. "Your hair."

He glowered, fisting his hand at his side. "Your friend owes me free cuts for life."

I gave Linc a hard time a lot, but at the moment, I truly felt the depth of our friendship. The man definitely had my back.

"I don't care if a wasp landed on him. Hell, even if it had stung him, the guy should be professional and not flinch half my hair away."

With a hand to my mouth, I coughed to keep myself from laughing. The man could *not* pull off a buzz cut. I'd always said he was pretty, but now it was more pretty *awkward*.

"What are you doing here?" Jake snapped after a long beat where I just stood, trying not to giggle.

I took a breath, steadying myself, and lowered my hand. "Emerson had a ticket, so instead of sitting with you, I'm sitting with him and his friends."

"Emerson?" He squinted as he repeated the name, like he had no idea who I was talking about. But my brother was always talking about his best friend. There was no way he wouldn't recognize the name. Actually, there was. Jake probably didn't bother to pay attention when Chris was speaking. That was on-brand for the asshole.

"Emerson, my brother's"—this was where I should have lied, but the idea of labeling Emerson as mine in any way, shape, or form made my stomach flip. Not because I thought Jake would care, but because I cared—"friend."

"Emerson Knight, number twenty-one, the Revs' third baseman?" His voice went up at the end, and he glared across the room.

I followed his line of sight and found Emerson watching us with a tentative look on his face. I gave him a nod, silently signaling that I was okay, then I turned back to my ex.

"Yeah."

Libby shifted and crossed her arms over her black dress. "I need to sit. My feet are starting to hurt." Her whiny tone dug into my eardrums. How the hell could Jake stand to listen to her talk regularly?

"Go sit, baby. I'll be right there." He dropped his arm from around her shoulders and pressed a hand to her back like he was gently urging her to move.

"Fine," she huffed, stomping off.

Jake watched her go for a moment, then turned back to me, giving me a once-over. He paused his perusal at the square neckline of my dress, then worked his way down to my hips and back up again.

I knew the look. It was full of interest. I'd seen it from him plenty of times, but at the moment it just felt gross. Arms crossed, I donned my armor and narrowed my eyes at him.

"What do you want?" I demanded.

He slipped his hands into his pockets and hit me with a smarmy smirk. "Thought you were dating someone."

"Yeah," I agreed. "Emerson." The lie was so much easier now that I was pissed. "We've been dating for a couple of weeks."

In response to my admission, the man *fucking* laughed. He full-on belly laughed for a solid thirty seconds before finally getting himself under control. "Funny, Gigi."

"What?"

He rolled his eyes and chuckled again. "There is no way. Guy like him could have anyone. No way he picks someone"—he waved a hand up and down, gesturing to my body—"like you."

My first instinct was to explode on him, but I tempered my response. Honestly, I could see his point. Emerson was a famous baseball player, and women threw themselves at him daily. Me? I was an average Jill.

Annoyance flared inside me. Putting myself down wasn't something I really ever did. I was pretty and loved my curves, but Emerson...

I turned, feeling his attention still on me. Green eyes seared my skin, so full of concern, and one eyebrow lifted in a silent question. *Are you okay?* I was. I didn't need to be rescued. Pride, or maybe self-perseveration, had my mouth moving.

"We've been friends for a long time." I rolled my eyes. "Honestly, if I hadn't been with you—"

Jake's mouth turned down.

"It probably would have happened sooner."

The scoff that left him was full of disbelief. "Or you're pretending so you don't look stupid or have to admit you can't get over us."

That statement fueled the fire that had been missing. Over him? The idea that I wasn't was laughable.

"Are you kidding me?" I ground out. "I couldn't give a single fuck what you think. Get over yourself. I certainly have."

"Like I said on the phone, I'll believe it when I see it. It's pretty pathetic. Humorous, really." He smiled a condescending smile, and something inside me snapped.

"Right." Without another word, I turned on my heel and stomped across the room, rage fueling every step.

Emerson watched me carefully as I came closer, his expression open, but a hair of confusions in his brow.

Jake needed proof? Then I'd give it to him. Without slowing down or allowing myself another thought about it. I stepped up to Emerson, grabbed the sides of his face, and pressed my lips to his.

The second his warm lips pressed into mine, every cell inside me shifted.

He sucked in a breath, clearly shocked. I couldn't blame him. I was shocked too. But surprise fled quickly, and then he brought a gentle hand to my cheek and opened his mouth against mine. In the next heartbeat, he took control of the kiss, running his tongue along the seam of my lips and guiding me to open.

Without hesitation, I did. With a sigh, I let him explore every inch of mouth and dominate my tongue.

I melted against him, my knees going weak. Holy hell. The man could kiss.

It was more than I expected. More than I'd ever felt. Need flooded my body and settled deep in my core.

With that same hand, he ghosted over my rib cage, then my waist. His fingers barely pressed against the fabric of my dress, but I shivered in response anyway. In a quick move, he snaked an arm around me and pulled me tight to him.

There was no denying how turned on he was. Not with the way his erection pressed long and hard into my hip. My immediate reaction was a gasp, but that quickly faded into a whimper as a fierce need to feel him filling me up pounded through me. I never wanted this moment to end. But he had other ideas. After one more slow exploration, he slipped his tongue out of my mouth.

I pulled back, though I remained pressed tight against his hard body, staring into the fathomless depths of those emerald eyes, where I swore I found a desperate need that matched my own. For one second, I wanted to lean back in. Take more from this man. But in a blink, reality set in.

This wasn't real.

Even so, that kiss might have been the realest thing I'd ever experienced. I was in so much trouble.

Emerson
16

I FOUGHT THE NEED TO LEAN BACK IN AND CLAIM HER MOUTH AGAIN. I hadn't gotten anywhere near enough of the unbelievably sexy woman in front of me. As I continued battling with myself, she grabbed my arm and yanked me toward the dance floor. For the last twenty minutes or so, a DJ had been playing music, and a few couples speckled the temporary wooden surface.

"Don't you dare turn back," she muttered, her nails biting into my arm as she dragged me behind her. The woman had to realize everyone we knew was wondering what was going on. Especially her brother.

But even though I could feel the scrutiny of my friends and team-mates, I couldn't pull my eyes from the sway of her full hips in the tight red dress as she stomped to the dance floor. I was mesmerized. All I could do was follow. Damn, I wanted to smack her ass. Pat it. Squeeze it. Touch it. Hell, pet it. I wasn't picky. If it meant my hand got to be on those round globes of perfection, then I was game.

"Emerson," she snapped.

I swallowed and willed my head to get back in the game. Trying to control the hard-on raging in my pants. Trying to hide the evidence of how this woman made me feel from the people around us. I'd gone from nervous as hell, to trying my best to make it work, to confused, to turned the fuck on. But there was a truth I couldn't deny.

"The guys are gonna ask a lot of fucking questions, Gi." Because it was not normally my style to attack my date's mouth at the table. Especially when she was my best friend's sister.

I winced at the realization. But as I sucked in my bottom lip, I could still taste her, and I couldn't muster any regret.

That kiss might have actually shut my brain off completely. All my life, my thoughts had moved quickly. Sometimes too quickly. But for that ten seconds or ten minutes or whatever length of time her plush lips had been pressed against mine—existing in a vacuum where time didn't exist—I didn't think.

"What do you mean?" Just as we stepped onto the wooden dance floor, she whirled on me. "We're supposed to be fake dating, so why can't I fake kiss you?"

Chest tightening, I watched her, taking in that gorgeous mouth. "Nothing about that kiss was fake, and don't try to bullshit me into thinking you believe any different."

As I said the words, I expected her to put up a fight. But as those fierce brown eyes swimming with desire met mine, my heart leaped. It was impossible to sum up what made everything, including Gianna's bad attitude, so attractive, but it was starting to feel dumb to fight it. Apart from the complications—her ultimately living in New York, my best friend probably killing me, the impending loss of my job and any means to support anyone in a few months—maybe, just maybe, she was meant for me.

She huffed a hard breath, but instead of fighting, she shocked the hell out of me by wrapping her arms around my neck. "Shut up and dance with me."

"Gladly." Slipping my hands along her hips, I pulled her close and crossed my wrists just above her ass.

She hard-core fought against the shiver that the brush of my fingertips against the curve of her ass caused, making it hard not to grin.

"Are we going to pretend that was fake too?"

"I hate you," she muttered.

I laughed, because she absolutely didn't. "What happened, Mariposa?" I was the easy target, but not the real one.

"I tell myself I don't care what he thinks, and then he says the one thing that sets me off."

My hold tightened around her automatically. I hated that she cared about some other guy. Especially when he wasn't worth her time.

"No. I see what you're assuming," she said, "but that isn't what I meant, exactly."

I took a slow breath. Normally, I didn't have a temper, and flying off the handle wasn't going to win me any points with her, so I locked down the urge to let out a long breath. "So explain," I said calmly, swaying to the slow music but not loosening my hold on her.

Hearing the story didn't help with my anger. In fact, it had the opposite effect. Rage burned deeper with every word out of her mouth.

"He's a fucking tool bag." The words escaped in clipped tones, beating from deep inside me as I grasped one of her hands and squeezed. "You are a goddess. Way too good for me."

"He's an idiot." She shrugged. "I shouldn't let him get to me. But yet he does."

The warning bells rang inside my head. If he still had the power to upset her, then it was likely there were unsettled feelings there. That was reasonable, since they'd only broken up a few weeks ago. Still, the thought caused an ache in my chest. If she was going to put effort into a man, it should be a man who cherished her. Not some asshole who said she couldn't possibly land a professional athlete. What the hell? This woman could have anyone she wanted. Anyone with half a brain would know they were lucky to be blessed with her time.

"It's backward," I mumbled as I tucked her in closer. Her hair brushed my jaw, and for one second, I let myself inhale her. Pull a piece of her into me. Soak in the way it felt to have her body pressed to mine. Our linked fingers rested above her right tit, and the swell of it pressed into the back of my hand. As we continued to sway to the music, her hip brushed my thigh, sending a rush of heat through me.

"What's backward?" Her forehead brushed my jaw as she tilted her head up to look at me. For a second, I got lost in her deep brown eyes.

They were swimming with so much emotion and vulnerability it hurt to be this close.

She was good at hiding her true feelings, but I'd studied her enough to know that her eyes always gave her away. Like the keys to a kingdom, one glance gave me so much.

"The idea that you're not good enough for me. It's so backward."

Breath hitching, she wet her lips. Between her scent in the air, the press of her body to mine, and her mouth just inches from me, my body was screaming for me to reach out and take her. To devour her mouth and show her exactly how much someone like me could actively want her. "Because you're smart and sexy as fuck."

Her eyes went wide, and her body stiffened in my arms, but she didn't pull away.

"Half the guys here haven't been able to take their eyes off you since we walked in. And I don't need to be a vice president of anything to know any guy would be lucky as fuck to get to call you theirs."

I pulled her closer and pressed my lips to her temple, relishing the shiver that raced through her.

"If things were different, Gi," I whispered against her skin, "I wouldn't be trying so hard to keep myself away from you."

If she didn't have plans to be back in New York. If I wasn't facing so many unknowns. If she wasn't my best friend's sister and the last person I'd ever want to hurt. If I was settled enough to be the kind of partner she deserved. Then I would have already taken her to my bed.

"Em," she whispered, that single word running across my skin, burrowing into me, claiming a space that might forever belong to her.

I swallowed the lust and genuine need for this woman. Fought the feelings that were getting harder to ignore.

As the song came to an end, I loosened my hold, and she stepped back, glancing over my shoulder at our table.

"Chris is all glary." Her shoulders tightened, and her chin rose a fraction. In a matter of one breath, she donned the armor she wore so no one would see the tired or vulnerable or hurt woman hiding below and scowled his way.

Fuck, I wished she could see that she didn't have to fight every battle alone.

Teeth gritted, she said, "I'll just tell him—"

"I've got your brother." I turned so I was at her side and pressed my hand back into the small of her back, then guided her to our table and pulled out a chair. Once she was settled, I made a beeline for my best friend.

He tilted his head, silently indicating the space on one side of the dance floor. With a nod, I followed. I owed him a conversation.

"What the fuck is going on?" he snapped, rounding on me. He wanted answers about what was going on between his sister and me. There was no way I'd admit my true feelings, but I couldn't lie to him. So I'd explain something else.

"See Jake." I kept my back turned to the douche, but Chris scanned the room, and when he stopped and narrowed his eyes, I said, "See the blond he's with?"

Chris nodded.

"His very pregnant date?" I prompted.

Chris's face turned to stone.

"That would be his baby."

Like a current of electricity had jumped through him, his whole body jolted. He opened his mouth and then shut it again. His fists tightened into thick balls.

"Are you telling me that fucker cheated on my sister?" Chris growled through clenched teeth. "Are you saying that while I welcomed the asshat into my house, gave him tickets to games, signed shit for him, he was fucking around on her?"

I gave a clipped nod, and that's all it took for Chris to growl and take a step to the side like he was going to barrel past me. I grasped his arm, stopping him before he could storm over to Jake and do something stupid. Then I pulled in a cleansing breath, searching for a calmness I didn't feel.

"Then," I said, "he told her she had to be lying about dating me. That there was no way a guy like me would date someone as unappealing as her."

He yanked his arm away, trying to free himself from my grasp, but I tightened my grip.

"Listen to me," I demanded. "If you go over there screaming instead of letting me take care of it, it'll only prove his point."

"The fuck?" Chris fixed the glare he was so well known for on me.

"Dragon, if someone picked on Avery, if a man said something awful about her, what would you do?" I lifted one brow.

"Go after him."

"Right. So Gi's date should be the one to take care of the Jake problem. And that's exactly what I'll do if you back off and let me."

He blinked, and the hard lines on his face softened a fraction. "Oh." He glanced over at Gi, then focused on me again. "Oh." With one hand, he rubbed at the back of his neck. "Comfort your girl. Kill the ass. Right. That's what you're doing." He shook his head. "Damn, you really are good at the fake out. After the way you kissed her, and then the looks between you two on the dance on the floor, I really thought…"

I said nothing. Not admitting to something wasn't the same as denying it. At least that's what I was telling myself.

He shook his head and blew out a breath. "Guess I'll let you do your thing."

I nodded. "I'm going to deal with Jake and then get her out of here."

With the hint of a grateful smile, he dipped his chin. "Thanks."

"Don't need to thank me," I assured him, and then I was off, headed back to Gianna, whose eyes hadn't left her brother and me. "Want a drink, Mariposa?" I asked, bending at the waist and looming over her.

"White wine?" she asked, like she really thought there was a right answer here. Didn't she know that I didn't care what she wanted? That I'd get her anything?

I gauged the crowd, looking for the idiot. I wouldn't ever forget the man. Not after the way he drank Gi in when he saw her in that dress. The way the material molded to her body was sinful. The slit that ran up, showing off the thighs I wanted wrapped around my hips. Every curve made my mouth water. But I'd forced myself to sit in my damn chair and brood silently as he eye-fucked her. The dude had one of those pretty faces that screamed he was owed a good nose breaking.

Just to take away the shiny perfection and symmetry there. If not for the buzz cut that was more fitting for an eight-year-old than a grown-ass man, I would have had to admit the guy was good-looking. In that too perfect Ken doll type way, of course.

It only took a minute to spot the douche bag at the bar on the other side of the room.

"Streaks."

He snapped his head up, pulling his attention away from the chick he was with. I didn't recognize her, not that he ever brought the same date twice. His agent had probably set him up with her. He didn't care who he took to these events. They were just arm candy. Someone to make him look good. He'd drop them as quickly as he found them. He lived by the friends before chicks mantra in life. The guy was almost thirty-five, and it wasn't looking like he'd ever settle down.

"Sup, Bambi?" he asked, strolling over.

I tipped my head to the bar and took off toward it. He stuck to my side, and as we made our way across the room, I explained what I needed.

"Asshole," Kyle muttered. "Learn how to treat women. All women"—he waved, gesturing to the whole outdoor space—"or your hand should be your only pleasure."

I nodded. He was fucking right. But as we sidled up to the bar next to Gi's ex, I jumped into character. "I don't know, man. I'm just so fucking happy."

"Probably because you finally got the girl."

In that moment, I could be honest about the woman who haunted my brain. "I don't get how I got so lucky. I've been waiting a year, maybe more, for this." I shook my head. "And when she looks at me and smiles, damn. I didn't know that kind of feeling existed."

He smirked, resting his elbow on the bar. "Getting to fuck those tits and that pretty mouth? Must feel like you've died and gone to heaven."

I frowned at the way he'd gone off script, but my irritation was forgotten when the guy behind me scoffed.

"Don't get your hopes up. Gianna's not a get-on-her-knees girl."

When I turned, Jake smirked. "At least not one who gives good head. She's more of a cold, selfish bitch."

I locked my hands into tight fists. Who the fuck talked about a woman that way? Especially Gi. Sure, she was salty and tough, but she was the opposite of cold. The woman was all fire and heart. But I kept my anger in check and continued with the ruse. "Huh," I said with a shrug. "That must be a you thing. She and I don't have that issue."

A choked sound escaped him as he scrutinized me through slitted eyes.

"Jake, right? Nice to you meet you." I held my hand out.

The guy looked like he was made from plastic. The skin of his face was too smooth, his eyebrows too sculpted. And the haircut was definitely worse up close.

"Wait, is this pencil dick?" Kyle peered around me, pointedly looking at Jake's stubby fingers resting on the bar top. "Dude, he's got toddler hands." Then his eyes dropped to his crotch. "I get why she traded up."

Rather than shake my hand, which was still extended, Jake balled his fists and tucked them into his pockets. He rocked back on his heels and frowned at me. The slight crease between his brows screamed confused, so I wanted to be clear.

"For the record." I met his eyes. "Gianna is exactly my type of woman. Go right ahead and piss her off, because damn if I don't love when she's fired up. But hurt her." Stepping close, I lowered my voice. "Hurt her, and you and I will have issues. Because I'm all fun and games until my girl gets hurt."

With a thick swallow, Jake blinked twice. Then he spun and walked away.

"Damn, dude. You're scary as fuck when you want to be." Kyle chuckled. "That had unhinged written all over it."

I turned back to my teammate and sent him a smirk. "Don't fuck with people I care about."

"Well, we totally made him feel like an ass." Kyle laughed, holding a fist out for a bump. "We crushed that."

Though I tapped my knuckles to his, I wasn't sure I agreed. I was still fighting the urge to cut Kyle's tongue out for even thinking about

Gianna's mouth or tits. And yet I couldn't even bring it up without making him suspicious. Because normally I could take a joke. "Not a fan of the improv," I said instead.

He shrugged. "Got us where we needed to go. Just don't tell Chris. He'd deck me." Kyle laughed.

I rubbed my palm over the top of his head, mussing his hair. He batted me away, but I half jumped on him and wrapped him in a bear hug.

With a firm push, he backed away and ran his hand over his head, smoothing out his hair. "Fuck off." With that, he strode away, leaving me alone at the bar.

I called the bartender over and convinced him to pop the cork of a bottle of wine and hand it over. Then, with it in one hand and two plastic cups in the other, I headed back to Gi. She'd suffered enough tonight. Although the zoo staff had gushed about her signs and so had all the Revs and the donors in attendance, not a single person from the douchey firm's table had even bothered to come congratulate her. Her company sucked. I always gave Chris shit for butting in and telling her she needed a new job, but the truth of it was that he was right.

"Come on." I pulled her to her feet and guided her away from the crowd. As we left, the weight of at least a dozen sets of eyes landed on me, but I couldn't make myself care who was watching us.

Emerson

17

"WHERE ARE WE GOING?" GI ASKED AS WE WANDERED TOWARD THE water.

Although it was a quiet night, we were in Boston, and cars rushed past on the street surrounding the harbor. If we moved down away from the center, there was a breakwater in the salty ocean that protected the harbor from the waves of the Atlantic.

"I thought you might want some downtime. There's a quiet place where you can see the stars and hear the waves." Two things I missed. Growing up, I spent a lot of time by the water. Especially when I wanted peace from my large family and noisy younger siblings. My dad swore that the water quieted all the noise inside. And even though he'd been gone for almost a decade, those words always echoed in my heart.

"Are we in a hurry?" she asked, her breathing choppy.

I assessed her, taking in the way her chest was heaving and how she was almost jogging in stilettos to keep up, and quickly slowed my steps.

"Thanks," she said. "All that lankiness isn't something I was blessed with."

"Thank God for that."

She tipped her head, and a small line appeared between her brows.

125

"You without those killer curves would be sad."

She rolled her eyes at me, but she couldn't hide the slight lift to the corner of her mouth. Her heels tapped along the concrete as we moved farther from the noise of the zoo and the road. When we reached the end of the sidewalk and came to the five-foot brick wall. She glanced around, confused.

"Trust me?" I asked, setting the wine and cups on the ground beside me.

With a slow nod, like she wanted to but wasn't totally convinced she could, she studied me. Good enough.

"Okay." I grabbed her waist and turned her so her back was to the wall. "When I say three, jump."

Her big brown eyes widened, and she locked her hands around my wrists. "Wait. Wait." She looked over her shoulder, then zeroed in on me, her mouth parted in disbelief. "You do not think I'm going up there, do you?"

I tightened my hold on her waist, my fingers digging into the softness there, keeping her from escaping. "No, I don't think it. I *know* you're going up there. Trust me."

"You can't lift me," she scoffed.

I frowned at her. I wasn't the scrawny seventeen-year-old who'd been picked up by a triple-A team anymore. Even at six-two, I still barely tipped the scale at 190, but I was just as strong as any of the guys on the team. "Try me."

"I'm heavy," she pleaded, her eyes full of fear and what I swore was embarrassment.

That was nonsense. I didn't lift a lot because I didn't want to wreck my shoulders by pushing it. But I could bench 305. I was a professional athlete; it was insulting that she thought I couldn't help her jump up a couple of feet.

Brows lifted, I tightened my grip on her. "So on three?"

"Fine." She glared, sliding her hands to my shoulders. "But I warned you."

I counted, and when she jumped lamely, I lifted her the rest of the way and settled her on the ledge.

She shrieked. "I can't believe you did that."

I set the wine and cups on the wall, then pulled myself up next to her with little effort. "I told you I could."

She rolled her eyes at me, scoffing, but I just grinned as I slipped over the side.

Once I'd dropped down onto the rocky ledge that ran out into the dark water of the harbor, I rested my hands on her waist again. "Gonna actually trust me this time?"

Head tipped to one side, she studied me. I could see the eye roll before it happened, so rather than wait for it, I lifted and pulled her down beside me.

She squeaked again as she settled on the rocks. "I can't believe you just did that," she said again, this time her tone filled with awe rather than incredulity.

I didn't get it. It was like no one had ever lifted her before. She peered around me, taking in the water and the horizon. Then she focused on me once more, carefully stepping forward onto the uneven surface.

"What is this?"

"A breakwater. Goes a half mile into the bay." I tipped my chin toward the rocky path. "It's a bit uneven, so you might want to take those off." I pointed to her heels.

Part of me thought she might fight me on it. Barefoot, outside, in the dirt. But without a word, she slipped the sky-high heels off and hooked them over her finger.

"This way." I guided her silently down the rocky wall. About halfway, I stopped and set the bottle of wine and glasses down. Then I shrugged my suit jacket off my shoulders and laid it out.

"Wanna sit?" I nodded to my jacket and held out a hand for hers. Once she settled, I plopped down beside her. Our legs dangled off the edge, not even coming close to the water below. The only sound was the lapping of the small waves against the rocks as I poured wine into both cups and handed her one.

She took it and brought it to her lips for a slow sip as she surveyed the dark water.

"How often do you come out here?" she asked, setting the cup on a flat rock beside her. She was perceptive, quickly understanding that this wasn't a new thing for me.

"About once a week. Maybe more often in the summer," I admitted. This last year, I discovered that December and January were cold as fuck in Boston. "The city can be overstimulating." It was overwhelming at first. The smells, sounds, lights. Even the people.

Having this quiet space centered me. In high school, I'd been given labels to explain why my thoughts ran wild. Why I couldn't focus in class and why I struggled to pay attention, which so often led to walking into furniture and tripping over things.

The second I stepped onto the baseball diamond, though, all the chaos faded away. At first, teachers assumed I was doing it on purpose, begging for attention, because the jump between being unable to focus and being hyper-focused was so severe it was hard for many to comprehend. As it turned out, my brain just worked differently. Neurodiverse. I was nowhere near the only athlete who fit that bill.

"I like that you can see a few stars here." Gianna leaned back on her palms and tipped her head back. The smooth skin at the column of her neck called to me. Begged me to press my lips to it. To taste her softness. "I always wanted to paint a good night sky. Not a city skyline. I've done that more times than I can count. But the sky in the middle of nowhere."

"You should see the view from back home."

She twisted, focusing on me, and the lights of the city created a glow that highlighted the long lashes that brushed her cheekbones as she blinked. "Where is home?"

"Currently Boston," I joked.

Her lips pulled into a line and her eyes narrowed. Once again, she wasn't impressed with me and my jokes.

"Can't get you to crack a smile," I teased.

"Are we joking or talking?" she countered.

That question hit me hard. Though joking was my go-to, I wanted this woman to really know me. I wanted to open up.

"I grew up in Pole Ojea."

With a hum, she lowered her brows.

"It's in Puerto Rico. A small coastal town. Not much there. But my dad loved it. He loved the water. We stayed there until I was fourteen."

"Why did you leave?"

With a thick swallow, I jumped right into the hard part. "My dad died."

She leaned forward, and suddenly, her warm palm was resting on my thigh. "I'm so sorry." She shook her head. "Wow, that's a dumb thing to say. I know that."

Was there really a right thing to say? Her mom had died when she was eight, so she knew that as well as I did.

"People always say that when you tell them one of your parents is dead." She frowned out at the water. "They act like that simple apology—for something that couldn't possibly be their fault—makes it better." She shook her head and then focused on me. "Was he sick?"

I took a breath. Rehashing was a challenge for me. Normally, I didn't like to harp on the past. I just worked to focus on the good that had come out of it. But more than anyone, I wanted Gi to understand me.

"He owned a fishing boat. That's what he did for work. Sometimes he'd take me out on the shorter trips with him. It was fun."

My brother had vague memories of my dad, and my sisters had almost none. So we didn't talk about him a lot. It felt strange to be doing it now. I cracked my knuckles, and in response, Gi squeezed my thigh lightly.

"He went out for a long weekend. There was a storm. His boat went missing."

A sharp intake of breath echoed around us, and I covered her hand with mine to comfort her. As if on instinct, she flipped hers palm up. Her hand was warm and soft. Even with the two rings on her finger biting into mine, that connection soothed me.

"Did they ever find him?" She whispered the question, her words hesitant, like she wasn't sure it was appropriate. Still, she didn't stop herself.

I winced as a memory surfaced. The call I got a few months after I started with the Diamond Hawks, the Revs farm team. As hard as the news was to take, it had been a blessing. It meant my mother could finally collect the insurance money our family desperately needed.

The first few months in Pole Ojea without Dad had been a nightmare. On top of losing him so suddenly, the insurance company wouldn't pay out. At the time of my dad's death, my parents had a small cushion, but not a lot, and it was nearly impossible for Mom to find a steady job to support us.

Gianna squeezed my hand lightly, reminding me I hadn't answered her question.

"They didn't find the boat for four years. And no boat meant no life insurance. In that time, my mom tried to support us, but she couldn't find work in our small town." I swallowed. "We moved to Jersey with my mom's sister and her husband. Lived in the same apartment complex. My aunt and uncle helped while my mom worked long hours at a law firm. I spent a lot of time taking care of my younger brother and sisters." While I spoke, I focused on the way my big hand swallowed hers up. The contrast of my slightly darker skin against hers. It kept me grounded. Kept my emotions in check. "Worked out, though, because the second the baseball coach saw me chase one of the team's fly balls, I had a spot on the team."

"Wow, that's pretty convenient. My dad coached for a long time, and I don't think he ever had talent fall into his lap like that."

I chuckled. "I doubt it was that convenient. I was fast, and I loved the game, but I couldn't hit for shit. He tossed me in center field. I had no issue racing every one of my teammates to every ball." I shook my head. "I annoyed them all, and I constantly begged to be put in. Swore I was ready to play, even when I had no clue what I was doing."

"You must have had some idea. Otherwise, I doubt you would have been recruited in high school."

"Coach Nelson put in a lot of time, teaching and working with me. And I was fast and threw the ball like a rocket." I joked the way Coach N had about the power in my throw. With a smirk, I took a swig of my wine before setting it down on the rocks. "But, honestly, without baseball, I wouldn't have made it through high school."

"I felt that way about art class," she said, so quietly I almost missed it. "It was my mom's and my thing, before she died. I painted more after she died because it was a way to feel close to her. And it turned into my peaceful place."

The ache in my chest that formed every time I thought about losing my dad and those high school days morphed at the sound of her voice and the sadness in her expression as she looked out over the water. But I understood her, because my peace had always been on the baseball diamond. Where everything but playing the game slipped away.

Rarely did anything break through my hyper-focus the second I stepped onto the grass.

"I wasn't like you, though. I was afraid to leave. I got into SCAD and the RI Institute of Art, but I was terrified to go somewhere new for college. So I convinced my dad I didn't want to go to college at all." She shrugged one shoulder. "I wish I had been brave like you."

It was my turn to squeeze her hand. "I was terrified. I wasn't even eighteen. But my family needed the money from my contract. So I didn't have a choice. Even though I wasn't making much, every cent I earned was a huge help to my mom. And the team's batting coach let me stay in the apartment above his garage."

She shifted my way, closing the space between us, teeth sinking into her bottom lip. Then she dipped her head and took in the water two feet below our legs dangling off the edge of the breakwater. "I may act like it, but I'm not brave enough to make a leap like that. Hell, I'm not even brave enough to leave my awful job now."

Pivoting so I was facing her, I cupped her cheek with my free hand, forcing her to look at me. "Gi, you are brave enough. You can do anything you set your mind to. You amaze me."

Her eyes didn't leave mine for a full minute before they floated down to my mouth and rose again.

That tiny movement had my heart hammering in my chest.

As if she could hear it, her plump lips separated slightly and her breathing went shallow.

Damn, I wanted her mouth. I wanted to feel it pressed to mine. I wanted her taste on my tongue. I rubbed my thumb lightly against her cheek, and with a long breath out, I dropped my hand and shifted back.

"You say all these big, nice things." She swallowed, her focus once again fixed on the surface of the water, but then she straightened her shoulders and forced her eyes back up to me. "You make it seem like you want something from me. But do you?" Her eyes swam with uncertainty. The vulnerability in her tone hit me like a wave, almost knocking me over. For a minute, all I could do was stare at her and consider how the hell to put my feelings into words.

In the time it took to sort my emotions, her eyes hardened and she locked her jaw. Her chin rose just a fraction. All of her became defensive.

Fuck. I wanted the walls the down.

"You're all I think about lately, Gi." The honesty flew out of my mouth.

Her eyes widened just slightly, giving away her surprise.

"But you are a forever girl, and all I can do is casual. In the six years I've known your brother, I've never known you to not be in a relationship. Jake, Ron, Steve, Teddy."

She gasped. "You remember their names?"

"My interest isn't new. It's just more intense."

Tilting her head to one side, she shifted imperceptibly closer. I wanted to answer that invitation, lean in too. Desperately. To kiss those soft lips I'd only gotten a small taste of earlier.

But I couldn't.

I sighed and squeezed her hand again. "But I'm not ready to be half of something. I have to be selfishly devoted to baseball for the next five months and earn a contract. Or earn the attention of another team. Even after that, I can't drag someone across the country and leave them pretty much alone all season. I won't take a person I care about away from everything they know and love." I shook my head. "I'm not a good bet right now, Gi. I care about you too much—and I respect your brother too much—to do something that could hurt either of you."

She watched me silently, her eyes brimming with both disappointment and understanding. Slowly, she pulled her hand from mine. The loss was like a knife to my chest. A mask of indifference covered her face, as if she were completely unaffected.

She turned and picked up her drink, and as she set it back down, she said, "Someday I'd like to paint the moon over the harbor."

My heart panged in the most painful way at that simple statement. It was a shift. But at least she wasn't shutting down completely. Because I did want her words, her thoughts, as much as I wanted to touch her. Everything about her utterly hypnotized me. I'd told her we had to have lines. She was merely accepting them. So that left me with no choice but to move forward too.

I shook off the disappointment. I had no right to be upset. Because what did I want her to say? That she'd be down for a casual situation, since that was all I could do? Would I even have taken her up on it?

I refocused on her words. The moon. The night.

"You should do it. One night in the apartment, when it's reflecting on the harbor, just drop everything and paint it."

"Maybe." She took another sip of wine, keeping her eyes averted.

"I've heard you can see the northern lights sometimes. I check every night, because I've always wanted to see them."

She turned, her brows arched. "What?"

I shrugged. "They fascinate me. There is this place in Finland I've always wanted to visit. You can stay in a glass house and watch them—"

Her mouth fell open.

"What?" I froze. Shit. That was a stupid thing to admit. When I'd mentioned it to the guys, they'd taunted me. We'd had a whole conversation about where we'd go if we could pick up and leave right then. Most of the guys threw out locations like Vegas or Iceland. But the idea of the flashes of color lighting up the sky above me thrilled me.

Gianna licked her lips. "The Kakslauttanen Resort."

I nodded, lowering my head and cracking my knuckles. "Yeah."

"That's my dream trip."

My heart stuttered as a vision swamped me. An image of Gi beside me as the greens and blues danced across her bare skin. Rolling her so she straddled me with the aurora borealis glowing behind her, reflecting off her long brown hair.

"Mine too," I whispered. My mouth was suddenly dry. The wine really didn't help, but I took a sip anyway.

She looked back at the water. "What else is on your list?"

"The underwater hotel in the Maldives, Bocas del Toro in Panama."

She chuckled darkly, but she wasn't smiling.

"What?" I asked again.

"Let me guess." She pressed her lips together and studied me with a thoughtful look. "The Tree House Lodge in the Amazon."

I nodded.

"Sounds like we have the same list. All the hot spots for extreme natural travel. I've always wanted to paint them." She shook her head. "I never realized how alike the two of us are."

I wanted to laugh, but the sound caught in my throat. Because suddenly, the idea of seeing those places without her seemed underwhelming. More than the sights, I wanted to witness the smile that would spread across her face as fish swam above her and watch her experience a torrid rain from the top of a tree in the forest. I wanted to study her paintings of each moment. To soak in the emotions she experienced as she discovered and explored each place.

Hand trembling, I grasped hers and held it gently again. "I hope I can see the paintings." Because that was as close as I'd get to any of it.

She shook her head. "I doubt I'll ever go. I've never left the East Coast."

It was on the tip of my tongue to say that I'd take her. But no matter how badly I wanted to, that wasn't a promise I could make.

Gianna

18

THIS VERY EASILY COULD HAVE BEEN THE PERFECT NIGHT. SITTING ON A breakwater, in the dark, under the stars with Emerson. Sharing deeply personal things. And not only did he listen, but he really heard me. Like he hung on each statement, waiting with bated breath for my next admission. The words that I didn't say as much as the ones I did. I'd opened up to him more tonight than I had to any other man in my entire life. And he had trusted me with his own vulnerabilities. From there, our conversation was easy, and our shared dreams were a pleasant surprise. It was unlike any date I'd ever been on, and yet it wasn't a date at all. He'd made that clear.

"We should probably head back."

Although I didn't want to agree, he was right. It had to be getting close to midnight. I didn't want the night to end. I'd never felt like I had the power to bewitch another person, but the way Emerson's eyes locked on to me? The way he clung to my hand?

Yeah. Tonight felt special.

After I nodded, he released my hand and pulled out his phone, probably to text the car service. Then he stood and helped me to my feet. Once I straightened, my attention got hung up on the pull of the material of his dress shirt against his shoulders. The lines of his lean, sculpted body were hypnotizing. He swiped up the wine bottle and

135

plastic cups, then hooked my shoes over one finger and led me to the wall we'd have to once again hop.

Just like last time, Emerson set the stuff on the wall and then turned to me. I didn't want to be annoying, but being picked up like that was foreign and strange. I hadn't been lifted off the ground since I was a child.

My heart pounded out a nervous rhythm, and I found myself twirling a strand of hair in a way I did subconsciously when I was nervous.

"What's wrong?" he asked. The frown he gave me was full of concern and so foreign on his always content face.

I sighed. This was ridiculous. He acted like he didn't get that I wasn't a small girl. "Emerson, I'm not super comfortable being lifted."

His brows lowered as that frown deepened. "Why?"

Huffing, I flung my arms out. Was he seriously going to make me say it? "You know I'm big, right?" I glanced at the black Oxfords on his feet, cringing at the blunt way I'd phrased the question.

For a beat, he was silent. All I could hear was the hammering of my heart.

The pounding lost its rhythm as he moved closer and brushed his thumb under my chin, forcing it up.

Green eyes burning into mine, he whispered, "I hate that you don't see what I see."

I glared. It was better than crying, which I was concerned I would do if I didn't rein in my emotions. "I love myself, but I know I weigh as much as two small women combined."

"Why does that matter? You. Are. Beautiful." His green eyes flashed. "Every inch of you is fucking perfect. And I'm more than capable of helping you over a wall. Or tossing you over my shoulder. Or picking you up and throwing you onto my bed." That last phrase came out as a growl I never would have expected from him.

My breath caught, and my stomach flipped at the image he'd painted.

"So trust me, trust yourself. And don't look at me like I'm suddenly going to say something awful."

I froze and forced a neutral expression to my face. Was that what I was doing? Maybe I was. Maybe I expected him to help me up and then throw in a comment like "damn, you weigh a ton." Or worse, maybe he'd drop me. Or hurt himself and then harp on how I'd injured him.

He was still standing close, watching me with an intent expression on his face. He'd lifted me once before, and he'd acted like it was no big deal.

Being afraid got me nowhere. So I relaxed my shoulders and dipped my chin once.

"So get over here and jump on three." He snaked a hand around my waist and pulled me to him.

My stomach flipped as I stumbled into him, my chest brushing his. The cedar scent of his cologne hit my nose, and suddenly, all I wanted to do was bury my face in his neck.

"Three."

I hopped a bit, and once again, he lifted me without much effort. Once I was settled on the wall, he pulled himself up and over to the other side.

With his feet planted shoulder-width apart, he held his hands to me.

Once again, I hesitated, nerves coursing through me at the thought of him having such intimate knowledge of my weight.

"I'll say it as many times as you need to hear it, Mariposa," Emerson assured.

His expression was so earnest. But having to constantly reassure someone could very easily get frustrating. He was right. I needed to trust him. And more importantly, I had to trust myself. I was worthy of the respect and care of another person. I was worthy of affection and desire. And there was a man out there who could enjoy being with me. Emerson enjoyed me. And at this point, I knew him well enough to know he'd be honest about what he could and couldn't do.

So I shifted toward him, and with minimal effort and not a single word, he helped me down.

The black Mercedes was waiting on the road just past the wall. Once we were settled in the back seat, we rode home quietly. Though the car was silent, my thoughts ran wild.

He pressed his leg against mine, and from hip to knee, I could feel the heat of him. His hand rested on my thigh near my knee. Silently, I begged him to slip it lower and move it up my dress. Slip under and touch me.

His words on the breakwater played in my mind. I got it. He wasn't wrong. I was normally a relationship girl. I didn't fling. But what had that gotten me, other than a slew of boyfriends who treated me as if I was barely worth their time or energy?

In my periphery, I studied Emerson.

What if I wanted to try a fling?

Would he feel differently?

The idea of asking was scary. It was possible he'd said those things in order to let me down easy.

His eyes drifted my way, and he gave my leg a light squeeze.

But what if he did mean it?

My breath came faster. What if I asked for one night, and he gave it to me? The idea of his strong hands roaming over me even for one night created an ache that throbbed almost violently between my thighs. All I had to do was be brave.

I swallowed. "Em."

He turned my way.

The car jerked to a stop.

"Is this okay?" the driver asked from the front as he pulled into the circular driveway of Emerson's building.

"Yeah, thanks." With a polite nod, he pulled the door open. Out on the sidewalk, he turned and held out a hand to me.

As I straightened my dress, keeping my chin tucked as I worked up the nerve to ask, he stepped closer. "What's the matter?" he urged, his green eyes astute, like he could see right through me.

Under his scrutiny, I lost my nerve. "Nothing." Turning on my heel, I headed for the front door.

Emerson followed me to the elevator. We silently rode up to his floor, and when we made it to his apartment, he unlocked the door and held it for me, letting me pass by into the foyer.

"Gi," he said as we stepped inside and he shut the door. With one hand, he cupped my face and angled in, pressing his hot lips against my forehead.

My pulse stuttered, and a burn started deep in my stomach. An aching throb that silently pounded as I became more and more sure that I needed more than just his hands on my face. More of his mouth.

I wanted the press of his hard body against my own. His bare skin on mine. I wanted his hands running down my body. Slipping low to cup my pussy, to slip inside me. To soothe the need he'd created.

"Thank you for tonight," he whispered, his warm breath skating over my skin.

Shuddering at the sensation, I rushed the words out, no longer able to keep them to myself. "I want us to have a fling."

Emerson
19

HER WORDS JERKED THROUGH MY ENTIRE BODY. MY GUT REACTION WAS TO tell myself that she didn't mean it. But I bit down hard on that. Because who the fuck was I to tell any woman what she meant?

"Gi," I muttered. My lips hadn't moved from her forehead, so the single syllable vibrated against us both.

She yanked back, her big brown eyes sparking, and glared at me. "Don't tell me I don't know what I want."

I released her and held both hands up. "I wasn't going to."

Putting words to my emotions wasn't easy. While I collected my thoughts, I ran my hands through my hair.

She must have taken that as a rejection, because she took a step away from me. Dammit. If I didn't move quick, she would storm out.

Breathing deep as desire coursed through me, I gave her a once-over, taking in the skintight dress that had been a temptation all night. I dragged my focus back up the red material, cataloging her wide hips and soft stomach. Running over the swell of her breasts, past the pounding pulse in her neck. Pausing on her lips for a heartbeat before meeting her brown eyes. Nothing good would come from a fling with her, but I found myself leaning in and snaking my hand behind her neck anyway.

As I pulled her soft body to mine, her eyes snapped wide, and she

141

wet her lips. And I swore that simple swipe of her tongue rocked through my entire body. My dick jumped in my pants, and as if she could feel it, victory flashed across her face. My breathing picked up. Damn, I wanted this so bad.

"Define fling." My tone was choked, desperate. I needed a clear picture. And not the one in my head, which was her naked below me.

She swallowed. "Just tonight. Em, please just make me feel good for one night." She sank her teeth into her bottom lip.

There was no way I'd deny those pleading brown eyes. I was so tired of fighting this thing between us.

"Saying no feels impossible, I give up." I tilted her head back and crushed my mouth to hers.

She moaned in response, and I swallowed the sound. Her lips were full and soft and tasted like the wine we'd shared, and I ran my tongue across the seam. The throaty moan as her lips parted was the only invitation I needed; I surged inside. Like the desperate man I was, I devoured her, demanding more. Because her mouth was not enough.

She ran her hands up along my chest and pushed the jacket off my shoulders. I released her for the millisecond it took to slip it off. Then she lifted her arms, clinging to my shoulders as my hands slipped lower. She was the type of woman who deserved all my attention, so I slowed down, paying attention to every soft curve. Every slope and plane of her body needed to be worshipped. I skimmed over the swell of her tits, then slowly down her rib cage, eliciting a shiver in response. The way her body responded to me was a high I couldn't get enough of. The tips of my fingers danced past her hips to that ass I craved and pulled her closer, pressing her hard against my dick.

"Emerson," she whimpered, rocking against me. I wanted to lay her out in front of me. See every inch of skin I'd been craving.

"I need space." I yanked my mouth away, but I sank my fingers into the flesh of her ass. I loved that it was more than a handful. I wanted to see if it would bounce when I took her from behind. "I need room to strip you down. Touch and taste every inch of you. Smack this ass and then work that hot pussy over with my tongue until you're begging for my cock."

In response, her breath caught, and her body clenched tight. I bunched the dress in my fists and tugged it up, desperate to touch the silky skin of her cheeks, but instead of skin, all I found was another layer of fabric covering her ass and thighs.

"What the fuck is this?" I pinched the tight fabric and pulled, but it snapped back.

"It's what made the dress look so good." She rolled her eyes and pulled back, but I locked my arms around her. There was no way I'd let her escape me.

Her full tits and incredible ass were what made the dress looked good, but I wasn't going to fight with her about the details right now. "It needs to go." I ran my hand over the garment—it was skin-colored and like underwear, biker shorts, and a leotard all in one—and slipped my fingers between her thighs, finding a slit in the stupid spandex. "Wait, it has an access channel?"

"Access channel?" She tossed her head back and roared with laughter, but as I ran my finger through her very wet pussy, the sound quickly morphed into a moan.

My dick jumped at the idea that it would soon be surrounded by all that heavenly perfection. I needed to settle the fuck down, though, because my mouth planned to spend a good amount of time devouring her before my cock got its turn. I spread the material wider, and she bucked against my hand.

"Damn, you're soaked, Mariposa."

Her heated gaze met mine. Desire pounded in the brown depths. "You make me feel desperate for you." The breathless words wound through me, spurring me on. I dropped my mouth to hers again.

Fucking hell. She was going to be my undoing.

I walked her backward, desperate for my bed. My foot landed on something that was definitely not tile, and I slipped, causing both of us to list to one side. I'd just righted us when we crashed into something else. I was too lost in her to bother to see what the object was. Reluctantly, I pulled my mouth from her but rocked my erection against the apex of her thighs, groaning at the sensation.

"I need a bed, now."

She giggled, half-pressed to a table and kinda arched into the wall.

I shook my head at myself. I'd love to say I was normally smoother, but that would be a lie.

"You seem crazy frantic."

"You have no idea," I assured her. Releasing her, I stepped away from the side table I'd backed her into and pointed. "My room. Let's move."

She sauntered past me with her dress bunched around her waist, a fucking tease if I'd ever seen one.

I couldn't resist smacking my palm against her ass as she wandered by. The crack echoed around us, and for a heartbeat, I worried she'd be pissed. But her long hair swung over her shoulder as she peeked at me.

"Yes, sir." Smirking, she batted her long lashes, then she took off.

Oh, fuck me.

I raced down the hall after her and practically tackled her on my bed. She giggled again as we bounced on the mattress. Arms planted on either side of her, I smiled down. The way her brown eyes sparkled up at me made my chest feel funny. When she wrapped her legs around my waist and pulled me tight, that sensation turned into a bolt of need that coursed straight to my cock.

I rubbed against her core, relishing her heat. "I repeat, the unitard needs to go."

She laughed, tipping her head back against the comforter. "Ya know, I never knew this could be fun."

I cocked my head to the side. What did that mean?

"I don't think I've ever laughed one minute and moaned the next."

For a second, nervousness flitted across her face. There was no reason for her to be apprehensive, so, making eye contact, I brushed a silky lock of hair from her cheek with my finger and tucked it behind her ear.

"That's because you've been with the wrong man." I lowered and ran my tongue up her neck, fighting back a smile at the way her heart pounded, until I reached her ear. "Sex should be hot *and* fun. It should be everything that makes you feel good. And I intend to show you that." I pulled her lobe between my teeth, eliciting a whimper from her that slipped through her lips and ran down my spine. "So tell me where the zipper is, because we need all the layers gone."

She shifted and raised one arm. "Here."

Once I'd found the tiny zipper, I gripped it awkwardly between my big fingers and slid it down. The sight of her with the dress bunched up around her waist and the nude spandex that caged her like an awful trap, or maybe a chastity belt, made me grin. I shook my head, eager to focus on the task at hand.

I'd taken my tie off a while ago. It was probably in the pocket of my jacket out in the entryway. But I still had too much shit on too.

I pushed off and hopped off the bed.

Eyes widening in panic, she sat up. "Wait, what did I do?"

"Nothing," I assured her. "I don't want to make an ass of myself while I try to get all these layers off us both. If I'm not careful, I'll knock us both off the bed while I'm fumbling around."

She giggled at me while I yanked my shirt and tee over my head in one motion. As the clothing fluttered to the floor, the sound stopped abruptly, and she zeroed in on my chest. She pulled her lips in, and desire burned in her gaze as she drank me in.

Pride welling up inside me, I snatched her ankles and pulled her to the edge of the bed. Once she was in front of me, I skated my thumbs up along her ribs. Hypnotized by the dark depths of her eyes swirling with desire, I brushed the underside of her tits. Her pupils dilated, and her breath sped up. But there was also a hint of vulnerability in her gaze, like she worried I'd be disappointed the moment her clothes were off. I couldn't imagine how she could feel that way. And I wanted to show her how wrong that assumption was.

"You want to know why I'm such a frantic, clumsy dumbass right now? It's because you're so fucking gorgeous. Getting to worship every inch of you is every erotic daydream I never thought I'd get to experience."

Her breath hitched, and her eyes glistened. Now I was the one choking back emotion. This moment was unlike any I'd ever experienced. The air was thick, heavy, but with so much more than just sexual tension.

"It'll all slide down if you take it off my shoulders," she whispered.

Obediently, I hooked my fingers into both the dress and the torture device, and for an instant, her body tensed. I stopped there, focused

145

once again on her face to gauge whether she was really okay with this. When a small smile crept over her face and her body went pliant, I continued slowly working both pieces of clothing down her arms.

When her arms were free, I stepped closer and released both of her tits. They were big and perfectly round, the dark nipples calling me to tease, to pinch, to taste. But it wasn't what she needed right now. Instead of giving in to the temptation, I bent and gave both breasts a chaste kiss, then lowered the dress down her waist. I dropped to my knees and placed a row of kisses down her soft stomach. Then on each hip. When the dress puddled at her feet, I rolled the spandex down, smiling up at her to reassure her that I loved what I saw.

Once she was completely free of the stupid unitard, I pressed my lips to one thigh, then the other, and stood back up.

When we were eye to eye again, her expression was guarded.

"Every part of you is better than I could have imagined. Thank you for letting me be the lucky fuck who gets to give you pleasure."

She blinked, and her breathing faltered. "Em—"

I cut her off by slamming my lips to hers. Her nipples brushed my chest, and behind my zipper, my dick jumped. Slowly this time, I backed her to the bed and laid her down. Her big, bubbly curls spread across my gray comforter, and as I quickly got rid of my pants and boxer briefs, I couldn't pull my eyes off her. The rosy nipples, the swell of her hips, all tan, soft skin. Gorgeous. After her reticence, I expected her to cover herself, but instead, she took a small breath and slowly separated her thighs.

"Fuck," I mumbled the second my eyes locked on her glistening pink pussy. Instantly insanely desperate for her, I hovered over her, pressing my entire body against hers and delving into her mouth again. Bracing myself with one arm, I skated my fingers up her thigh and to her wet heat.

Shuddering, she arched against my touch. "I need you to touch me," she panted against my mouth. "Please touch me."

But I didn't want to just touch. I wanted to taste.

"Patience, Mariposa. We have time," I assured her, lowering myself. Lips pressed to her neck, I savored the scent of orange blossoms and the slightly salty flavor of her skin.

Continuing lower, I skimmed one breast, then the other, but when she arched her back, thrusting a nipple against me, I couldn't stop myself from latching on. Her responding throaty whimper nearly broke me. I was racked with a pounding need to slam into her pussy until I finally exploded, but at the same time, I was hit with the desperate desire to drag this out for as long as she'd let me. I lapped at her nipple, then switched to show the other attention. Two perfect points that I couldn't possibly pick between.

She rocked against my thigh, coating my skin with her desire. But I didn't want her to come on my thigh. I palmed her hip, holding it down.

"Please." Whimpering, she grasped at my hair and pulled.

A thrill shot through me at the move. Smirking, I flicked my tongue against her nipple a few more times, torturing her.

"Emerson," she growled now.

"What does my dirty girl need?" I asked.

"Your mouth on my pussy," she demanded.

Never in my life had I heard more perfect words. And I was more than happy to comply. I dropped my mouth to kiss her stomach, sinking my tongue into her belly button, then moved lower, separating her thighs to make room for myself. I ran my nose along her pussy, taking in her scent before I finally let myself have one long lap. The rich, salty taste of her on my tongue sapped any control I had left, and I dove in.

"Please, I—" she begged, clutching at my hair with more desperation.

I zeroed in on the bud of sensation that made her arch off the bed and deeper against my face. I circled her clit with my tongue before sucking it between my lips. I teased and played, and she thrashed under me as I curled two fingers inside her, pressing right on her G-spot.

"Yes, Emerson. Yes, right there." Her cry echoed around the room and vibrated through me.

I flattened my tongue against her clit, then flicked twice. That was all it took to have her falling apart. She tilted her head back, her eyes squeezing shut as she came hard on my tongue.

I'd never seen anything as beautiful as this woman being consumed by pleasure. I worked her through her orgasm, lapping up every drop of her release until her body sagged into the bed. Looking up from her still glistening pussy, I was overtaken by a surge of emotions. I wanted to wrap her in my arms and hold her forever. Never let her go. See her come again and again. Make her smile. Make her laugh. I never wanted her taste to fade from my tongue.

What the fuck was going on with me? I wasn't the kind of guy who got attached.

I was all over the place, and I couldn't make this emotional. She'd asked me for one night, and that was what I promised. So this needed to be hot and fast. If it became anything more, I might never recover.

"Head down, ass up," I demanded, flipping her onto her stomach. Her normal sass was noticeably missing, and fuck if I didn't love how she followed my commands without blinking. I ran my hands up her waist and along her ribs to cup her breasts. With the weight of them heavy in my hands, I pinched both nipples, teasing her, pushing her back toward the brink.

"Emerson, I need your cock. Inside me now." Her voice had both an edge and pleading to it as she rocked against me.

As my dick wept, begging to finally be unleashed, I pulled away to grab a condom out of the nightstand. In record time, I had it on and was behind her, rubbing my tip along her lips.

"Damn, Gi. Your pussy is crying for my cock."

"So stop being so damn stingy with it."

The sass was back, and it had me chuckling. But the second I let myself slip into her, all humor evaporated. She was heaven. Hot, wet, and gripping me like a tight fist.

I groaned as I bottomed out inside her and her ass cheeks pressed into my thighs.

"Move, Emerson," she pleaded. "I need you to move."

That made two of us. With a quick motion, I slipped out and plunged back in. Electricity zapped through me, igniting a fire that licked up my spine. *"Damn."*

With every thrust, her ass bounced, mesmerizing me. Driving me on. Like an animal, I rutted over and over. I smacked the soft flesh as I thrust balls deep, and she whimpered as the cracking sound echoed against the walls and ceiling. Faster, harder, I pistoned my hips against her.

"Emerson." The moan of my name had me on edge, but I was determined to make her come first.

"One more," I demanded through clenched teeth as her pussy quivered and tightened.

She was so close. I spanked her ass one more time, and she clenched around me so tight, over and over, until I thought I might die from the sheer pleasure of the moment.

"Oh my God," she cried, her arms slipping and her body tipping so her cheek was pressed against the mattress. A burning need to see her face had me pulling out and flipping her over.

Eyes glazed with pleasure, she peered up at me softly. Walls down. At my mercy.

That right there, that open vulnerability, was my downfall. The whole world shifted, and in that moment, I fell hard. Epically. Off an edge and into an abyss. My perspective was forever changed. Looking into her eyes as I slipped inside her, I knew there was no going back.

I pumped my hips, consumed by the feeling of being inside her soft, warm body. Without slowing, I linked our hands and lifted them over her head, bracing myself on my elbows changing the angle. Her eyes flitted shut, and I dropped my mouth to hers, needing to be as close to this woman as possible.

And like that, linked to her, I came. In a violent burst of pleasure that raced through me. That all-out euphoria wasn't contained to just my dick. No, the sensation settled firmly in my chest. I pulled away from her mouth and buried my face in the crook of her neck, holding on to this moment for as long as I could. I wanted to hold it forever, remember it when I was eighty. Because in this moment, I finally understood the difference between sex and making love. When emotions were involved, it was a joke to think that anything between us could be casual.

I brushed my nose along the sensitive spot under her ear, and she shivered. Then I pressed my lips to the soft skin of her neck. Finally, I forced myself to lift up and give her one more kiss before I pulled out.

I hated leaving her even for a second.

"I'm going to get rid of the condom."

She nodded.

Heart pounding in my ears, I slipped out of the room and into the bathroom. There was still an open hole in the wall, and only the toilet and the sink worked. But sharing a bathroom was no longer an annoyance. Maybe I'd even talk her into the shower now. Gi wasn't as big a germophobe as her brother, but I knew she preferred sleeping in her own sheets, so we'd at least have to switch beds.

Once the condom was disposed of, I washed my hands, then stepped out into the hall. Across the way, Gi's door was shut. I stumbled to a stop, and disappointment hit me like a punch to the gut. I could have sworn the door was open when I stepped into the bathroom. No way she just left. Three steps, and I turned into my room. My comforter was mussed and bunched where her hands had fisted it, and my clothes were strewn on the floor. But otherwise, the room was empty.

I blinked twice. She had asked for a good time. But it had become so much more than that. My heart thunked weirdly in my chest. Had it really only been a quick fuck to her?

Fuck that. I knew it was more. The chemistry between us went way beyond just sex. Way beyond even good sex. But what was I going to do about it?

Gianna
20

As the door clicked shut, I gripped the red fabric to my chest. I wasn't super comfortable walking around naked, but I hadn't wanted to pause to put on my dress. Besides, all I had to do was cross the hall. Walking out might not have been the right choice, but I didn't want it to be weird when he came back. Flings meant leaving. But I was terrible at flinging, apparently, because I was already being hit with a wave of emotion. I blinked back the tears and the disappointment crashing through me. I desperately wanted a hug. And that wasn't a fling thing. Cuddles were for couples.

Plus, I had a hang-up about sheets. That was far too much to get into with a fling, so giving him space seemed like the best bet.

But now my legs were shaky, and I was swinging between sore and blissed out. Part of me wanted to go back to his potentially germy sheets just so I could bask in the comfort of his arms around me.

I sighed. I'd asked for one night, and he'd given it to me. No matter how great it was, it didn't seem fair to ask for more. I got his reasons for not wanting a situation that came with strings. And there was no way I'd interfere with his baseball career. So, swallowing down my unease, I dropped my red dress on the chair and pulled on a T-shirt.

I was scrutinizing my bed, considering whether I was really going to climb in, when my door opened. Emerson strode in wearing nothing but a pair of black boxer briefs and headed straight to me. He tipped my chin up and placed his lips over mine. Of its own volition, my body sagged against him.

"We'll sleep in here, and I'll get new sheets tomorrow," he promised against my lips, pulling me toward the bed. "I'm big on cuddling, Mariposa, so I need some snuggles."

He pulled the comforter back and helped me in. Then he climbed in and spooned right up to me. With his knees cupped against the backs of my legs, he looped an arm around my middle and tucked me tightly against the hard wall of his chest. It was exactly what I needed, and yet—

"Emerson?" I whispered.

"Night's not over until the sun is up. We can figure out the rest tomorrow," he mumbled into my hair, keeping me locked in his arms. "You feel really good like this, Gi," he whispered against the back of my neck, his lips finding the skin there.

And although he kissed me when he woke me up to tell me he was leaving for his game, we never actually talked.

Gianna
21

Linc: Since it's been a million and two hours and we've still heard nothing I'm assuming that the night ended with the exact kind of bang I like.

Mila: Or they got kidnapped. That happens to famous people sometimes.

Linc: What famous people do you know who've been kidnapped?

Mila: I mean I don't keep a list but isn't that a thing?

Me: No one was kidnapped.

Linc: She rises from the orgasm bliss. Can you walk upright?

Me: GIF of a woman flipping the camera off

Mila: We still doing breakfast before we drive back this morning?

Linc: Of course we are. I want all details.

Me: 9:30 at Mama P's - sound good?

Mila: Yay! I wanna try those banana pancakes.

Linc: Also I have an apartment possibility. A dude in our building with a one-bedroom is looking to sublet. He texted me this morning asking if Eli and I had any interest in getting a bigger place. I gave him your number.

Mila: Wait what? OMG why didn't you tell me?

Linc: Because it's for Gi. Why would I tell you?

Mila: GIF a woman rolling her eyes

Me: Yes give him my number - Mila don't get your hopes up - who knows if I can afford it.

Mila: Hope's already flying high!

Linc: See why I didn't tell you? You're practically screaming in my ear now.

Gianna
22

THE ELEVATOR RIDE UP WAS ALMOST TOO QUICK. THESE HIGH-RISES IN Boston all had elevators that moved at warp speed so that twenty floors went in a blink. I'd been tortured for details all through breakfast with my friends, and although I'd given them a few, I'd kept them vague. Neither of them believed I could do one night. And I spent most of the meal claiming I wasn't attached to the guy. Lying through my teeth was exhausting.

Right now, the only thing I wanted to do was crawl back into bed, but I'd promised Pop that I'd pick him up and take him to Chris's game.

"Pop." I smiled at my dad, who answered the door wearing jeans and a pin-striped jersey with the number 35 on the back. Ever since his heart attack, the relief I felt just seeing him was intense.

"Heard last night went great. Proud of you, girlie." He smiled at me. "I saw a ton of pictures."

Pictures? I hadn't sent him a single one. Hell, I'd barely taken any. And I couldn't see Chris doing it.

"Avery sent me a few, and Emerson sent about fifty."

Fifty? I forced myself to not react, but holy hell. I knew he'd taken several, but I assumed he was just sending them to his mom.

"You're the spitting image of your mother." My dad patted my shoulder. "But yeah, Emerson's been the one keeping me in the loop for years. When Chris has a good game or when he snaps a good one of him and some fans. Even photos of the places they travel." Pop shrugged. "He says his mom insists on not missing out, so he figures I shouldn't have to either. Nice kid."

I swallowed, because he was definitely nice, but I wouldn't call him a kid. He was *all* man. That single thought pulled me back into memories of the way his hands had run over me. How he'd used his tongue to make me see stars.

Heat crept into my cheeks, and I shifted, taking in Dad's apartment and avoiding his gaze.

"Why's the cat got your tongue today?" My father cocked his head to the side, the move causing the light to play off the grays that were getting more and more prevalent in his normally dark hair.

"I'm fine." I frowned.

His responding smirk was full of mirth. "There's my little ray of storm clouds."

On instinct, I lifted a hand, ready to whack his arm the way I had for years, but I froze and clutched it to my chest instead. At this point, I was certain that the memory of finding him passed out of the floor wouldn't ever leave me completely.

He sighed. "Gianna, I am getting stronger every day. I won't break. I'm even in my own apartment now."

A small one-bedroom that allowed him the option of making meals or eating in a group dining room.

"And in another month or two, I'll be able to leave the rehab facility completely and be back on my own."

"I know. And it's good." But it wouldn't erase the way it had felt to be so close to losing him.

Chris had been asking about apartments in Avery's building. He was hoping he and Avery could get one of the bigger apartments and Pop could take over Avery's one-bedroom. I wasn't sure whether Dad knew my brother was planning for them to be neighbors, but I didn't blame my brother for wanting him close by. Especially since money wasn't an issue. Chris had more than enough to put Pop up anywhere, and he was too stubborn and overprotective to take no for an answer. If I were in his shoes, I'd do the same.

"Are we standing here all day or moving?" He herded me out into the hall and to the elevator.

His movements were so much more fluid than they'd been even a few weeks ago. What would have taken us an hour a month ago—because he'd need breaks—was now an easy walk.

It took us almost no time to get over to the stadium, and with my dad's handicap parking pass, we were settled in the box with plenty of time to spare before the game was scheduled to start.

"Hey, Pop!" Avery chirped from across the open space. "Ready to kick some Trident butt?"

Beside her, Wren shook her head. "Ass, Avery. We kick *ass*."

Avery huffed at her best friend. "It feels weird to say that to a parent."

Wren snickered, bringing her glass of wine to her lips, but Avery stood up and all but skipped toward us. She gave Pop a quick hug.

"How are my great grandkids doing?"

Avery's entire face brightened at Pop's mention of Puff's soon-to-be babies. "We're seeing real movement, so the eggs will be hatching soon. Have you watched the feed?"

Avery had set up a live stream so Pop could keep tabs on the hatchlings.

"I check it all the time. I can't wait to see the little guys."

Puffette, Puff's mate—my brother's name choices; clearly, his creative talent was limited—had laid three eggs.

"I'm crossing my fingers for tonight, otherwise, it will probably happen while Chris is gone."

My dad shot me a quick look and frowned but schooled his features quickly and turned back to Avery.

Chris was stressed about it, although he was trying to keep that from Avery. He'd been planning to propose and wanted to do it when Puff's pufflings hatched. It was nuts to me that he was counting on a bird, and it was so unlike him to create a plan where he had no control over the timing. But he was almost as obsessed with his bird as he was with his soon-to-be fiancée.

"Dad's outside if you want to go bake in the sun with him," Wren called.

"Where's your mother?" Pop asked.

"She flew out to see Lottie," Wren said, referring to her sister. "My niece has a dance competition, so she's helping with the baby."

"Aw, grandkids." My dad smiled. "I can't wait to have more of those."

"Hopefully you mean the feathered ones," I muttered.

As much as my brother was all about making Avery his wife, I wasn't sure he was ready for kids. And my father understood already that I wasn't anywhere close to that point. I'd wasted the first four years after high school being afraid to do what I truly wanted, so even though I was thirty, I wanted more me time before kids. Maybe that was selfish, but wasn't it better than having kids I didn't feel ready for?

"I'll take feathered, scaled, furred, or haired. I'm not picky. More love is never bad." Patting me roughly on the shoulder, Pop moved down the stairs toward the glass door that led to the open-air seats.

"So, is the rumor true?" Wren rubbed her hands together and waggled a brow.

My spine snapped straight at the insinuation. Rumors about Emerson and me couldn't already be flying, could they? I darted a glance at Avery as my heart beat unevenly in my chest.

She shrugged at Wren. "I told you they looked super cute and coupley at the zoo."

Oh shit. Did we? My stomach flipped at the idea. Though I supposed we were pretending to be. But was it all really pretend? I swallowed as visions of last night flooded my mind. There was nothing about the connection Emerson and I had that wasn't real. From the way he kissed me to the look in his eye from across the room. I didn't want it to be over. But I had no idea what to do about that. The only thing I knew was that I didn't want rumors.

"Looking coupley doesn't mean anything," I hurried out.

"Maybe, but it's hard to fake the kind of vibes he was giving off."

Emerson was giving off vibes? At the zoo? How had I missed that? Sure, we'd had that kiss. But Emerson had assured me that he'd explained to Chris that it was for show.

"I don't know." Wren lifted her wineglass again. "I feel like everyone associated with a player must love Puff, so I'd hate if that wasn't the case."

"What?" My stomach sank. I didn't gush over the darn bird, but that didn't mean I didn't like him. I broke out in a cold sweat. Did people really think I didn't love my brother's bird? If that were the case, then why hadn't Chris called me out on it? He'd never been known for his subtlety. "I love Puff."

Both women cocked their heads and eyed me with matching looks of confusion.

Avery cleared her throat. "Yeah…we know *you* do."

So what was the issue? Surely, they couldn't think Emerson didn't love him.

"Em's obsession almost rivals my dad's."

Avery nodded slowly. "Yeah. Everyone on the team loves Puff. Even Tristian, who's a total jackass, can't help but have a soft spot for him."

"Right." I nodded. Tristian…Tristian. It took me a minute to place him. He was the left fielder and a prick. Thought he was better than everyone else.

"So it's annoying that Rory doesn't seem to like him."

"Rory?" I scanned my brain, searching for a memory of a person named Rory on the roster.

Wren flicked a hand. "The chick Mason's dating."

"We think." Avery dropped her voice low and took a step closer, like someone might overhear, even though we were the only people in the room. "She's a trainer for the team, and after last year, I have a very good understanding of Langfield Corp's rules." She smirked. "Although I can get away with dating one of Dad's players, a trainer dating a player is a big no-no. But we've seen them interacting a few times now, and it seems like a thing…"

"Oh." They weren't talking about Emerson and me at all. Relief washed over me, but I did my best to keep a straight face. Even so, my cheeks heated. Because, of course, they weren't discussing us. No one could know anything. It happened once, and now it was over.

My chest panged at that thought. Shit. My stupid self needed to get on board with that idea.

Ugh. Why wasn't I built for one-night stands? People did them all the time. Stupid me getting attached.

They were both staring at me.

"Who…" Avery glanced from me to the field and back. "Who did *you* think we were talking about?"

Wren's eyes widened just slightly, and she lifted her wineglass, though not before I saw one side of her mouth lift in a smirk. Last time I was here, she was talking about Emerson looking at us. My heart pounded again.

"I-I don't know. I'm not really into the Revs gossip," I stammered.

"That might change real quick," Wren sang, her eyes dancing.

"Don't be so sure." Avery waved her off. "She's going back to New York next month, right?"

Nodding, probably too aggressively, I agreed. "I actually just got a text from a guy about possibly subleasing his place starting August first."

The price was high, but I might be able to swing it. Especially if I got rid of my car. And I'd be in the city, so I wouldn't need it.

"That's awesome." Avery beamed.

Wren's eyes narrowed. "So nothing about Boston makes you want to stay?"

I shifted on my feet. Who knew why Wren seemed to see through me, but her questions were cutting a bit too close.

"My job is in New York." I shrugged. Although working mostly remotely didn't seem to be a problem. Plus, I hated my job. But my résumé still had no hits on it. So I didn't have a lot of hope of getting out of that hell.

I pointed lamely outside, looking for an excuse to get out of the conversation. "I'm just gonna check on Pop."

The second I was through the glass door, the June humidity hit me. Being on the water often helped keep the temperature mild, but today's game was at one, and already, the air was thick and the sun was beating down.

Slipping my sunglasses on, I wandered over to Pop and said

hello to Mr. Jacobs before moving to the far side of the area and leaning on the half wall between our box and the one next to it. As much as I wasn't a baseball fan, I had to admit that the field was gorgeous. The dark green grass, classically raked sand, and bright white lines stood out, creating the perfect stage in front of Boston Harbor. The view from this stadium was unlike any other in the league. Not that I was surprised. The Langfields always insisted on the best.

Nearby, a throat cleared, causing me to straighten.

"Gianna."

At the sound of my name, I spun, then looked up—way up—to the team's general manager, Cortney Miller. He was supposedly a nice guy, but he was also the one who had yet to extend Emerson's contract, so I couldn't help but wonder if he might be a dumbass.

Before I could get annoyed, he twisted, and a tiny bundle donning a pink pin-striped number 8 Boston Revs jersey appeared.

With a hand to my mouth, I cooed. "Willow." There was no stopping the response. I'd heard she was adorable, but that was an understatement. She might have been the cutest baby I'd ever seen. Chubby cheeks, tiny bow lips, big blue eyes, and a full head of red hair. "It's wild that she already has all that hair."

Cortney smiled. "She's been full of that fiery ginger, just like her mother since the day she was born."

"She's precious," I assured him, taking a small step closer. I'd heard he was weird about letting people touch her, so I didn't ask.

"Thanks." He gave me a nod, causing his man bun to wobble a bit. "My fiancée," he said, locking me in a stern blue-eyed glare, "is patiently waiting for you to show up at our brownstone. She swears it's gonna happen." His lips pulled up slightly at the corner. "I try not to doubt her, because she *is* normally right, but she desperately wants you to design her logo, and all I want is to make sure she's happy."

All thought left me at his comments. She'd told me to just show up, and he was really encouraging it? "Um…" I glanced around, hoping we'd be interrupted and I could avoid continuing this conversation, but my dad was still chatting away, and the girls were still inside. "Okay."

"So tell me what I need to do to ensure you'll design her logo," Cortney said, his tone far too desperate for something so simple.

I opened my mouth and then closed it again. "I mean...I was going to call her. I'm not opposed to doing it," I assured him. "But it's been, like, eighteen hours."

Did she expect me to call last night or first thing this morning? Because I was under the impression that it was a more like a *sometime in the next week or so* thing.

He blew out a hard breath. "Okay. So she's right, and you'll design it for her? Because unknowns stress me out. I just want to control the stuff that makes my family happy."

My heart melted a little at that. Not only did I understand his stress, but it was endearing as hell. The love he had for Dylan was clear in that one statement.

"I promise I'll call her this week." Probably Wednesday. But maybe I'd squeeze her in before to keep him from freaking out too badly.

"Thank you." He hit me with a genuinely grateful smile. Between that and the way he cared for his family, I was having a really hard time still thinking of him as the idiot who hadn't bothered to lock Emerson in yet.

The door opened behind him, and a handsome dark-haired man sporting the Revs 00 appeared. Ah. Beckett Langfield. I'd never met him—he hadn't been at the zoo event because he had a family thing—but I'd seen plenty of photos of the billionaire. His family was Boston royalty.

He homed in on me, his eyes narrowing. "Gianna Damiano?" His voice lifted at the end like he was happy to see me, though I didn't have a clue why, and his serious expression contradicted the idea.

"Beckett." Cortney growled.

"I know. I know." He waved Cortney off and held a hand out to me over the half wall. "I haven't gotten to meet you yet, but I've heard good things."

For some people, a charming man's attention would be flattering, but for me, alarm bells went off. "Why?" I demanded, keeping my hands at my sides.

Cortney tipped his head back and laughed.

162

That reaction only made me even more suspicious. Teeth gritted, I looked from one man to the other, scrutinizing them for their motivation. Why the fuck were these men talking about me at all? "What do you want?"

Cortney rocked back, looking at Beckett. "I like her. Dylan was right. Reminds me of Delia."

Beckett huffed. "Dippy Doo is rarely wrong."

"Did it hurt to say that?" Cortney asked.

Beckett glared. "No. I love your fiancée." He shook his head and turned back to me. "Your brother has spoken highly of you."

"Bossman." Cortney's voice was a growly warning. "Dylan first."

I crossed my arms, my guard rising further. These two had some agenda, and I didn't like it.

"What do you want?" I asked again.

Beckett crossed his arms, mimicking my posture, and narrowed his eyes right back at me. "We need a designer to create a new city jersey, and your name has been tossed around."

I sucked in a breath. A project for the Revs? That would be huge. I knew nothing about jersey design, but ideas were already swirling in my mind. Play into the city, the team, and make it interesting. It wasn't that I couldn't do it. And if I did that and the logo for Little Fingers, I might get more side jobs. My contract with Doucette didn't allow me to set up a website for myself or promote that I took on side jobs. They didn't make them forbidden; I just couldn't advertise myself. But if I could pick up a few more commissions, then maybe leaving Doucette wasn't a crazy idea.

"I'd love to hear more about it," I agreed.

"But…" Beckett cleared his throat.

Cortney puffed up, towering over him and looking like the only reason he wasn't pummeling the Revs' owner was because his arms were currently occupied by his sweet infant daughter.

"We aren't looking to release until next season. Langfield Corp needs a Little Fingers logo first. And apparently Dippy Doo won't work with anyone but you."

My breath caught at that tidbit of information. She only wanted *me*? I couldn't fathom how she even knew about me.

"So after you design for Little Fingers and Langfield Corp"—he smiled, clearly proud of himself—"the Revs want to chat. We want to be first in line." Then he turned to Cortney. "See how well I did that?"

Cortney sighed. "Yeah, Beckett, you're amazing." The sarcasm was so thick I didn't get how Beckett missed it.

"I am." His green eyes flicked to Willow. "Now let me hold her." He held his arms out.

"No." Cortney stepped back and brought his daughter closer to his chest.

Beckett slumped, his shoulders sinking. "But I need practice."

"Not on *my* child." Cortney turned back to me. "We'll see you soon?"

The question was laced with the need for assurance, so I nodded.

Seemingly content with that response, the two walked back into their box, bickering with each other the whole way.

"What was that about?" Pop asked.

"A logo for a daycare," I said, leaving it at that. I didn't want to get his hopes up. If I told him they mentioned the city jersey idea, he'd go nuts. He'd be so proud, and he'd tell everyone. The problem with that was that I didn't have the job yet. Worse? I wasn't sure I really had the capabilities. It was definitely outside my wheelhouse.

And people might have a lot to say about me doing it. My mind heard screams of nepotism because Chris was my brother. Or lack of experience or talent. Or just lack of the right look to be part of professional sports. Because I wasn't athletic and definitely didn't look like I was.

"Look at my girl, getting attention everywhere she goes," Pop boasted proudly to Mr. Jacobs.

That was exactly why I didn't want to say too much.

Dad's eyes were still alight, like he was ready to launch into a game of twenty questions about the logo, but I was saved from having to answer a single one when Avery came squealing out the door.

"Oh man, Chris is so mad," she said, grinning at her phone. "Hannah is making him do a team dance!" She bounced on her toes. "He hates Hannah, but I love her. She's so fun."

"What are they doing?" Pop asked.

"Is it about Dumpty? Because he's listed as possible," Mr. Jacobs said.

"Mason's playing. I'd bet my car on it," Wren stated, smirking.

"Your expensive shoes aren't conducive to walking, child of mine, so I'd be careful about reckless bets," her father warned.

Our conversation was cut short when the opening bars of "Center-field" blasted, and Emerson and three mascots trotted out onto the field, clapping their hands over their heads.

Warmth spread through me at the sight of him, and the sensation only deepened at the happiness in his expression.

I knew the song. Who didn't, really? But after what Emerson had told me about his high school experience, it took on a whole new meaning. Begging the coach, dreaming of playing center field—it all pulled at me.

Below us, the Revs mascots danced around. One trotted around on its fake horse. Another beat on its drum, and the third was doing the Floss. One by one, they tried to drag Emerson into their antics, but instead, he swung an invisible bat and tilted his head back like he was watching his ball fly through the air. Then he took off, running the bases.

Dressed for the game in his pin-striped jersey with a big number 21 on his back, he worked the crowd as he rounded home plate, getting them up on their feet, clapping and dancing with him. Fans loved him. It was crazy to think that he didn't see it. He literally had the attention of the entire stadium, me included. Although he had mine a lot lately.

As that thought crossed my mind, he turned and looked up my way. I swore that as his smile grew, my heart skipped.

Last night had been intense. And the way he'd held me through the night made it hard not to think that he might have also been thinking that once wasn't enough. So what if I asked for more? A slightly longer-term fling? Could I?

"Put me in coach!" Wren called when a glaring Coach Wilson came up on the Jumbotron, standing next to Price and Martinez.

Emerson ran back to the dugout just as the chorus started, clasping his hands in front of him and begging Coach Wilson—who looked anything but amused by the situation—to let him play center field.

Coach Wilson waved the catcher and shortstop onto the field, and both Price and Martinez trotted over to a row of bins near the stands, Sharpies in their hands. There, they got busy signing balls and T-shirts, then they handed them off so the mascots could fire them into the stands.

Emerson was still dancing on the other side of the field, whole-heartedly fulfilling his role and engaging as many people as he could. He worked his way back along the first base line, and then home plate, putting him right back in front of Coach Wilson as the chorus hit. Dropping to his knees, he launched back into pleading to play center field. The whole thing made me laugh.

Instead of giving in, Coach waved two more players onto the field. Kyle Bosco and Jasper Quinn stepped up and headed over to sign the shit the mascots were shooting up into the stand.

"Is Chris doing this?" I asked. I couldn't imagine him goofing off like the rest of the guys.

Avery shrugged while she clapped and bounced to the beat. "I think he has to. It's team building."

Just about every person in attendance was dancing now. Emerson had that effect on people. Even I was smiling and clapping.

The coach waved a few more players onto the field until only the pitcher and center fielder were missing from the roster.

Chris was pitching today. But until Emerson danced down the steps and clasped my brother's wrist, I doubted he'd join this game. Chris waved to fans half-heartedly, clapped, and, fighting a glare, strode over and got to work signing balls, all while keeping his head down.

Just before the last chorus began, Emerson centered himself in front of the dugout, and as the words "Centerfield" echoed around the ball-park, the entire starting lineup pointed to the dugout, and Mason Dumpty ran up the steps.

The fans had been enjoying the song, but the noise level was insane when the center fielder who had been listed as IL came trotting up the steps. Everyone was on their feet. They hadn't seen him in a week, and by their reaction, it was clear Boston loved the guy.

He ran straight to Emerson and bro hugged him before they trotted to the bin of balls. There, Mason started signing, and Emerson began tossing them into the stands.

What a way to introduce him.

Movement near the dugout caught my eye, pulling me away from ogling Emerson's ass in those baseball pants. Hannah was recording the fans as the entire stadium screamed. Talk about marketing. The woman was genius.

As I slid my attention back to Emerson, my heart sank a little. Although he had been on the field for the entire song, leading it even. He'd yet to sign a single thing.

"Does Emerson not sign merch like the rest of them?" I asked.

"I've never seen him do it," Avery said.

"He's usually busy throwing for the guys who need shoulder rest. The pitchers, the catcher, guys in situations like Mason's," Wren explained.

Mason had been out for days with his head and shoulder injuries. And clearly everyone was glad he was back.

"That is true," Avery agreed. "He does it for Price or Chris pretty regularly, but I don't think I've ever seen him sign anything. Weird." Avery shrugged.

No, not weird. It was so on-brand for Emerson. I'd bet money he didn't think anyone wanted his autograph. The comments from the building super a few weeks ago floated in my mind, along with a few offhanded remarks Emerson had made. Had anyone ever actually told him how much of a fan fave he was, or how important he was to the team? It hurt to think that they hadn't. Emerson was always taking care of the people around him. His team, his friends, his family, me. Putting those he cared about above himself. We might have been nothing more than a fling, but I wouldn't leave Boston without making sure he understood that he was worth so much more than he realized.

Emerson
23

With Mason's return, the game was a gimme, and I'd had a blast announcing him. Hannah had asked for a big idea this morning, and Bosco and I had come up with the perfect song. Even Chris and Coach had joined in, because no one could deny having our center back was season changing.

I spent the entire day smiling, though it had little to do with winning and everything to do with waking up with Gi in my arms this morning. The happiness was bordering on euphoria, knowing she was up in the box with Avery. I'd never really understood the idea of having a girl who was special to me watch me play until today.

The way she bopped along with my dance and jumped out of her seat cheering when I stole second was intoxicating. I was on a freaking high, and damn if I didn't want another hit of that feeling.

She'd even appeared in the team room with Avery after the game. Probably to see her brother. I knew that. Even so, I couldn't let go of the possibility that she was there for me *too*.

When I walked into the team room and saw her in her black Revs cropped shirt and leggings, my stupid heart surged. Last night, I had played off the idea of us being anything more than a night. Mostly because I wanted to give her time to come around to the idea, but also because I was terrified that she'd be like *What the fuck dude? One night means just that.* Yet I wanted so much more.

As of this moment, I had no idea where we stood, but I planned to talk to her tonight. And that moment couldn't come fast enough. All day, she had been the only thought in my head besides baseball.

"Who wants to hit the bar before we fly out?" Bosco dropped into the seat between Mason and me. Most of the team had headed home with their families, and I was working on my exit since I had a plan for the night.

"I'm out," Mason said, hardly looking up from his phone.

"Out?" Bosco practically shouted, his brows pulled low.

"No drinking, no flashing lights, no noise for another few days." Mason shrugged. He was all about the bar on a normal day, but staying on the field meant taking care of himself. I understood that.

Bosco huffed. "Dragon has dinner plans with Avery and her dad. And Price and Martinez will want family time. Guess it's just me and you, Bambi."

"Out," I said quickly.

He crossed his arms. "Dude, what the hell? You haven't gone out with us in like a month."

I actually hadn't been out with any regularity since before Christmas. I'd buckled down and dedicated all my excess energy to baseball. I wanted to be on my game and get a new contract. Once I did, I could mess around again.

"I gotta do some shopping. Pick up new sheets."

Both guys blinked at me, looking like a pair of owls.

"What?" Mason cocked a brow. "What happened to yours?"

Shit. Should have worked out an answer before spewing that bull-shit. Because they were perfectly fine.

"You know me. I thrash around and always trip on them getting out of bed. I go through them pretty quickly." That was a convenient truth, even if I hadn't technically damaged my current set.

Mason shook his head. "I'd call you a liar, but I've seen you do it so many times."

Kyle frowned. "I don't get how you make diving catches up the third baseline like it's easy, yet simple things like not falling out of bed are so damn hard."

"He can fucking dance too."

"I know." The smirk that crept up Bosco's face was a little evil. "You should have seen him dancing with Gianna last night."

Mason's eyes widened, and he pocketed his phone, suddenly very interested. "Dragon's sister?"

I held up a hand. "Don't start shit." Forcing a chuckle, because if I got mad, Bosco would think something was up, I sat up straighter. "I took her to the zoo thing last night as a favor because her ex is an asshole."

Bosco nodded. "Yeah, total tool bag. But that doesn't change how damn real that kiss looked."

Mason jerked up in his chair and spun to me. "You kissed her?"

Multiple times. All over her body. Not that I'd tell them that. Those details were best kept between her and me. But I hated having to lie. So I just shrugged. "Gentlemen don't kiss and tell."

"And you're a gentleman since when?" Bosco chuckled.

"Probably since it's his best friend's sister." Mason shook his head. "Dragon's weird about that shit."

I was very aware of that. "Anyway," I said, ready to end this conversation. "I'm out. Got shopping to do. See ya on the flight." Without giving them a chance to comment, I stood and headed out of the team room.

I used the car service the Revs had given players access to so I could do a quick run for sheets and a few other supplies so I could make dinner for Gi and me. We needed to talk.

But when I opened the door of our apartment, I was hit with the scent of sauteed onion.

"Gi?" I called as I headed for the kitchen.

She stood barefoot, still in her game outfit, at the stove, stirring while her head bounced slightly to music I couldn't hear. The messy bun she'd tossed her hair up into since I'd last seen her wobbled precariously with every tilt of her chin. She looked so damn cute. I stuck the food I'd brought home into the fridge, then snuck up behind her and gave her ass a quick pat.

Jumping about a foot in the air, she shrieked and stumbled into me. "Holy shit."

I steadied her, savoring the feel of her in my arms for a heartbeat or two. When she yanked her AirPods out, I released her and held my hands up. "Sorry."

"No." She took a breath and placed her hand on her chest. "I just didn't hear you come in."

I tipped to one side and peered into the pan full of chicken and vegetables. "Whatcha making?"

She shifted on her feet, nervously lifting a hand before dropping it again. "Well." With an audible swallow, she looked from me to the pan, dipping her chin just a fraction. "I thought you might like dinner, and I wasn't sure about your diet restriction during the season. Chris has always had a lot. So I stuck with sautéed chicken and veggies with brown rice."

"It smells great," I assured her. I kept my tone easy and my reaction tempered, but my stomach flipped at the idea that she'd done this for me.

She'd made dinner for *me*. That realization rocked through me. And I tried not to be weird about it.

"Oh, good. Since Pop worked full time teaching and then coaching both football and baseball, he wasn't home a lot, so I did most of the cooking growing up." Gianna rushed the words out, but her eyes grew wary. "What's wrong?"

"Absolutely nothing." The urge to hold her was so strong, and I was overwhelmed by her gesture, so I gave in and pulled her into my chest for a hug.

She didn't fight me like I thought she might. In fact, just like the night before, she melted into me.

"Thank you." I closed my eyes and inhaled, loving the feel of her in my arms, inhaling her scent and letting it bring with it a sense of peace I'd never known before. "No one but my mom and aunt has ever made dinner for me before."

Her head snapped up and she glared at me. "No one?"

It hit me then, though I should have recognized it sooner, that her glares, although directed my way, weren't always meant for me. Like right at this moment, she seemed upset on my behalf rather than angry at me.

"You know better than to think your brother has ever cooked." I didn't want to knock Chris, but I wouldn't lie to her either. "You know he'd rather be alone, but he agreed to live with me when he discovered that I liked to cook and clean. And I was lonely. He was the first person who treated me like more than an annoyance. I would have done any amount of cooking to ensure someone would pick me as their friend."

My gut clenched as those last words left me. It sounded pathetic, but it was true.

Gi's eyes softened, but not with pity. No, they were filled with a tenderness and understanding I couldn't understand. "I would pick you," she whispered.

I squeezed her tighter and pressed my lips to the top of her head. "I would pick you too."

The chicken on the stove popped, startling her, and she pulled away slightly, so I released her and let her deal with the food. Though I did it begrudgingly, because honestly, I hated letting her go. She scooped the food onto two plates, and I took them from her hands.

"Want to grab drinks?" I suggested.

"Sure, what do you want?" she asked, opening the fridge as I moved around the bar to the table.

"Water," I called over my shoulder.

A second later, she appeared with a bottle of water and one glass of white wine.

"Did you have a plan for dinner? I see you got food," she asked, worrying her bottom lip as she dropped into her seat.

"My only firm plan was to eat with you." I reached across the table to place my hand over hers. I couldn't care less what we ate. The important part was that we got to talk.

My eyes landed on the Revs logo on her chest.

"What?" she asked.

I couldn't explain it. Like it somehow marked her as mine, even though she wasn't wearing my Revs jersey. Although I'd really like my name on her back. It was an idea that had been making my brain itch since I'd seen her standing next to Avery, who was sporting Chris's 35. I wanted to see 21 resting above her breast and blasted across her back.

I shook my head. "I just like seeing you in Revs blue."

She flushed slightly, the corner of her mouth pulling up, and my heart pinched. I loved making her smile.

"You should eat before it gets cold." She nodded at my plate and pulled her hand away to pick up her fork, but she didn't take a bite. I picked up my own and dug in. For something that aligned with a strict MLB meal plan, it sure tasted good.

I swallowed and reached for my water. "This is excellent."

With a shrug, she ducked her head. "I learned to do a lot with veggies and chicken because it's all Chris ate in high school."

Understanding worked its way through me. She and I had both shouldered a lot of the responsibility for our siblings and homes when we were in high school.

Now that I'd had that first bite, it hit me how hungry I was, so I scooped another bite onto my fork.

"Emerson."

I paused with the fork halfway to my mouth. "Yes, Mariposa?"

"Can we talk about last night?"

I set my fork down. The food could wait. "I definitely want to."

Her eyes snapped up to meet mine. "You do?"

I nodded, swallowing back the nerves threatening to silence me. "I know we said one night, but I'd really like to change that."

"Really?" Her eyes went wide. "I was thinking the same thing." She wet her lips and let out a relieved breath.

I nodded, not fighting the smile that overtook my face. It felt so fucking good to know we were on the same page.

She cleared her throat, her lips trembling as she gave me a small smile. "And I understand your reasons for not wanting anything serious…"

I had meant those things when I said them yesterday. But today? Shit, I wasn't sure I did anymore.

"I understand that if Chris finds out, that will mess things up for you, so he never needs to know."

Holding my breath, I assessed her. Was she serious? I didn't see how that would be the case. There was no way I wanted to hide a relationship from her father or her brother. Or my friends or family. Secret relationships did not serve to create solid foundations. I forced myself to breathe again, but before I could tell her that, she continued.

"I mean." She swallowed, her breaths coming out a little shaky. "I figured that if we extended the fling until I move back to New York..."

It was like a physical blow. That sentence. Wow. So we weren't at all on the same page. Turning my attention to the windows that overlooked the Boston Harbor, I blinked back my disappointment and hurt. Fuck, I had to get it together, even if a painful fissure had formed in the middle of my chest. For the first time ever, I wanted to dive into something real, but the woman I wanted to do that with didn't see me that way.

"Unless you just meant one more night," she rushed out.

I sighed and reached across the table for her hand again. "I'd take all the time you'd give me." It was the truth. I squeezed her hand. "But—"

My words were cut off by the annoyingly high-pitched ping of her phone.

"That's Avery's ringtone." She pulled away and darted for the counter. She glanced down at the screen and winced. "The pufflings are hatching."

"That's great." Really. All week, my best friend had been stressing that we'd be on the road when the moment came. Chris had planned this perfect proposal for his girl, and I sure as shit wanted it to go off without a hitch. Not to mention most of the city of Boston was on puffling watch at this point.

"My dad's not going to want to miss it."

"Me either," I agreed.

"So we should get him?" she asked, a line forming between her brows.

This was important. But so was the conversation we were having. "Yeah, we can pick him up, but Gi." I stepped up next to her. "If we need to skip this because you feel like we have to talk first, I'm okay with that."

Her eyes popped wide. "No," she said quickly. "Chris is getting engaged, and Puff's having babies. We can't miss that."

I didn't disagree, but one thing needed to be clear. "You matter too. I want you to know that. And if you feel like this conversation can't wait. Then we miss what we miss."

She shook her head and glanced at her phone once more. Then she peered up at me through thick lashes. "We're on the same page, though, right? We keep this going while I'm here, but I'm not putting any pressure on a future. This can just be fun?"

No, we weren't on the same page. We weren't even reading from the same book. But the hope in her eyes yanked hard at my heart. She needed this. And it turned out that what mattered most to me was that she was happy. So I nodded.

"I want you to have so much joy and fun in life."

The smile she gave me squeezed my chest. Although my heart hurt at the idea that for her, I was just a for now, her smile made it worth it. So we picked up Pop and made our way over to watch my best friend get his girl. And that had an entirely new meaning to me now.

"We didn't miss it, did we?" I asked as I practically danced into the puffin exhibit.

"No."

"For as excited as you are, you'd think one of them was your kid," Gianna muttered next to me.

Okay, maybe I was being extra. But I was trying to be happy.

"I'd rather be home with you," I whispered, leaning in close. "Either talking or naked. At this point, I'd be perfectly happy with either."

She flushed and stepped away, and since we were with her family, I turned away too, giving her space.

By the way the eggs were rocking, this wasn't a false alarm. Excitement coursed through me, because my best friend had been desperate for this moment for over a week. I couldn't fault him either. Not when he was about to ask *the one* to marry him. Chris was ready, and he and Avery would go the distance. I had no doubts.

As we waited, I couldn't help but watch Gi where she stood next to her dad. If only I were anywhere close to being that confident about what was happening between the two of us. Because I had no doubt that she had the potential to be *the one* for me. But I wasn't sure how to convince her to feel the same way about me.

Emerson
24

"So, how's it feel?" I asked as Chris and I settled into our seats on the team plane.

"Really good." Chris shook his head. "Nothing has actually changed, I guess. She's always been all I wanted. But having my ring on her finger." His lips pulled up, the expression almost a smile. "Yeah, man. It's good."

"I'm happy for you both. *Long* time coming." I chuckled, though the action quickly became a yawn. It was only six a.m., and we were all loaded up and ready to leave Boston.

Nodding, he shifted in his seat and grimaced a little. "So, uh…" He cleared his throat, clearly stalling. "We need to talk."

My entire body stiffened. Because he'd gotten engaged twelve hours ago, and all of a sudden, he didn't sound happy. Gianna and I had kept our distance at the zoo with Puff and the pufflings last night, so it was hard to believe he suspected anything, but even so, I broke out in a cold sweat.

Last night, the second we were home, I changed my sheets and got her into my bed. The amount of sleep we got was minimal, but it was worth it. I only had a limited amount of time with Gi, and I was going to make the most of it. Slipping out of bed this morning may have been one of the hardest things I'd ever done, because the way it felt to have

179

her body pressed to mine was better than anything I'd ever experienced.

"I don't want this to be a big thing, but apparently, it is," he grumbled.

"Okay…" I didn't want to lie to him. I really didn't. But damn if I wanted to tell him that his sister couldn't get enough of my dick, yet didn't want anything serious, so we'd agreed to have a fling for the next few weeks. I wouldn't want to know that shit about Isabella or Yevette, so as much as I hated being untruthful, I was gearing myself up to do just that.

If I could say *hey, I really like your sister, and I want to try to be the guy she has a future with*, I wouldn't sweat it. Unfortunately, I couldn't imagine him being okay with a casual hookup with an expiration date.

"I thought it was pretty obvious, but Avery said we should hash it out. So…" Chris glared at me, and I thought my heart might have stopped.

I cracked my knuckles and waited, my breathing suddenly shallow.

"I need a best man." His jaw tightened. "I told her it was implied that you'd do it, but apparently, I need to come out and ask."

Instantly, my entire body relaxed, and I threw my head back and laughed. "Dude, there is no world in which I wouldn't be your best man. You know that."

"That's what I told Avery." He shook his head and blew out a breath. "But she made me nervous as fuck, worrying that you might not want to." He shrugged. "So this is probably a given too, but I'm not gonna be renewing the lease for our apartment."

That hit harder, but I tempered my reaction. Obviously, he and Avery would be living together officially, but we'd been roommates for almost six years. The thought of once again being on my own cut deep. There were very few things I'd experienced that were worse than being lonely.

"We can continue month to month until October, so if you want to just take it over then, that's an option." He shrugged again. "I'm going to keep month to month going until Gi moves out regardless. But after that…"

"Right." I nodded. I'd still heard nothing about a contract extension from the team. I couldn't lock myself into a lease. Our place wasn't ideal anyway. It was too big for one person and way too formal and fancy. Not to mention it was more expensive than I could afford alone with my current contract. Mason had a guest room, and so did Kyle. So once Gi moved out...

Fuck. Every time I thought about her leaving, it was like a knife to the gut. But it was reality. She'd even been chatting with her dad about a possible place in New York last night.

So once she was gone, I could probably crash with one of them until the end of the season. Go back to Jersey for a month or so and figure out where to go from there.

I swallowed back the wave of sadness threatening to make itself known. I'd have to start over. Alone again. I took a deep breath and let it out, pushing away the emotions. I'd done it at seventeen; I could damn well do it now.

"So." Chris popped in one earbud. "Since that's all settled, I'm crashing. I didn't get much sleep last night." Smirking, he popped in the second earbud and leaned back, shutting his eyes.

I turned to the window and looked out over the tarmac. Normally, I was a champ at napping on planes, but there was no way I was getting any sleep today. Although we weren't even at the all-star break, the uncertainties of next season loomed. And the idea of a new team, making connections, feeling at home, haunted me.

Halfway through the flight to the West Coast, I pulled out my phone.

> Me: How'd the call with Dylan go?

> Gi: It was quick - I'm going to meet with her on Wednesday.

> Me: That's great.

> Gi: Might be silly - but I'm really excited to see her house.

I could understand that. The place had chill vibes. It was like walking into the calmest house on earth. It was well decorated, without being over-the-top, and the roof deck was killer. Not to mention the basement was full of every game a guy could want. Pool, ping-pong, darts, basketball, air hockey. We'd had the best time when he'd had the team over for a housewarming party.

> Gi: I'm obsessed with brownstones.

> Me: I like the feel of them. The room without too much dead space.

> Gi: Exactly - and the mix of the old and new that some people create is killer.

> Me: Dylan rocked hers.

> Gi: I've always wanted to own one.

The scene played out before my eyes. Her at the stove in the long, thin, open space. Old woodwork and clean white subway tile. White cabinets. Black hardware. Leggings, a cropped shirt, and a messy bun, with the steam coming off the pot on the burner. Gianna bouncing to a beat in a way she wouldn't if she knew she wasn't alone. It was her future.

I swallowed.

> Me: If that's what you want, then you will, and I want to see your painting of it.

"Are you texting with my sister?" Chris asked, startling me.

My first instinct was to hide the phone. But nothing in the message was anything other than friendly. So I forced myself not to move.

"Nosy much?" I asked, forcing a smile.

For a moment, he leaned closer and read through the messages still on the screen. "Why are you talking to my sister about houses?"

"She's going over to Miller's to talk about a graphic design project Dylan wants to hire her for—"

"What?" His brows slammed together.

What the hell? Pop told him and Avery about this last night, and Avery went on and on about what a good job she'd do.

Annoyance coursed through me. The idiot was so overprotective of his sister, and he really did care, but obviously, he didn't pay attention. And although it made hiding my feelings for Gi easier, it was frustrating.

"Yeah," I said, affecting an even tone. "She's trying to pretend she's not nervous, but she is. So I was checking in on her. Then she deflected by bringing the conversation around to houses."

Jaw locked, he glared at the row of seats in front of us. He finally turned to me. "Should I do something to help her?"

Like what? Chris wasn't a bad artist, but his talent was nowhere near as impressive as his sister's.

So I shrugged. "Maybe just listen to her."

"What?" he snapped.

"Listen," I repeated. "When she talks or has something to say. Don't hear blah, blah, blah. Maybe just listen to what she's actually talking about."

He nodded and pulled out his phone. "Avery can do that. I'll have her call."

I shook my head, fighting the laugh. The guy meant well, but he was a fucking idiot.

Gianna hadn't replied to my message, so I tucked the phone away and turned back to watch the clouds and enjoy the view. I soaked in as much as I could, vowing not to forget little things like the view of the Rockies below me and focusing on the moment and my surroundings and the sound of my teammates laughing. I stopped worrying about next season. It was months away, so I was determined to enjoy the present.

Gianna
25

THIS WAS NOT A BIG DEAL. THAT'S WHAT I TOLD MYSELF, EVEN AS MY heart pounded away in my chest. The brownstone I was staring up at was my dream house. I'd been told repeatedly and pretty bluntly that Dylan wanted to work with me. And on the phone, she'd sounded excited, so there was no reason for my stomach to be in knots.

My phone buzzed, pulling me from my spiraling thoughts, so I pulled it out and tapped the screen.

> Emerson: You got this, Mariposa. Just be yourself. Can't wait to hear about it.

My shoulders relaxed just a little, and I took a breath.

> Me: Thanks

With my head held high, I headed up the steps and rang the bell. Instead of the typical *ding-dong*, a sound like a wind chime brushed through the air, and an instant later, the heavy wooden door swung open.

"Who is you?" A little girl stood in the doorway, her brown pigtails bouncing as she tipped her head one way and then the other.

185

"Addie." A blond girl who looked about ten with bubble braids skipped to the door and scooped her up. They wobbled in the way a ten-year-old does when holding another child who's almost half their size. "I've explained repeatedly that the probability of opening the door to someone you know is only about 9 percent."

"What about the probability that it's not gonna be a murderer?" A boy with dark curly hair appeared beside the blond.

I rolled my lips but couldn't stop myself from smiling at his head-to-toe denim ensemble. His jean jacket was buttoned up to the neck, and his pants were the same shade. He was sporting a pair of aviator sunglasses and three gold chains around his neck. The kid looked like a bad eighties rapper.

Cute as hell and thoroughly himself.

Behind them, another boy sauntered up. This one was tall enough to ride a roller coaster. The teenager stepped into the light from the sun behind me and flicked his red hair out of his eyes.

"Ma says this is an important meeting and we're supposed to be at the park. Let's go, rugrats."

The teenager ushered all three younger kids out the door.

"The term rugrats implies that we crawl." Another blond girl who looked identical to the first one followed them out the door.

I stepped back to give the kids space as they tumbled out and clambered down the stairs to the sidewalk.

"No, it means you're shorter than me." The teenager shook his head, his shaggy red hair falling into his eyes again. "Come on, Addie. Up ya go." He scooped the little pigtailed girl up and popped her up on his shoulders, then turned back. "Kai! Win! Let's move it."

Two more kids came flying out the door, chasing the others.

"Ma's inside." He tipped his chin as the four-year-old pulled his hair. "Just go in."

For one second, I was frozen to the spot, watching the seven kids skip down the road, laughing and pushing each other.

They couldn't all be Dylan's, right? Or was she running the daycare out of her house until the space at Langfield Corp was ready?

"Oh, hi!" Dylan chirped, peeking her head out the door. "The kids get off okay?" She shook her head, her curly red hair dancing around her shoulders. "What am I saying? Of course they did. Liam is as much of a drill sergeant as Becks these days." She pulled the door open wider and stepped back. "Come in."

The moment I crossed the threshold, I could swear the air lightened. The crystal blue on the walls, the original but refinished woodwork, and the stone fireplace created a serene calm that was palpable. How it was possible was a wonder after the way those seven freaking kids had just left the house like a pack of Tasmanian devils. Child number eight was here, babbling from a play mat in front of the entertainment center.

But the high ceilings, the crown molding, and the original fireplace, mixed in with the modern sectional and artwork, were perfection. This was the type of brownstone dreams were made of.

"It's beautiful."

She nodded. "We wanted the aquamarine energy. Cortney suffers from anxiety, so it's important to have the calm, healing energy to give him peace."

"Sure." I nodded. Though I had no idea what she meant, she'd done an amazing job with the place.

She pointed toward the sofa, so I moved that way and sat, placing my portfolio on the floor next to me. Dylan gracefully pranced across the floor, scooped up Willow, and dropped onto the couch, criss-crossing her legs. As she settled Willow in her lap, the baby cooed up at her.

"Oh, shoot." Dylan's eyes went wide. "I have the manners of a six-year-old. Can I get you something to drink? Coffee? Tea? Water?"

"No, thanks," I assured her. My stomach was still a mess of knots, so empty was the way to go.

She pursed her lips. "My friend Shay left some swamp sludge for the kids that they don't want. If that's your jam?"

"I'm sorry. Swamp what?"

Dylan shrugged. "It's like bone broth and spinach and cat puke or something."

Hmm. That was…different. "I think I'll have to pass."

"Me too. Every damn time." Holding the baby with one arm, she used her free hand to grasp the crystal pendant that hung from her neck and slide it across its chain. "And Cort went with the team, so he's not here to be the bigger person."

"Does he not normally travel with them?" I asked.

She shook her head. "That was a big ask when they offered him the GM position. He wanted to be home, so he is for the most part. They're checking out a reliever on the Kansas City Roasters this week, though. They're trying to lower the payroll for next year or something."

I worked not to frown in response to that comment. That didn't sound good for Emerson's contract being renewed.

"Plus, he's worried about Mason and the trainer. He thinks they're banging behind everyone's back." Dylan laughed, the sound a light tinkling. "He did it with me behind Becks's back, so he isn't really one to talk."

Willow reached up and grabbed a fistful of her mother's red hair.

Dylan just tipped her head down, still smiling, like it didn't faze her. "Anyway, enough team talk. About the design…" She lifted one brow.

"I brought some samples of my work." I reached down to my leather bag.

She waved me off. "I've seen so much of your work. Honestly, your charcoal of Cortney sold it for me."

Confused, I frowned and studied her. My what?

She pointed up to the entertainment center with a smile, and I followed her line of sight. When I saw it, I rose. There were two frames and a magnet of the firefly from the Disney movie *The Princess and the Frog*. In the first frame was a note that said *Puzzles are fun, but not as fun as a game of pool with you. Thanks for an unforgettable night.* ♥ *D.*

"I gave Cort that the night we met. I can't believe he kept it, but he never wants to lose it." Dylan shrugged. "He's much more sentimental than people realize."

In the second frame was a sketch. I lifted it off the shelf and took in the details of the black-and-white sketch I'd done last season. I'd left it at Chris's apartment because I wanted the charcoal to set before I moved it. Then I'd forgotten it completely.

Chris was on the mound, mid-pitch. Behind the plate, Cortney was sporting his number 8 pinstripes. Behind them, a boat floated in the Boston harbor.

"Gano, right?" she asked.

I'd started signing pictures at four or five, back when my drawing ability was better than writing and I was still learning to spell my name. My mom had suggested shortening it, maybe because she got tired of repeatedly telling me how to spell Damiano. But now, every time I signed a piece, she was there with me.

I nodded and spun, a question on the tip of my tongue.

Before I could ask it, she answered, as if she could read my mind. "Emerson and Chris gave it to Cortney when he retired. You are really good with details. Even Cort's ass in his baseball pants." She giggled.

My stomach twisted as I took in the image again. The frame matched the one the oil painting of Puff had been matted in. It had Emerson's mark all over it. My heart flipped over itself. What was I supposed to do with this idea that Emerson thought my work was good enough to gift a friend?

"I want something similar for the background of the Little Fingers logo, but I want kids playing the part instead of the guys."

As she went on, describing the colors and her vision, the picture played out in my head.

"Maybe the shaded areas could be imperfect," I suggested. "Like a child colored outside the lines?"

"Yes." Dylan beamed. "I knew you'd be perfect for the job."

I set the frame down and moved back to the sofa. "So here is what I'm thinking…" I pulled my sketch pad and a pencil out of my bag and got to work drawing the baseball diamond. Then I smudged the middle line and worked the rink in on the far right. From there, I went on, smudging and sketching until I had the backdrop. Then I flipped it. "I thought since Langfield Corp owns both the Bolts and the Revs, we could play on both teams."

"Perfect." Dylan had adjusted Willow in her arms and scooted closer. "I get the feeling we've got lots of new souls joining the Bolts family soon."

I had no idea what she meant by that, but she and I played around with a few ideas. Dylan had to be one of the most open, honest, genuine people I'd ever met, and she was very easy to please. When I left the house forty-five minutes later with a promise to send her drafts over soon, I was riding a high. I pulled out my phone, and I wasn't the least bit surprised to find a text from Emerson asking me to let him know how it went.

> Me: It went really well

> Me: She officially hired me - I'll have the first round of drafts to her next week - I'm excited.

I hadn't been this excited to start a new project since the meeting with the Boston Zoo over six months ago. Maybe it was because, in both instances, I had the opportunity to meet with the client and see their excitement about their work directly. Through the firm, I was never included in that part of the process. I supposed it made projects feel more impersonal. My phone buzzed in my palm as I headed away from the house.

> Emerson: GIF of a guy dancing in celebration

> Emerson: Headed out for batting practice, but I'll call you after. I want to hear all about it.

He was just like my dad in that respect. Anytime I was excited about a project, Pop got antsy to hear all about it. And all my life, he'd been the first person I'd call or text over big news, good or bad. Guilt crept up when I realized I hadn't even thought to text him. I hadn't talked to him since Sunday. That in and of itself wasn't strange, but how could I so quickly have moved Emerson up to the top of the list of people I wanted to share good news with? Maybe because I'd never dated a guy who hyped me up and got excited about my work. Not that I was dating Emerson.

I headed down the steps into the subway in a rush, since I had a Zoom call at noon with Jake and the team. As I hit the last step, my phone buzzed again.

> Emerson: Excited for you.

Me: Thanks.

I couldn't stop the smile that lifted my lips. My friends and Chris and Pop, even Avery, had made the same remark, but from Emerson, it hit so much more potently. And I didn't hate the feeling.

I boarded the train and found a seat, all the while thinking about how I could make him feel just as supported as he's made me. His comment about seeing me in Revs blue and the glint in his eye left me wondering. Athletes had a thing about their women dressing in their jerseys. Everyone knew it. I couldn't wear his number to a game without garnering way too much suspicion, but I could wear it for him. I didn't have the type of body that looked cute in a buttoned-up jersey, but I'd once seen a TikTok video with the perfect idea. After a quick internet search, I found the Revs site, and two clicks later, I'd purchased an XXXL number 21 for pickup from the store next to the stadium. I could run by after my meeting and grab it. There was no way I had time before.

In fact…I peeked at my watch. *Shit.* I only had ten minutes to make it back to my computer and log in to the meeting. I flew off the train and ran up the stairs to the street level. I bolted the half block to the building, and by the time I got on the elevator, I was sweating. The distance had been short, sure, but it was almost ninety degrees today.

Inside the apartment, I pushed my hair back from my sweaty face and glanced in the mirror, swiping the mascara from under my eyes, and then fanned myself to minimize the bright red flush.

Two minutes later and one minute early, I sat down in front of my computer and pulled up the Zoom link.

"Why do you look like shit?" Jake asked the second my video feed appeared on the screen. "Jesus, Gianna."

A few of the seven other people on the call covered their chuckles with coughs, and my stomach bottomed out.

"And to think I was going to ask you to meet with the people from the Java NY account." He shook his head. "Regardless of the new relationship status," he sneered, "this bedhead, rode hard and put away wet look isn't professional."

My mouth fell open and my stomach lurched as a few gasps echoed from my coworkers.

My eyes stung, but I locked my jaw. There was no way I'd allow this man to make me cry. I focused on the anger brewing inside me and hit him with a glare. "Actually, I had to run back from another meeting. I wanted to be responsible and not be late. Unlike some people, I care about being professional."

Jake blinked twice and ran his thumb and pointer finger over his lips. "Julie," he said smugly. "Putting you onto the Java account. Gianna, please pass on the Java files."

A sharp breath escaped me. "What?"

"We'll talk later." He reached forward and pressed a button, and in the next second, my screen went black.

Had he seriously just disconnected me from the team meeting? My shoulders tightened, and I blinked repeatedly to keep the tears at bay. Mad. I wanted to be mad. But the moisture wouldn't stop pooling in my eyes. I ground my teeth and forced my eyes closed.

So what if I'd put over a hundred hours of design work into the account? So what if it was the third time he'd taken me off a project? I bit fiercely into my bottom lip to stop it from quivering.

An email lit my inbox.

From: Julie Cartright
To: Gianna Damiano

I'm so sorry. Want me to say no?

~J

IT WASN'T HER FAULT. SHE'D ALWAYS BEEN NICE. AND WE'D WORKED WELL together. I tried for a deep breath, but it caught in my throat, and my breath hitched.

I replied to the email quickly, telling her good luck with the asshole, and shared the drive with the files. Then I dropped my head into my hands. This wasn't the end of the world. It was one account. I needed to get a grip.

My phone buzzed on the high-top counter in front of me, dancing and lighting up as Emerson's name flashed across the screen. Shit, I'd forgotten that I told him we could talk.

With another deep, centering breath, I wiped under my eyes again. Jake's comment about my hair floated into my mind, so I yanked my portfolio bag open and frantically searched for a hair tie. By the third long buzz, I had my hair up in a topknot. Shoulders pulled back, I swallowed down all my upset and answered the FaceTime request.

"Hey."

Emerson appeared, already smiling. He was framed by a concrete wall, like he was standing in the tunnels. In the space of a breath, the smile slid from his face, and he tilted his head to the side. His long lashes brushed his cheeks as he blinked twice.

I glared at my own video on the screen, channeling all the composure I could muster.

"What's wrong?" he finally asked.

I shook my head. "Nothing."

He hummed. "Angry face. Sad eyes. So tell me what happened. Or, if you'd prefer, I could track down Miller and find out from his girl."

"What?"

"Miller's on the road with us, so I can find out what happened between *I'm so excited* and *I'm trying my best not to cry* from him, or you can tell me." He leaned back and crossed his free arm over his chest.

"Dylan was wonderful. It's just." I swallowed and then started at the beginning, filling him in on the morning and my meeting with Dylan, the rush to get home, and then the Zoom call.

I didn't know what I expected when I poured it all out for him. Maybe some sort of reassurance that I looked professional. Or maybe a little anger. Some kind of reaction I'd have to deal with or possibly talk him down from. But all I got was an eerie calm.

Emerson
26

MY BODY TINGLED AND RAGE PULSED THROUGH EVERY CELL OF MY BEING. The urge to get on a plane and fly to New York to beat the life out of the man who'd made Gianna sad was intense. Almost as intense as the need to wrap her up in my arms and hold her until she forgot all about the stupid shit the guy said. But I was halfway across the fucking country. And the last thing she needed was for me to go off on a rant. So I focused on her needs. And the first one was a new fucking job.

For years, Chris had nothing but shitty things to say about the douches design firm. Then I witnessed the way every person from the firm behaved at the zoo event. Jake was an ass, of course, and so was his fiancée, but not one person Gianna worked with had congratulated her. Hell, they didn't even speak to her. If, for some reason, this place was the firm of her dreams, then that had to change. If she felt like it was the place where she could make a name for herself, then I'd figure out how to decimate Jake while supporting her dream.

"Why do you work for the douches?" I asked, forcing my voice to sound relaxed.

"It's Doucette, and for the obvious reasons," she snarked, hitting me with that glare that I understood hid her vulnerability. "Money."

That was such a sassy Gi answer. Though the attitude didn't last. It only took a moment for her walls to melt slightly. Chin lowered, she focused on something below the screen and sighed.

"Health insurance. Income stability." She shrugged. "Since I've been in Boston, I've sent my résumé out to dozens of firms, but I haven't gotten a single hit. Even if I get more jobs like Little Fingers, I'd need to bring in at least two projects a month to pay the bills."

That was understandable. "You need to prove to yourself that you can survive on those jobs before you can quit."

One of my worst qualities was that I harped on things. I became single-mindedly focused to an annoying degree. Sometimes it wasn't all bad. It's how I'd gotten so good at baseball so quickly. It became my obsession. Now, though, I had a new obsession, one with big brown eyes and gorgeous curves and a place in my heart I never thought anyone would fill. But she also had a boss who needed to be socially castrated and a talent that she downplayed and dismissed at every turn. And I intended to fix all these things.

"Isn't that what people do before they quit their jobs? Find a new one?" She cocked a brow. That simple response was so very unreactive, so very un-Damiano, that it threw me off. Though maybe it shouldn't have. She wasn't as hotheaded as everyone made her seem.

"Smart, rational people." I cracked my knuckles and took a breath. "Let's look at your résumé when I get back and see how we can make it pop. You deserve a job you love." I forced a smile.

She rolled her eyes. "Not everyone gets a job they love."

That might be true, but no one deserved the way Jake Caderson was treating Gianna.

"Eh, fine. But we're gonna make it happen for you. Don't you know I'm like Micky Mouse? I make all the dreams come true," I assured her with a tease.

Finally, she cracked the smallest smile. It definitely had a *you're such a dumbass* vibe to it, but it was genuine.

"Well, thanks for…" She pressed her lips together and ducked her head again. "For not freaking out. I needed to feel better. And some-how, you did that."

"I would paint myself blue, hop around like a monkey, or stand on my head if it made your day better."

"I could paint you blue," she teased.

My blood heated at the thought of her brush on my skin. "Don't make promises you don't want me to hold you to."

She smirked. "Who says I don't want you to hold me to them?"

All I could do in response was groan. I was too lost in the fantasy.

"Go play your game, Emerson." She smiled. "Text me after."

I nodded. Of course I'd text her. She didn't have to ask. Eventually, she'd figure that out.

As soon as she ended the call, my smile fell and my body heated again. And not in the way it had when she mentioned painting my body. No, the rage I'd put aside for her still existed in my core, and it flared back to life. I didn't know how to deal with it. Anger and punishment weren't my norm. And I couldn't hide down in the tunnels much longer, or someone would find me.

I'd wanted to hear about Gi's meeting with Dylan, but with my locker right next to Chris's, I couldn't FaceTime her there. So I'd wandered out and down the hall far enough that it was unlikely anybody would stumble upon me. But eventually, someone would notice I was missing from pregame shit and come looking.

I moved back toward the locker room, tucking my phone into my uniform pocket. Pushing through the door, I scanned my teammates until I found the one I needed.

I moved straight to the dark-haired man who was tapping away on his own phone.

"What's up, Bambi?" Asher Price tipped his head up and cocked a brow at me from the folding chair where he sat.

"Zara is a professional fixer, right?" I asked. Supposedly, Asher's wife used to work with athletes, actors, and singers, setting the record straight after bad publicity and stuff like that.

"She backed off once we had kids," he said, frowning, "but she's playing with the idea of working more often."

That's exactly what I'd heard. "So if I needed a truth set free, she might help me?"

That frown of concentration turned into one of concern. "You personally?"

I cleared my throat and shifted slightly so I was closer to him. "Not exactly me."

His eyes widened. "About the Revs?"

Slowly, I shook my head. I had nothing bad to say about a single member of this organization. They had always been great to me. He craned his neck, surveying the room over my shoulder.

When he focused on me again, he was wearing a knowing expression. "About the reason you want to hang at your apartment so much lately?"

It was a backhanded way of asking me whether I was talking about Gianna. The carefully worded question gave him the ability to deny that he knew anything more than that there was a reason I didn't go out lately.

I gave him a clipped nod.

He returned the gesture. "I'll have Zara text you."

I gave him a murmured thanks, then moved back to my locker. I needed my wallet.

"You okay, Bambi?" Chris asked from next to me.

"Yup." I flipped through cards until I found the one I was looking for. White. Embossed. Gold letters. I scanned the number, then plugged it into my phone.

A moment later, a response came through, and the tension in my shoulders eased. Fixing the issues took away some of this throbbing anger. I set my phone on the shelf and sank into my chair, attempting to steer my thoughts to the game. It was no use. Over and over, my mind kept shifting back to Gi.

Was she okay? Or was she sitting by herself, crying again?

Her friends were in New York. She'd left them.

I'd agreed to a fling, but I wanted more. For days, I'd been running through ways I could win her over and get her to see me as a relationship possibility. But even if I got us past this fling and we committed to trying for a real relationship, what would that mean for her? In a year, I could be playing for the Tridents. If I dragged her with me, she'd be stuck in Vancouver. Alone. Even farther from her friends and family. In a country she didn't know.

Boy, was I familiar with that concept. Unease churned in my gut as I tried to block out the thoughts. Now was not the time.

"Hey," Chris said, pulling me from my moment of panic.

I looked up at him hovering over me and blinked.

"You okay?" he asked, his brow furrowed.

With a steadying breath, I cracked my knuckles and went for easy. "What do you mean?"

"I don't know. Did the team cancel your off days for your sister's thing next week or something? You looked furious a minute ago, and now you look like someone ran over your dog."

"You won't let us get a dog." Deflection. It was a great tool.

He crossed his arms and kept his eyes locked on me. Apparently, the tactic wouldn't work today.

"But no," I assured him. "I'm off after the Metros game next week."

Chris would be pissed on my behalf if the Revs didn't approve my time off for Isabella's graduation. He knew how much that shit mattered to me, and he'd have my back.

Hooking his foot around one leg of the folding chair by his locker, he pulled it closer. Then he dropped into it and rested his elbows on his knees.

"I don't know what, but something is going on." He lifted his head, surveyed the guys who were milling around, ignoring us, then lowered his voice. "You've been weird. Distracted. And the only thing I can come up with is woman drama. But from where I'm standing, it seems like the only woman you've been hanging out with is Gi." He shifted slightly. "So what's up?"

Fuck.

The idea of lying to my best friend just about killed me. But rocking the boat with Chris over something that had an expiration date? Causing issues between him and his sister? Did I really want to do that? I didn't see how Gi and I could be more than a fling. I wouldn't push her into uprooting her life. No matter what, I'd never put her through what I went through.

Maybe it would be easier to start over as an adult. Regardless, the dread that consumed me on my first day of high school in New Jersey still haunted me. The stares, the loneliness. The fear that hit me every time I had to speak, since the teachers insisted I only use a language I wasn't even completely comfortable with.

My accent, although barely noticeable now, had been thick back then. I didn't understand half of the slang terms the other kids used, and I ended up in mostly ESL classes. Taunted for being slow to read. Teased for sounding funny. Fourteen-year-olds were just mean.

Baseball had been my saving grace. And by my senior year, I was almost comfortable. And then, once again, my life flipped.

I'd never regret moving to Triple-A and helping my mom, but starting over again that time was even harder than in high school.

I cracked the knuckles on my other hand. "No problems with Gi. She's easy."

Chris scoffed and roughed a hand down his face. "She's not. But is there something going on between you two?" His lips dropped to a straight line.

Any lie was acid on my tongue, and I was terrible at it. "Between us? Like are we together?" Giving up the idea was so hard. But I had to. "Nah. I mean, she's great." Nerves made my words spew out too fast. "Totally cool chick. But she's headed back to New York. She doesn't need anything derailing her plans." Least of all me. I could enjoy what little time we had together, but that was it. "Not that I have any intention of derailing anything." I'd hold on to the moments, because they would be fleeting. "I just want to support her in stuff." Too fast. I was talking too fast. Like I did when I let anger get the best of me. "Unless it's her boss. That man needs to be hit by a bus." I clenched my teeth to make myself shut up.

Chris snorted. "Hell yeah, he does." Quickly, his expression went serious again. "So what's the deal? You're not yourself."

Was I not? Maybe I wasn't putting enough effort into my forced cheerfulness.

"You don't go out anymore."

That was an odd statement coming from him, though I kept that to myself. "I just agreed to go to the bar tonight."

He frowned, clearly not ready to let this go. "You're currently fully dressed, which is never a thing."

Because I knew I'd have to leave the damn room to call his sister, and I couldn't walk around the hall in boxers.

"I don't even know when the last time you flung yourself at me was."

My eyes widened at that. He was right. "Aw, you miss it." With a painted-on smirk, I jumped up. "Bring it in, man." I leaped over the space and smothered him. He jerked back, pushing his chair onto its back legs.

"Oh, shit." Bosco barked a laugh.

I was attacking him the way I had for years when the chair tilted to one side. It hovered there for one breath, and then we toppled over.

I slammed down, banging my shoulder into the wall of his chest as we crashed in a heap.

"Jesus," he snapped, shoving me off him.

I rolled around on the Roaster's red carpet, laughing.

He tried to glare, but even my grumpy best friend struggled to fight a smile. "How do you always make this shit happen?"

I lay flat on my back, then pushed myself up on my elbows. "Just lucky, I guess."

"Seems like the same old Bambi to me." With a chuckle, Mason reached down and pulled me off the floor.

Coach Wilson stood at the door to the coach's room, shaking his head. "Dumbasses," he muttered before turning and leaving.

Martinez pulled Chris to his feet. "Did you offer him your hand in marriage or something?"

Chris snorted. "No, I told him he was being weird, and his response was to fucking tackle me."

"What can I say? I love being noticed," I joked.

Discreetly, I breathed out a sigh of relief. My antics had successfully ended the conversation about my weirdness. Because this goofball of a guy was who they expected me to be.

Emerson
27

Wren: Both Hank and Tim approved all three paintings.

Me: Wow, in two days? You said it would take at least a week.

Wren: They loved them. It took no convincing at all.

Me: Were they okay with the prices?

Wren: Yes. No fight there either. We'll list all three on the July 20th date.

Me: Great. When do you need them?

Wren: Probably week after next for photos. Can you make that happen?

Me: Hopefully.

Gianna
28

"Stupid or not stupid?" I asked for a second time, rubbing my hands along the hem of the pin-striped jersey. It fell just above my knee, so it wasn't too short. Although I never planned to wear it out of the house, so I supposed it didn't matter.

"You made that?" Mila cocked her head as she leaned closer to the screen. "How?"

"TikTok taught me." That didn't matter. I just wanted to know if this was a dumb idea before I embarrassed myself. "Linc?"

"I'm with Mila. How did you make a dress out of his jersey?"

With a sigh, I rushed through the explanation so we could get back to my question. "I bought a jersey a few sizes too big so I'd get a good amount of length. Then I trimmed the extra fabric off the sides to fit it to me. After I did that, I squared the neckline, because if you have boobs you need cleavage, or it's just unflattering. Then I stitched it up with my serger and sewed up the button line so it wouldn't pull open."

"You brought your serger to Boston?" Mila asked.

"Mi, I brought everything I didn't sell to Boston. I don't own anything that isn't with me." I shifted from one foot to the other on my wedges. "So, is this dumb? He texted me fifteen minutes ago to say he landed. He should be here soon." I waved my hands up and down the dress.

"I mean..." Linc looked me over from top to bottom and back. "Hair is perfection. You wanded that shit up. I'm always jealous of your lashes. Like, babe, people pay for the length God just gave you."

Although I appreciated the compliments, I'd gone to school for hair and makeup, so that wasn't my worry.

"The dress looks super hot." Mila nodded.

"And the red lips are a nice touch. Every straight male dreams of red lips around his cock." Linc shrugged.

Sighing, I flopped onto the chair. "Guys, I meant the idea. Is this stupid?"

Mila shook her head. "It's a thing. At least in books." She sat up straight and clasped her hands, all formal-like, as if she was teaching a class. "Men who play sports like to see the girl they're sleeping with wearing their jersey. Brings out that alpha dominance."

"True," Linc jumped in. "Whereas I prefer—"

"I don't want to know." Mila cut him off, and they both cracked up.

"So leave it on?" I asked.

"Yes. And we want all the details." Linc waggled his brow.

"Some details. I don't need nor *want* them all." Mila frowned.

"Nope, we want them all. Every single one, down to exactly how veiny his cock is." Linc smirked.

"Never going to happen, but thanks." I tapped the End button on my phone, and the image of my friends was replaced with my home screen. With a glance at the time, I changed the oven from bake to warm so the manicotti wouldn't burn and then tossed a wet paper towel over the salad and stuck it in the fridge. The wine was open and breathing on the counter. Everything was perfect.

The small click of the lock hit me a second before the door pushed open.

"Damn, it smells good in here," Emerson said, his voice quiet.

I leaned against the counter and cocked a hip.

"Gi?" his deep voice called.

Second-guessing my pose, I crossed my legs so they'd look smaller, then I shifted again and was half in a new position when he walked into the kitchen space. So rather than looking sexy, I looked like a cat, frozen and wide-eyed, ready to pounce.

For one second, he paused. Then his eyes snapped to my outfit, and the corner of his mouth kicked up.

"I was planning to look cute when you walked in." I sighed, shoulders slumping.

He strode over and stopped in front of me. Then he lifted his finger to trace the blue 21 on my breast. The touch sent goose bumps skittering down my arms.

"You look like everything I want and can't call mine." With that same hand, he gripped the back of my neck, his callused hand biting into my skin. "You look like the dream I'll hang on to and pull out on a bad day."

He pressed his lips lightly to mine for a heartbeat, then pulled back and rested his forehead against mine. "This is what coming home should feel like."

Really? How could he feel that way if he'd closed himself off to anything but a casual fling?

"Feel better today?" he asked, not moving away. He tipped his head slightly and nuzzled into my hair, and when he pulled in a deep breath and held it like he was savoring it, my whole body buzzed.

He'd checked in on me more than once over the last two days. But I was fine. Jake was a jerk. He'd always be a jerk. And a new project had come in. That was keeping me busy and keeping my mind occupied. It was better than the uncertainty of no income. Plus, I was having fun with the Little Fingers logo.

"Today was good, but it's better now that you're here."

"Is that so?" he asked, a smile in his voice as he kept his face pressed to mine. His hands skimmed down my body and rested on my ass, and with a jerk, he yanked me against him. Behind his zipper, he was hard and warm. As he ground his cock against my thigh, his leg vibrated. Pulling back, he dug his phone out of his pocket.

Zara. The name flashed on the screen.

"Give me one sec. This is important," he said to me as he wandered out of the room. "Hey, bebé."

God, I hated that term. Why was everyone and their mother his baby *except* me?

His voice faded as he moved farther away, and I clenched my jaw, choking back my anger and hurt. Had he really just walked away in the middle of *that* to talk to some other girl?

My heart raced. Who left their—

Shit. Their what? Roommate? Fling? Possible hookup? Yeah, everyone left those kinds of people for important phone calls. Because all of those terms described someone who was expendable.

I turned and took in the skyline outside the huge windows across the open room, annoyed with myself. There I was, hair and makeup all done. Attempting perfection but just being not good enough. With the sun almost set, the windows reflected my image. Me in the stupid jersey dress. I glared at myself and shook my head. Dinner, wine, a homemade dress. I was doing it again. Going all-in for someone who wasn't there with me.

Swallowing back the emotion pricking behind my eyes, I poured wine into one stemless glass I'd set out on the quartz countertop. Why did I ever think this was a good idea? I stormed back to my room and took off the jersey opting for shorts and crop top. Then heading back to the kitchen, I grabbed my drink and I moved to the window taking in the harbor spread out below. With a deep gulp of wine, I shut my eyes.

Emerson returned to the kitchen, fumbling around noisily as always, but I didn't move. Not even as he padded toward me. It wasn't until he put a hand on my hip that I opened my eyes and moved away.

Before I could even open my mouth, he spoke.

"Settle down." He put his hand on my hip again and gave it a quick squeeze before releasing me. "You too the jersey off?"

"Dumb idea." I snapped.

"Zara is Asher Price's wife. She does corporate investigations and media spin."

That statement took the wind out of my sails. The hurt was still there, but it was mixed with confusion and maybe a hint of relief.

"I asked her to look into something for me."

I spun and frowned at him, trying to decode his words.

"Jake's an ass." He sighed. "I doubted you were the first person he'd treated badly at the douche firm. So I had her ask some questions."

My stomach twisted in a knot. Why was he doing this? And would it come back to bite me once Jake caught wind that I had something to do with it?

"Turns out he's made a few people upset over the years."

"Wait." I held a hand up. "You asked her to do that for me?"

He weighed the statement, tipping his head one way, then the other, before finally saying, "I asked her to find a way to ruin the fucker that didn't involve you at all." Hands fisted at his sides, he grunted. "I can't stand the fact that he hurt you. But I refuse to mess anything up for you, so I made sure to keep you out of it."

My heart cracked. All the mad that had been there seconds ago disappeared, and in its place was this swamping emotion I couldn't name. No one had ever done anything like that for me.

"I'm sorry if I overstepped. But I can't live with the idea of him not suffering for making you cry."

I rushed forward and threw my arms around him. "I'm sorry," I mumbled against his chest.

"For what?" he asked, tucking me into his body.

"I was pissed at you for leaving me to talk to a girl, but it was all about me," I admitted, my cheeks heating with embarrassment.

He chuckled. "I love when you're fired up. Don't ever apologize for being pissed. But I am sad you took off my jersey because I've been dying to see my number on you."

"Well…" The idea he didn't sign things had haunted me for awhile now. Maybe…

I pulled out of his arms and moved to the counter reaching for a sharpie from the cup before coming back to him. My stomach fluttered slightly once again worried he'd think this was dumb.

"Think you could give me an autograph?"

He cocked his head to the side as I passed him the marker then I slowly lowered my shorts and spun to face the window.

He sucked in a hard breath but I heard him uncap the marker. "Damn Gi, I love the idea of my name on you." His warm palm hit the bare skin of my ass pushing my shorts down so I could step out of them completely before the cold marker touched me. It moved quickly along my skin then it was gone. He bent and pressed his lips to the same spot and I shivered. "Mine." The words were barely a whisper against me before he stood. But the idea of being his lingered, it felt too good for the casual we were supposed to be and I couldn't let myself get caught up in that.

"Thank you." Popping up on my toes, I pressed my lips to his. Quickly, desire took over, and I ran my tongue along the seam of his mouth.

With a groan, he yanked away. "What am I eating first, dinner or you?"

"Home team's choice."

The deep chuckle that reverberated through him made me shudder in the best way. "That's you every time."

A whimper rumbled in my throat as his mouth met mine. I parted my lips, and his tongue invaded, thrusting deep, desperate to meet mine. Leaning in, he pressed me tight to the cool glasses with his hard chest and smooth stomach. He snaked one hand down and grasped my thigh, hooking it over his hip.

He rocked his long erection against me, using his free hand to tug my hair and tip my chin up. My head banged against the glass, and I moaned. With a grunt, he pulled his lips from mine, then ran them along my jaw, his teeth nipping at my skin.

"You're hot and wet already, aren't you?" He swirled his hips against me and I thrust against him. His cock, so hard, pushed against the thin material of his dress pants, begging to be free, to sink into me. "You need my cock, don't you? Did you think about me coming home and fucking you real good, Gi?"

"Yes." I moaned. I needed nothing between us.

He nipped at my neck again, sending a zap of electricity to my core. "Did you touch this pussy, fuck your fingers, and pretend it was me?" He lapped against my collarbone, his tongue running along the swell of my breast. Then, abruptly, he released me and dropped to his knee.

My body buzzed with a pounding desire, but all coherent thought had left me.

"Because I fucked my hand thinking about you."

"Em." I whimpered.

As he slowly slid his fingers up my bare legs, I shivered with antici-pation. I was desperate for him to touch me. He looked up, eyes dark with need, for an instant before he lowered his face and ran his nose along my thigh. It was almost embarrassing, the way my body was primed for him.

He ran his nose along the white lace covering me.

"Mmm, you smell so fucking good, all needy and ready for me." His fingers bit into my ass cheeks as he pulled me closer, then he released his grip and hooked them into the waistband of my thong. "Now be my good girl and step out of these so I can have some of my favorite flavor." He yanked the lace down my legs, and then his mouth was pressed to my skin. Slowly, his lips roamed up my inner thigh.

"Emerson, please," I begged.

He smiled against my skin. "I know, Mariposa. I'll make your body sing for me."

Slowly, he lifted my leg over his shoulder and hovered, his breath brushing against my pussy. And when I thought I couldn't stand it one more second, he took one long, painfully slow swipe along my slit.

"Oh God." I leaned back, the glass cool against my ass cheeks as his hot mouth covered me. I was so close already. Two swipes of his tongue, and my legs were quivering. I grabbed his hair, holding him against me.

He chuckled, and the vibration shot up my spine. With another long lap, he sucked hard on my clit, making my whole body tighten. Buzz. He alternated between slow laps and sucks until I was on the edge, and tight swirling need rushed through my body. Finally, I broke and bucked against his face, coming hard.

"Emerson," I called.

"Yes. That's it. Drown me," he moaned against my pussy. As soon as the last wave of pleasure stopped, he was on his feet, pressing his lips to mine, owning my mouth the way he'd owned my pussy.

"I need to feel you inside me," I begged, reaching between us to release him from his pants.

"Condom." He started to pull away, but I stopped him.

"I'm on birth control. And after…" I shook my head. "I was tested. I'm good."

He nodded. "Me too. But if I'm taking you bare, I want all your skin." He pulled the tank top over my head, then ran a finger down the center of my chest to the bra clasp between them. As he released it and my breasts spilled out, a shiver racked through me.

"Looking at you steals the breath from my body." He perused every inch of my skin. "I just need one taste." Angling forward, he wrapped his lips around my nipple.

I whimpered at the thrill that raced down my body. "More," I begged.

He switched to the other side for one moment before pulling back and yanking the Revs polo over his head. As it fell to the floor and he went to work on the button and zipper of his pants, he kept his eyes on me. Once he'd kicked off his shoes and his pants, only stumbling once, he lifted my leg and hooked it over his hip.

Eyes locked with mine, he sank into me.

My head fell back against the glass and I moaned.

"Fuck, Gi," he gritted out, tipping back and watching the place we were joined. His breath picked up, and he thrust, swirling his hips. "Nothing is prettier than your pussy taking my cock against the night sky."

The glass was more of a mirror from the outside, and no one could see us. Even so, the idea of Boston behind me made me throb.

He dropped his hands to my ass, gripping tight, as he slowly slid back out before thrusting deep. "The way you feel against me. Around me," he groaned. "I'm not going to last." With that, he quickened his pace, slamming into me hard and deep.

Every thrust of his hips pressed me harder into the glass. Over and over, rocking deep. My stomach tightened. My legs quivered.

"Come on, Gi. Come for me," he begged as he thrust hard.

The cold behind me biting against my skin, his hot body pressing against my breasts, the feel of him deep inside me—it was all too much. But at the same time, it wasn't enough. All I could do was cling to him as I clenched around him.

"Oh yeah. That's it." He thrust once more, twice, and on the third, he groaned my name, pulsing inside me and filling me up.

He collapsed against me, panting into my neck. And we stood there for just one minute, but that minute felt perfect.

"Come on," he mumbled. "I need to clean you up."

He finally pulled away and led me down the hall to the bathroom.

Ten minutes later, I was in one of his Boston Revs T-shirts and he was in a pair of black boxers, forking bites of manicotti straight out of the dish.

"Second best thing I've had all day," Emerson said, shoving another bite into his mouth.

I rolled my eyes. "First being the salad?"

"First being your pussy as you came all over my face."

A shot of heat rushed through me at the image he painted. "Emerson!"

"You asked." He chuckled, stabbing another forkful of manicotti. "What are your plans for the week?"

I shrugged. "I don't have much. I need to send Dylan some mockups before the end of the week."

He set the fork down and shifted, his focus drifting to something just over my shoulder. "We have a game in New York on Tuesday, and then I'm taking a couple of days off." Popping his knuckles, he cleared his throat. "I'm going home for my sister's graduation and party. And I, uh…" He paused, his expression uncertain. "Want to come?"

My heart stuttered in my chest, and my eyes shot wide. "To the graduation?"

"The game…" He sighed. "Zara's going, and she'd love for you to come with her. She won't mention it to Chris…"

Oh. Not to meet his family. Just go to the game. I fought the way my shoulders wanted to slump and swallowed back the disappointment that shouldn't have hit me over a possibility that didn't even exist two minutes ago.

"But yeah. After, I'd love it if you came home to my mom's with me for a couple of days…" He ducked his head and used his fork to toy with the manicotti in the dish. "Unless you don't want to."

How badly I wanted to go wasn't even rational. Because people having flings didn't hang out with one another's families. I'd only met Jake's parents once in the almost two years we'd dated.

"You don't have to," he said, his cheeks going pink.

I reached a hand out and put it over his. "Em, I'd love to."

His eyes shot to mine. "Yeah?"

"Yes."

His answering smile burrowed its way into my heart. I gave him a soft smile in return. All the while, my emotions were in overdrive, because everything about this moment made it feel like we could have more.

Gianna
29

Emerson: Did you and Mila get here okay?

Me: She lives in the city.

Emerson: She's from Kansas.

Me: Yeah she grew up there - what's that have to do with anything?

Emerson: I thought we were just stating Mila facts. I don't see how living in the city has anything to do with you two getting to the ballpark…

Me: You think you're funny.

Emerson: So I didn't make you smile?

Me: That's irrelevant.

Emerson: Your smiles are never irrelevant to me.

Me: GIF of an eye roll

Me: Picture of the front of the stadium.

215

Emerson: Glad you're here safe.

Me: Have a good game.

Gianna
30

"YOU READY TO ADMIT THAT THINGS WITH BASEBALL BOY ARE SERIOUS?" Mila asked as we weaved our way through the throng of people.

"What do you mean?" As we approached the gate, I tucked my phone into my pocket.

"You're smiling. I'd swear you're almost giddy." Mila shook her head. "And that happens every time he texts you. I've never seen you like this. Now, if that apartment had been in your price range, maybe I'd believe it was the reason…"

Yeah. The apartment. We had seen two. The one today was ridiculously unaffordable. The rent the guy had quoted via text didn't include the building fees, which added another four hundred dollars to the price. The one yesterday had potential. It was a studio and at the very top of my price range, but it was smack dab in the middle of the city and surrounded by buildings. Not to mention the traffic down Fourth was insane. In the last couple of weeks, I'd gotten used to the harbor view and the slightly slower pace of Boston. But I couldn't stay there.

"Emerson and I are good with what we are. And I'm still looking at moving back to New York."

The thing I'd come to realize about Emerson was that he didn't want to label a relationship as serious, even though he was as actively willing to be involved with me for as long as I was. I had his unwavering support and so much of his attention. So if he didn't want to put an official name on what we had, I could live with that. Because often, things worth having were worth waiting for.

And Emerson was more than worth it.

"I'm not sure I get it." Mila frowned over her shoulder as we lined up to go through security.

For the first time in my life, I didn't feel the need to justify what I was doing, so I answered her with a simple shrug.

We were barely through the metal detectors when someone called my name from several feet away.

I turned in that direction and was met by a tiny woman headed our way.

Her long black hair was twisted into a braid that hung over her thin shoulder. Her collared shirtdress was all black, with a small white Revs logo over her right breast that matched the white Nikes on her feet. The woman barely came up to my shoulder, but she carried herself with confidence, shoulders back and head high, as she made her way to me. A ray of light caught on the silver and diamond watch on her wrist as she held up her hand. Between that, the diamond around her neck, the studs in her ears, and the massive rock on her finger, she was a walking jewelry store.

"Zara Price." Beneath her dark Bulla sunglasses, her lips lifted into a smile that showed off straight white teeth that glowed as brightly as all her diamonds.

"Gianna. And this is my friend Mila." I nodded at my bestie.

Zara released my hand and then shook Mila's. "Nice to meet you both."

The Prices had gotten a box suite at the field and had invited Emerson's family, as well as Mila and me, to sit with them.

"Emerson mentioned you were heading in through this gate, so I figured it would be easier to grab you here. The layout of this bloody ballpark is ridiculously convoluted," she said in a light British accent.

Zara wasn't kidding. She led us through a maze of escalators and corridors that I never could have navigated on my own before we finally got to suite 311.

A man in all black stood on either side of the door. Entrance into boxes was monitored, sure, but I'd never seen this level of security at a baseball game.

"Don't mind the suits. They're here with our friends." She pushed the door open and lifted her glasses to the top of her head. "Do you know the Matthewses or the Demodas?"

I didn't, but I quickly met the wives of the Metros player and coach. Two more tiny women. One was dressed in cutoffs and a Metros tank top and the other in a green Metros fitted T-shirt dress. All three women fit the stereotypical look of a professional athlete's wife. Tiny, pretty, and confident. And aggressive in their support of their husband's team.

I glanced down at my own clothes. I'd gone for jeans and a blue T-shirt—*without* a Revs logo—clearly nowhere near as supportive as the other women. I had wanted to wear the dress I'd made, but I couldn't. There was little chance I'd see any of the guys on the team, but if I did, they'd ask why I was wearing Emerson's number. There was also the issue of me spending the day with Emerson's family. I wasn't sure exactly what he'd told them, and I had zero interest in fielding questions regarding our situationship.

Zara had barely dropped into the chair before she popped up, phone in hand. "Mama Knight is here. I'll grab them too. Be right back."

The woman was probably so thin because she never stopped moving.

"Either of you want a drink?" the blond Zara had introduced as Beth asked.

"I'd love a water for now," I said.

Taran, the dark-haired woman with a southern accent, hopped up and grabbed one for each of us from a refrigerator in the kitchen area of the suite.

"So," Taran said, her drawl faint, "what do you all do?" Her eyes were bright and full of curiosity as she settled on her stool again.

"I'm an art teacher." Mila picked nervously at the water bottle, probably as intimidated by these two well-dressed, confident women as I was.

"Really?" Taran perked up, sitting high on her stool. "Have you heard of School First?"

Mila nodded. "Oh, I adore the organization."

The woman's smile split her face. "I work for them."

Right in front of me, Mila's nerves melted away, and the two dove into a conversation about getting more art programs into schools. As I listened silently, the Boston Revs' blue jerseys appeared in my periphery, so I stepped away from the table so I could get a good look at the field.

Emerson and Eddie Martinez lined up and took off, doing sprints along the grass. Eddie was the only guy on the team who had any chance of competing with Emerson for speed. But even he couldn't beat the third baseman. Emerson very dramatically glanced at his watch when Martinez stopped next to him. The shortstop flicked Emerson's hat off, and they both laughed.

I wouldn't get to see Emerson today. He knew I was here, and his family would head down to see him after the game, but I couldn't go down. Chris and Pop knew I was in New York, but I let them believe I was here to visit Mila and to hunt for apartments only. I had no reasonable excuse to be at today's game. Though this wasn't the first Metros game I attended in my life, it *was* the first I'd come to totally voluntarily. And yeah, they'd ask far too many questions if they knew I was here.

"Gianna Damiano."

I turned at the sound of my name and smiled.

Mrs. Knight rushed across the sitting area toward the glass where I stood. She was decked out in jeans, a pin-striped number 21 Revs jersey, and a Boston Revs baseball cap. Beaded bracelets circled both wrists, making her by far the most devoted-looking fan in the suite. She had to be close to sixty, but by the way she looked like she was going to hurdle the seats in a rush to get across the room, you'd never know it.

Without a pause, she wrapped her arms around me and squeezed me tight.

"You are just as perfect in person," she said, patting my cheek, her accent thick.

My face heated. "Um, thank you?"

"I'm obsessed with your eyelashes."

Behind her, the other three Knights were all sporting number 21 as well. My stomach spun. Shit. I was the only one in the suite not sporting Revs or Metros gear. Even Mila had on a Boston tee.

One of Emerson's sisters, Yvette, I thought, stepped closer and invaded my space as much as her mother had. "I want all the lash secrets. Because those look real."

"Way to have chill," her sister snickered.

"None of you have chill." The deep voice was so similar to Emerson's, I might have been fooled if I didn't know he was down on the field. "I'm Andre. The better-looking Knight brother."

I didn't agree. Not that I'd tell him that. The brothers were probably the same height, but where Emerson was all lean lines and tight muscle, Andre was softer. His features weren't as defined, and he sported none of the scruff that peppered Emerson's jaw.

"The look on Gianna's face totally called you a liar, Andre," Yvette teased.

Isabella giggled. "Pretty and smart. What a combo."

The back-and-forth felt so normal, so much like the way Chris and I had bantered my entire life. I'd known these people for minutes, and already, I understood how Emerson fit so well with Avery, Pop, and Chris.

"Enough." Mrs. Knight snapped her fingers at her children. "Leave the poor girl alone. Your brother will skin you all if you scare her off."

She shooed them away and turned back to me. "Come sit with me. We will get to know each other."

She reached up and patted my cheek again. And although I knew I was about to sit through an inquisition. The warmth that flooded off Mrs. Knight in waves put me at ease. Until the first question, that was.

"Tell me about my son." She cocked her head, studying me with knowing hazel eyes.

Tell her about her own son? How could I even begin? There were so many things I could say, but she probably knew him better than anyone.

I looked down onto the field where he stood with his team and considered the options. What wouldn't she get to see?

"He's the giver in every situation. Always passing out smiles or high fives or offering a supportive shoulder to lean on. He'll happily cook for his friends and always offers himself up when someone is in need." I couldn't pull my eyes from him as he tossed ball after ball into the stands after Mason Dumpty had signed them. "I just want him to learn he's worth enough to receive that kind of kindness too. He deserves as much joy as he spreads every day." My voice cracked on the last word, so I cleared my throat. Why the hell was I getting emotional about this? "Sorry." I turned back to her, only to find her blinking back tears.

"You and me? We are good." She grasped my hand and gently tugged it closer. "But you don't let him go on stealing the eggs for long, mi hija."

I had no idea what *me ha* meant, nor did I have any idea what eggs he was stealing, but I didn't want to upset her.

"Uh?" I worried my lower lip, racking my brain for an appropriate response.

She chuckled, the skin at her temples crinkling. "It's milk." With a pat to my hand, she released me and fanned herself. "The saying is about buying cows and stealing milk. But personally, I don't see why any woman would want to be a cow. I'd much rather be the chicken."

"The chicken?" I asked, confusion swirling inside me.

She nodded. "Yes. Because the hens get all the good cocks."

My mouth fell open, and my face heated, but I couldn't help but laugh. "Mrs. Knight!"

She smirked. "Mama Knight, mi hija. Everyone calls me Mama knight."

I nodded, hit with a wave of gentle affection for the woman. "Okay. Mama Knight."

"The world now, there are free eggs." She shook her head. "All over, free eggs." Angling closer, she stuck a finger in the air. "But you must remember, even the best men need a good shove in the right direction. Including my son." With a firm nod, she patted my thigh. Then she pivoted, changing the subject altogether. "Tell me about your family."

"Uh..." The way she jumped from topic to topic left my head spinning.

She waved me off. "I've met them, of course. But I want to see them through your eyes."

I looked out over the field, finding Emerson again. He was laughing with Mason, craning his neck like he was searching the stadium for something. Maybe he was looking for his family, but his gaze didn't stop on anything, including us. And I couldn't wave, because I wasn't supposed to be here. Because Chris would be too much about it. I looked back at Mama Knight, who was watching me, wearing a patient smile.

"My brother is annoying."

She chuckled. "Aren't they all?"

And from the there, the conversation was much easier. It wasn't until halfway through the second inning when Andre stopped by to drop a water off for his mother that the questions stopped.

"Emerson will be up this inning, Mama."

She patted my leg. "Thank you for humoring me. You are as lovely as my son promised."

With a smile, she stood and followed her other son into the open-air seats.

Zara dropped into Mama Knight's seat beside me before I could even get up. "The mother stamp of approval. That's a big hurdle."

"Oh, uh, no." I flushed.

Apparently, Emerson had talked to his mom about me, but I didn't know what he'd told Zara. And since her husband played for the Revs, I didn't want to give her the wrong idea.

Flicking at a piece of fuzz on my jeans, I lowered my gaze. "It's really not a thing."

"Trust me, it's a thing. I've been married almost ten years, and I still don't have it." Zara shook her head.

"Really?" How could anyone with half a brain not approve of her?

She and Asher were the sports world's favorite couple. They were all over magazines and TV, always smiling and put-together.

"In my mother-in-law's opinion, no one will ever be good enough for her angel boy." She frowned. "But most certainly not some English girl. And she has no trouble reminding me of that. Heaven forbid her grandchildren don't love apple pie and baseball."

From the bite in her tone, it was obvious there was a real issue there, but I didn't know her well enough to pry, so I just forced a smile.

"But," she said, splaying her hands on her thighs, "I came over to talk about you."

"Me?"

With a nod, she launched into details about what Emerson had told her when he first reached out about Jake.

"Leopards never change their spots, and since Emerson wanted to keep you out of this completely, I went back to his last two employers and starting asking questions. Pretty quickly, a pattern emerged." She scowled.

"Emerson mentioned that you found some people who were upset with him."

"This goes way beyond upset. These weren't just coworkers who didn't like him. No, he stole their designs, used them in his portfolio. Literally stepped on people to get ahead. Harassed them, forced them to quit. I've been in touch with a few people at *Socials Weekly* and *Into Design*."

Both magazines were huge in the graphic design field. Even now, when people were forgoing magazines for websites, Doucette Designs still subscribed to both.

"They're both interested in researching how often credit is stolen, especially from new designers." She smirked and sat back in her seat. "Turns out Jake's a great illustration of such issues. They are reaching out for quotes in the next couple of days. Give it a couple of weeks, and the guy will be out of a job."

The pressure in my chest made it hard to breathe as I absorbed the implications of what she'd said. "I don't even know what to say."

A cheer echoed around us, interrupting my thoughts and pulling my attention to the field. Emerson was rounding first and headed to second. He pulled to a stop after stepping on the bag and smirked at the guy next to him.

"I'll let you watch Emerson. But I just wanted to say thanks for letting me do this." She smiled at me as she pushed to her feet.

"Don't thank me," I assured her, standing up too. "I feel like I owe you."

She shook her head, and her black braid flicked over her shoulder. "You owe me nothing. I forgot how much I loved digging for the truth and exposing it. This is the most fun I've had in a long time." With a pat to my arm, she wandered across the space and sat beside Beth.

On the field, Emerson was taunting the pitcher. Three strides from the base wasn't much, but Em didn't need much of a lead to beat a throw. Two pitches later, his squat deepened. This was it. He was ready to move. And the moment the pitcher released the ball, he took off.

My heart skipped at the sound of the ball smacking into the catcher's glove. Emerson was two-thirds of the way to the base. It was going to be close.

I held my breath as he dove. His hand skimmed the top of bag only a second or two before the Declan Lowery's glove swiped across his back.

A smile lit Emerson's face, and I couldn't help the one that flooded mine.

"He's so good at that." Isabella came to stand beside me. "Makes me nervous every time, though."

"Yeah," I agreed. My heart was still working its way back down from my throat. Where he found the nerve to take off on a wing and prayer was a mystery.

"He said we're not supposed to say anything because of the whole Chris issue." With a scoff, she rolled her green eyes. "And I kinda get it. I mean Andre"—she flicked her hand out the window at her brother —"would murder any of his friends in their sleep if I hooked up with them."

She huffed hard, pushing her hair back from her face.

"He can hook up with girls without judgment, but somehow, I can't do the same." She snorted. "Whatever."

"Brothers can be annoying." I had too much firsthand experience to not throw that out there.

"Not Em." She smiled down at where he was standing at third base. "He's always just been there for us. I was little when he went to triple-A, and for a long time, I didn't realize what a big deal it was. He was younger than I am now. Yet here I am, too scared to even go farther than Montclair, New Jersey, for school because I don't want to leave my mom." She laughed at herself, then schooled her expression and pulled in a big breath. "I understand it now. How much he did for us. And I'm really happy that when he talks about you, he smiles. Like really smiles."

I wasn't prepared for that statement, and it stole the breath from my lungs.

She rolled her eyes again. "It's not that deep. You just make him happy, and that's cool."

"Oh." I cleared my throat and shifted on my feet. "Thanks?"

"Yeah." She nodded. "It's a good thing. So…" She glanced outside at her brother and sister. "Now that Vet isn't here, what's the deal with the lashes?"

I laughed, my heart feeling so light. Was there a person in this world who didn't love the Knights? Because this family was the definition of perfectly imperfect.

Emerson
31

THE SECOND THE UBER PULLED TO A STOP, I HOPPED OUT AND TOOK IN THE sight of the women on the sidewalk. Gi looked so damn good in the light dress that showed off the curve of her hips. I wanted to yank her into my arms and finally touch her. It had been literal days since I'd seen her.

We'd played at home twice last week, then we'd headed to DC for the weekend and New York for the Metros game after that. This was how life went for MLB players. We were constantly moving, and it wasn't something I'd never minded until recently.

Because until recently, I was never leaving anyone important behind. Now, every time I left Gi asleep in my bed so I could head to the airport, I left a piece of myself behind.

"Hey." She smiled shyly at me.

"Good game yesterday," Mila said.

"Thanks." I tipped my chin at the two bags on the sidewalk. "Just these?"

"*Just*?" Mila shook her head. "It's a two-day trip, and she's taking *two* full bags. And a jacket."

"Hey, it's three days, and don't mock me." Gi frowned. "I might need that coat. You never know if it'll get cold at night."

"It's practically July," Mila huffed.

She wasn't wrong. The high for today was supposed to be ninety-eight, but Gianna should be comfortable, and if bringing along a coat made her happy, then I would lug it around.

I grabbed the bags and hefted them into the open trunk. "Mama and Tia Camilia love their AC, so you never know."

Gi glared at me.

I didn't bother trying not to smile. "Your chariot awaits, Mariposa." I waved my hand toward the Tesla.

Gianna responded with a sigh and a giant eye roll. Then she turned back to Mila to say her goodbyes. Once we were settled in the car, I leaned in and pressed my lips to hers. This time, the sigh that escaped her was soft, and her body sagged against me. Instantly, my own body relaxed. Just having her near me lit me up and calmed my mind. I pulled back and brushed a curl off her face.

"Did missing me make you cranky?" I teased.

"Shut up," she huffed, though she was pliant in my arms as we left the city and headed for Jersey.

The longer we drove, the more relaxed I felt. Coming home felt like nothing else. And this time, I was bringing Gi. The second I mentioned that she was coming, my family knew there was something going on with us. So for the next two days, we didn't have to hide. It was mind-blowing how good it felt knowing I could be affectionate out in the open.

We didn't speak much on the forty-minute drive, but just having her resting her head on my shoulder and filling my nose with that orange blossom scent was enough.

When the Uber pulled up beside my mother's Subaru, I helped Gi out and circled to the trunk to get our bags.

"Where are we putting our stuff?" She glanced around the parking lot.

"Mama's car." I pulled her two bags out and set them on the asphalt before grabbing mine.

"She leaves it unlocked?" Gi asked, her voice pitched high in disbelief.

"Don't bother trying to tell my mother that we live in a world where people need to lock their doors. She won't believe you."

My mom was the reason I always looked for the positive side of things. No matter what happened in life, she always found the bright side. Every day, I worked to be like her and be that light for the people around me.

Unsurprisingly, Gi scoffed. My girl lived in a world full of locks. Oddly enough, I respected and admired the carefully crafted walls that Gi lived behind just as greatly as I did my mom's sunny outlook.

"What?" she snapped.

I smiled. "You're pretty."

With a roll of her eyes, she picked up one of her bags. "Which car? Can we lock it after we put our stuff in? I'd hate for someone to take her car."

I pointed. "We can. We just need to take the keys out."

Her brown eyes widened and her spine snapped straight. "She left the keys *in it*?"

All I could do was laugh at her reaction. Grasping her hand, I pulled her in for a kiss, but we were interrupted a moment later when the Uber driver honked.

"What's his problem?" Gianna snapped, affecting her patented glower.

The guy probably wanted to leave, but we were in his way. Regardless, nothing could wreck my mood today. I popped Mama's trunk and put our bags in the back while Gianna got the keys out of the console in the front. Once the Subaru was locked up tight, we headed for the football field.

At the entrance, I flashed the two blue tickets, then we were engulfed in a sea of people.

"Emerson!" Tia Camilia called as we wandered, looking for my family. They'd set themselves up in the second to last row of bleachers.

With my hand on Gi's back, I guided her up the steps, weaving through people until we reached them.

"Tia Cam, Tio Paulo, this is Gianna." I nodded. "Gi. This is my aunt and uncle."

My aunt wasn't shy about her appraisal of Gianna. She looked her up and down, then looked back at me with a slight brow raise and a tip of her lips. Approval.

My uncle just smirked. Another win.

The ceremony was shorter than I thought it would be, and before I knew it, we were all back at the house.

Everyone had piled out of the car and headed inside already, leaving Gi and me to grab our stuff in peace. Thank fuck. I could use a minute alone with her.

After I pulled her in for a long, slow kiss, I slung my small duffel over my shoulder and grabbed her two bags. Then I led her up the pavers to the two-family house brimming with the comfort of home. The sensation was odd, since I'd never lived in this place, but I wouldn't question the blessing.

"My mom lives on the bottom floor, and my aunt and uncle live on the second floor." When I signed with the Diamond Hawks, I used the bulk of the bonus they offered as a down payment for the two-family house for Mama and her sister. A year later, when the insurance money from my dad's accident finally came in, my mom offered to pay me back, but I refused. Instead, she used it to pay off the rest of mortgage, and in the eight and a half years since, they had turned the place into a home.

Tio's green thumb had the gardens blooming, even this early in the summer. A huge tree with a tire swing hung in the front yard, and the porch was full of rockers.

"It's so cute." Gi glanced up at me out of the corner of her eye. "And I love the yellow with the brick."

"Jeez, old man. You're slow as hell. Should I help you?" From the doorway, Andre reached out to grab a bag. "Shit, what's in this, rocks?"

"Maybe." Gi smirked and batted her eyes. "Never know what a woman will need."

I chuckled.

"Fucked," my brother mouthed to me.

"Gianna's staying upstairs with us," my uncle said when I headed down the hall that led to my room.

"What?" I spun on my heel and zeroed in on my mother.

"We have the sheets you had the Amazon man drop off, and we put them on her bed up there."

Their daughter was a year older than Andre and lived in an apartment across town now, so they had an empty room, but I'd never considered having Gi sleep anywhere but with me.

"No free milk," my brother joked.

"Tell that to Bels," Yvette teased.

Isabella's eyes widened. "No way. I was the one home last night while Vet was out. Tell me, Vet, was that Todd's car I saw drop you off?"

Yevette blushed.

"Wait, what?" At the mention of his friend's name, Andre shot a glare at Isabella, then turned it on Yvette.

"Don't think you can get away with shit because of their chaos." Tia Camilia raised a brow and pointed at the bag I had just slipped into my unofficial room in the house.

With a sigh, I picked it up again.

"Em," Gi said, shifting on her feet.

Dammit. My family was extra, and she didn't know them well enough to understand the dynamic, so she was beginning to panic.

"Fine," I said, holding her bag out to my brother. "Take them up."

"Me?" he asked, rearing back.

"Yeah. I'm old, remember?" I shoved the bag into his chest. "Stairs are bad for my knees."

The curse was on the tip of his tongue, but before he could let it fly, my mom whacked him with the spoon in her hand. "No, sir."

Wincing, he snatched the second bag and headed out the door and upstairs.

"I'll give you a tour." My mother set her spoon down, then took Gianna's hand and pulled her past me down the hall to my sister's room.

The place wasn't huge, so it would be a quick tour. She and Yvette had bedrooms on this floor. Along with the guest room for when I visited, which they also used as a second living room. Andre and Isabella had bedrooms and a shared bathroom in the basement.

"Your mother is already in love with her and the idea of you two giving her grandkids." My aunt sighed, her eyes going soft.

I cracked my knuckles, ignoring the heat that crept up my neck. "Tia, I've been clear. We're friends."

"Friends who sleep in the same bed?" Tio chuckled. "Weren't you just arguing with your mother about that?"

So on-brand for Tio to cut through the bullshit.

My heart clenched, but I locked an easy expression in place. "We'll be going in two different directions in a few months."

"Anything on a contract for next season?" he asked.

I shook my head, the ease slipping.

"Estúpidos dirigiendo el equipo," my aunt muttered.

That was the issue, though. Every person I'd told had sworn that Beckett Langfield and Cortney Miller were idiots if they didn't bring me back. But from my experience, that couldn't be true. In the time I'd been with the Revs, the pair had never even come close to making a poor decision. If they didn't bring me back, it was because I wasn't bringing what they were looking for to the table. Not only did they recognize skill and potential in players, but Miller was very focused on team dynamic. He knew his shit, and that's what cut even more harshly. I'd worked my ass off to be the teammate who could always be counted on, yet I was pretty certain either they didn't see it or I'd been focusing on the wrong priorities.

The basement door opened, and Mama appeared, still dragging Gianna by the arm.

"And this is my favorite space. See this?" She pointed to the brick fireplace. "It works, and not on that dumb switch that people have now. My house smells like a wood fire all winter."

I bit back a laugh. I wasn't sure if that was something to brag about.

But Gianna's smile was genuine, not amused. "I'm obsessed with working fireplaces. I've always wanted one."

Every time she mentioned a detail like that, my brain adjusted the picture of her future I'd created. Automatically, a fire crackled in the fireplace of her dream house in my mind.

"Oh, whoa." Gianna's face went slack with shock as she stepped up to the painting on the wall in the corner.

"Oh, yes. That is such a lovely picture of Lang Field. It was a gift from Emerson." My mother folded her hands at her waist and beamed.

With my heart in my throat, I watched Gianna, unsure of how she would take this. I'd gifted several of her paintings and drawings over the last couple of years, but I'd never told her I was doing it.

Gianna ran a finger along the frame, and my body tightened in anticipation. "Emerson gave it to you?"

"Mmm. Maybe a year ago?" My mom shrugged, oblivious to the significance. "He's always obsessed with the most random things. Somewhere along the way, he decided this artist—I don't know how to pronounce the name—Gano?" My mother frowned. "Anyway, he became fixated on this artist's work. I can't blame him, I suppose. The emotion in the painting is impressive."

"The dynamic she created in the way she depicted the stadium," I said, my voice hoarse. "How she portrays the loneliness of the person on the way, the person who's looking in on the crowd. The way the loneliness is expressed in water. The 'not quite in' vibe." I took a breath. "I feel that."

"I just think it's pretty." Yevette shrugged, head tilted and eyes squinted like she was trying to see the deeper meaning but having no luck.

With an audible swallow, Gi dropped her hand from the frame.

She turned toward me, her eyes brimming with awe and acceptance and a sense of being seen. With amazement and surprise, maybe because her painting was prominently displayed in the home of someone she'd never met until today. Disbelief that my family could love the piece without knowing she'd created it. Gratitude for the moment she clearly hadn't expected.

The relief that washed through me made me wobble. This moment was what I needed. A sign that she was open to the idea of sharing her work with the world. She just needed a push.

I closed the distance between us and brought my lips to her ear. "So fucking talented."

Blinking hard, she tucked her face into my shoulder. Still flying high after her reaction, I wrapped her up and held her close. It felt so good, like this was where she belonged.

"Now that that's done, we all pitch in to get ready for Bels's party," my mother announced, just as Andre returned.

"I have to help?" Isabella whined, her shoulders slumping dramatically.

"Of course you have to help. You're the reason we're doing this. You insisted everyone celebrate you." Andre threw out the words almost too fast to catch.

She huffed and crossed her arms over her chest.

"I swear to God," he said, "if you don't help, I'm posting that video I took the other day and tagging you."

"Uh, I look gross. You can't do that."

"Then help."

"I hate you." With that, she stomped away.

My mother yelled at them both in rapid-fire Spanish. I glanced down at Gi's face to make sure she wasn't overwhelmed by the madness, but instead of finding apprehension, all I found was a mischievous smirk. Like she found the chaos funny instead of too much.

And by the end of the day, it was clear that she not only found them funny, but was totally comfortable in the chaos. Even when I needed to translate, she never got overwhelmed. She just fit in with them like she'd been here all along.

And that night, as I lay on my back on the pull-out sofa, staring at the ceiling in the room we called mine when I was home, that sense of home had disappeared. I twisted, tugging at the sheet, frustrated. Normally, I felt settled here.

This was ridiculous. We had plenty of issues with no easy solutions, but this was a problem I could fix. If I couldn't sleep in this bed knowing Gi was a floor above me, then I'd go to her.

I was a grown-ass man; my mother could deal. I snapped the covers back and surveyed the door for a moment. Ultimately, I decided to go for the window. Mama would deal better if she didn't know.

In less than a minute, I had it open, and I hopping out onto the porch railing. From there, the pull up to the porch roof was nothing. Six feet later, I tapped on her window.

Gi pushed it opened, her brows pulled low. "Emerson? What are you doing?"

I ducked inside and pulled her close. "Apparently, I'm stealing milk."

Emerson
32

Andre: I see how it is. Didn't even wake me to say goodbye.

Bels: I saw him go into your room and jump on you.

Vet: You told him to get out.

Bels: We all heard you.

> Me: You all knew what time my flight left. Those who love me got up to see me off.

Andre: Drama much?

Bels: Plus, he wanted to get his girlfriend on the train.

> Me: Not my girlfriend.

Andre: Keep telling yourself that.

Andre: GIF of a river in Africa

Vet: Yup totally in denial.

Vet: GIF of the word duh

Bels: Well I love her.

Vet: Me too.

Bels: I vote she stays.

Me: GIF of guy shaking his head

Andre: Dude that girl has you sprung. Don't deny it.

Me: GIF of a middle finger

Vet: I'm telling Mom.

Andre: Grow up.

Bels: She's grown up enough for Todd.

Andre: Not funny.

Vet: He drove me home. That's actually all that happened.

Andre: I'm aware. Trust me. I already talked to him.

Bels: He could be lying. Look at Em. He's not telling Chris that he's totally into Gi. And for the record Em I totally saw you climb onto the porch roof last night.

Vet: This conversation isn't getting us anywhere.

Me: Agreed.

Andre: Fine.

Bels: You all are no fun. I'll stop but...PS - I got Gi's number so I'll be texting her.

Vet: GIF of a crowd laughing

Emerson
33

"Avery said she got them."

"Cool." I ran a hand over my face. I still had no idea if I was doing the right thing. "And you're cool with me selling them?"

Chris shrugged. "You're giving the money to her, so yeah, I'm okay with it. Though *she* might hate you for it. She has a thing about selling her stuff."

My stomach sank. That was my worry. Though my perspective was a little different. Chris thought that she didn't want to sell them. In reality, she was afraid no one would buy them. But he was right. She might hate me for making the decision for her. Because Gi was stubbornly independent and hated vulnerability.

I sighed. "If they sell, then she'll see that her art is valuable. That people enjoy it. And if that happens, then it'll be worth it, even if she hates me."

We only had a short time left anyway. August was creeping up on us too quickly. She hadn't found an affordable place yet, but as much as I hated the idea of her leaving, the auction would give her the cushion she'd need to move back to New York and get her life back on track.

Time wasn't my friend these days. Not at home, and not on the field. With each passing day, my time with the Revs was running out

239

and Gi was getting closer to moving out. Since I was on the road as much as I was home, I spent every free moment while I was in Boston with her. Watching TV, talking, making dinner, making her come with my tongue or my hand or my dick. Any way and anywhere I could.

The mixture of emotions I felt was overwhelming. Trying to enjoy the time with her while holding a piece of myself back. Trying to keep myself at the top of my game so maybe Beckett Langfield would see me as an asset while trying not get my hopes up that I'd get the honor of putting on the blue pinstripes next season. It was a tightrope.

"When are we telling her?" Chris's question jarred me back to the visiting team locker room at the Bandits' stadium in Denver.

"What are we telling who?" Kyle asked.

"Gi." Chris hardly looked at him as he scrolled on his phone. "Emerson got Wren to list some of her artwork in an auction next week. I had Avery and a moving crew get the rest of my crap out of the apartment, and while they were there, they picked up the paintings." Chris dropped his phone onto his chair. "We should let Wilson know that a bunch of us are going. It's a day game, but they like to know when we do cultured shit so they can promote that we aren't just dumbasses who can hit a ball. Plus, I think Asher and I are going to leave a day later for the all-star game."

I nodded. Not that I was going to the all-star game. That was Chris, Asher Price, and Mason Dumpty.

Chris moved across the room to his fiancée's father's office.

"So..." Kyle shook his head and dropped into Chris's chair. "When are *you* going to tell *him*?"

I pressed down hard on the knuckles of my left hand and relished the way they cracked. "Tell who what?"

He snorted. "There are things men do for friends. Paying for drinks at the bar, maybe giving them a ride to the airport, if it's a normal hour and you've got nothing else to do. You might water their plants while they're on vacation..."

"I'd do any of that stuff for anyone."

He rolled his eyes. "That's true, but still. Even if we use you as the bar. Setting up an art auction to sell her work? That's *I'm sleeping with her and my dick isn't the only thing enjoying it* kind of shit."

Heat crept up my neck, and I let out a growl.

"And you're testy." Kyle was entirely too happy about my issues.

I sighed and hung my head. "Do you want to lie to him?"

Kyle shook his head. "Hell no."

"Then don't ask me a question you don't want to know the answer to."

Because somewhere along the way, vague answers and omissions had turned into lies and actively hiding shit from my best friend. Although I hated it, I wasn't willing to give Gi up yet, and I couldn't apologize or be remorseful if I wasn't sorry. So hopefully Chris would never find out. If he did? Then maybe it would be far enough down the road that I could fake an acceptable reaction.

"For the record, we aren't telling Gi about this until we get there." I had been forced to tell Chris and Avery. When Wren texted to tell me she needed to get them over to the auction for presale photos, I was in Minneapolis, so I had no choice but to ask for their help.

"Oh, this is going to be such a shit show." Kyle laughed. "Can I come?"

Gianna
34

"I WOULD HAVE MADE DINNER," I SAID, LOOKING AT EMERSON WORKING IN the kitchen. "You had a game today."

"I like feeding people." Shrugging, he held up a spoon for me.

"What is it?" I asked, eyeing the yellow mush on the spoon and taking half a step back.

"Mofongo." He chuckled at my reaction.

Returning to where I had been, I forced myself to unscrunch my nose.

"It's not poison. It's garlic mashed plantain. Try it." He lifted the spoon higher.

I parted my lips for a small taste. It wasn't bad. Like a potato, but richer. It didn't have a lot of flavor, but the garlic gave it a savory taste.

"It's good."

"Chris likes it. And he loves the fried pork on top."

Apparently, my brother had invited himself over for dinner tonight. He and Avery had done it a few times since I'd moved in, so it wasn't totally out of the blue. But it had been a while since they were here. And rather than just showing up like they usually do, they actually gave Em a heads-up.

"Can I do anything for you?" The plates were stacked by the stove, and he looked like he had the food managed, but I'd feel guilty if he did all the work himself.

In true Emerson fashion, he glanced over his shoulder and waggled his brow.

Huffing, I shook my head. "If Chris is on his way, then anything that results in that kind of happy face is off the table."

He full-on laughed, the sound one I'd come to love. And it managed to always make me respond with an answering smile of my own. Even on a bad day. Not that today was bad. The last few days had been uneventful. I hadn't had to deal with Jake at all, and I'd worked on a logo for a pitch next week and a full branding project that was due the week after.

I had finalized the logo for Dylan a few days before, and she was thrilled with it, so that was off my plate. The only stressor still eating at me was the apartment situation. But at this point, I could admit that I was actively putting off the hunt. Every time I thought about it, the idea of locking into a lease gave me a stomachache. So I was in full-on avoidance. Though I had to face reality soon. Eventually, my brother would want to get rid of this place, since he was living with Avery.

Emerson had turned back to the stove, his broad, bare shoulders on display. A shirt was in a heap on the counter for when Avery and Chris arrived, but he rarely wore a shirt at home, and I wasn't complaining. Until the idea of leaving popped up again. I had a lot of complaints about that.

"Is this more of a wine meal or beer?" I pulled open the fridge and ducked to peruse its contents.

"Beer," he said from behind me, "but I'll have water."

I grabbed an IPA out of the fridge for myself and filled a glass with water for him.

He'd probably prefer the beer, but lately, he'd been following his diet plan pretty strictly, only stealing a sip of my beer or wine here or there. His game was on fire, his on base percentage was the highest of his career, and he was leading the league in steals, but none of that stopped him from pushing himself. The lack of a contract was eating at him. And it hurt to know there was nothing I could do about it.

I popped the top of my beer, and as I set his water on the counter next to him, he snaked an arm out and pulled me in tight.

"One more before your brother gets here." His mouth settled against mine. But instead of the peck I anticipated, he cuffed the back of my neck, locking me in against him. He coaxed my lips open and invaded my mouth. Teasing me. Tempting me with an idea he had no time to follow through with.

With his other hand, he grabbed my ass, fingers biting into me as he squeezed. He slipped a thigh between my legs, and I rocked against him. The groan that vibrated deep in his chest in response to that move flipped my stomach. When he swatted my ass, I moaned.

Maybe we had time…

"Em." I whimpered against his lips.

Instead of tightening his grasp, he pulled back, releasing me.

"Hold that thought. Your brother's about to be here." He smirked.

I narrowed my eyes. "Ass."

He chuckled and kissed me one more time before turning back to the stove.

"I'm not sharing my beer now." I pulled it off the counter next to his water and moved around to sit on one of the stools at the high counter behind the sink.

"You wound me," he teased.

Behind me, the apartment door swung open. "Bambi! Where my mashed bananas at? My mouth has been watering all day," my brother called.

"You know," I called back, "since you moved all your stuff out, seems like you should give back your key."

Chris scowled as he walked into the open living area. "I still pay half the rent. That shit means I don't need to stand outside a door, waiting to be let in."

"They might want privacy, babe." Avery hopped up onto the barstool at the counter next to me.

"Who?" Chris whipped his head one way, glaring at me, then the other, so he could hit Em with the same expression. He pointed a finger between us. "Are you saying you need privacy from me?"

I forced myself not to react to that statement, but Emerson just chuckled.

He peered over his shoulder with a smirk. "Nah, man. Nothing you can't see. You see my dick all the time."

"Not by choice. Jesus," Chris muttered, shuffling to the fridge. "Wear clothes in the locker room, and we wouldn't have a problem." He bent at the waist and pulled out a beer.

Em shrugged. "I tried that. You called me weird."

"Hmm." Avery pressed her lips together like she was fighting a smile as she took the beer from my brother.

"You better not be picturing Bambi naked, Blondie," Chris growled.

She giggled. "No, I was picturing my dad's face when he has to deal with you all not wanting to wear clothes."

Emerson laughed again, and Chris huffed.

"Can I help?" Avery asked.

"Nah. Gi offered. She wants to see how I plate the mofongo."

That was entirely untrue. I hadn't said that at all, but I wasn't going to complain about spending a few minutes at his side. I loved that I was his go-to when he needed a hand.

"Are we watching a movie or a show or what?" Chris asked, moving across the room to the sectional and coffee table. The end tables were gone now.

Last week, Chris had moved out almost all of his stuff. It left the place feeling empty. Most of the pictures and paintings were gone, since they had been Chris's, and the stark walls made it feel too sterile.

Emerson had framed the skyline I'd painted when I first moved in, and that hung where the stadium used to be, but only half as many photos and books sat on the shelves now. And apart from the bed, Chris's room was completely empty of anything that wasn't mine.

"We've been watching *Foyle's War*."

The brightness in Emerson's eyes when he mentioned the show surprised me. He hadn't been thrilled with it when I first put it on.

"What?" Chris glared my way.

"It's a detective show set in World War II." It was something I had picked. So, of course, my brother would hate it.

"Why the hell would you watch that?" Chris asked. "Nothing about that sounds appealing."

"You know, I kinda thought that too, but it's got the feels, man." Emerson didn't turn away from the stove. "Not the tingles of a good happily ever after, but the emotion will choke you up."

Chris scoffed. "I'm not going to cry over a television show."

"I do sometimes. I love a good cry once in a while," Avery chirped.

"Me too," Emerson agreed.

In unison, Chris and I scoffed. And then glared at each other.

"It's funny how the two of you can be so different sometimes, and then others, you're practically the same person." Avery's bright blue eyes danced between my brother and me.

"I know, right?" Emerson laughed, the sound echoing around the kitchen.

The buzz of my phone on the counter stole my attention. It danced on the quartz as the firm's number flashed on the screen.

"We can watch whatever, but give me a sec. This might be important."

Normally I was pretty opinionated when it came to movies and TV shows, but tonight, I really didn't care what we watched. If Avery and Em chose some sappy romance, then I was okay with that. Emerson would love it, so I'd be happy that he was happy. And yes, I realized that made me almost as sappy as the stupid movie we'd be watching. But not many people in his life did things with the goal of making him happy, and I wanted to be someone who did. "Em and Avery, you pick."

My brother handed Avery the remote as I stepped down the hall and shut the bedroom door.

As I swiped the screen to answer, I braced myself, expecting Jake. "Hello?"

"Ms. Damiano?" A voice I didn't recognize greeted me.

"Yes?"

"This is Jonathan Whittemore."

My heart dropped right out of my chest. Why was the president of the company calling me?

"We met at the Boston Zoo event."

247

I cleared my throat. "Yes, I remember."

"I wanted to meet with you in person, but I've been advised that you're working remotely for another few weeks."

There was no official end date to my remote employment. We'd left it open-ended so I could return on my own time. But I wasn't going to correct the guy that was my super boss.

"What can I do for you, sir?"

"I'm not sure you've heard yet that Mr. Caderson and Doucette Design parted ways earlier today."

My lungs seized and my knees wobbled. Seriously? Jake had been fired? Zara mentioned that it would likely eventually happen, but the article wasn't slated to come out until next week. Zara had asked if I wanted to be a part of it, but I'd decided against it. The story here should revolve around the people who'd been brushed aside, whose ideas and designs had been credited to others. That was the story. Yes, I was one of those people, but there were many more, and if I was mentioned. I worried the focus would turn to the scorned girlfriend.

The long pause on the line meant I should speak.

"I hadn't heard."

"We kept it quiet." He sighed. "We're dealing with an issue regarding designs being poached, so to get ahead of the problem, we're reorganizing. We want designers, the artists, in management roles. Guiding and fostering our young talent. We want to have a very proactive approach."

Getting ahead? Meaning they'd been clued in to the article, so they were reacting? That didn't seem like being proactive. That seemed like damage control.

"Okay," I said carefully, scanning the room without really seeing anything. I loved the feel of this room. Between the heavy furniture, the family photos, and Revs gear, it was a soothing, comforting space. I took a deep breath and refocused on the conversation.

"We were impressed with how you handled the Boston Zoo's account. Not only the designs, but your interactions with the zoo's marketing team."

"Th-thank you." I stuttered the words, shocked by the compliment. At the zoo event, this man acted like he had no idea who I was, and so did every other person from Doucette in attendance. Besides Jake and Libby, of course.

"I will be honest," he said with a sigh, "there is some bad press headed our way. And although, through our own internal investigation, we noted that you could have joined the impending smear campaign, you didn't, and that shows loyalty."

An icky feeling started to crawl across my skin. I didn't like where this was headed.

"We appreciate and reward that kind of commitment to the organization, so we'd like to offer you a management role. You'd be overseeing the designers and meeting with clients."

They were offering me a promotion because I'd kept my mouth shut about Jake? The shudder that worked its way down my spine felt nothing like the kind I experienced around Emerson.

"Ms. Damiano?"

I cleared my throat. "Sorry, I'm just surprised." I rushed the words out.

"Understandable. When we floated your name, we hadn't realized you were working remotely. I just want to be clear that this isn't a remote position. But it comes with a drastic salary increase, and you'll receive a bonus for every project your team completes, not just for your own accounts."

"Right." I swallowed, the pressure in my chest making my breathing labored.

He threw out some numbers, and I shut my eyes. Because that kind of salary would easily make the apartments I'd looked at in New York affordable.

"I'll email an official offer, but why don't you take a few days to think it over? Let's set up a meeting for Monday morning. Say my office, eight thirty?"

"Sure," I agreed, because though he'd framed it as a suggestion, it was a directive. The five o'clock train would suck, but it would get me into New York on time. The end of the conversation was a blur. And then I was saying goodbye and promising to see him on Monday.

I swallowed past the boulder lodged in my throat and set the phone down on the bed. A job offer I didn't want from a company I didn't want to work for, but with a salary that would make life so much easier.

"Gi," my brother barked.

Heart lurching, I rushed out of the room and hurried down the hall. When I stepped into the living area, they were all sitting at the table, waiting for me.

"Did you just come out of Emerson's room?" My brother's brows jumped as he looked from me to the hallway and back again.

"Why would I be in his room?" I asked, even though that's exactly where I'd just come from. I hadn't even thought about it when I walked in there to take the call. I'd been sleeping in his room for weeks. Even when he wasn't home. I guess it was habit at this point.

Chris glared at me. Emerson lowered his focus to his plate. Avery eyed each one of us, her gaze calculating, before she jumped in.

"How can you possibly tell what room she was in? Can you even see either door?" Avery leaned across him. "Doesn't look like it from here."

"Whatever," Chris huffed and then waved at my seat. "Can we eat now?"

"Did we decide not to watch a movie?" I dropped into the chair next to Em.

"Avery wanted to sit at the table. What was the call about? Must have been important if you kept us waiting to eat," Chris said, but his shoulders relaxed as he took his first bite.

"Jake was fired," I mumbled, picking up my fork.

Emerson brought his ice water to his lips, but I swore he was smiling behind the glass.

"Good," Chris said.

"They offered me his job."

"That's great," Chris said, cracking the smallest smile.

On my other side, Emerson choked. He barely had his glass steady on the table before he launched into a coughing fit.

Snapping up straight, I whacked his back. "You okay?"

He nodded, and with one final cough, he turned to me. "They offered you his job?" His normally bright green eyes were a little muddy. It happened when he wore a yellow or beige like he was wearing now, but the contrast was so drastic in this moment that it made him seem sad.

"Did you take the job?" Chris demanded.

After I gave Emerson a quick scan, searching for what the issue could be, I turned back to my brother. "No. I said I'd think about it."

"What?" His fist fell to the table, rattling the dishes. "What's there to think about?"

A lot of things. Starting with how wrong it felt when he'd made the offer. I couldn't pinpoint the problem, but my gut was telling me to think it through.

"It's a big decision," I hedged and left it at that. I couldn't even begin to explain the way my intuition was nagging at me.

"It comes with a big raise, right?" Chris dropped his elbows to the table and hit me with his patented grumpy face. "More money means you can afford a place in New York. You'd be stupid to say no."

"She hasn't said no, and it's reasonable for her to take time to think it through," Emerson gritted out, his jaw rigid and his eyes harder than I'd ever seen them. I wasn't used to the look. Mad Emerson wasn't a norm.

While I thought Chris would be as shocked as I was about Emerson's obvious change in demeanor, he only scoffed, like he hadn't even noticed it. "Since when do you believe that? You're the king of just act on an idea."

My heart panged at the flash of hurt in Em's eyes. Sure, he could be impulsive, but typically only when it came to run-of-the-mill things that didn't matter. Like jumping up to hug someone when he was excited or offering his help without a second of hesitation. But saying he never thought things through was grossly unfair.

With my hands balled into fists on my lap, I forced myself to focus on the table while I worked to get my temper under control.

My focus shifted to Emerson's white plate, only then noticing that he wasn't eating the same thing we were. But the grilled chicken and broccoli made sense. He wouldn't have fried pork when he was focused on being at the top of his game.

"No," I gritted out, throwing figurative daggers at my brother.

"No?" His eyes flashed with the same kind of challenge I'd seen from him all my life.

"No, he's not the king of just act on an idea," I growled.

That single sentence made my brother sit back, his jaw dropping.

"Don't pretend to be shocked. Why do you think you two are such good friends? You are both focused and have consciously made choices and sacrifices that have driven your careers."

A warm palm covered my fist in my lap. At his touch, my body released most of the tension it was holding tight to. Emerson slipped his fingers into mine and gave me a squeeze, silently communicating his gratitude. I couldn't look at him. If I did, I had no doubt my brother would pick up on the fact that he was holding my hand.

"And now I'm taking time to make smart choices with my own career. So don't give either of us shit." My voice was calmer, but I kept my expression hard.

Chris worked his jaw back and forth, his eyes moving between his best friend and me. After he'd scrutinized each of us a couple of times, Emerson went rigid next to me.

"Chris, she's right. You wouldn't want her to jump into a shitty job. So let's eat, and maybe the hangry will go away." Avery rubbed my brother's shoulder. "Anyway, congrats on the offer, Gianna. If you decide it's what you want to do, I have no doubt you'll be great at it."

"I never said she wouldn't be," Chris mumbled.

Emerson was still wound tight, like he was ready to spring at any second and he'd yet to release my hand. The awkward way he'd positioned his arm so the contact wasn't visible above the table had to be uncomfortable, so I loosened my hold, ready to release him, but he kept his fingers locked around mine.

Across from me, Avery was forcing a smile so hard that her face must hurt.

"Oh, guess what?" she chirped.

It took a pretty decent amount of willpower not to snap at her. The atmosphere was still tense, and my defenses were still raised high, but none of that was her fault, and I could appreciate her efforts to smooth things over.

"What?" I fought against the resting bitch face, shooting for cheerful.

My efforts must have been a little too over-the-top, because Emerson squeezed my hand and cleared his throat in a way that sounded almost like a chuckle.

I side-eyed him, and sure enough, he was totally fighting a laugh. His eyes danced, and he finally released my hand to cover his mouth.

I rolled my eyes. Me smiling wasn't that funny.

"You actually want us to guess, Blondie, or are you going to tell us?" Chris shoved another bit of pork into his mouth.

She smirked. "Sorry. No. I just got distracted." With a shake of her head, she straightened in her seat. "Wren's going to run her first art auction this weekend, and she has extra tickets."

"Cool." I finally dug into my dinner. The moment the pork hit my tongue, the most incredible flavor burst in my mouth. Damn. No wonder Chris liked this so much. Quickly, I scooped another bite.

"She's worried it'll be an empty house, so she wants us to come fill the seats. Are you available on Sunday night?" Avery asked. "Kyle is coming too, and so are Asher and Zara."

I shrugged. Sounded like fun.

Beside me, Emerson cracked his knuckles. "I told Wren I would go."

"Yay!" Avery tapped the tips of her fingers in front of her chin, smiling wide. "We'll all go."

Her reaction was a bit overzealous, but my brother just smiled at her like she was the cutest thing he'd ever seen. Whatever. At least the tension had faded.

After dinner, Avery even convinced Chris to watch one episode of *Foyle's War* before he was ready to go.

"Hey, Bambi," Chris called as they were putting their shoes on in the entryway. "Did you decide what you want to do about signing a new lease?"

Emerson's shoulders sagged, the movement so small, I was positive my brother had missed it. "I'm not going to lock into another year."

He couldn't while his contract was still up in the air. Didn't Chris know that?

"Okay, cool." Chris held out a fist. "I'll let them know we're done after October."

"Sounds good." Emerson forced a smile and pounded my brother's knuckles.

Seriously? My teeth ground with so much force my jaw throbbed. Did Chris not realize how insensitive he was being?

The second Chris pulled the door shut behind him and Avery, I turned to Emerson.

"Have you made any more decisions about what you're doing after October?" I asked.

Emerson shook his head. "I'll probably spend some time in Jersey while I wait for another team to pick me up."

"Does Chris know you might not play for the Revs next season?"

"I'm not sure." He gave a half-hearted shrug. "It's common knowledge that my contract is up. The baseball world has been talking about it. A lot of people are speculating that I'll end up in Vancouver." He swallowed audibly, his throat working, and averted his gaze.

That was far. My heart hurt for him. The unknown, as well as the thought of starting over, seemed awful and scary.

I shuffled up to him, and without hesitation, he wrapped his arms around me. With my head on his chest, I listened to the steady pounding of his heart.

"But it doesn't seem like I'm any team's first choice." The words were soft and laced with hurt.

I pulled back and studied him, but he looked past me out at the skyline, his eyes flooding with emotion. "That's not true."

He pulled back, looking me straight in the eye. "Gi. It's okay. It's part of the game." He released me and stepped away. "Besides, I'm used to it."

The statement was gutting. Because he meant it, and he was okay with it. He'd learned to expect it. But he deserved to be put first once in a while.

"After my dad died, my mom had to focus on my siblings. They were so young and needed her more. Then we moved when I was in high school. Worst time to lose all your friends." He cracked his knuckles. "And I was the gawky weirdo. Trust me, no one liked me." The chuckle that escaped him was dark and so unfamiliar. "And then I moved to triple-A and was the baby of the group."

He sighed and scanned the horizon, so lost and in so much pain. I'd seen hints of the hurt he kept buried, but this was the first time he was purposely showing me all of it.

"Literally, my first real friend since I was fourteen was your brother. And now he has Avery."

"But—"

He held up a hand, cutting me off. "I'm so damn happy for him. Because she is everything he needs."

"But you quickly became less."

"I'm not sure I ever ranked above you or Pop." He swallowed. "And I shouldn't have. But you weren't around."

"She was."

He shrugged. "I don't have the 'it' factor to be a fan or coach's favorite. Those are your once-in-a-lifetime stars. But I'm here, playing on a professional team. I'm lucky to be on the list at all. I don't need to top it. I'm not anyone's first choice. But I'll say it again. I'm lucky to just be on the list."

"After all that, how can you be this way?"

He cocked his head to the side, his lips turning down in a confused frown.

"Happy. Grateful." I gave in to the instinct to glare. Why the hell hadn't anyone ever fought for him? He clearly wasn't going to do it. "Even when all you get is scraps."

His shoulders sank. "I don't know how else to be."

And that's what made him so incredible.

"That's good, because I never want you to change." I swallowed back the emotion rising up inside me. Damn if I didn't want to cry for this man. But I wouldn't ruin the moment. Because when I thought back to this time with him, I wanted to remember the perfection and not tears.

Emerson
35

I walked out of the bathroom with a towel around my waist, and my heart tripped over itself. Gi stood across the room, dressed in a black halter dress. Her hair was pinned up so it cascaded down her back in big, loose curls. The smooth skin of her bare shoulders and back contrasted with the black of the dress that tucked in at her waist and flared over her hips, draping perfectly over my favorite ass on the planet. And damn, her legs looked good in those sky-high heels.

The only time they looked better was when they were slung over my shoulders or wrapped around my waist.

I stalked toward her, eating up the space between us until I cupped one shoulder, relishing the sensation of her silky skin against my callused palm. Dipping in close, I pressed my lips to her neck.

In response, she tilted her head, giving me better access.

"You're stunning," I whispered against her skin. "Every guy in the place will have their sights set on you."

"You're ridiculous." She snorted delicately.

My chest pinched at the way she brushed off the compliment. She didn't get it. She didn't see what I saw when I looked at her.

257

Beautiful, talented, determined, caring, and fierce. A complete package of a woman.

My heart clenched, because she was so close to slipping away.

Tomorrow was the deadline. She'd have to give the stupid douche firm an answer about the job in New York. And although she hadn't come out and told me she wasn't taking it—not that I'd asked; the last thing I wanted to do was push—she hadn't said she wasn't either.

After tonight, she'd have money from the auction as well. That would probably come into play when she had to make that final decision. Wren had texted yesterday to tell me she'd received early interest in Gi's work. The Puff painting had been so popular that they'd raised the starting bid on it.

"Are you planning on wearing a towel?" She smirked, skimming a hand over my abs.

I would absolutely not wear a towel to the big night she had no idea was *her* big night. But teasing her was in my wheelhouse, so I shrugged. "It's more comfortable."

Lips pursed, she squinted at me. "People will be there."

"And?"

She crossed her arms over her chest, causing her breasts to lift into the deep V of her dress. I lifted a finger to trace the swell, but she batted my hand away.

"There's no way you'd let me wear just a towel anywhere."

My smile bloomed, along with a warmth in my chest. "Is this your way of saying you're feeling possessive of me?"

She rolled her eyes and opened her mouth, but before she could retort, the doorbell chimed. I turned, ready to answer it, but she grabbed my arm.

"*I'm dressed.* I'll get it," she huffed, every word dripping with exasperation.

I chuckled as she sauntered out of the room, taking the time to drink her in from behind, but my laughter died when her voice echoed down the hall.

"Why are you here?"

Her tone was full of disgust, which meant it couldn't be her brother or her dad. And there was no way she'd talk to her friends that way either. Linc and Mila were meeting us at the auction house, so they were in town, but she didn't know that, and they wouldn't ruin the surprise by coming over beforehand.

"I hate surprises."

I winced. That didn't bode well for my night. Maybe I'd be better off telling her before we left. Holding my breath, I moved down the hall to get a look at the unhappy surprise that had shown up.

At the sound of a man clearing his throat, my back went ramrod straight. Who the fuck was here?

"My attorney said I should get you your money back. So I brought a check."

I gritted my teeth and pushed away the bolt of rage that hit me when his voice registered. Jake.

"You drove three hours to hand deliver it? Why didn't you just stick it in the mail?"

I padded down the hall quietly and hovered just out of sight. The gentlemanly thing to do would be to give her privacy, but every instinct told me to storm out there, lick her, and yell *mine*. So standing out of sight wasn't that bad in the scheme of things. I wasn't charging out and peeing a circle around her.

"I wanted to see you."

My entire body went from tense to full-on alert.

"You look amazing, Gigi."

I wasn't sure what I wanted to do first: cut out his tongue for talking to her or remove his eyes from their sockets. I could envision the exact expression on the dude's face. It was the same one he'd worn when he saw her at the zoo. The one that made me want to break his nose.

"I missed you. My life has gone to shit since we broke up. I know I made a mistake…"

Hands balled into tight fists, I warred with myself. She was fierce and independent. She'd want to handle this on her own. My head knew that. My heart was really struggling, though.

I took a deep breath to calm my racing heart, but it did no good.

"Mistake?" That small whisper made my heart skip.

There was no way she'd fall for his bullshit. She wouldn't. She couldn't. The two seconds of silence that followed that one word felt like an eternity. My heart hammered so hard I was worried it'd beat its way out of my chest.

"Well, isn't that…disgusting?" she snapped.

Instantly, my shoulders sagged in relief, and I let out the breath I hadn't realized I'd been holding.

"What the hell is wrong with you?"

I could picture the look on her face. Chin up, eyes heated. I couldn't help but smile.

"You have a pregnant fiancée at home. Who, for some unknown reason, *likes* you. And you're here telling me, the woman you cheated on for seven months with said fiancée, that you miss me?"

"Don't you miss me?"

"No!" She scoffed, clearly thinking the question was as absurd as I thought it was. That one word gave me all the happy tingles. "Not at all. You should go."

"Gigi." His voice dropped low.

"Don't touch me."

Those three words were all it took for my vision to go red. That was my line. She'd made it clear to him, and not only wasn't he leaving, but now he'd put a hand on her.

I turned the corner and strode right up behind her.

"She said you should go," I growled, reining in the urge to knock him out.

Gi turned, her eyes snapping to mine.

I found her waist and grabbed hold of her, my fingers biting into the fabric of her dress.

"I can handle Jake," she huffed at me.

"Well aware, Mariposa. But I still have that being a gentleman problem that you put up with so patiently for me."

A small laugh slipped from her lips.

I stepped around her and loomed over him, forcing him to back out the door. "Bye, Jake." Once he was over the threshold, I pushed the door closed. Then I spun and took Gianna's face in my hands, pressing my lips to hers so I could prove to myself that she was still here and still mine.

I pulled her into my body. "You deserve so much better than that idiot."

"I've learned that." She smiled against my lips. There was a peace in the fact that although she'd been annoyed and possibly exasperated by his appearance, she didn't seem to care. At all. "And you need to get dressed so we can see some art."

"Yup." I pulled back. "Looking forward to it. One of my favorite artists is going to be there," I joked as I turned and headed down the hall.

"Who is that?" she called from where she was still standing in the entryway.

"You'll see." I kept my tone light, but unease swirled in my stomach again, because she might not be smiling later.

Gianna
36

"You okay?" I asked as Emerson parked the car in the parking garage under the auction house.

"I'm good," he assured me, though he didn't smile. He looked formal in his navy suit and white dress shirt. He'd skipped the tie, but he still looked buttoned-up. Not only were the clothes out of place—though I wouldn't complain; the man looked good—but the normal lightness that surrounded him was missing.

The man had been tense since Jake had shown up. And there was an edge to his kiss. Lately, every kiss was laced with a hint of goodbye. But I didn't want to say goodbye.

His strong hands were locked on the wheel, and he oozed competence. There was a security in the certainty with which Emerson moved through the world. Even when he was impulsive, he was confident. Being so close to that strength bolstered me in ways I'd never known existed.

Once he'd helped me out of the car—insisting it was the gentlemanly thing to do—we walked up the ramp to the street. As I reached for the entrance, his hand brushed mine. He simply raised a brow, the look sending sparks through me, and I let him open the door. The way Emerson approached each task made it clear that he didn't think me

263

less capable than he was. No, he went out of his way for me because he wanted to.

He loved showering people he cared about with physical affection like a hug or a squeeze of the hand. He was touchy. It was still foreign to me, since I'd grown up in a home where hugs weren't common, despite how loving and supportive Pop was in every other way. But even though it hadn't been my norm for so long, Emerson's touch quieted this yearning inside me.

He also showered people with love through his actions. Ways he communicated his feelings without words. And those in particular locked tight in my chest.

I picked up a program and turned, ready to head in, but he grasped my wrist and locked it between his strong fingers. Forcing me to face him.

"Before we go in," he said with a thick swallow, "I need to tell you something."

My heart panged in my chest at the anxiety and fear etched into every line on his face. "Okay."

He sucked in a deep breath, and when he opened his mouth, his words poured out fast. "I probably should have told you before now, but I worried you'd say no. And I want this moment for you. And I know you want it for you too."

I tipped my head, confused, as my pulse quickened.

"The artist I'm excited to see featured tonight is…" He took a breath. "It's you."

My lung seized up as I gaped at him. "What?"

"Your work is on the block tonight."

Wobbling, I grasped his arm to steady myself. My paintings were here? He released my hand and cupped my upper arms, like he was worried I'd fall over. Or maybe bolt. With a roll of my shoulders, I stepped out of his gasp and flipped through the program.

Page eight. I cleared my throat, but it was no use. My heart had firmly lodged itself there.

There in front of me were three of my paintings. One of Puff. The second was of the stadium. The third, New York City in the snow. Each had a price listed as well. The New York street scene was listed for five hundred dollars, but the one of Puff was four thousand. A burst of air escaped me. Who would pay that?

"How?" I blinked at the page, then up at him.

Guilt emanated from him, in the look on his face, in his eyes. "I gave them to Wren."

Bits and pieces of the conversation I'd had with her about selling my work floated through my brain. She'd asked…

But what if no one wanted them? My heart hammered in my ears, and my chest felt tight. A warm palm pressed to my cheek and Emerson tilted my head, forcing me to focus on him.

"Trust me. You are talented." His green eyes were flooded with nothing but open honesty. "Trust *yourself*. And your own skill. Gi, the auction house was swamped with so much early interest that they upped the starting bid for the painting of Puff."

"What?"

"She listed each one for five hundred originally, but they got so many calls once she displayed them on their website that she raised the price before they even moved to the block."

My body had gone numb, and though I could hear his words, I was struggling to comprehend the meaning. This couldn't be real.

"You are amazing and talented," he pleaded with me. "Trust yourself."

Stunned speechless, all I could do was stare at the page in the book. Three of my paintings were listed there. Up for auction. I swallowed, thinking about all the hours of painting and sketching that had gone into each one. The hundreds of pictures I'd made. My breath caught when I zeroed in on a name. Four simple letters. Gano. Listed as an up-and-coming artist in the Boston area.

"I believe in you. But if you don't want to do this, then let's go." He pulled me toward the door.

Finally finding my wits, I yanked back, holding us in place. "It's always been a dream," I whispered.

Head tilted, he angled in closer. "What?"

"This has always been a dream." One that I only voiced to my mother. One that seemed more like a child's daydream than a possibility, so it had lived deep inside.

Breaths coming quickly, I studied him. This gorgeous man in front of me. No one had ever been as excited about my painting as Emerson was. He was more passionate about every single work of art than even I was. I hid them away. He framed them and put them on display. He gifted them. He offered them up for sale when I was too scared to do it myself. He was the support I never knew I needed.

"Thank you." I choked out the words and leaned into him.

Automatically, he wrapped his arms around me. "So we are going in?" He sounded so unsure.

But I nodded.

"Hell yeah we are." He held me closer for another moment, and when he released me, he put a hand to the small of my back and guided me down a hallway.

We'd barely made it through the next set of doors when Hannah appeared.

"Let me grab a picture," she said. The directive was clearly a demand, rather than a suggestion.

"Here?" I asked, my voice still shaky.

"Yes, I like to document it when our boys look cultured. Posting pictures of them at events like this one and other formal shit. Makes them look like they know more than just how to throw a ball." She held up her phone. "So hop over there by the art and smile."

"Dance, monkey, dance." Emerson clapped his hands and spun in a circle, making Hannah laugh.

I rolled my eyes. He was such a ham.

"Come here." He tucked an arm around my waist.

"Me?" I asked, rearing back.

Hannah stepped back and held up her phone, nodding. "Pose with the handsome baseball player."

"Wait, you're posting this on social media?" I asked, my feet locked on the floor. "I'm not sure I should be in the picture."

"If anyone should be in a picture tonight, it's you." Emerson yanked me by the waist and positioned me where Hannah wanted us to be. Lowering his head, he whispered, "I don't give a shit about the social media post. I don't give a shit about seeming cultured. But I give *a lot* of shits about you. And that's what tonight is about. You." As he

266

stood to his full height, his green eyes shone bright. "So smile," he said, tucking me into his body.

Giving in, I placed a hand on his chest and smiled for Hannah.

"That was perfect." She smirked at her phone's screen. "Culture achieved. Thanks, Em."

"Anytime, bebé," he called over his shoulder as he led me away.

My entire body shuddered at the word, and he froze mid-step.

"What's wrong?"

"Why?" I whispered, standing stock still in the middle of the doorway to the massive auction room.

He blinked down at me, his lips pulled down at the corners.

"Why is everyone baby but me?" I whispered.

With one side of his bottom lip caught between his teeth, he surveyed the crowded room, and instead of stepping in, he pulled me off to the side by the bathrooms.

"Look at me," he demanded. When I couldn't, he used two fingers to tip my chin up. "Bebé is anyone. A dime dozen. Could be a friend or a stranger. She doesn't matter." He swallowed. "You, Gi." He shook his head. "You could never be just anyone."

As his words sank in, my stomach flipped.

"From the second we met, I knew you were special. You were my butterfly. Always meant to soar." His smile was soft. "You just needed some time and some Boston air to come out of the cocoon." With a slow breath in, he studied my face, his eyes warm and full of affection. "But Mariposa—*butterfly*," he said, "you are soaring."

Butterfly. He'd been calling me that for as long as I'd known him. It just became the norm, and I never wondered why. I shut my eyes, fighting back emotion. Because fuck. I'd gotten upset, and once again, he'd proven there was no reason to be. This man was far and away the best one I knew.

"I didn't need Boston air," I whispered. "Just you."

The corner of his mouth kicked up. "So you want to go in now? I promise to work on using bebé less. I didn't realize it bothered you, or I would have stopped long ago."

I shook my head. "Let them be your bebés." I swallowed. "As long as I'm your only mariposa."

He brushed a thumb over my cheek. "Always and forever."

And once again, nothing about our connection felt casual.

The moment we finally stepped into the auction room, my heart leaped, and I took off as fast as my shoes would let me.

"Oh my gosh!" Linc and Eli were dressed in white suits, and Mila wore a gorgeous blue dress. "I cannot believe you're here." I glanced over my shoulder and found Emerson sauntering up behind me. "You are full of surprises today."

"Like we'd miss your big day." Linc tilted and peered around me, taking Emerson in. "And there is the man of my dreams."

"You're an asshole," Eli muttered.

"I'm *your* asshole." He smirked at his boyfriend.

Eli's face didn't change. He simply leaned over to kiss me on the cheek. "Congrats, babe." Then he shifted his attention to Emerson and held out a hand. "I'm Eli, the very patient boyfriend."

"I heard we're doing Spain Jazz, as a throuple, in the fall," Emerson teased.

Eli dropped his head back and groaned. "Oh hell, that's why he loves you."

The whole group laughed so loudly the people around us turned to stare.

"I'll get the drinks," Eli muttered once we'd composed ourselves.

"Bubbly for the girl of the hour," Linc shouted after him.

"I'm going to…" Emerson nodded at the Revs players who were mingling on the other side of the room. It made sense that he should be with them. He and I weren't pretending tonight. He squeezed my shoulder when I nodded.

But even as I agreed and let him go, pain lanced my chest. Because I liked it better when he was beside me.

"So, it's still…?" Mila watched Em as he walked away.

I shrugged.

"There's my girl."

I spun at my father's voice. He stepped up beside me and gave my shoulder a squeeze. "I'm so proud of you. Did you see them?"

"Uh…" I shook my head.

"Damn, Gi." He chuckled. "Come here." Turning on his heel, he dragged me over to the set of paintings. There were about twenty lined up in frames along the front of the room.

My three pieces were set up side by side in beautiful gold frames. I swallowed at the sight of them lined up with paintings by other artists. Wow. My work was currently sitting on the auction block.

My eyes pricked with emotion, and I bit it down hard to stop the tears from forming. Blinking furiously, I cleared my throat. "It's cool."

"It's talent and hard work," my father corrected. "Your mom would be so proud." Pop shook his head. "Not to say she wouldn't be proud every day, because she would, but she always hoped you'd stay as excited and confident."

As a kid, I had been. Always demanding they frame and hang my creations. Somewhere along the way, I had lost that. But someone was determined I get it back. I glanced over my shoulder. Across the room, Emerson met my gaze and gave me a quick nod before turning back to his conversation with Asher Price.

"She'd like him too," my dad said quietly.

I spun back to him. That wasn't a statement my father had ever made about one of my boyfriends, and yet…

"We're not…" I swallowed and shook my head. "A thing."

Pop cocked a brow, and I braced myself for twenty questions.

"Who's ready for a toast?" Linc called, with Mila and Eli on his heels. I couldn't say I minded the interruption as he handed out drinks. "Don't worry," he said as he handed one to Pop, "yours is club soda. So you get the sparkle and none of the bad heart no-no."

We all clinked, and just as we were taking that first sip, a small bell rang, signaling that the auction would begin in five minutes. My stomach fluttered. I wanted to be confident in the moment, so I forced my shoulders back and inhaled deeply.

"So what's the etiquette for this shit? Like clap or jump up and yell 'hell yeah'?" Linc asked.

Mila sighed. "We went through this."

"He knows." Eli shook his head.

"You're going to behave, right?" I asked Linc. If he got up and started a wave or something when my first painting sold, then I could guarantee this would be my first and last auction here.

"We discussed rules." Eli raised a brow.

"Don't worry, I won't embarrass you, babe." He gave me a small shimmy. "We are full of classy today."

"Eli and I have a plan to keep a lid on him," Mila assured me, pulling me in for a side hug.

"Gianna!" Avery whisper-yelled as she approached. When she looped her arms around me, I took a heartbeat to savor the gesture. "This is so amazing. I can't wait to hear the gavel bang when you sell your first painting."

Behind her, the rest of the Revs appeared.

"Hey, Gi." Chris held a fist out to me. "Congrats."

I smiled at my brother, but my focus was quickly stolen when Emerson stepped out from behind him, eyes shining. For a long moment, I couldn't look away. My palms were clammy and my heart was racing. What I needed in this instant was a real hug. And maybe a pep talk. But Chris was here, and Em and I weren't supposed to be a thing. Kyle elbowed Em, pulling his attention away from me and breaking our connection.

"We should sit," Avery said. "I'm totally getting the eye from Wren."

We slowly shuffled to the section that had been roped off for us. As I waited for Mila to fill the next open seat, I rubbed a hand over my stomach.

Chill, Gi. This is going to be amazing.

Letting go of these nerves was easier said than done.

Once Mila was sitting, I settled beside her, and Pop took the seat beside me. After a second, he frowned and turned in his chair, scanning the people around us.

"What's wrong?" I asked, leaning in and keeping my voice low.

"Nothing," he said. But he stood up and tipped forward so he could see down the row. "I need an aisle seat. I can't be cramped up like this. It makes me hurt."

Hurt? My stomach sank. He hadn't complained about pain in weeks.

"What?" I asked, scooting forward in my chair, ready to help him out of here.

"Don't worry." He waved me off. "I just want more room." He looked at Emerson, who had taken the aisle seat. "Switch with me?"

Emerson popped out of his chair and moved instantly so Pop could sit down. "Is that better?" he asked when my father was settled.

Pop nodded and shooed him away. Emerson chuckled at him, then turned and moved toward me. My mouth lifted slightly as the rich scent of his cologne filled the air.

"Hey," I said as he sat beside me. Instantly, I was enveloped in his warmth and scent, and my nerves drifted away.

"Hey." He smirked, leaning back in his seat. As he adjusted, our arms grazed, and his pinkie twitched, brushing against mine.

I glanced down at the sensation, and he did it again.

"Nervous?" he asked.

I shrugged, feeling much more settled than I had only a moment ago. "People will bid on them, right?"

"Hell yeah, they will," he agreed, ghosting that finger along the side of my hand.

And they did. When my first painting sold for eight thousand dollars, he locked his pinkie with mine and grinned so wide it hurt to look at him.

Damn, was I glad he was here with me.

Emerson
37

THIRTY-FOUR THOUSAND DOLLARS. HOLY SHIT. BETWEEN THE THREE paintings up for auction, Gianna had made thirty-four thousand dollars tonight.

I was so fucking proud of her.

Sitting next to her, feeling the excitement and nerves bubble off her, might have been the single best experience of my life. She glowed all night long, pressing her teeth into her lip as the bids went higher and higher. When the auctioneer banged the gavel, she beamed brighter than I'd ever seen.

My heart ached in the best way as I watched those big brown eyes shut for one second while she collected herself.

It had been the best night.

And yet, I'd been trapped on the outside. As desperate as I was to pull her into my arms, kiss her, tell her how proud I was of her, I was forced to keep my distance.

I couldn't act like she was mine. And even now, as I waited while she said goodbye to my teammates, I had to pretend I was just her ride home. Just the temporary roommate.

"Big night for her." I yanked my gaze from Gianna when her dad suddenly appeared next to me.

I cleared my throat and straightened the cuffs of my jacket. "Yeah."

"Chris is pulling the car around." Pop rolled his eyes. "Both my kids will baby me forever."

"Because they love you," I said honestly.

"Not sure I really want to live down the hall from Mr. Overprotective." He frowned.

Chris and Avery had just signed a lease for a two-bedroom apartment on the same floor as Avery's. They were moving all their things four doors down, and as soon as Pop left rehab, Chris planned to move him into Avery's place so they would be close.

"Avery will keep him in check."

Pop nodded and then blew out a breath. "I'm going to overstep, but she's my girl, so I have to."

I turned to him, confusion whirling inside me as I worked to process his statement.

His brown eye cut into me, sharper than I usually saw from the laid-back man. "I didn't fall off the turnip truck yesterday. I can see there is something going on between you and my daughter." He sighed. "So I'm asking, what's your plan there?"

My heart hiccupped. That was the question I asked myself every day. The one I had no good answer for.

I shrugged. "She's got a life in New York." Like a magnet pulling me in, Gi caught my attention, and there was no way I could look away as she hugged her friends. "And God knows where I'll be next year."

"Won't that always be the case for you? The unknown of professional sports?"

I nodded.

"You've liked her for a long time."

I could lie to a lot of people, but not to her father. "Years." I swallowed.

"And you're worried about how Chris would feel."

A dip of my chin. Of course I was. Thank fuck Chris paid so little attention to anything that didn't involve Avery. It had made it relatively easy to hide my feelings for Gianna all these years. But when he figured it out, he'd lose his shit.

"Well, when the dumbass freaks out"—Pop patted my shoulder— "tell him I approve."

My heart lurched, and my breath escaped me. The shock that hit me was enough to finally pull me away from watching Gi.

He lifted his chin in his daughter's direction. "See that smile?"

I did. I drank in that expression as often as I could. Gi wasn't quick to offer it, and she didn't laugh a whole lot, so when she did, I damn well noticed. Because when she smiled at me, my day got better.

"I've seen that smile a lot more often lately. And you're a lot of the reason. So as long as you make my girl happy, then we're good." With a pat to my shoulder, he sighed. "You're a good man, and you have a huge heart, Emerson. And the way you look at her." He shook his head. "Damn. I don't see how my son hasn't noticed. But when he does?" Turning to face me, he held out a hand. "Remember, tell him you have my blessing."

My throat felt thick, and I swallowed hard as I slipped my hand in his. "Thanks."

"Pop, you coming?" Chris called from the door.

They flagged Avery down and headed out. Not long after, I found myself headed home too, with the scent of orange blossoms filing the air.

"You have a good night?" I reached across the armrest and set my hand on her thigh, finally able to touch her.

"The best." She smiled.

"Good."

We made our way up into the apartment, but Gi seemed anxious. Not really nervous, but somehow on edge. Multiple times, she reached for her hair to twirl it, and she shifted constantly, which was normally my thing, not hers. It felt vaguely familiar, but I wasn't sure when she'd been this kind of twitchy.

"You okay?" I asked when my apartment door shut behind us.

She nodded. "I just... have something for you. Or something I think you'll like."

In a flash, it came back, her in the kitchen, shifting on her feet, in my jersey. Unsure of how I'd feel about it. She had no reason to be nervous then or now.

I reached out and pulled her tight against me, the black fabric of her dress scratching against my navy suit. She needed to feel my affection, as well as hear it. "Anything that involves you, I know I like."

She pulled back slowly, looking up at me with a small smile that felt a lot bigger in my chest than on her face. She released all but my hand and guided me toward the area of our living room that had become her studio.

"So." She released me and reached for a brown box. "Not long ago, you mentioned painting yourself blue." She lifted the flaps of the brown box and pulled out a pack of paint.

Body paint.

Edible body paint.

A thrill raced up my spine, the tingles of a good adrenaline rush. This was one hundred times better than any stolen base. I tossed my coat off my shoulders, then yanked my shirt over my head, popping a button or two as I went. The idea of her brush on my skin had my body going from zero to sixty in half a second.

"What are you doing?" Gi asked.

"Getting naked." My pants were next. In my rush, I tried to slip out of my shoes at the same time. My pants caught on my ankles, and I teetered, almost falling over.

Gi grabbed my arm, laughing as she stopped me from ending up on my ass. "I love that you can always make me laugh." She leaned up and pressed her lips to mine.

That L-word that had slipped out of her mouth echoed around oddly in my chest. I wasn't sure why. I normally wanted to know all the things she liked, so it felt weird that it put me on edge.

She pulled back, her smile settling the nerves in my system.

"I like making you happy. And the idea of being your canvas makes me tingle."

She rolled her eyes. "Then sit down." She nodded toward the stool where she normally sat to paint.

More carefully this time, I shucked my shoes, then my pants, and when I was down to my boxer briefs, I dropped onto my assigned seat and waited.

She pulled out a new palette and brushes and set herself up to work. Blue mixed with a purple to create a dark shade of navy, and then blue and green to make a teal-ish blue. It was something I'd seen her do plenty of times before, yet at this moment, I was riveted. Dying to know what the colors would create. Dying to be the focus of her creativity, of her passion.

I'd watched her paint many times over the last almost two months. But from the outside. From across the room or over her shoulder. I'd never gotten to view what I was about to see.

She moved toward me, her attention focused on my chest, and my mouth went dry. All the blood in my body surged to my cock as she dropped to her knees between my legs. I was practically naked while she was still fully clothed. It was the opposite of how our nights usually went. Normally, it was her body I was worshipping. But the way her eyes took in every inch of me made me feel like I was being worshipped. I swallowed down the intense thrill that gave me. But my heart pounded as she looked up from under her long lashes.

"It might be cold." She warned, lifting her brush.

The first stroke against my pec was icy, but it didn't feel cold. It like a branding. Fire ripped across my chest, like each brush of color was marking more than my skin. Every experience with Gi was unlike anything I'd known. Her touch always turned me on, and right now, my cock was beating against the seam of my boxers, trying to reach for her.

But this intensity that was more than physical hung over each moment. I should have known it would be this way, because a haircut with her had felt life-alternating. And yet I felt hypnotized watching her paint my chest. Experiencing the creative spark in her eye from this side was thrilling. Her free hand came to rest on my thigh, and my muscles clenched in response. Her breasts barely brushed my cock. Once. Then again. My blood raged. I was desperate to touch her. To feel her body against mine. But I locked myself in place.

I balled my hands into fist to keep myself from reaching out. I wanted to see what she'd paint. But once the wall started to form, with waves along the edge. I couldn't stop myself.

I titled her face to mine. "The breakwater."

The corner of her mouth kicked up, but she looked back at my chest. "If there was a moment between us that I wanted marked in time, it would be that one, because that night I learned what it felt like to be enchanting to someone. To have a man not be able to look away from me, but want my words just as much as my body."

Her statement easily spilled from her lips, but it cracked at my soul.

"Gi, I'm forever enchanted by you—" My whispered confession was cut short when a large, cold drop of paint hit my stomach.

"Oops." She looked up to my eyes as she leaned closer. The breath hissed between my teeth as she licked lightly against me, taking the glob of paint away. "Hmm," she murmured against my skin. "I'm not sure the end of the rocks is right." She trailed her lips up my abs, less than a breath from my skin.

My thighs spread on their own as her breasts moved closer. My body thrummed a beat along with the pounding in my ears.

"This needs to go." Her tongue flattened against my left pec, right beside my nipple. A groan rose from deep in my chest, and the second she made contact with my nipple, my hips thrust up.

"Gi," I moaned.

Slowly, she moved back down toward the elastic of my boxers. My cock jumped, pressing into her tits. Big teasing eyes danced as she glanced up at me before pressing a kiss to my tip. Even through the thin material, it was too much.

"Please, Mariposa. I need your lips around me," I begged.

She pulled me out, and my cock sprang toward her like he knew exactly where he belonged.

As she wrapped her soft hands around me, a deep groan escaped my lips. And when she touched her tongue to my tip, I almost fell out of the chair.

When her lips circled me, I fisted her hair at the back of her head and guided her to take me deep. The stroke of her mouth on my cock made me feel cherished, worshipped. My chest tightened. Every part of my being wanted to thrust forward and own her, encourage her to work me over until I couldn't see straight, until every part of me belonged to her. But I couldn't do that.

I tightened my hold on her hair and pulled her back. She released me with a pop, her eyes wide. Fuck. Seeing her on her knees with desire flooding her gaze was just too much.

"Get the layers off." I unhooked the material behind her neck that held the dress up. "I need you naked and under me."

Without moving to help me, she smirked.

"So get the dress and the elastic trap under it *off*."

With one brow cocked, she scrutinized me, humor dancing in her eyes.

"Mariposa, I know every inch of your body, so you can be damn sure I know when you've wrapped my favorite curves in cellophane."

She laughed. "Em, it's not cellophane" But she let the dress fall around her waist as she leaned forward to lick my chest again.

I shivered, loving the feeling, but I needed to do it for her. "Gi," I growled.

"Okay. Okay." She pulled back, giving me an incredible view of her bouncing tits as she shimmied out of the bodysuit.

Once it hit the floor, I stood and swiped my fingers through the blue paint on the palette. The thrill of seeing her shiver as I traced her collarbone with a finger, then dipped between her full breasts, was worth putting my own needs on hold. Goose bumps broke out under the layer of blue coating her skin, and her nipples hardened, jumping out to me. I pressed my thumb into the yellow paint, then lifted both hands to her tits. A moan slipped between her lips as I pinched hard. I worked her over until her breasts were coated in yellow and blue, and she was begging for me to fuck her.

Then I licked her clean. The sweet tart of the paint mixed with the saltiness of her skin was like a drug. I licked over her ribs and stomach, moving lower. But before I could continue farther, she dropped to her knees next to me and pulled me down to the floor with her.

"I need you inside me. I need it so bad," she whispered.

Fuck. There was no way I could deny her. She lay back, chest heaving, and wrapped her legs around my hips.

Inch by inch, I sank into her, and she pulsed around me as I moved.

"Gi," I whispered. My chest pressed against hers, my blue paint mixing with her yellow. Pieces of us blended together, mixing into something new. Combining to become one, something that could never be separated again. That thought gripped tight at my chest, pulling me under, this feeling that was so much more than the heat that was coursing through me.

I rocked deep, relishing our connection, drinking in the way pleasure flashed in her eyes every time I was fully inside her. Hitting that spot that made her moan gave me this indescribable pleasure. Not in my dick; in my chest. As I locked eyes with her, it bloomed and throbbed, and then it cracked. Because I never wanted to let her go. I never wanted another moment without her.

"Em. I'm so close." Her moan vibrated through me. Her lids started to drift closed.

"Don't," I demanded. "Look at me. Give me this moment."

Her eyes were molten when they met mine. Emotions warred in them as her pussy quivered around my cock. I swirled my hips and rocked my pelvis against her, then thrust hard.

"Em," she cried, pulsing around me. She dug her nails into my shoulders as she came on my dick.

As I came inside her, my heart exploded and my entire soul burst with an intense emotion I didn't want to name. I wanted to give her everything. Everything she wanted, everything she needed. Everything she deserved. But I couldn't. Not without her having to sacrifice for me.

As she came back down, her pulsing slowing, she took a breath, and her eyes softened.

"Em, I l—"

I placed my hand over her mouth and shook my head. "Don't say it, Gi."

The way she shook off my hand and blinked hard, fighting the moisture pooling in her eyes, squeezed my chest like a vise.

"Once you say it..." My voice cracked. Once those words left her lips, I'd never walk away. And that meant dragging her with me to wherever I ended up. It meant leaving her while I traveled with the team. It meant leaving her alone and lonely. The idea of hurting her like that? It was like a knife to the chest. I cleared my throat. "Please don't say it."

She met my gaze, her eyes still glassy but full of understanding. Slowly, she nodded and then she pressed her lips to mine. She didn't say a single word, but she didn't have to. I felt them in the press of our lips, in the warmth of her body against mine, and in the openness in her eyes when she pulled back.

She felt the same way.

Gianna
38

I couldn't decode his thoughts or emotions, but I could see the desperation in his eyes. For some ridiculous reason, he didn't believe in us. Or maybe he wouldn't fight for us. Regardless of how obvious it was that a whole jumble of emotions was warring inside him, he wasn't giving in to them. He was still holding that wall up, keeping me from getting past.

"We should go clean up." He helped me to my feet.

The paint was sticky on my skin. Smears of blues and yellows mingled, creating swirls of green.

He didn't let go of my hand as he pulled me down the hall to the bathroom, or even as he turned on the shower. An eerie silence descended on us while we waited for the water to heat.

With capable hands, he squeezed the body wash onto my loofa. Then he worked painstakingly to gently scrub every inch of my skin. The paint colored the water green as it circled down the drain under my feet. When it ran mostly clear, he moved on to my hair, tenderly massaging my scalp. And in almost no time, we were in his bed, his arms locked around me, pulling me tight against him.

Every night, he held me like he'd never let me go. Even as his breathing evened out, he never loosened his grip. Normally, I fell asleep enveloped in the peace of being with him. But tonight, I didn't feel peaceful.

Emerson was used to being alone. Was that the issue? That the idea of hoping for a life with someone was scary to him? Or was it something he didn't want? Maybe he didn't want the pressure of having another person to worry about.

Or maybe he just needed to be chosen for once.

According to the clock on the nightstand, it was after one. On Monday. My meeting with Mr. Whittemore was in a few hours. Did I want to go back to New York? I'd always been scared to go after the things I really wanted in life. I'd always taken the safest path. Nothing about leaving Doucette Design was safe. My paintings had done well last night, but there was no guarantee that would happen again. And although I had a meeting next week with the Revs to talk about designing a city jersey, they very easily could go with another artist. After that? Who knew when another opportunity would pop up.

I'd have to depend on selling my art for income, but who was to say there would be any interest? Creativity was weird. It came in bursts and sometimes it didn't come at all. Some days, I struggled to find the inspiration to paint or the motivation to force the brush to move. And yet if I took the plunge, then I'd have to do it, even when it was hard. I didn't feel brave enough to make that decision.

I squirmed, and Emerson's arms loosened in response. Holding my breath, I slowly eased my way over so I was facing him. Then I ran my fingers along the scruff of his jaw. His long eyelashes fluttered, and warm breaths slipped through his full lips.

I sighed. Of course making decisions that would alter the whole trajectory of my life would be scary. But he'd tell me to be brave and to believe in myself. Right now, though, I wasn't sure what that meant.

By the time I slipped out of bed, though, long before the sun was up, I knew what I was going to do. But I couldn't wake him. If I did, I was afraid he'd try to talk me out of my decision.

Emerson
39

I ROLLED ONTO MY BACK AND BLINKED UP AT THE CEILING, INSTANTLY feeling off. Lolling my head to one side, I took in the empty space beside me. Gi was already up?

I tossed the blanket back and stood.

"Gi?" I called. But I was met with silence. After a quick lap through the empty apartment, I searched for my phone. Finding the living room and kitchen empty, I headed back to my room, only to find it on my dresser, next to a neat pile of clothes I'd worn last night.

A pile I hadn't put there.

With a tap on my phone's screen, I squinted at the time. Eight fifteen. My heart plummeted. Fuck. Her meeting started in fifteen minutes. She was in New York.

I ran a hand down my face and cursed again. I'd planned to set an alarm and walk her to the train, but my mind had been singularly focused on holding her last night. I'd upset her. I knew it. She hadn't said a single word after I told her not to love me, and the silence had crushed me, leaving my heart in shards. With a hand pressed to my aching chest, I lowered my head and closed my eyes. Every moment after that one felt like the beginning of the end.

One that I'd created and now had to live with.

I'd just set foot in the locker room when Tom Wilson appeared in the doorway of his office and sent me to Hannah. Shoulders drooping, I'd turned on my heel and headed her way. Regardless of what she needed today, I didn't have it in me to be her dancing monkey. There wasn't an ounce of fun, happy Emerson accessible at this moment.

"Rough morning?" Hannah asked as I stalked into her office.

I shrugged, brushing a serious question off in a way I was far too good at. "What's up?" I wasn't in the mood for a game. Waking up alone this morning had been the most painful experience I'd had in a long, long time. Gianna still hadn't replied to my text, but she'd viewed it.

So what the hell did that mean?

She spun her computer monitor toward me. On the screen was the picture of Gi and me that Hannah had taken last night.

The shards of my heart crumbled further. We looked so fucking happy in that moment. My arms around her. Her hand on my chest. I wanted to go back in time. Soak in that sensation.

"I wasn't sure how you'd want to respond."

"To what?" I asked, squinting at the image again.

She hummed and adjusted the screen a little. "Did you read any of the comments?"

I shook my head and angled over her desk so I could focus on the words. The first comment had my jaw locking.

"What the fuck?" I snapped as I skimmed another. One after another, I read them, my body winding tighter and tighter until I was ready to snap. Although some were typical comments about how hot I looked in a suit or genuine comments about their love of the Revs, they were mixed in with hundreds of nasty comments. The trolls attacked Gi for not being the type of girl a professional athlete would want. Some saying she'd better up her game or I'd lose interest. Some outright calling her fat.

"So we can ignore it," Hannah said, "or say something. I'm happy to help you work it out. But I wasn't even sure you two were together." She tilted her head, scrutinizing me knowingly. "Although by the rage on your face, I'd say you are."

"Send me the picture," I gritted out through my teeth. "I'll make my own statement."

My hands shook, and my heart pounded as I pulled out my phone. Had Gi seen this? Was this why she'd gone radio silent?

My phone buzzed as the picture landed in my inbox. A second later, it was downloaded, and I was clicking over to my own Instagram. From there, the words poured out so easily. Naturally. But when I was done, I didn't feel any better.

Choking back the outrage growing inside me, I stood. "Did you need anything else?"

Slowly, Hannah shook her head. So I turned on my heel and stormed back down to the locker room. On my way, I called Gianna, but she didn't pick up.

> Me: Hey, I don't know if you're upset or mad at me, but just call me. Please.

I slammed through the door and stomped to my locker. Once I got close, I tossed the phone inside.

"So…" Kyle spun the chair next to my locker and dropped into it.

"What?" I snapped. I had zero patience to deal with anything right now. No, that wasn't true. But the only thing I wanted to do was go to fucking New York and track her down.

"You just posted some heavy shit."

I nodded, hit with a wave of unease. Until this moment, I hadn't even considered how the guys would react. And I hadn't thought about Chris.

Rather than give me shit like I expected, Kyle did the damnedest thing. He stood up and wrapped his arms around me. My body went rigid, but it only took a second to relax and allow myself to sag against him.

Fuck, I was tired.

He patted my back twice and pulled back.

I took a deep breath and roughed a hand down my face. I hadn't realized how much I needed a hug. "Thanks," I said.

"I'm not going to touch the other shit yet." He pulled back. "But, uh, you're really not sure about playing with us next year?"

"My agent hasn't heard anything." I sank into my chair with a shrug.

"I thought the media was just stirring shit up." Kyle scratched his head.

The locker room door flew open and banged into the wall behind it. "What the fuck is this?" Chris demanded.

Heart lurching, I blinked at the phone in his hand.

Kyle took two steps back, holding both hands up as Chris stalked across the room.

"What the fuck is this?" he asked again, looming over me.

With a sigh, I ran a hand over my face. "I know you asked, and I know I said nothing was going on between us, but…" I swallowed and tipped my head back to meet his eye. "It's not nothing."

Chris worked his jaw back and forth, then blinked twice and dropped into the chair next to me. "So what is it?"

Damn if I didn't want to tell him everything. But I had to talk to Gi first.

"A mess," I said, dropping my elbows to my knees. "And I know you don't think I'm good enough for Gi—"

"What?" Chris spun in his seat so he was facing me head-on. "Why wouldn't you be good enough?"

I snapped up straight, at a loss for how to respond to that question.

"Dude, you're my best friend. One of the best damn people I know. You're loyal. You're caring." He shook his head. "Fucking hell. If you put half the effort into a relationship with my sister as you do our friendship, you'd be better than every other guy she's ever dated put together. You're beyond good enough."

I blinked and forced air into my lungs to keep my emotions tempered. "You told us to stay away from her…"

Chris frowned. "No, I told Streaks to stay the fuck away."

My heart stuttered. "So you don't care if Gi and I are together?"

"Are you?" His brows rose high on his forehead.

I shrugged, lowering my head again. "I don't know."

"What the fuck?" he muttered, kicking at my foot to get my attention.

"She doesn't want a serious relationship since she's going back to New York."

Eyes narrowing, he leaned forward. "What do you want?"

I dropped my focus to the post still called up on his phone.

"Yeah, that's what I thought." Chris sat back and crossed his arms. "Tell her."

I shook my head. "Dragon." I cleared my throat, willing my voice to stay steady. "I don't even know where I'll be next year. I can't drag her all over the country."

He glanced past me for an instant, then studied me with a look more earnest than I was used to seeing on his face. "We'll come back to that. Let's focus on Gi a second."

I cracked my knuckles and looked up at the ceiling. "She's all I focus on, man."

"Let me ask you something, then," he said. "If you could do your job from anywhere, would you follow her?"

My spine snapped straight. "Anywhere. But how could I ask her to leave her life behind and come with me?"

Lips pressed together, he nodded. "A few months ago, Avery thought they might trade me. And she didn't hesitate to come flying in here, screaming that she was going with me."

It was a pretty epic moment, and since the media was here, it turned into a big thing they spent days talking about.

"Some things in life are replaceable. A job. A house. Some things you can't live without. And when you find the person you can't live without, rearranging plans to be with them isn't a sacrifice." He shook his head. "It a joy."

My heart lurched, because he wasn't wrong. But—

"You won't know if you don't ask her," Chris said. "I love my sister. She deserves the best." He leaned forward and placed a hand on my knee. Shit. That move choked me up. From him, that was the equivalent of the biggest hug. "And I can't think of anyone better than you."

My phone buzzed, and I jumped up to grab it.

Gi: On the train back to Boston. We'll talk
when I get there.

I shut my eyes and sagged against the wooden side of the locker. Because that didn't sound like good news.

"Tell her how you feel. It could change everything." Chris clapped my shoulder, then he was gone.

And I dug deep, searching for the courage to do just that.

@happyfeet21

• • •

12.5k likes

happyfeet21 Congrats to the best person I know. Last night, I got to watch this talented, amazing woman shine. This might be my last season in Boston, and there is no better way to spend my days than I have been. There are days when her beauty takes my breath away. There are moments when she lights me up with her smile. There are times when the world around us disappears because I'm lost in her. There is nowhere I'd rather have spent the last few months than beside her. I'm blessed that she puts up with me, because she's entirely too good for me. Anyone worth anything would see that. So thank you, **@Gidamiano** for giving me the honor of being the man on your arm while you shine.

Gianna
41

I REREAD THE POST AS I RODE THE ELEVATOR TO EMERSON'S FLOOR.

What was the deeper meaning here? It was in response to something, because Emerson wouldn't have issued a statement to the entire world, including my brother, without reason. But I wasn't sure what he was saying. Was this a declaration of love or a goodbye? My stomach churned. Not only was I unsure about Emerson's feelings, I was also freaked out that maybe I'd made the wrong decision today. No. I pushed that thought away. If I was ever going to have the life I wanted, then I had to start doing the scary stuff.

The elevator dinged, and the heavy metal doors parted. My feet felt like they were encased in cement as I walked down the hall to the Emerson's apartment. The last text he'd sent said he'd be waiting for me.

I took a big breath and pushed through the door.

"Gi?" Emerson called before I'd even crossed the threshold. And before I was even out of the entryway, his arms were around me. He clung to me there, arms shaking and breathing choppy.

"Are you okay?" I pulled back, forcing the words out past the giant lump lodged in my throat.

"No." With both hands, he snatched mine and held it, still trembling. "I waited way too long to say this. And I'm worried I might

293

have missed my chance." He shut his eyes, sucked in a long breath, and then opened them again. "Feel this," he demanded as he splayed my hand over his chest. Directly over his heart. "This belongs to you." Pressing more intensely, he covered my hand with his. The steady pounding echoed against my palm. "It pounds for you. It skips when you walk into a room. And it breaks when you're hurting."

My knees went a little wobbly, but I forced myself to remain upright.

"I can't stomach the idea of letting you go." With his free hand, he cupped my cheek. "I know you could do better than me, but Gi, I'll spend forever doing everything I can to be enough."

"Emerson." I wrapped my arms around him. "There is no one better for me than you. I just didn't think you wanted it."

He shook his head, his chin brushing my temple. "Biggest fake out of my life was trying to convince myself that you weren't my everything the first time your lips touched mine. I've never worked harder at faking anything than I did at faking casual with you."

My heart skipped. "Em."

"No, wait." He stepped back and held a hand up. "You need to understand—I'm still not a good bet. There's a good chance I'll have to move in a few months. I'm going to be gone most of time. You might be lonely. And hate it." He brushed his knuckles under his nose and sniffed. "I'm not a good bet..." His eyes met mine, and finally, all the walls were down, and pure love shone in his gaze. "But I'm asking you to take it anyway."

I shook my head, and in response, he jerked, and his face crumpled.

"Em," I whispered, taking a step closer. "You are the surest bet of my life."

His body sagged, and he blinked hard. Clearly, he thought I was going to say something different.

"You are the surest bet I could make, because I'm not just betting on you. You'll always bet on me too." I tapped his chest, right over his heart. "It'll never be just you again. Now it's us. Together, you and me."

"Together." With a long breath out, he shut his eyes and nodded. Then he reached out and pulled me tight into his arms. "Have you been on Insta today?" The words were careful. "Because there was some stuff."

"I saw your post."

His arms tightened around me. "What about on the Revs page?"

The picture Hannah posted last night. Of us. Between his post and his hesitancy now, I was getting the idea. I wasn't what people expected when they thought of an athlete's date.

"They're wrong," he muttered into my hair. "You are perfect."

That was ridiculous. I wasn't perfect. I might be his perfect match, but I wasn't perfect.

"Em." I tried to pull back, but he clung to me. "Look at me, please."

He sighed but loosened his arms enough so I could see his face. The angry crank in front of me didn't seem like Emerson.

"You're a professional athlete."

"So?" He frowned.

"So people are always going to have opinions. And we have to learn to ignore them." I didn't doubt how Emerson felt about me. And critics who didn't know us shouldn't get that kind of control in our relationship. "Both of us."

He cupped my cheek. "I don't want you to be upset."

"I'm not," I promised. "I'm not going to read random people's comments on social media. I saw the comment I needed to see. Yours."

His eyes softened.

"I'm going to listen to voices that matter and drown out the noise that doesn't."

"I love you so much."

My heart tripped as he pressed his lips against my forehead.

"Can I say it now?" I asked.

With a chuckle, he nodded, his chin brushing against my cheek. "I love you too."

His arms tightened, and he breathed me in, sending a spark of awareness through me.

"And I quit my job today."

He jerked back, clasping my upper arms. "What?"

"I didn't just not take the promotion. I quit." I licked my lips and surveyed the skyline behind him. "It's scary, but I want to paint. And sell my work. I don't want to be in that toxic work environment anymore. And I want to trust myself."

He smiled. "So if I have to ask you to follow me to Timbuktu, you might be free to do it?"

"I'd follow you anywhere," I promised.

He pulled me in and squeezed me tight again. But as relieved as he was in this moment, I knew he didn't want leave the Revs.

I hoped the team was smart enough to realize that Emerson shouldn't be going anywhere.

Emerson
42

I CLIMBED OUT OF THE BLACK MERCEDES LIKE I DID EVERY TIME I ARRIVED at Lang Field. But this time, Chris was leaning against the fence that surrounded the stadium, a jersey tossed over one shoulder.

"So?" He straightened and cocked a brow.

"I'm totally in love with your sister."

He rolled his eyes. "I got that yesterday. Is it safe to assume, since you're practically spitting happiness, that you talked to her?"

I tackle-hugged him, almost knocking him over.

"Jesus." He shook loose and shoved me back.

"She quit her job. And she wants to focus on art and stay in Boston for a while." I smiled, my heart practically bursting out of my chest. "Because she wants to be with me."

"Smart woman." He clapped a hand on my shoulder, but then he hit me with the glare I was so familiar with. "And I want no more details ever."

I laughed. "Fair enough, but I have to say one thing."

His brow knitted. "What?"

I stopped walking and gave myself a minute to say this right. Because it would probably be the biggest problem in our relationship moving forward. "I'd never say a single bad thing about Avery or ever be mean to her."

"I know that." He crossed his arms and frowned at me.

"'Cause that would be really sucky for you to deal with."

He grunted.

"So it makes sense to you that it's really hard for me not to throw something at you when you aren't nice to Gi."

"Oh." His eyes narrowed. "Yeah, okay. I get it." He sighed. "She and I have always butted heads, but I'll try."

"Thanks, man." Still floating on damn air, I followed him to the elevator, and he hit the up button instead of down, where the locker room was.

"Where are we going?"

"I have a meeting with Langfield." Focus set on the stainless-steel doors in front of us, Chris worked his jaw back and forth. "He asked me to bring you."

Odd. But whatever. If they wanted me to be their trained monkey today, I was willing.

"Hold it for me." Kyle trotted over with his jersey bunched in one hand.

"We're going up," I warned.

He nodded. "Me too."

"Is this a team meeting?" I asked, looking from one guy to the other.

"Hell yeah, it is," Chris growled. "Most important one we've had."

For the first time today, a little niggle of worry wormed its way through me. With a cleansing breath, I pushed it away. It wasn't that weird that I didn't know about it. I wasn't usually involved in the serious stuff that went on with the Revs.

Though I did my best to keep my thinking positive, that worry returned. As we rode, I cracked my knuckles.

The doors opened, and we stepped off on the top floor, finding Asher and Mason, both with their jerseys slung over their shoulders.

"Should I run to the locker room and grab my jersey? I think I missed the email." I glanced farther down to where Eddie and Jasper chatted, both also holding their jerseys.

"Don't worry. We've got you." Chris clasped my shoulder.

That worry turned into dread. What did that mean?

"Come on." He tipped his chin, gesturing to Beckett's office.

When I didn't move, Kyle gave me a shove in the back, sending me stumbling through the door. Beckett was behind his desk, and Cortney stood at the windows that overlooked the harbor.

As I righted myself, Beckett glanced up, his brows pulled together. "What's going on?"

He gave me a cursory glance, then leaned to one side, his eyes widening. Frowning, I turned around to see the rest of my teammates filing in.

Cortney Miller turned completely and crossed his arms over his massive chest.

"It came to our attention yesterday that one of our teammates doesn't have a contract for next year." Mason stepped up in front of the desk. "As the captain, it seemed odd to me that management would be dumb enough to get rid of him. But apparently, it's a thing."

He dropped his jersey on the desk. "My bat is on fire this season, but it's only because that man"—he turned and pointed at me, and my heart jumped—"is always on base, stealing second or even third. Making the pitcher nervous and twitchy. I get easy pitches because they're distracted. My bat's on fire because he's supporting me." He stepped close and pulled me in for a hug. Then he turned back to Beckett. "I need him on the team. Take 5 percent of my contract for him."

My breath caught in my lungs. *What?*

Before I could argue with him, Eddie stepped up to the desk.

"You say I own the infield, but the truth is the only reason I can cover so much is because I don't need to worry about anything up the left side. Em owns the third baseline. If it's catchable, he's got it. He's a wall. And I don't want anyone else beside me. Take five from my contract too." Eddie dropped his jersey on the desk and then hugged me.

My legs were numb, and the rest of my body was heavy, frozen in shock.

Kyle dropped his jersey on the pile next. "Fans love the Revs and the show we put on. But dude"—he shook his head—"we all know it's really the Emerson show. I couldn't do it without him. And truthfully, I won't act like a dumbass for publicity with anyone else." He turned and hugged me. "Love you, bro." Then he glanced back. "Take five from me too."

One by one, my teammates dropped their jerseys on the pile and offered up small percentages of their contracts to keep me on the team. As stunned as I was at the gesture, when Tom Wilson pushed through, I thought I might pass out.

He tossed his hat onto the desk. "I love the kid. Not only is he good on the field, but he's good for morale." He clapped my shoulder before stepping aside.

Hannah walked up to the desk and took in the pile of shirts. Then, with a sigh, she carefully stepped out of her sky-high heels.

As the shoes hit the pile, she said, "He is literally the only one of these guys who makes my job easy. Do not get rid of the heart of the team." She turned to me and smiled. "I'm not sure any of us have ever said this to you, but thank you. There isn't a single person on this team or in this organization who doesn't realize that if they need a yes-man, you're it. So thank you."

I scanned the room, blinking hard. My heart had never felt so full. There was a good chance that this dog and pony show would have no effect on the decisions made in the front office, but fucking hell, this was a moment I'd never forget. My eyes welled.

"Shit." I sniffed. "I'm gonna cry."

With a snort, Chris shook his head. Then he turned to Beckett's desk and tossed his jersey on top of Hannah's shoes. "Take 10 percent of my contract. Hell, twenty if you need it. I'd really like my future brother-in-law to stay in Boston."

With that, he turned and hugged me. I couldn't stop the sob that worked its way up my throat.

"Jesus. Don't leak on me." Chris pushed me away, chuckling.

Wiping at my eyes, I couldn't help but laugh.

Beckett slammed his hand on the desk and stood. "I told you," he snapped over his shoulder. "First of all, I was right about Damiano's sister and this one." With a finger jabbed at me, he turned back to

Miller. "And second, I *told* you they would all freak out about his contract."

Cortney sighed. "Okay. It pains me to say it, but you were right."

"As always." Beckett smirked. "For the record," he said, raising his voice, "we're all glad you love Emerson. But Man Bun and I have been working all season to free up the money to give our third baseman the contract he deserves."

Cortney stepped past Hannah and the guys and towered over me. With a pat to my shoulder, he said, "Your agent will have it next week at the latest."

I froze. "Really?"

He nodded. He might have been our general manager, and what I was doing was probably anything but professional, but I couldn't help myself. I jumped up and squeezed him tight. He staggered back and banged into the desk, but kept us upright.

"And look, I created another happy ending." Beckett dropped into his chair with a smirk.

Cortney extricated himself and gently pushed me away. "Don't even start."

I ignored their bickering. I was too busy floating on cloud nine. Never in my life had I been so happy. Now that I had both my girl and my team, life was perfect.

Emerson
43

THE ENTIRE STREET WAS FRONT STOOPS AND WIDE SIDEWALKS. A LONG LINE of stone steps and wrought-iron railings. Brick buildings and trees.

A dog barked at the far end, and Beckett Langfield bellowed, "Deogi, get back here!"

"Bossman," came a little voice, "he's just chasing Junior because she stole the trash lid again."

A smile pulled at my lips. I loved my street. The guys on the team thought it was nuts of me to buy a house two doors down from the momcom. But no one could ever claim my street was boring.

The crisp fall air blew, rattling the trees, and a few leaves drifted down onto the stones.

I trotted past the line of pumpkins along the stoop and opened the door on the left.

We'd only moved into the brownstone a week ago, but it was already feeling like home.

The first week of August, my agent called me about the deal the Revs had sent over. I had been blown away by the number of zeros on the five-year contract. But it opened the door for me to purchase Gi's dream house.

Not that she needed my money. In the three months since her show, she'd been offered a contract with the Revs to design their new city jerseys, and she'd sold two more paintings. And although she could have afforded to take care of herself, I loved spoiling her.

Since it was just the two of us for the foreseeable future, we didn't need all four floors of a traditional brownstone, but we'd found one that had been split into two homes. So we had enough space with the three-bedroom brownstone to give her an art studio and still have a guest room for my mom.

I climbed the steps to the second floor and pushed the door open.

Some kind of angry girl music was blasting. Something about ruling the world.

Gianna was standing at the stove, stirring what smelled like stir-fry.

The white cabinets and subway tile brightened up the dark wide-board floors and moldings.

I stood in the doorway, watching her silently for a minute, enjoying the way she rocked her hips to the beat. The loud crackling pop from the fireplace made her jump, and that, in turn, made me chuckle.

Alerted to my presence, she turned and gifted me with the welcome home smile I loved.

"You got home fast."

The flight had only landed thirty minutes ago, but I hadn't stopped at Lang Field today. If I had, Kyle would have totally tried to drag me out to a bar for a celebration drink.

The entire team was stoked that we'd officially come home the east conference champs and were heading to the national league championship for the first time in almost twenty years.

Game one was tomorrow at home, and I had big plans.

"Couldn't wait to see my girl." I ate up the distance between us, pulled her into my arms, and pressed her into the counter, giving her a kiss.

"Mmm. I'm glad you're home."

"Missing me make you cranky?" I teased.

She swatted my stomach, but smirked. "Come on, let's eat."

"Dinner or you?"

She rolled her eyes. "Well, I'll hold, but the stir-fry will burn."

"Okay. Dinner. Then you show me that painting you've been telling me about. And then bed."

She laughed. It was my favorite sound to come home to. Nothing was more real in life than the sound of Gianna Damiano's laugh.

Epilogue

"HE'S ADORABLE." AVERY SHOOK THE BOBBLEHEAD.

Wren hugged hers to her chest. "Totally. I love it."

It was game one of the championship, and the Revs, apparently trying to still prove how much they loved him, had made today Emerson bobblehead day.

"They never do this for playoff games. He should feel special." Hannah tapped her foot impatiently.

The Revs were doing a special introduction for Emerson tonight, so we were sitting to the right of the dugout rather than in the box.

"He's been so nervous all day." It was weird. When the forecast called for drizzle, Emerson freaked out, certain that I wouldn't come. Like I would ever not show up to an event that was important to him, regardless of the weather.

"I laughed so hard when he switched from *you have to come* to *I'm worried you'll get sick if you sit out in the rain*." Isabella giggled next to me.

It wasn't even currently raining. If it started, we'd head up to the box, so I didn't understand what he was so stressed about.

"Like I said, he's nervous." His entire family had come up for today's game. Most of them were in the box with Pop, but Isabella had asked to sit down here with Hannah, Wren, Avery, and me. She and Hannah had been glued to my side all damn morning. "I'm gonna run to the bathroom before—"

"No!" Isabella and Hannah shouted in unison as each grabbed one of my arms, sending me jerking forward.

"Good thing she wasn't holding her beer," Wren said, rolling her eyes at the jump scare they'd just given me.

"Seriously. Is it something in the air today? You're being just as weird as Em."

"We just don't want you to miss anything." Avery waved the bobblehead at me. "It's Em's big day."

And yet it didn't seem to warrant their brand of weird.

Less than five minutes later, the mascots were out on the field with their normal bins of balls and T-shirts.

The synthesized beat blared from the speakers around the stadium. Then, in a shocking turn of events, my brother was the first to trot up the steps, clapping and looking almost happy. He glanced our way and gave his fiancée a smile as he shook his rose gold Sharpie at her.

"Why is he the only one allowed to use a color other than black?" Wren asked.

"He utterly refuses to use anything but rose gold. I can only assume it has something to do with you." Hannah arched a brow at Avery.

"It's the best color," she said unapologetically, her eyes locked on Chris.

Mason, Kyle, Asher Price, and Eddie Martinez were right behind my brother, all clapping and dancing as they moved toward the mascots. Black Sharpies came out, and they all started signing.

I took a sip of my beer. As I set it down, a cacophony of beeps and buzzes sounded around me, and I swore everyone near us was pulling out their phones.

Wren pulled hers out, but I couldn't see the screen.

"What's going on?" I asked, reaching for my pocket before remembering my number 21 jersey dress didn't have any.

"I think you left your phone up in the box," Isabella said. "I saw you set it down when we dropped Mama and Pop off up there."

"It's an Amber alert." Wren tipped forward and tucked her phone back into her pocket.

"Yeah," Hannah agreed, barely looking up from her own device.

The music suddenly changed, and in the next second, Emerson came up the steps, clapping like all the other guys. His eyes met mine, and the tension visibly drained from his shoulders. The smile on his face became less forced, and he moved toward his best friend, dancing the entire way.

"I missed 'Shut Up and Dance.' He and Mason haven't done it since the playoffs started." Wren craned her neck and clapped. "Let's see those moves, boys," she called.

Coach Wilson spun our way and glowered at her.

She simply gave him a small finger wave and batted her eyes.

"Don't make it worse. Dad's already annoyed today." Avery rolled her eyes.

"I legit cannot believe that Christian Damiano is dancing right now."

"I keep telling you, Han," Avery said, "I'm not the only one he does these things for. Emerson is his best friend, and it's a big day."

Emerson moved down the line, dancing and signing shirts rather than throwing them for his teammates. In turn, the guys were the ones tossing the shirts he was signing into the crowd. After he made it down the line, he did what he does best. He got the crowd on their feet and got them making all kinds of noise.

The Amber alert must have had an update, because as he was engaging the crowd, phones started beeping again.

"Why is he shaking his phone?" I asked Hannah. As he danced, he kept lifting his phone and pointing.

Her eyes widened. "Um, he must want them to see the message?"

I narrowed my eyes at her. Why the hell was she being weird now too?

Halfway through the song, he bounced our way. The chorus was blasting as he hopped onto the roof of the dugout and held his hand out to me.

I shook my head, but he just moved closer and reached out. Avery and Hannah hauled me out of my seat and shoved me closer.

Begrudgingly, I held out a hand. He pulled me up onto the dugout and into his arms, his smile blinding.

Attention wasn't my thing. I broke out in a sweat as I clung to him. The lyrics were up on the Jumbotron for the chorus, and the crowd was all locked in and singing along.

"Eyes on me, Mariposa. You are my destiny. The only thing I need. So dance with me, Gi," he whispered in my ear.

In the next instant, he released me and spun me around. Just as the song was about to demand that I shut up and dance with him, he dropped to one knee, and the entire stadium shouted. "Marry him!"

Heart leaping in my chest, I slapped my hands over my mouth. *Marry him!* flashed on all the screens around the stadium.

My heart skipped, and I lost my breath as Emerson looked up at me with a massive diamond pinched between his fingers.

He smirked and cocked a brow, silently asking *well?*

I nodded, fighting back tears, and the crowd around us broke into a thunderous cheer. He rose and slipped the ring onto my finger.

"Emerson," I choked out, holding my hand up, "it's huge."

He shrugged, then leaned to whisper in my ear. "It's the flashing sign that tells the world you're mine."

He kissed me quickly, and the entire stadium went nuts, screaming and cheering again.

"How the hell did you plan this?"

He leaned in. "Hannah helped, and so did the stadium messaging system. Told you I wouldn't be stealing free milk for long."

I snorted. Him and that dumb expression.

He smiled. "I totally faked you out, though, didn't I? I had you thinking we were doing something completely different."

"Yeah." I inspected the ring again. Damn, the huge circle-cut diamond sitting on a full band of smaller diamonds was really mine. "I thought today was about you."

"Any day about me is about you too, Gi." He gave me one more quick kiss. "But now I've got a game to win. And then we'll head home to celebrate."

"Another first day of forever."

Curious to see who could possibly convince Kyle Bosco to settle down?
Preorder The Foul Out here!

DEAR READER

Dear Reader,

First, let me just say a massive THANK YOU! Thank you for reading *The Fake Out*, these two were just meant to be from the second Emerson opened the door to her. And who didn't love getting to see more Puff, and of course Cortney and Beckett, who love to jump into every story and try to steal the show. But seriously, THANK YOU for supporting me. It's only because readers exist that writers get to live out their dreams.

Some characters are hard, and some are easy, and when I set out to write Em and Gi's story I thought it would be Gi the difficult one. I'm not the best at writing the black cat female. But it turned out Em was actually the hard one. Having to decide what that man was thinking when he said the things he would say was a challenge. Can you explain what a grown man is thinking when he pretends to be an airplane? It sure gave me some fits.

And there is plenty more baseball fun to come! Yes, Kyle is next.... I'm having a great time setting up that man with a single mom and her two kids. Hopefully you'll join me on the entire Boston Revs ride because we have so many more to go this year!

If you haven't yet, definitely jump back to the Momcoms for

Beckett and Liv's and Cortney and Dylan's stories. And then check out Mason and his trainer's story in Gracie York's (My pen name with AJ Ranney) *Back Together Again*. Spend the fall with Kyle Bosco when the playboy finally falls, and then get snowed in before the holidays with Coach Wilson and someone...

Finally, remember: Live in your world, fall in love in mine.

Jenni

ACKNOWLEDGMENTS

A big thank you my kids who have to hear, "Hold on a second, mom is writing." Or "I have one more signing this weekend." You big guys have become constant babysitters for lives, and have manager to learn to fend for yourselves while I'm at signing but you all always more excited than I am when the next book releases. I'm so grateful for all four of you!

Thank you to my parents, who support me in all I do all the time. I couldn't get through life without you guys. Being able to count on you both all the time for help or support, or encouragement, is the best gift. Thank you for being examples I can strive to be with my kidsand being the best grandparents ever.

Beth, thank you for being you. Detailed, and organized because I am not. And your series bibles are amazing. You are friend and such an amazing supporter of me. I will never stop singing your praises from the rooftop. Don't doubt yourself because you rock at your job, and we all know it! Thank you for being the wonderful person you are.

Becca and the rest of the Author agency you all are the best. You keep up with me and always keep things under control. I'm chaos and I'm sure I make you nuts with the wait, when is the cover reveal messages, I constantly send your way.

Sara, thank you for everything. There aren't enough words to explain what you are. A friend, a support, a cheerleader, an amazing visually creative gem, I'm so lucky to have you. You wear so many hats, not just for me but for all the authors you support. You do it all and juggle so many things it makes my head spin. But whenever I need one more thing you get it done. And I'm so proud of the amazing business you created and I cant wait to watch you keep flying.

Jeff, thank you for being the final nit-picky check to make sure everything is perfect. Becoming a romance reader wasn't on your to do list, but I'm grateful you did it anyway!

Britt, thank you for being you. I probably could do things without you, but I wouldn't want to. I cant believe I was lucky enough that you recognized a random beach one February day. Your support is never ending even when you are so busy with your own stuff. And watching you soar in your success is inspiring. I love getting to be part of every new idea you have. You are thebest.

Jess, thank you for being with me this entire story. Every single time I sent you a few more chapters and the question are they annoying. Is Emerson the way you think he should be? You talked me through it every time without pause and I'm so grateful to not only get to work with you but get to call you a friend.

Amy, thank you for being the organized one, the one that keeps us on track, and the one that makes sure we get it done. For putting up with my chaos and my next 'fun' thing. I'm so lucky to get to call you one of my best friends. Daphne thank you for all your support and help. Anna thank you for being a great friend and helping whenever I need beta reader. And making sure my zoo stuff tracked on this book. For having so many TikTok accounts that I cant even keep track and shouting to the world to read my books. I'm grateful for your support and friendship.

To all my author friends and beta readers, thank you for being supportive and inspiring writers. Haley Cook, AJ Ranney, Kristin Lee, Alexandra Hale, Amanda Zook, Kat Long, Bethany Monaco Smith, Elyse Kelly, and so many, many more.

And big thank you to the rest of my friends and family who have helped me with encouragement and feedback. I love you all and am so thankful for your support.

ABOUT THE AUTHOR

Jenni Bara lives in New Jersey, working as a paralegal in family law, writing real-life unhappily ever-afters every day. In turn, she spends her free time with anything that keeps her laughing, including life with four kids. She is just starting her career as a romance author writing books with an outstanding balance of life, love, and laughter

ALSO BY JENNI BARA

Want more Boston Revs Baseball?

Cortney Miller

Mother Maker

Christian Damiano

The Fall Out (The Boston Revs Three Outs Book 1)

Emerson Knight

The Fake Out (The Boston Revs Three Outs Book 2)

Kyle Bosco

The Foul Out (The Boston Revs Three Outs Book 3)

coming October 2024

Coach Wilson

Finding Out (The Boston Revs Three Outs Book 4)

coming December 2024

Curious about the baseball boys from the NY Metros

NY Metros Baseball

More than the Game

More than a Story

Wishing for More

Romcoms written as Gracie York

Goldilocks and the Grumpy Bear

Tumbling Head over Heels

Along Came the Girl

Peter Pumpkined Out

Back Together Again (Part of the REVS Universe)

Printed in Great Britain
by Amazon